For Adele
05/18/2024
David McGraw

THE DELIVERANCE OF THE HEROINES

THE DELIVERANCE OF THE HEROINES

Volume One of Escape from the Night World

David McGraw

Escape from the Night World is a work of fiction, a visionary novel, of the kind known as science fantasy, both as a whole and in all its separately titled volumes. All references to real persons, events, and doctrines in history are fictitious usages only. All other characters and incidents are imaginative constructs by the author. Any resemblance of such imaginary beings and happenings to actual persons and events in real life, whether past or present, is wholly accidental and unintentional.

ISBN-13: 9781977569387
ISBN-10: 1977569382

Library of Congress Control Number: 2017915578
CreateSpace Independent Publishing Platform
North Charleston, South Carolina

Escape from The Night World:
The Deliverance of the Heroines

CHAPTER ONE

It has been many years now since the musician pointed out, rightly, that sickness may "surely take the mind where minds" cannot ordinarily go. If there was any weakness in his insight, it was only in imagining (if he did imagine) that this thesis applies exclusively to human minds. Then again, perhaps he knew better but understood that most human minds are too weak to face reality apart from some special gift, whether of sickness or whatever. Be that as it may, the young lady's destiny was to illustrate this point by her own example, as she would find.

Her name in her own language and among her own people was outside the range and functioning of human senses. When transposed as nearly as may be into sounds audible to human ears, her name would be an inarticulate squeal. However, the nearest translation of her name into human languages would be Beatrice.

In the present context, the great question was how someone like Beatrice could ever fall sick in the first place. The answer was that sickness for her was very different from sickness for a human subject. Indeed, to speak of what happened to her as sickness is correct more as a loose analogy than anything else. It is just that one must speak of it that way.

It was not that sickness was unknown among her people. Sickness, deterioration, and death had occurred very often among her people in the course of history, and there were plenty of such cases among her people at the time Beatrice fell sick. But it was extremely rare among her people, or perhaps even unheard of, for someone to suffer in these ways unless something else had already gone wrong. Nothing like that had happened with Beatrice. Her sickness occurred only through the wrongdoing of another, and then only because her own heroism made it possible. Yet this too was exotic and extraordinary among her people.

What happened to her occurred in the first days after her initial coming-of-age as an adult person. Both her mother and her principal mentor had agreed with Beatrice's intuition concerning what her appointed destiny was. All three had agreed that Beatrice had something exotic to fulfill, although much remained obscure. So, it was arranged that she should receive appropriate specialized advanced instruction from one of the great theoreticians of her people. This instruction was to be carefully tailored to Beatrice's personal concerns, based on what the mother and the mentor told the theoretician. It was just after Beatrice had concluded the first level of advanced learning that her great adventure began.

The very fact that the preparation for the adventure—which was to be accomplished by means of sickness!—involved specialized tutoring from a theoretician calls for explanation. Beatrice did not need to learn more about the right order of genuine reality in order to be made ready. She knew that well enough, as did her people in general. What she needed was to learn much more than was generally known among her people about those people who turn things upside down, and about the twisted worlds of unreality they weave around themselves and insist on living in, and about how they might—or might not—be brought back. As for why she needed such knowledge—well, that is the story to be told.

Upon receiving the details about Beatrice, the teacher who guided her advanced learning had much more than a suspicion of what the exotic destiny was. Upon being consulted, the teacher's colleagues concurred with this view. Consequently, the teacher started by saying, very mildly, "So, your mother and your old principal mentor believe you have some exotic destiny to fulfill. I have two questions for you about that. First, what do you believe?"

"I too believe that."

"Do you, now? Do you really?"

"Yes, really. Do you think I have misunderstood?"

"When I know what to think about it, I shall tell you. For now, you tell me what you think this exotic destiny is."

"Well, I have always found that puzzling. Somehow, it seems almost as if I should be both an advanced theoretician and also a Traveler, and yet neither, and then again a third thing that is some sort of combination of the two. I rejoice at the honor of being sent to you as a theoretician for training, but I wonder whether I should also be trained by a Traveler, either in conjunction with you or later on. Or perhaps some third form of training might be more reasonable. As I say, I find myself puzzled."

"All right, so far, so good. Second, is that what you yourself would want or prefer or choose? Let me clarify by putting it this way. If God, by some miracle, were to reach down from Heaven and offer you the choice of any path through life—any path at all—what would you say? How would you answer?"

"Oh, that is hard. Let me think...to tell the truth, I think the question is too much hypothetical. I find it hard to imagine

God would do such a thing. My impression is that it would be too much like mere cruelty. Since I was old enough to think about it at all, I have always had in mind simply to trust that this appointed path on which I find myself is leading me to something wondrous beyond my own dreams, far better than I could have chosen for myself. I have always rejoiced that this is so. To be challenged as you said would be—well, I do not know what it would be. If I had to think in those terms at all, I reckon at most I would ask whether I had understood rightly. If so, then I would keep to this present path on which I find myself."

"Very good, and I am sure you have considered the consequences and implications, but I need to have you speak to me about that."

"I know that to follow one path is to give up others. I know that other paths have their own joys and benefits, and I rejoice for other women, who prosper and flourish by following those paths. They are following their appointed destinies. But those paths are not for me. I know that based on what I told you, even though I do not know what shape my path could have."

The point of leading Beatrice though this conversation was to test what the teacher had suspected. This was done by finding what she had to say to being asked, just straight out. But it was also by observing what words she selected and how she combined them, how she held and carried herself, what her face displayed, and what the tone and quality of her voice were.

So now the teacher said, "All right, then. Yes, I agree with you and your mother and your mentor. Quite clearly, you have some exotic destiny to fulfill. There is no question about that. The question is what that destiny may be. I have suspected the answer since I first heard about you. I have consulted my colleagues, and they agree. This conversation has reinforced my impression. But it would be premature to tell you just now. However, I can tell you this much. There is something to be fulfilled that calls for what is kind of like a combination of a theoretician and a Traveler. Now, I think this may be your appointed destiny."

At this, Beatrice's mind stopped for a brief moment. She prayed inwardly for guidance and then said simply, "In that case, I am at a loss."

"Yes, of course. For a little while, you will have to take my word. In the meantime, we shall have lunch, and then your training proper begins."

After lunch, the teacher began. "I know you have learned the truth well enough. What you must do now is to think about an extraordinary question. How would you prove the truth if you had to do so, starting from point zero? First of all, do you understand the question?"

"No, I do not think so. What is point zero in this context?"

"Well, there are the basic things about life and reality you learned as a child. How would you prove all that if you had to?"

"Do you mean, how would I, as an adult person, teach all that to a child? I reckon the same way my mother taught me."

"Yes, of course, but that is not what I meant. Your mother had only to guide you through the process of developing and exploring and understanding your own experience. But what if that were not enough?"

"Now I am puzzled. Why should anyone have to prove what is obvious to everyone?"

"Good, good. But the truth is not obvious to everyone. As I said, your mother had only to guide you through your own experience. What if there were people for whom that would not work, people whose experience is very wrong, grossly distorted, severely misleading? Such people could not simply be guided through as you were and as other children are. What then?"

"Is this merely hypothetical, or are there in fact people like that?"

"It is not merely hypothetical. There are in fact such people."

"I am accepting on your word that it is so, but I do not understand."

"Well, to begin with, what about the Renegades?"

"Well, but even they know better. It is just that they choose wrongly. Yet even they can be brought back and restored, exactly *because* they know better underneath."

"Yes, of course, among us. That is because they remember what it was like before. But what if there were Renegades who had never known anything else?"

Beatrice's mind stood still for a long moment at the very idea. Finally she asked, "Is that even theoretically possible? It sounds like you are asking what follows from an absurd supposition. Is that the point of your question?"

"No, that is not what I am doing—not at all. Yes, it is possible, I assure you. What then? Where does it go from there? How would you prove the truth to a Renegade who had never known anything other than life as a Renegade?"

"What truth would I have to prove?"

"Well, what is it that makes someone a Renegade?"

"Defiance based on insolence and arrogance. But all that is obviously wrong as soon as one stops and thinks. They choose to look away from that fact, and that is all. What is there to prove, even to them?"

"What is there to prove? Plenty, for a Renegade who had never known anything else. Someone like that might think there is nothing in life to do apart from glorifying and exalting oneself in the way you call insolence and arrogance. Whether it makes sense to you or not, you can see at least how the logic of the situation could work itself out in that way."

Beatrice pondered this and then replied, "Yes, yes; of course. If there could be a Renegade who had never known anything other than life as a Renegade, then it might well work out the way you said." After a long pause, she went on. "But then, in that case, your whole proposal breaks down, for there would be nothing whatsoever left as a starting point for proving the truth to such people. Anyhow, it sounds very much like you are asking after all what follows from an absurd supposition, even though I am accepting on your word that you are not."

"No, I am not doing that. Quite the opposite. As for your claim that my proposal to teach such Renegades breaks down, no. Almost, but that is not quite correct. Even someone like that may be genuinely concerned to honor and follow the real truth. But that one may believe that, in terms of the real truth, there is no reason not to glorify and exalt oneself. For that one does not start with any awareness of dishonoring or opposing the truth by magnifying oneself."

Given what she had learned as a child, Beatrice figured this was nonsense, and she was ready to argue the point on that basis. Then she remembered the teacher already knew all the reasons she could give. So instead, she blurted out, "Dear teacher, what is it you are not telling me?" Beatrice had not known this was in her mind until she said it.

"Very good. I was waiting for you to ask me that. Yes, there is something important. First of all, you have to remember that you understand much because your mind is illuminated, since you are not a Renegade. The question is, how would you prove all that to someone whose mind is not *and has never been* illuminated? In point of fact, there are such people, and those are the Renegades who have never known anything else.—Yes, it is actually real, not merely possible."

From the teacher's tone of voice and manner of speaking, it was very obvious to Beatrice that she had deliberately been left hanging. As soon as she realized this, it became obvious the teacher was waiting for her to respond. With the peculiar calm of one who is expecting and awaiting something too horrible to anticipate, she asked simply, "What else?"

"Moreover, the truth is even worse than you imagine. For you see, some of those people believe, quite sincerely from their own standpoint, that—well, what is the worst thing you can imagine that they might believe? Perhaps that is the soft and easy way to lead you into it."

"Is it worse than the nonsense the Renegades among us spout?"

"Oh, yes, very much so."

"Then I have no idea."

"Some of them believe there is no God. You must keep in mind what I told you: their minds are not illuminated."

"No God? *No God?!* Are you joking or playing around?"

"No, not at all. I am speaking totally seriously."

"Is this some sort of—of story or poetry?"

"No, it is the plain statement of blunt fact."

"Well, but then—but then—I am at a loss. Is that what you are asking me to prove from point zero? That God exists?"

"Yes, child, it is. You need to understand what it is like for them."

Beatrice thought about it for a moment and then said, "No. I am sorry, but you must explain it to me very elaborately. It is almost too much for the mind to accept."

"Yes, I know." Then, weighing words very carefully, the teacher began, "This denial of God is really much less absurd than it may seem. You have to consider that you start out having your mind illuminated. Given the basic awareness this involves, you can then go back and pick up the right answers to other questions very easily. But they do not have this benefit. Therefore, they have to do it the other way around. In other words, they have to start from point zero, and observe various things, and work through how those things point up to God. That is doing it the hard way."

Beatrice thought about it and said, "Once again, I can see how the logic of it could work out as you said. But that is all."

"Perhaps that is as much as can be expected for the first session. All right, then; that will be all for today. Until the next session, here is something for you to think about. Why do you find the denial of God to be obviously and overwhelmingly absurd?"

At their next session, Beatrice replied, "I thought about your question. Of course, really, it is absurd first and foremost because we experience Her constantly. But I assume you meant *why* in terms that one who has never been illuminated could appreciate. Well, then, it is absurd because there is the clear and very blatant dependency of things on God."

"Yes, exactly so. Now what about this dependency?"

"Well, the lower level depends on the higher level. That is all."

"Good. That answer makes it easy to show the problem. You speak of higher and lower levels and of dependency. That is the very thing that all too often they do not understand—or at least not as you mean it in this context."

"What are you saying? Do you mean they do not understand the idea of having the lower level depend on the higher level?"

"No, even they know that much. But you see, the world of lesser beings works out rightly on its own terms, almost as if it were a stand-alone structure. Now, *you* would say this fact shows the wisdom and goodness of God, to set up this world as having its own perfection as far as may be. *They* say this world is able to work of itself, apart from any need for God to interfere with it in order to have it work right, and so there is no need to speak of the world as depending on God. In other words, given that the lower level works out rightly on its own terms, they think that ends the question. All too often, they fail to appreciate the more subtle or sophisticated dependency of the lower levels on the higher."

Now one of the great breakthroughs among her people, just twenty generations before Beatrice's life had begun, was the design and construction of a device that worked automatically. Once this had been accomplished and publicized, other people had taken up the basic ideas involved and had developed these ideas in other ways. By the time Beatrice first met with the theoretician, there was among her people a wide variety of automatic devices, with different attributes and functions. So, after a long pause, Beatrice said, "Dear teacher, I am accepting on your word that those people think that way. But what they think is totally ridiculous. An automatic device is able to work rightly apart from any interference by the artisan or craftswoman who made it. Indeed, the very fact that no interference is required shows she made it right. It does not begin to show that no one made the device."

"Yes, to be sure, what you just said is correct on its own terms."

"Well, then?" And then she knew in part. "You want me to think it through." And then she understood. "You said I need to know what it is like for them."

"Exactly so. Very good. For example, you think of the world as reflecting the wisdom and goodness of God, in that She set up the world to have its own perfection as far as may be."

"Yes, of course. That should be obvious just by working through the logic of it."

"Well, in one way, yes, it is. The problem is that those people do not see the world as a realm of beauty and perfection, or at least not in any way that would point up to God. Quite the opposite, in fact. They see the world as empty and desolate, which they are right to do from their own perspective. Apart from God, the world is empty and desolate—or it would be if it could be apart from God."

"Again, I see your point, in the sense that I see how the logic goes."

"All right. They see the world, but they do not see that the world is an image of Divine wisdom. Nor are their minds ordinarily illuminated, for they are Renegades. Moreover, unlike the Renegades among us, they find themselves in that situation apart from any choice of their own. So, since their experience seems to show the absence of God from the world, and to show such absence as something simply given, the natural and obvious conclusion for them to draw is that there is no God. That is where those people start from."

Beatrice thought about it for a long time and then objected. "No. I am sorry, but as I turn it over and over in my mind, I cannot find any way in which it is not just obviously ridiculous. I mean, yes, to be sure, I can see from what you said how their experience seems to show the absence of God from the world. But still, no. The world is *not* an image of Divine wisdom, they say. Then, do they say the world is the realm of random chaos?"

"Well, some of them go so far as to say even that, but many do not. Many recognize the world as a system of regular order and lawful structure. As for how that can be if there is no God, some of those people say one thing, and some say another. Their answers range from the very clever to the blatantly stupid."

"So what then? Do they think the world is orderly of itself?"

"Some of them do, yes."

"Then they must also say the world exists of itself."

"Yes, that too."

"Then it is all nonsense. Only God exists of Herself. If the world were to exist of itself—by an impossible supposition—then it would have to enjoy the exalted attributes and privileges that only God enjoys. But that is clearly false and totally absurd. Even they must know that."

"Yes, dear child, they do know it. Or at least those among them with the best insight and deepest understanding know it. The problem is, because they are Renegades, their minds are weak and limited as well as being darkened. Therefore, it is very difficult for them—first to be aware of all this and then to take the implications seriously. This is so especially because, as I have explained, their experience seems to point in the opposite direction."

Once again, Beatrice thought about the teacher's comments for a long time. Then she said, "On this point also, I understand, but only in the limited sense of seeing how the logic goes through. But still, something seems to be very wrong here. I think what is basically wrong is this whole idea of Renegades who have never known anything else. For I reckon, given the idea of such Renegades, then all the rest follows, as you keep indicating."

"Yes, of course it seems wrong to you. You have enough to think about for this session. At this point, then, let us pause for a quick retrospective. How does all this stuff from these first two sessions add up in your mind so far?"

"Well, a Renegade is one who has failed to learn the basic lesson about the experience of real life in the real world. In an obvious way, the denial of God is the end of the line for that failure. The false view of the nature of reality that supports this denial is then a further development of this same basic error. Among us, the Renegades know better. But for a Renegade who has never known anything else, all this might seem kind of reasonable." It was in responding to the teacher's question that all this was thus clearly formed in Beatrice's mind, as the teacher had hoped. She had not known so well how it all added up until she worked it through in this way.

"Good—very good indeed. You understand perhaps even better than I expected. I think, if anything, both your mother and your old principal mentor underestimated you."

"I thank you. But many questions remain."

"Yes, to be sure. So until the next session, you should think about all this. But you should also think about what is involved in having someone be a Renegade in the first place. How does that happen among us? You start with that and go from there.—Meanwhile, I have to tell you that the easy part of the course is now over."

CHAPTER TWO

At their third session, Beatrice said, "As I turn it over and over in my mind, I can see more fully how what you said all comes together to make some kind of sense. But it comes together only in an upside-down or backward way. It is like having a coherent structure, but of twisted pieces. It is almost as if someone were to make up a logic, not to work through the truth, but to work through falsehoods and negations in order to avoid the truth."

"Yes, exactly so! That is very much the mentality of the Renegade. Or at least it is the mentality except insofar as the person has been corrected."

"I thought about that too. Yes, I reckon it would be, when it is carried through fully and consistently. Yet that is not what we observe with the Renegades among us."

"Only because they do not carry it through fully and consistently. That is because they know better underneath and also because there are plenty of Normals around to guide them. Along this line, have you thought about how there come to be Renegades among us?"

"Yes, I have, but my thinking has not led me to any serious insight. Of course I know what everyone knows, but I do not see where it leads."

"Right, then. The easy way is to think back to one's own childhood. Gradually, you became aware of various things, and then of yourself as a separate being, and of your own desires as your own, not necessarily shared by others. You became aware of yourself as able to choose. Eventually, you became aware that you could insist on looking to your own desires, just because they were directly given in your own mind, and you could carry this insistence even to the point of standing against God Herself. But you chose the other way instead. That is the difference between a normal or regular person and a Renegade."

Beatrice knew all this, although she had not previously found these points set forth so cleanly and systematically. "Yes, I know, but what then?"

"Well, the insistence on what one happens to want is what makes someone a Renegade. But of course, this same insistence narrows the focus of the mind. The natural tendency for a Renegade is to understand truth, not in terms of recognizing and respecting genuine reality or anything like that, but only in terms of what will work out to fulfill that one's desires. Again, the tendency is to understand reasoning, not in terms of working through the truth or anything like that, but only in terms of being clever to fulfill desires. Quite obviously, this kind of mentality would make it very difficult to appreciate any serious reality. In the present context, only insofar as they get past that way of thinking can they begin to see these things as pointing up to God."

"Well, I had not thought of it in those terms, but yes, I reckon that would follow."

"Now for the punch line. Among us, the Renegades have the memory of what it was like before to help them. But a Renegade who has never known anything else has an enormous task just to begin to look to the real truth."

After a long pause, Beatrice replied, "Yes, I can see that, at least in theory. But I see it only in terms of taking what I know about the Renegades among us and subtracting out the memory of what it was like before."

"Very good. That is exactly how you should think of it. But there is also something else, something I have held off on telling you until you were ready. They see the world as empty and desolate, given that it looks to them like the absence of God is just given. But it is not just that the world is there as a perfectly good system, only not inhabited by God. If you were to see the world as being apart from God, what do you think it would look like? By which I mean, what would its basic character appear to be?"

"Well, first of all, I expect it would be very hard to avoid saying the world is a realm of random chaos, as we have discussed."

"Yes, that too. But in one way, there is something even deeper."

"Hmm. Given that there is no God to support or maintain or even establish the world, and given also that the world does *not* exist of itself, what then? One thing is kind of obvious just from the terms in which all this has to be stated. The whole basis for the world to be what it is and do what it does would be profoundly negative. A negative basis—how would that work? The world cannot be an outgrowth of nothingness, for nothingness is not something positive that it could exist at all in the first place. But what then? Hmm…no, there is no other way to say it. With what you said, one would have to say that the primary fact of concrete reality is deadness, crazy as that sounds. A thing just *is*, based only on what just happens to be so, and that is all. Since the basis for a thing to exist at all is also the basis for it to be what it is, what the thing is turns out be a lump of deadness, and that is all. The nearest it could have to any positive function would be to disrupt or displace other things, all of which would also be equally dead."

"Good. Very good indeed. You understand very well and quite easily. Now, given this primacy of deadness, you can perhaps see why they might go on to say the world is a realm of random chaos."

"Yes, of course. Indeed, as I think it through along that line, all you have told me about their ideas falls into place.—But it sounds like they will think or say anything to justify their position as Renegades."

"No, not at all. In fact, that is the worst of it. With some of them, yes, but with others, no. Quite the opposite—they are trying to be honest. That is really how the world looks to them, and so that is what they think they have to conclude. You must remember what they are."

Beatrice stopped and thought. Then she said, "Well, yes, right. But it is all nonsense. If deadness were truly the primary fact of concrete reality, then only lumps of deadness would exist. Everything would be dead. They themselves are not dead, and they know it. That one fact should be enough to settle it even for them."

"With some of them, yes, it is, although how it works may take different forms for different individual people. With others, well...some do not manage to carry their thinking through that far, for whatever reason. Still others imagine that life can somehow be built up from the functioning of deadness."

"What did you just say?!"

The teacher repeated it.

"That is what I thought you said. But that is just too much. You were right about one thing. Their errors are far worse than the stuff the Renegades among us spout."

"Yes, that too. But now, why is it just too much?"

"Let me think. Hmm...hmm...hmm. I want to say that it makes a kind of sense to say the functioning of dead objects is like the zero level, so to speak, of the functioning that living beings have, but it will not work to say it is the other way around. But I do not know how to develop the point, let alone prove it."

"There is no need. Another theoretician among us, a woman named Astrid, worked it all out on this point long ago." This had happened dozens of centuries before Beatrice's life had begun. "Here is the easy way to think of it. Given that the only positive functioning is to disrupt or displace other things, there is then no room for any interior functioning among things. But to be alive is to have one's own interior functioning. So there is no room for life, except perhaps at the lowest levels, where no serious interior functioning of the being as a unified whole is required."

"Well, there you go! Given that, all the rest follows."

"Not so fast, Beatrice. Where does it follow that I should go there? Before you answer, you must first stop and calm down."

After a short pause, Beatrice answered, "Well, to begin with, it seems at least very questionable whether a lump of deadness could really exist at all in the first place. It seems almost like such a lump would be a chunk of nothingness raised up to be a positive something. And even if it could exist, what then? A rational animal, and even a higher animal among the dumb beasts, has a very rich mental life. This involves strong interior functioning, far beyond the low levels you said. Since there would be no room for this given what they would have to say, their whole structure of ideas collapses."

"Yes, you do understand very well and quite easily.—The problem is that when those of them who think this way contemplate building up higher levels out of lower levels, very commonly they do not think of the lower levels *as realms of deadness* in the way you mean, although perhaps they should in order to be consistent.

They imagine there to be some serious, positive character or functioning, and this allows them to hope it could be made to work, if only they knew enough, or were clever enough, or something like that."

Beatrice became aware suddenly that, once again, she had been deliberately left hanging, and the teacher was waiting for her to respond, but differently. She was supposed to see for herself and to say what came next. "No, I am sorry, but you will have to tell me what else."

"You said they know they are alive, and that should settle it for them. But do they, now? Do they really? Or at least, do they know it seriously enough so as to appreciate it? Among us, Renegades can degenerate and deteriorate quickly, so as to be almost like they are dead inside. Of course, this is only insofar as they have yet to be corrected. Well, that kind of thing can and does happen among them as well. Given that, as you say, all the rest follows."

With this, the teacher concluded the session, saying Beatrice had plenty to think about for the time being. Beatrice agreed, and so they parted.

At their next meeting, Beatrice said, "I have been thinking. Given that those people are Renegades who have sunk to the level of being dead inside, it is kind of reasonable to expect they would not acknowledge God or much of anything else—at least given that they do not have the advantages the Renegades among us have to help them be corrected."

"Good. I think now you understand."

"Yes, but then all this serves to reinforce a larger and deeper concern. I think most of the reason I find it difficult is the basic problem with this whole line of conversations. The very idea of a Renegade who has never known anything other than life as a Renegade remains deeply puzzling."

"Yes, indeed. I am sure it does. I told you before that the easy part of the course was over. Now begins the hard part. First of all, you were right about something important. No such Renegade could arise or exist among our people or anyone like us."

"This gets more and more remarkable!"

"Oh yes, certainly. A Renegade who has never known anything else must be based on radically different principles from what there is among our people. Among us, nothing like that is possible. You were right about that."

"Then what?"

"Among us, we are all the same kind or species of being, but each of us is separately created. On the other side—among them—what happens is very different. They arise through breeding and reproduction, like the dumb beasts. In other words, those people arise through animal generation."

Beatrice spoke slowly and carefully. "I have wondered sometimes whether, just as a theoretical possibility, God might do it that way." After pondering for another moment, she asked, "What difference exactly does that make? Why does it make possible what you said about Renegades who have never known anything else? Or have I misunderstood?"

"No, not at all. You understand rightly. But you must be very clear in your mind about the fact here before you can work through the implications. Now, you say you have wondered about it as a theoretical possibility. Good—that makes it easier. But still, you find the fact to be extraordinary, even anomalous."

"Yes, very much so. Only through direct action by God can any rational being come into existence. A person is a sheer jump above dumb beasts and all other lower beings."

The teacher interrupted. "Why should one believe that? Many of them do not."

"Well, reasoning is too exalted to be constructed from any other processes, including even the kind of low-level cleverness that dumb beasts can share."

"In fact, yes. But to know that depends on knowing reasoning to be a kind of superior awareness of reality, which it is. The problem is that many of them do not know that. As I told you a little while ago, they think of truth in terms of what works to fulfill their desires and of reasoning in terms of cleverness. Along that line, they think of reasoning as just a further extension or development of animal cleverness, or perhaps as something even less exalted." Then, after a brief pause, "But yes, what you said is correct. So, given that, you are wondering how one can get from animal generation to having a person come into existence. Well, in fact, it is possible, since it is actually real. So, you think about it and tell me how it is possible."

"Hmm...hmm...hmm. There are only so many possibilities. Since rationality cannot be constructed, it must be given directly by God. Something made directly by God must either be directly created, or else...what?" After a very long pause, Beatrice answered, "Or there must be some special intervention to make the thing by transmuting something else. So, given that those people arrive through animal generation, it must be that God intervenes to transmute animal organisms into genuine persons."

"Very good indeed. All that you have said just now is correct. Yes, that is exactly how those persons arise."

Before the teacher could say more, Beatrice found herself so overwhelmed that she blurted out, "No—I am sorry, but I need to say something. May I speak?"

"Yes, of course."

"Those people imagine reasoning can be constructed from the lower levels of life, and then they imagine life can be constructed from the functioning of deadness. Putting these ideas together, the exalted function of reason is built up from deadness. No. I am sorry, but somehow it seems even a Renegade who is dead inside should know better than that."

"Yes, certainly, and those of them with the best insight and clearest thinking would at least appreciate your concern, even if they might not agree with your answers. As for the others...well, Renegades do and say and think all kinds of things."

Then it hit her. "No, not so fast. You said some of them think of reasoning as an extension or development of something even less exalted than animal cleverness. Is this point connected with the concern I just raised?"

"Yes, of course it is. Very good, Beatrice. Here is the way to sum it up: there is the work of reasoning as a function of deadness, but that is all right, for what has to be known through reasoning is just the dead world of dead things.—No, no more questions right now. Next time. You have enough to think about for a while."

CHAPTER THREE

At the fifth session, Beatrice began by saying, "Once again, I have been thinking, and it seems to get worse the more I think about it. There is the positive fact of being actually real, and this is supposed to have a purely negative basis. Do they really not see anything wrong here?"

"Well, of course something is obviously wrong when it is stated that way. The problem is that very often, they do not exactly think of being actually real as something positive in the strong way you mean. Of course, to be actually real is a genuine fact, good as far as it goes, but often they think of that fact as kind of empty."

Instead of arguing further along this line, Beatrice said, "To be actually real is empty. Then do they think the difference between being real and unreal is empty?"

"Well, they would probably not speak of it in those terms, but some of them seem to think something like that, yes."

"Then they would also have to say the difference between truth and falsehood is empty."

"Yes, of course, that too, although they might not want to say that exactly."

"Oh, well, in that case, it is clear why they think reasoning can be just a function of deadness. I understand now."

"Yes, you do understand. Very good indeed, Beatrice."

"But it is just too much. Is all this really how they think?"

"Yes, all too often. The problem is that for Renegades who have never known anything else, there is the serious temptation to see the basis for the world as what you would call purely or deeply negative, and from there, there is the temptation for them to see real things as empty, and their existence as empty, and truth as empty, and there they go."

"But why should it not work the other way around? I mean, why should they not see that things are not empty, and truth is not empty? And therefore, why should they not see that deadness cannot be the primary fact, and so the basis cannot be purely or deeply negative? If they did this, they might then come to know there is God at the top."

"First of all, they are Renegades who have never known anything else. Second, when all goes well, what you said is more or less what does happen among them. The problem is that all too often, not all goes well, and that is why some of them say there is no God."

With this, the teacher paused to let Beatrice digest all this. After a short while, Beatrice asked, "What then? Where does it go from there?"

"We were discussing Renegades who have never had or known any other life. As I told you, they experience the absence of God as just given, apart from any choice of their own. From there, they find that the natural and obvious conclusion to be drawn is that there is no God. We have been discussing what all this involves, and how it works, and what the implications are. Before that, we were discussing why the fact of arising through animal generation makes it possible for there to be Renegades who have never known anything else."

"Yes, right—I remember now. How does it work? What is the connection?"

"First of all, do you have any other questions or concerns before we get into that?"

"Come to think of it, yes, I do. Everything else seems clear enough, but I am not sure how even they can think reasoning is just an extension of animal cleverness. What I mean is this: if they were to imagine reasoning is just a function of deadness somehow and leave it at that, then so be it. But animal cleverness belongs to the inner mental life of an animal. So once they recognize knowledge and awareness as belong to the inner functioning of a living being as a living being, it seems strange they should stop there and not carry it through."

"Oh, well, as I told you—first of all, they imagine life can be constructed out of deadness, to put it crudely and oversimplify slightly, as we discussed. Second, they think of reasoning in terms of cleverness to fulfill their desires. Given that fact, the rest is fairly straightforward."

"Yes, I considered that. But then I wondered when I reflected that there is also more serious reasoning even among them. Are there mathematicians among those people?"

"Well, there are many societies full of such people. Some are more savage, and some are more advanced. But there are mathematicians among some of them, yes."

"Am I correct in thinking that they know, for example, that the series of prime numbers runs forever and why this is so or how it is proved?"

"The serious mathematicians know all that, yes."

"Along the same line, what about natural science? Even to understand elementary mathematical kinematics requires some fairly serious intellectual abstraction, far beyond what any dumb beast can do. Are there theoreticians among them who know all this?"

"Again, the societies of such people differ, but there are among some of them, yes."

"Then it is bizarre for them to say reasoning is an extension of animal cleverness."

The teacher thought a moment and then asked, "Well, but what else should it be?"

"Something on a higher level."

"Right, and so we come back to the question of higher and lower levels. This question came up the other day, with the question of God or no God. As I told you, they understand the idea of having the lower level depend on the higher. The problem is that they find it hard to think in terms of higher and lower levels in the way you mean. The other day, you pointed out that an automatic device may work rightly on its own terms, with no need for intervention, exactly because it was built and built rightly by someone. What this analogy illustrates is that the specific function of the higher level over the lower may be to make it possible for the lower level to work rightly on its own terms, as opposed to overriding or interfering with the lower level. Yes, indeed so. As regards the character or status of reasoning, there is another error they commit, slightly different but related. All too often, they fail to appreciate that the higher level may work *by means of* the lower. They see the lower level working, and they do not see the higher level working alongside it—as it would be if there were some intervention—and so they imagine the functioning of the lower level is all there is to it."

Beatrice thought about this explanation and then replied, "I understand what you just said in the abstract terms in which you have stated it. But, first of all, I do not see how even they could fail to appreciate this point. Second, I do not see how exactly it applies to the present case, although I have some vague idea."

"Why do you think even they should appreciate this point?"

"You said some of the societies of such people have mathematicians and natural scientists. Do they also have artisans and craftspeople—those who work with tools?"

"Some societies of such people do, yes."

"Then it should be obvious. An artisan does not act instead of working with tools, and the functions of the tools do not displace the action of the artisan. No, but the artisan works by means of the tools. That being so, it should be obvious even to them that the higher level can and does act by means of the lower level."

"Yes, and here too, those among them with the best understanding and deepest insight do know it, just as they know the point of your analogy about automatic devices. But once again, you must remember what it is to be a Renegade who has never known anything else. It is very difficult for them even to achieve the knowledge of these things, let alone to develop the implications, as we have discussed."

Beatrice conceded the point and then asked, "But how exactly does this concern about having the higher level work by means of the lower apply to the present concern about the status of reasoning?"

"Well, Beatrice, have you ever considered in what way, exactly, reasoning is superior to the kind of mere cleverness dumb beasts display?"

"Not explicitly, no."

"Well, as you said, reasoning is on a higher level than animal cleverness. So we are rational beings, but we are rational animals, and that includes being animals. Thus, we share with dumb animals lower cleverness, imagination, and other mental faculties and functions. Now, one who thinks about abstract points in mathematics or natural science must leave that behind, as you said. But for that very reason, it is somewhat difficult to think about those things. Serious exertion is required. More commonly, people think about the concrete facts of this or that particular situation. This is easier, for the lower levels serve to facilitate such thinking. Dumb beasts can also think about the concrete facts of particular situations, and that is what their animal cleverness amounts to. What they cannot do is to develop or entertain any abstract awareness. For example, a bird can be aware of a berry as tasting sweet, but it cannot think of berries in general as tasting sweet. The bird can be aware of other animals as dangerous to itself, but it cannot think of various kinds of animals in general as being dangerous. To think abstractly about things in general, berries or animals or anything else, is just what it cannot do. Again, there are higher animals among dumb beasts that can solve problems, sometimes in clever or crafty ways. What such an animal cannot do is be aware that the solution for this case will work for such cases as a general proposition. To think abstractly about having something apply in general is just what it cannot do. So with people, some measure of understanding is achieved based on the animal cleverness shared with dumb beasts, just as such beasts enjoy some measure of genuine knowledge. But then, with people, this understanding is taken up to a higher level, and that is what it is to be aware intellectually of the concrete facts of particular situations. Similarly with imagination, what can be achieved by forming and holding a picture in one's mind—which dumb beasts can also do—is then taken up to a higher level, and that is how imagination can serve to promote understanding. The point is that intellectual awareness, including the awareness involved in reasoning, works by means of the lower levels in this way. That is how the question of higher and lower levels applies here."

"Well, I guess all that sounds about right. Indeed, as I think about it, what you said seems like the only way it could possibly work. Now let me see whether I understand rightly. One thing people observe is that when a Renegade takes severely sick, she may become unable to think straight. Given what you said, the explanation would be that the sickness deranges the bodily functioning involved in exercising animal cleverness, and so there is the failure or weakness of what gets taken up to the higher level of intellectual activity, and that is why her thinking is degraded."

"Yes, all that is correct."

"And so, as for why they misunderstand, what then? Let me see. Since intellectual awareness is mixed with the other things as part of a package deal, its distinctive character or function may too easily be overlooked. Is that it?"

"Yes, right—exactly so."

"Well, but what about abstract points of mathematics and natural science?"

"Most of those people think about such things only rarely. They do not have occasion to think about them much. We people—we Normals—have plenty of occasion to think about what is beyond the reach of the senses and imagination, for we experience God constantly, as you said the other day. For them, however, it is very different, as we have discussed."

Beatrice thought about all this and said, "Yes, I guess it makes sense well enough, but perhaps only in the backward or upside-down way I spoke of earlier. What then?"

"First of all, it is just as well that we went through the question of higher and lower levels rather carefully, including this specific application. It will turn out to be very relevant, as you will see. But for now, we left off last time with the question of how the fact of having persons arise through animal generation is relevant to why there can be Renegades who have never known any other life. That is where it goes from here."

"Yes, right. So what is the answer?"

The teacher was about to tell her but then said, "No, I should like to see how far you can work it through for yourself, based on what we have discussed. You tell me instead."

With that, the teacher called an intermission for them to have lunch together. During lunch, Beatrice turned it over and over in her mind. After lunch, she answered, "No, I am sorry, but as I think about it, it is just too bizarre. There can be Renegades who have never known any other life, and that is possible because they arise through animal generation, even though they are full persons. I am accepting on your word that all this is so, but it sounds too much like saying, 'Here is one exotic wonder, and here is another exotic wonder to explain the first one.'"

"Yes, of course. I know it does. It sounded that way to me when I first learned of it. The easy way might be to approach it from another angle and work it through piece by piece."

"What do you have in mind?"

"You spoke a little while ago of artisans or craftspeople and their tools. When God accomplishes something by working through created beings, She is kind of like the artisan, and they are like the tools. There is the obvious application to the present case. Ultimately, as you said, any person who is inferior to God can arise only because God makes the person and does so directly in some way. But there is the question of, so to speak, how much of the work She gives to the created beings who serve as Her tools. The problem is that when the tools fail, the work is then to that extent ruined, as happens with artisans among created beings. Do you understand so far?"

"Yes, so far it is easy enough."

"All right. With rational animals, there can be basically three levels of motherhood. With all three, the mother is like one of the tools with which God accomplishes the work of raising up and providing for the child. Among us, all children are foundlings, and all cases of motherhood are by adoption only. But there is another level where God entrusts much more to the mother. There is natural motherhood simply as a function among animals, as opposed to adoptive motherhood. This involves contributing genetically to the offspring. But among mammals, it involves gestation and bearing as well—what is sometimes called pregnancy and childbirth. As you know, there are the rational animals on the third planet of the next yellow star over, and among those people, there is natural motherhood, gestational only and not genetic, along with the protracted care and nurturing involved in adoptive motherhood. Since more is given to them, motherhood among them is understood to be much more wondrous than among us, and more of an occasion for rejoicing. Again, do you understand so far?"

"Yes." Like all her people, Beatrice knew that third planet to be full of Renegades, much more than her own world, even though the Normals were numerous enough to be clearly dominant. The questions about the Renegades and the provisions for them were much more pointed than among Beatrice's people. On that third planet, the Renegades were numerous enough to make necessary serious distortions in the whole structure of that civilization. Beatrice's people often used that third planet as a point of comparison in discussions about Renegades.

"Well, those people are like us as being all of the same kind or species. They are also like us as being each separately created, since the child is established as a fully formed living being and then implanted into the mother. There is no merely animal organism that must then be transmuted. That is one of the implications of having no genetic motherhood among them. But there is also the third level of motherhood, with genetic contribution as well as gestation, and also the protracted care and nurturing. At this level, it is not true anymore that each one is separately created in the same way. Instead, even more is entrusted to the mother. The problem is, if there should then be some corruption or betrayal with the mother, it may work to the child's ruin, just as in general the work of an artisan may be ruined by some failure of the tools used to do the work."

Beatrice thought about this and said, slowly and carefully, "Once again, what you have said makes sense in the very abstract way you have stated it. But still, I am left wondering."

"Are you perhaps wondering where or why any corruption or betrayal would come into the situation, given that the mother sees herself entrusted with something so wondrous?"

"Yes, exactly so. I was merely having trouble articulating the question."

"Right. That was one of the things I wondered when I learned of it. The trick is that you are assuming the mother is herself a Normal and not a Renegade."

At this, Beatrice's mind stood still for a long moment. Then, "Are you saying She would entrust motherhood, and even the highest level of motherhood, to a Renegade?"

"In a word, yes. It is so. She would, and She does."

Before the teacher could speak further, Beatrice reacted. She found herself too deeply amazed to respond beyond stuttering and stammering incoherently.

"Well, I was going to say that I answered your question in the terms in which you asked it. But in fact, the question is based on—well, on wrongful oversimplification, although I see my words misled you. In the case of a Normal woman of such a species, the highest level of motherhood is entrusted to her, just straight out. But with a Renegade of such a species, one may still say such motherhood is entrusted to her, but it is very often also more complicated." The teacher paused to think and then continued. "Even among us, when a child goes wrong to become a Renegade, she does not immediately die. No, but by the mercy of God, her lower levels of functioning, such as metabolism, continue to work out on their own terms, and that is why she remains alive to be brought to contrition and conversion. Something like that applies here also. The lower levels of functioning of such a Renegade woman include the biological processes for animal generation. So then, in these cases also, God allows the lower levels of functioning to work out on their own terms, and then She takes it from there to provide for the people. Very often, that—or at least some version of that—is more or less how such motherhood is entrusted to those people."

"But you said the child may be ruined by the mother's corruption or betrayal. So how God provides for the people in such cases must be truly mysterious."

"In one way, yes, of course. But to ask that is to ask about the whole order of Divine Redemption, and we have so far only scraps and fragments of knowledge about that. So for now, I think it would be best to explain further about how it works and leave aside why She allows it. Do you have any question or concern before I continue?"

"No, not at all. Please, speak on."

"In an obvious way, the offspring of Renegades start out with the status of being spawned from filth and darkness. That status is the basis for them to exist at all. Therefore, they are already themselves Renegades. But they have never known any other life."

"Now, wait a minute. When you say they are spawned from filth and darkness, that has to refer to their origin through animal generation."

"Yes, of course."

"Well, but then when God transmutes the animal organisms into real persons, why does that not cancel out the Renegade status?"

The teacher thought for a moment and then answered, "Very good. But you see, this kind of transmutation does not work by simply wiping out everything. What happens is that something is raised up to a higher order of being. However, what was there before remains as the lower level of the new being. Therefore, the status that comes with it remains. In this case, that means the underlying evil remains."

"Also, why should they be spoken of as being spawned from filth and darkness just because they arise through animal generation? Surely they arise in that way only because that is what God has ordained. But if God has ordained it, then no evil is involved."

"Yes, what you just said is correct, but there is more to it than that. It is not that they arise through animal generation. It is how that function is exercised among those people. Such beings breed and reproduce *as Renegades*, instead of as God originally intended."

"Does that apply even to a Renegade mother whom She has brought to full contrition and conversion?"

"Sad to say, yes it does. This is so for the same reason the Renegades even among us are and remain subject to sickness and bodily deterioration. The restoration of the person does not exactly reach down to the lower levels of biological functioning, and so it does not reach down to the processes of reproduction or generation. In that way, they reproduce only as Renegades, and so their offspring may be said to arise from corruption." But quite clearly, Beatrice did not understand, so the teacher added, "Perhaps the easy way to see it is to view it somewhat crudely. You speak of God as transmuting animal organisms into real persons. Well, but what are real persons? They are persons as having the capabilities of intellect and will, above and beyond what dumb beasts have. But they are not full persons as having their inner lives governed by wisdom and moral concern in the way that a Normal person does. They can be thought of as almost like mere talking animals instead of as full persons. That is all the personhood this transmutation gives them. Again, you can see it easily enough if you stop and think about the Renegades among us and what they are like before they begin to be corrected. Along this line, you can see that if those among us who are like that could reproduce, it would be apart from any reference to any

Divine gift that would raise one up to be a full person instead of almost like a talking animal. Well, that is how it works among the Renegade women of such species. The problem is that even when such a woman is brought to contrition and conversion, the lower level functioning whereby she can reproduce remains degraded, as I have explained."

Beatrice understood this well enough, but she was deeply shaken and greatly horrified, and so the teacher concluded the session, seeing that she had enough—or even too much—to think about for a while.

CHAPTER FOUR

The sixth session was delayed for a few days. The teacher was called away on personal business having to do with a relative. Beatrice was not left alone, although she could have been, as a Normal adult. Instead, after thinking about it, the teacher gave her into the keeping of an old, personal friend. The reason for this was noteworthy. The teacher and the friend had agreed that the delay would come in handy, as giving Beatrice extra time to work through all she had learned, especially at the last session, and to turn it over and over in her mind. But they agreed further that what she had learned might well be almost too much for the mind to accept. ("I have had to teach her about Renegades on other worlds.") So it was decided that it would be well to have Beatrice supervised, and if need be comforted, in the teacher's absence.

Now this old friend was an artisan, a craftswoman. Beatrice understood such things in a general way, but she knew only what was commonly taught to any ordinary child among her people. So the friend took her up to the next level, having her perform easy tasks and work on simple things during those days. Beatrice found this work as a novice craftswoman to be a great pleasure. Indeed, although she did not articulate it until much later, she realized intuitively that this interlude was exactly what she had needed. The friend had suspected that this might be so, and the teacher had agreed.

Upon returning, the teacher was somehow clearly different from what Beatrice had seen before. In fact, as she thought about it, she found it puzzling, for she had never seen anything like it. The friend explained it to her. "Oh, well, you see, my old friend is in the early stages of recovering from great sorrow."

"Oh, dear. That is a very sad thing. I wish no cause for such sorrow had arisen."

"Very good. I thank you on my friend's behalf, and I hope you may never have cause for such sorrow."

Then the obvious suspicion came into Beatrice's mind. "Does this sorrow have to do with why my teacher was called away?"

"Yes, child, it does." That was all the explanation the friend offered, and Beatrice left it there. As it turned out, she never learned any more about it within her whole lifetime.

The sixth session began the next day. Beatrice started by saying, "I have been thinking about it, and it adds up much more cleanly and easily than I had realized, given what you told me at the end last time. If they are almost like mere talking animals, then I can see why some of them imagine there is no God. Of course, in order to say that and make it work, they have to have a twisted view of a whole lot of other things as well. But then that too is not strange, given what you said."

"Well, as I said at the time, I was speaking somewhat crudely to make it easier to see. In fact, the view of those people as almost like mere talking animals is in some ways seriously oversimplified. But as for the basic idea of what you just said—yes, right. Exactly so. You have understood very well. But I need to see also how well you understand about children of Renegade parents who are themselves Renegades and have never known anything else."

"Of course I have thought about that too—very much so. Yes, it makes sense in terms of having the logic work through. But it is still kind of bizarre. With what you said, God makes new persons who are already Renegades! Why would She do that? And before that, how is it even possible?"

"Once again, the way to understand it is to take what you know about the Renegades among us and then go on from there."

"Well, She is concerned to bring those among us to contrition and conversion. So it seems She would be concerned to bring them to contrition and conversion as well. But perhaps 'contrition' is a poor word for it, since they are not personally guilty as though they had themselves chosen wrongly. She would be concerned to bring them to look to Her, and submit to Divine mercy, and so forth."

"Yes, indeed. Exactly so. The point is not that there should be people who start out being Renegades. The point is that there should be people for whom God has provided. She is so great that She can accomplish this even through Renegade parents. And also, there is the answer to your question about how it is even possible. It is not contrary to Her wisdom and goodness to do that, just as it is not contrary to the wisdom and goodness of a craftswoman to make up perfectly good objects if she can manage to do so using tools damaged through another's wrong."

Beatrice thought about all this and agreed. Then she asked, "But in that case, why do some of them imagine they arrive through animal generation, as though that were all there is to it? For that seems to come out of what you said. Or have I misunderstood?"

"No, not at all. Many of them do imagine that. As for why, that is to ask why they imagine there is no God. Once again, you must think what it would be like to be one of those people." The teacher thought for a moment and then resumed. "Earlier, you spoke of regular order and lawful structure as pointing up to God. I assumed you were speaking of the laws of physics and chemistry at that time."

"Well, yes, although I had not developed it explicitly in my mind. But yes, since that would be obvious even to a Renegade. The orderly structure of reality may be said to start with physics and chemistry, and then go on from there."

"Yes, right—of course. But in another way, that is just the problem. When you say it goes on from there, you mean there is moral and spiritual reality, with its own laws and rules, as a much higher level of the same orderly structure. Well, you know that, and I know that, but they do not know it. Among them, what happens is very often—very often and not as a rare exception, mind you—grossly contrary to the right order defined by ethical law. To be sure, God will resolve everything in Her own good time and in Her own ways. But the process or function of having it resolved is largely hidden from them. You start out knowing enough to be sure that God will take care of it, without having to see it done. But they do not start out knowing that. Consequently, it could look to them almost as if there is no serious moral or spiritual reality. As for having God provide for them, instead of having animal generation be all there is to it—the problem is, they find it hard to see that God is concerned to provide for them, given where they have to start from."

The teacher paused to let Beatrice digest all this. At length, Beatrice said, "All right. Is that all?"

"No, not quite. Some of them would take seriously your points about the laws of physics and chemistry specifically and about the dependency of the world in general. On that basis, they would say that yes, there is God, and She set it all up and set it into motion. But they would also say God has no serious care or concern, or at least no concern that people can understand. They would say people are just talking animals, very much like other animals, and they arise and perish like any other animals, and that is all."

Beatrice thought about this and said, "My impression is mixed. I want to say what you just said is certainly more—more—well, more clear minded than the straight denial of God. But even so, it seems to be somehow more deeply wrong."

"Can you tell me why?"

"Hmm...yes. It has to be because it is too bizarre to affirm God but not as the Founder and Guardian of the moral order."

"Yes, indeed so. But again, that assumes there is enough reality to the moral order to be worth taking seriously, and that is what they find problematic."

Beatrice considered this and then said, "Well, all right. Once again, it adds up to some kind of sense, at least in terms of their own upside-down logic. Yes, as I turn it over in my mind, it does make sense, given that the opposition to moral and spiritual reality is what makes someone a Renegade in the first place."

"Now you understand. Very good, dear child."

"But still, it is all nonsense. What you said about their view of the world exists only because their experience is distorted and perverted. Some version of that fact should be obvious even to them. You said before that they measure truth in terms of their desires. Even they must know this is not the way to understand and appreciate genuine reality."

"Yes, they do know it, or at least the best of them do. The problem is what I told you before. Because they are Renegades, their minds are weak and limited, as well as lacking illumination and thus being darkened."

After a long pause, Beatrice said simply, "What then? Where does it go from there?"

"No, not yet. You have enough to think about for now. We shall discuss it next time. I think I can promise you the next session will be much more interesting." So indeed Beatrice found it to be—far beyond her own wildest dreams.

CHAPTER FIVE

Once again, the next session was delayed, but by just one day this time. One of the teacher's colleagues, a Traveler who had not previously been available to be consulted, came to visit on professional business. After this business had been concluded, she met with Beatrice. They exchanged customary greetings and pleasantries, and then Beatrice spoke of her lessons in answer to the Traveler's very gentle questioning. After about ten minutes of this, she glanced at the teacher as if to say, "You know we have to talk." Beatrice missed it, as the Traveler had intended, but the teacher picked up on it. So, later that day, while Beatrice slept, the Traveler began, "Surely you know what you have here."

"If you mean what I think you mean, then of course I do."

"She has all the makings of a truly great Traveler, perhaps even to be the leading Traveler in the history of our world. But she is more than that—much more. She is more like a theoretician, but she is also much more than that. Is there any question about this?"

"No, not at all. She knows it in some measure. I know it much more."

"Then you as a theoretician know even better than I do what all this means."

"Yes, I do. Even she has some vague awareness. I have already planned to tell her at our next session."

"Very good, my old friend. I only wish I could be there to see it. But I have to leave tomorrow morning on other business."

At her next session with Beatrice, the teacher began, "You must ask freely whatever you will."

Beatrice said, "Am I correct in thinking the existence of Renegades who have never known any other life is not generally known among our people?"

"Yes. Yes, that is correct. It is bad enough that Travelers and theoreticians have to know about it. There is an unspoken understanding among those of us who know that it is best to speak of it only as necessary."

"What is the answer for those people?"

"Well, of course, the short answer is that they are not forsaken, just as the Renegades among us are not forsaken."

"That is about what I figured, based on our past conversations." Then it spilled out of her. "Is the fact that you have told me about those people especially significant somehow?" She let this question stand, even though she wanted the teacher to explain much more about such Renegades instead of going on to other topics.

The teacher had long since learned to probe for the question behind the question the student asked. "Yes, indeed it is. But I want you to elaborate."

"All this has to be leading up to something important you have not yet told me. So, what is it?"

The teacher spoke slowly and carefully. "Right. Beatrice, you told me you know about the Renegades what everyone knows.

As you have just learned, there are things that not everyone knows." Then, weighing her words with special care, the teacher continued. "But that is not all. Beyond this, there is much about these questions not known at all among our people, not even to Travelers and theoreticians. Do you know where it goes from there?"

"No, of course not." Then something exotic came into her mind. "Or maybe I do!"

"Please, you must speak freely."

"There are old prophecies about some special explorer who is to arise among us."

"Indeed. When and where is this to happen? What about this explorer?"

"Let me think.—I believe it is to be in this age and in this part of our world. The explorer is not to be an ordinary Traveler. Instead, this person is to have extraordinary capabilities of mind, in order to observe and understand and yet not be overwhelmed."

"Yes, all that is correct. Beatrice, I have discussed the question with your mother and your principal mentor and also with my colleagues. We are all agreed. I can answer now the question about the exotic destiny you are to fulfill. Beatrice, it looks like you are the explorer who is to arise."

Beatrice closed her eyes and prayed for guidance. Then she said, "What shall I do, or what will happen? What should I expect?"

"First of all, there will be a vision in a dream. This will not be like ordinary dreams. Your ordinary bodily functioning will be disabled in order to make the vision possible. In particular, you will not be able to awake normally. I do not know how this will befall you or how it will work out. I know only that, as always, there will be nothing for you to fear, given that your mind is fixed on God and the things of God. She will see you through whatever may happen."

"Do you know whether this vision will concern those on the third planet of the next yellow star over? For there, the questions about the Renegades and the provisions for them are much more pointed than they are among us."

"Yes, I know the answer to that. No, Beatrice, it is not to be about those people. It is to be about something much more wondrous." The teacher paused and then said, slowly and carefully, "It is to be about the Home World of the Redemption."

"The Home World of the Redemption!" Her mind stood still in wonder. Finally she asked, "What more? If you know that, then there must be further prophecies that are not generally known. What else can you tell me?"

"Yes, certainly there are further prophecies. But I do not know much more. None of us does. Moreover, most of what I do know I have to keep from you until you awake from the vision. For you to know too much too soon would make it harder for you. However, I shall tell you what I can. You must ask freely."

"Is there anything more I need to learn before it starts?"

"No, not unless you yourself have some question or concern in your mind. I have told you now because I see you are ready."

Beatrice pondered and then said, "From various indications, and especially the fact that you have taught me so much about Renegades, I gather that world is full of Renegades. What about that?"

"Yes, that is correct."

"How does that world compare with the third planet of the next yellow star over?"

"Well, regarding what we discussed about God or no God and the related concerns, we do not rightly know how far they understand all that. Indeed, we know precious little, as I told you. One of the things we know is that that world is even worse than the third planet of the next yellow star. For you see, those people reproduce through animal generation, and so they breed people who know life only as Renegades, as we discussed. Furthermore, *that is all there is on that world.* There were the First Parents, who were created as pure and innocent. But they sinned against God and thereby ruined themselves and all their descendants as well as a further consequence. Eventually they died, just as the dumb beasts die. Since then, there are and have been only Renegades among them, save only for the special situation God set up for the Redemption itself. At this time, that world is totally void of Normals. Now, Beatrice, that is most of what we know, and how we know even that is something of a story in itself. Beyond that, all we have are scraps and fragments concerning that world, and I have to withhold those from you for now."

"You say they died, just like the dumb beasts."

"Yes, that is correct. That is what happened to them.—In answer to what you are thinking but have not yet asked, yes, that is also what happens with the Renegades among us, and with all the others on other planets as well."

Now it was Beatrice who spoke slowly and carefully. "From various indications, I guess I should have known that. But I had not thought it through." Once again, she closed her eyes and prayed for guidance. Then, "What about my own mission?"

"As I told you, first will be the vision in a dream. It will begin in the next few days, perhaps even this very night. But how it will happen, I do not know."

But it did not begin that night, although that had been the most reasonable surmise. Yet after the fact, the teacher saw why what really happened was the most reasonable way for the situation to develop.

When they awoke the next morning and nothing had yet befallen Beatrice, the teacher decided to visit a colleague and to take Beatrice along. This colleague specialized in providing for Renegades but was currently doing less practical work to engage for a time in theoretical research. On the way,

Beatrice and her teacher came upon one of the colleague's protégés, a Renegade who had wandered into deadly danger through her own folly. Happily, Beatrice and the teacher succeeded in delivering her from the fearful fate. But in the process, Beatrice had to strive beyond the limit, so that she spent herself and cracked her powers. The teacher and the rescued Renegade (now much chastened and sobered) managed to take Beatrice to the colleague's place. This colleague was gifted with special capabilities for healing (very useful in providing for Renegades). Upon their arrival, the colleague examined Beatrice quickly and then caused her to go into a deep sleep, explaining that this would allow the best chance for her body to heal itself.

And so she slept, and slept, and slept, for days. When finally she awoke, Beatrice found her body to be very feeble and her mind to be clouded. The colleague told her to relax as well as she could, warned her not to move or speak any more than she had to, and gave her food and water. This improved both her mind and body, and then Beatrice found herself astonished at what was happening.

The colleague explained, "Nothing is wrong. What you are feeling is the natural consequence of being severely and acutely overstressed with bodily exertion in the way you were." But Beatrice was still obviously puzzled, and so the colleague added, "It is just that it is very rare for Normals to be overstressed in that way. No, do not speak. Drink this mixture I have prepared. It will replace the specific chemicals of which your body has been depleted. It will also relax you, which is what you need just now. If you fall back asleep, that too will be just as well."

Beatrice did fall back asleep. She slept through the rest of that day, and through the night, and into the next morning. But there were no more visions—only the ordinary dreams of a mind processing its own experience.

When at last she awoke fully, Beatrice was more happy than she had ever been before, with deep joy that was almost heart-breaking. She was surprised at the relief of the others, since she had not known the severity of her own condition. After this concern had been talked out and resolved, Beatrice turned to comfort the Renegade. "Dear child, of course I forgive you. For you see, I have nothing to resent. Yes, you did wrong, but still, through that, Divine prophecy was fulfilled. No, I have only love for you. You do well to be sorry you did wrong, but that should make you look to God all the more. That is all." Beatrice also thought but left unsaid that her experience where the life or death of a person was at stake had prepared her mind to visit a world where people were constantly dying.

After an exercise of devotion in which all four of them took part, Beatrice asked the Renegade to take her leave. "I have much to tell my teacher and your guardian. I am afraid that for you to hear it without special preparation would both disturb your mind and lead you to misunderstand." The colleague smoothed over the situation by sending her on a lengthy errand. Then Beatrice spent the next few days telling the following story.

CHAPTER SIX

"Where to begin? First of all, there is that world itself, the planet on which all these things happened. It too is the third planet of a yellow star. Again, both the period of the planet's revolution around its star and the period of its rotation about its own axis are almost exactly the same as we have on our planet. But these facts, and almost all the other details, are already known among us from the reports of ancient Travelers.—One thing that is not known from those reports turns out to be important. The old Travelers did not speak of it because they did not know. I shall came back to this point later.

"There is also the dominant species of rational animals on that world, among whom God accomplished these wonders. Regarding their bodily shape, size, and character, they are not what most of our people imagine. They are very much like the Glarpesh Blagonto, apart from two things—one minor and one major." Like Beatrice's people, the Glarpesh Blagonto were all of the same kind or species, but each was separately created. However, as with the people on the third planet of the next yellow star over from Beatrice's world, they enjoyed gestational and not merely adoptive motherhood. Again, as with Beatrice's people, there were some Renegades among them, but an even smaller percentage than among Beatrice's people, and the Normals were clearly predominant. Like other peoples, they exchanged Travelers and knowledge with Beatrice's people, and there were what human societies would call full diplomatic relations.

"The minor point is that their skins are not multicolored checkerboards." Beatrice's people had other board games, but not checkers. However, "checkerboard" is the nearest equivalent to what she said in her own language. "Except as a rare aberration, or a special feature I shall describe in a moment, the skin of each one of those people is more or less uniform in color over the whole body, although the people differ in color from each other. There is, in fact, some rough grouping of those people by color. The special feature is that with those darker in color, the skin on their palms and the soles of their feet would commonly be noticeably lighter than the rest, but the rest is more or less uniform except as a rare aberration.—The major point is with how they breed and reproduce. I had wondered whether the animal generation among them would be parthenogenetic or hermaphroditic. The answer is neither. They have full differentiation of the sexes. They are mammals and fully viviparous—not even marsupials, but placental. By their standards, all of us would have to be considered biologically female, for we too are mammals, and our bodies are set up with full capabilities for adoptive motherhood but with no capability for natural fatherhood.

"However, their minds are perhaps even more remarkable. First of all, there is the distinction between—well, between what might be called underlying intellectual capability on one side and actual operating intelligence on the other. In terms of their underlying intellectual capability, those people of the Home World of the Redemption are clearly superior to us. But because they are Renegades who have never known any other life, and because there are no Normals among them to offer guidance, they are almost always clearly inferior in regards to their actual operating intelligence. In saying this, I mean to factor out the benefit of having the mind illuminated that a Normal person enjoys. The wisest among them are roughly on the level of our moderately bright penitent Renegades, apart from some special Divine gift.

"Yet it is more complicated than that. They are largely blind concerning moral and spiritual reality. As a further extension of this fact, they are lacking in wisdom and insight concerning any reality. On the other side, they are highly competent for things that do not require wisdom and deep insight. This is where they display their underlying superiority. Except in one specialized area that I shall speak of later, they are almost as sophisticated in mathematics as we are, for they can do much with mere cleverness. Some insight is needed, of course, but very little comparatively speaking. Indeed, except in that one area, they might well have been greatly ahead of us, but we have the advantage of being a much older civilization."

The civilization among Beatrice's people was much older for two reasons. First, her people were an older species than the other people—not vastly older, just a few dozen millennia, but that was enough to be significant. Second, and more important, their civilization had run continuously since ancient times. There had not been the disruptions and devastations, with the need to begin again, that the other people had suffered through the conflicts among Renegades.

"They are clearly less sophisticated than we are in natural science. Since this calls for a larger measure of insight and awareness regarding concrete reality, their mere cleverness gives them a lesser advantage. Also, of course, here too there is the advantage we have as an older civilization. Furthermore, there is what

I said about the weakness of the old reports. There are naturally occurring magnets available to be discovered and used. That is why those people discovered magnetism as quickly and easily as they did. Otherwise, they would be even further behind us—much further—in natural science. But the magnets and their attributes had not been discovered by those people in the times of those reports, and the Travelers were focused on observing the people rather than exploring the planet as such. I know the Travelers knew about the magnetic field that protects the planet as a whole, of course. That being so, it would have been easy to find the magnets. It is just that, as I said, they were not concerned to investigate.

"At this point, I come back to the question of mathematics. I said they were almost equal to us except in one specialized area. That area is the mathematical analysis of logic. This has been developed among them in some measure, but it is fairly recent in their history, and it is clearly inferior to what we have. I expect this is largely because they have a lesser appreciation of reasoning, as I discussed with my teacher before the vision began. Remarkably enough, there is a serious point along this line, having to do with a practical application they have developed, that I shall come back to in a moment.

"The one area where they are clearly ahead of us is in working with gadgets and devices, including automatic devices. The development of automatic devices is more recent among them than among us, but they have surpassed us, as with devices in general. Their progress here has been very rapid now that they have acquired the critical concepts and ideas, because they feel far greater practical urgency than we do, as do the Renegades among us, apart from being comforted. For they are confronted with the stark facts of misery and eventual death in the manner of dumb beasts. Then again, I have to qualify what I said. They are ahead of us insofar as there is the basis for comparison.

Among us, the work with gadgets and devices has been largely based on different principles and has proceeded along different lines.

"Now, before my vision, my teacher said Renegades might misunderstand reasoning as just an extension of animal cleverness such as dumb beasts have, or perhaps as something on an even lower level. I wondered about this lower-level business, but I failed to ask about it before the vision because I was too much caught up in the main thrust of the situation. But I found out in my vision. This is the practical application I spoke of a moment ago, having to do with their mathematical analysis of logic. They have devices whose functioning can be set up to mimic the work of tracing through logical structures by working automatically. Well, some of those people think of reasoning as an extension of such mechanized functioning. This involves looking upon reasoning as based on even *less* awareness of reality than what dumb beasts have—which is, of course, just a little too ridiculous—but that is what some of them think and even what has become somewhat popular among them to believe. Then again, since they are Renegades, all kinds of crazy ideas have to be expected."

The teacher's colleague spoke up. "We have long known about such devices and such errors on other worlds full of Renegades. And yes, there is the obvious explanation you just gave. But still, those other worlds outgrow such errors quickly enough. As you know, that analysis of reasoning will not work out even on its own terms when the technical details are worked through. Have the theoreticians on that world not yet discovered Rosemary's Theorem?" Rosemary had been a landmark mathematician of that civilization. A dozen generations before Beatrice had arisen, Rosemary had discovered a critical limitation on what can be done with the kind of formal protocols that can be implemented or mimicked with the mechanized functioning of automatic devices. Other worlds had "outgrown" the error of viewing reasoning as this kind of functioning as they had come to discover this limitation for themselves and to appreciate the implications.

"Well, yes, they have, but the implications have not yet been appreciated."

Then Beatrice paused briefly. She resumed, but now with a clear note of sadness in her voice. "There is also a point of history. No Traveler of any species who was a Normal person has visited the Home World of the Redemption since ancient times. This is generally known among our people. What is not generally known is why such visitations have been forbidden. But it was revealed to me in my vision. Quite simply, it was for our own sakes. It would have been contrary to Her plan to allow us to interfere, and it would have very cruel—for us, not for them—to have us watch and be forbidden to interfere. I myself was able to observe what happened only because I knew intellectually that it was already long since accomplished in times past, and especially because I knew that She had already long since turned everything right-side up. Otherwise it would have been unbearable. Even so, there would have been a tremendous urge to interfere if I had been able to do anything other than observe passively."

Beatrice's teacher confirmed all these points regarding their bodies, their minds, and the history by disclosing that all this was among the prophecies and the ancient reports from Travelers that had been kept hidden from her. The teacher's colleague concurred.

Then Beatrice resumed. "What was there to observe that was totally overwhelming in this way? There was enormous evil committed directly against God Herself. We are aware of perjury and blasphemy committed by Renegades on various worlds, and we find even that to be both horrifying and appalling to witness. Well, what happened on that Home World was far beyond all that." With this, she had to pause before she could continue. Then she said, "What She did to accomplish the Redemption was far beyond our hopes and dreams. More than that, it was beyond *their* hopes and dreams, even though there were mysterious prophecies among them speaking of what was to be."

Once again, Beatrice had to pause. Then she began a fast-paced, noninterruptible spiel of the kind someone spouts when she needs to say it quickly, and get it all out, and get it over with.

"That enormous evil was the very means by which the Redemption was accomplished. Your protégé did wrong, but through that, Divine prophecy was fulfilled. That is how it works in general. Out of evil, God brings good. Otherwise, She would not allow evil to arise or exist at all. Even children learn that among us. Well, this was the great case of all cases for that rule to apply. And so the Lady God set up the situation such that the evil was directed specifically against Herself in such manner that She could destroy it."

After Beatrice had paused again for a long time, her teacher's colleague asked simply, "What then?" This was said for Beatrice's sake, to get her past the blockage in her mind.

"In order to destroy the evil—well, how is any evil destroyed? People do evil because it has some aspect of being desirable, and that distracts them from taking seriously its character as evil. In order to be resolved and overcome, evil must be disclosed for what it is and experienced as the evil it is. But to experience evil as evil is to suffer. So, in order to destroy the evil—well, there is no other way to say it, She set up that She Herself could and—and *did* suffer through it, very horribly and totally undeservedly.—There, I have said it."

This time it was her own teacher who spoke up. "Be comforted, dear child. It was not for you to stop it. She could have stopped it forcibly, with uncontestable power, at any moment. But She chose to allow it and see it through."

"Yes, I know that, or else it would be unbearable, in spite of everything."

"All right, then," her teacher said, "tell us what you can. There are many questions."

Beatrice paused, then spoke again, but differently. She was more of an adult person now than her teacher had observed before. "First of all, you tell me. Prior to the Divine activity whereby the Redemption was accomplished, there was a lengthy preparation, stretching over many centuries and over dozens of generations. For them, this was a long series of life spans, so that all those involved in the beginning of the preparation were long dead when the Redemption occurred. This preparation involved its own line of prophecies. Now, the visitations to that world by Normal Travelers were ended before this process of preparation began. We knew that some new phase was going to begin among them, but not what or how. Yet even so, have any of those prophecies become known to us in any way whatever?"

"I assume you mean the prophecies from that preparation? No, not at all." Then the teacher turned to the colleague. "Your researches may have taken you further even than most theoreticians. Have you run across anything like that, among us or any other people?"

"No, not really. There are other things that may perhaps be relevant to the Redemption, but nothing of those old prophecies among them."

"Too bad," Beatrice replied. "That might have made it easier. All right, then. So be it. But what happened was too wondrous, too exotic, to lay it out systematically, in the manner of a scholarly exposition. So instead, I shall tell it as I myself learned it, by taking you through my vision."

"To begin with, there was one noteworthy difference from ordinary dreams. All of us on this world speak the same language. But some of the other peoples with whom we are involved have other languages, if only because they have different bodily organs for speaking. However, when we dream about those people, the dreams represent them as speaking in our own language. Well, those people on that Home World have a multitude of different languages among them, all of which are very different from both our language and also those of any of the peoples with whom we are involved. I observed those people as speaking in their own languages in all cases, although I was always able to understand effortlessly what was being said.—I mean that the correct translation always came into my mind effortlessly, not that I knew what was meant beyond what the words conveyed. If someone's words were weak or sloppy or otherwise inadequate or inappropriate to convey what he or she intended, then I would be puzzled or misled just as well as anyone else."

Both the teacher and the colleague found this multitude of languages among them to be remarkable indeed. Then the colleague remembered learning of something old and almost forgotten from a world very remote from their own. An especially brilliant theoretician there had long ago become aware of, and proceeded to explore, that multitude of languages by correlating the reports of many Travelers from many worlds. When this point had been smoothed over for the moment, Beatrice resumed her narrative.

"In addition, I always knew the correct evaluation of what someone was saying. What I mean is that I always knew both whether the person was speaking sincerely and also whether what the person said was factually correct." Beatrice and her people knew about both lying and also more crafty forms of deceit from their experience with the Renegades among them. To know in this way whether someone spoke sincerely was a special privilege of her vision.

"The way it worked was, I was attached to this one woman, to follow her as she learned and developed. I learned of the Redemption with her as she explored the history of what had been done and been taught. However, I had the advantage that, as part of my vision, my mind would be sent back to observe the relevant living history and then brought forward again to be with the woman."

With this, Beatrice had to pause and think how to proceed. Then, "Dear teacher, you had a whole lot to say to me about Renegades who imagine there is no God. But really, that turns out to be an oversimplification, as least regarding those people. Yes, to be sure—given what we mean in speaking of God, some of them say there is no God. We mean there is the Absolute Being at the top, Who exists of Herself and Who makes everything else exist according to Her wisdom and does so as a free gift based on the choice of Her will, such that those things are made to exist as an act of true creation from nothing. All right, many of those people deny that there is any Absolute Being at the top. But in a whole lot of cases, the denial is kind of worthless. You see, what happens in many cases is that even they understand there has to be some basis for things such that this basis has Divine attributes, and so they imagine that such attributes belong to other things, lesser beings. The more serious denial of God, wherein someone denies all Divine attributes as well, is perhaps relatively rare even among them, although it does occur sometimes. As it happened, this point turns out to be very relevant to that woman to whom I was attached."

Then she burst out, "There is also something else. It may come up as I tell the story, but I should tell you right now. We speak of God in the feminine exclusively, simply because all the people of our kind or species are female. Really, of course, God is far above and beyond the whole division of male versus female. We know that perfectly well, and it is also given to them within the right Faith pertaining to Divine Redemption. But within that Faith, and also within the preparation leading up to the events of the Redemption, God is spoken of almost exclusively in the masculine instead. Why this should be so is something I hope to explain as we go along."

With that, Beatrice began to tell the remarkable story of that remarkable woman.

CHAPTER SEVEN

Her name in her own language and among her own people was Wendy. She was born on the hundredth anniversary of the day one of the natural scientists of her species had first discovered radioactivity, which was many centuries after the critical events of the Redemption occurred. Wendy was born and raised on a volcanic island within a cluster of volcanic islands, near enough to the planetary equator to avoid being excessively cold. This fact turned out to be important for her moral and spiritual development.

Wendy was conceived and born as an application of the point that, as the saying goes, God writes straight with crooked lines. At that time and place, it was common for people to engage in sexual relations apart from the provisions established under Divine law, or even contrary to the arrangements they had entered into pursuant to such provisions. Wendy resulted from a union of two people who had not entered into any such arrangement. But the truth turned out to be worse than that. After the relationship had been going on for some time, the people found out they were brother and sister and had been separated when they were far too young to remember. Such relationships between brother and sister were almost universally recognized as forbidden. As soon as they learned their real history, they stopped having sexual relations with each other. But by then, the woman was already pregnant.

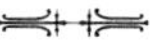

Beatrice had to explain it in this elaborate way because she did not have words to do otherwise. Sexual unions as well as sexual reproduction were foreign to her people. On her world, these things were observed only among dumb beasts. Consequently, among ordinary people of her species, there were no such words as "marriage," "fornication," or "adultery." Theoreticians and Travelers did have such words, but Beatrice had not learned this specialized vocabulary prior to her vision. However, when she had explained all this, her teacher and the colleague taught her the words right then, along with some other vocabulary as well.

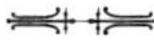

In spite of the sexual union, the pregnancy should not have happened. Many years before, when he was still a child under the guidance and protection of his adoptive parents, sterilization had been imposed on the natural father as a clinical procedure. This had been done, not by his will, nor by the will of the parents, but rather through error and confusion. But once it was done, it could not be undone. Reversal was tried and failed. However, it had been known to happen rarely in such cases that the patient's own body would repair the damage that had been inflicted and would restore its reproductive capability. That had happened in this case, although the natural father did not know about it.

The natural mother knew about the sterilization, but she did not know about the spontaneous recovery until she learned of her pregnancy.

The pregnancy was not discovered until six weeks after they had learned their real history. So, as it happened, Wendy's natural father died without knowing either of Wendy's existence or of his spontaneous recovery from that old procedure, having traveled to another part of the world and been murdered by bandits five days before the discovery. Specifically, he had found himself called upon to stand fast and be killed rather than deny the right Faith given within the order of Divine Redemption, and he did so. The mother learned of his death on the same day she learned of her pregnancy, just a few hours after learning of the pregnancy. At that point, she was not sure what to do or not do. She became only more agitated and confused as she turned the question over and over in her mind. Finally, in desperation, she turned to an old friend from her childhood, who was almost like an honorary sister.

The first thing the friend had to do was to get her past the weeping and blubbering in order to extract the straight story from her. When this had finally been accomplished, she began. "All right, Diana. The first thing you have to do now is to shut up and listen."

"But Alfreda, I think...I think...I think...I have no idea what to think."

"Exactly! You are not thinking right now. You are not even trying to think. You are too busy burning emotion instead. So what you need to do is shut up and listen." Then Alfreda stepped away, poured two vessels full of a red beverage, and returned with a vessel in each hand, saying, "The second thing you need is to drink with me." This would have a calming effect on Diana's mind.

After the beverage had taken effect, Alfreda said, "Now, let us see where we are. The whole problem is that you do not know either what you want or what you need. All right, so be it. We can come back to that later. Let us see whether you know what you believe in and where you stand. Perhaps we can start with that."

This approach panned out. As a child, Diana had been taught the right Faith given within the order of Divine Redemption, and she still followed that as much as she believed or followed anything. Moreover, in Diana's case, this was not just the line of least resistance. Even though she was a young woman, she had already found herself called upon to think about it and make at least some preliminary decision.

Late in her student days, Diana had heard a teacher say something very interesting about the popular idea that modern science had displaced the old stories about God. "Yes, they say that, and that is what you are supposed to accept. First of all, the very fact that you are supposed to accept it should make you suspicious. Exactly *because* it is one of the standard lines they run, you should be suspicious as to whether it is one of their many lines of phony baloney. Second, and more seriously, the hard-line proof is not really there, in spite of what they say. Sometimes, their answer to hard questions is that you are not supposed to think about that. Other times, they say they cannot prove it now, but they will someday. In other words, it comes down to faith. Well, the old stories about God also called for faith, but they told you that out front, instead of saying they had clear proof to wipe away any need for faith and then having to worm out of it. So the old way seems to have been more honest, which is exactly opposite to what you are supposed to believe.—Also, if we are going to talk about modern science, what does modern science really say? Modern science looks upon the material world as an orderly realm of applied mathematics. This view goes much better with the claim that the world is an image of Divine wisdom than with the claim that chance is the deepest basis for everything." Diana thought about all this, and it seemed right to her. From there, she made the decision in her mind to stay with the old stories she had been taught "until something better comes along." But as time went on and she learned more, her adherence to the Faith deepened.

"And so," Alfreda summed up, "is that where you still are now?"

"Well, yes—yes, it is."

"Then let us go through it, one step at a time and by the book. First of all, by the book, you know you were really not supposed to go out and play around with any man, your brother or anyone else. But you did. By the book you follow, that has to be resolved. So, where do you stand? By which I mean, do you take the book seriously enough to honor that point?"

"Yeah, I do. I was trying not to think about that. But yeah, what you said."

"All right, then. We can go on to something much harder. By the same book, there is at least an enormous presumption that you have to see it through, with no nonsense about it, to put it very mildly. What about that? Do you honor that point also?"

"Oh, well, an enormous presumption? Yeah, that too. But—."

"Then the question is, do you think you have some reason on the other side?"

Indeed she did, although Alfreda had to work to extract the truth from her in some coherent form. Diana had essentially two concerns. First, she had already known the man who impregnated her to be truly worthy, even before he stood and died for what he believed in. He would have done what he could to see both her and their child through. But now he was dead, which left her to face the situation alone, and so she was in an impossible situation. Second, it had turned out she had been playing around with her natural brother, although she had not known it at the time, and so there was the especially great danger of genetic sickness or deformity.

"All right, so far, so good. Is there anything else?"

"No, that is it."

"Well, your first reason is a fantasy, and your second reason is not based on wisdom. You said you were left to face it alone. No—not at all. You have friends and relatives and connections, starting with me, but not only me." There followed a lengthy discussion of Diana's other friends and relatives, as well as what other people she could look to. "The one serious problem will be with your own mother. But she can be guided through the shock and persuaded easily enough that the important thing is to bring you back, provided you remain willing to admit that you went spinning off.

"As for your second reason—yes, there is that danger, and what then? Any child might be born defective, either for genetic reasons or because something goes wrong in the course of the pregnancy. On the other side, there is no guarantee that this child will be defective. But then, that being so, there is not nearly enough serious reason not to see it through. No woman can go through life, let alone make big decisions like this, based on such ifs and maybes."

"So you say I have to see it through?"

"I say you must decide whether what you say you believe in is more than just words."

Alfreda kept Diana at her own place that night, seeing that she was in no fit condition to be left alone. The next morning, her rationality restored, Diana told Alfreda, "You are right, of course. That is what I have to decide."

The decision did not take her long, now that the issues were clarified. A few days later, Diana told Alfreda, "Yes, I do believe it is more than just words. In the present context, the specific form that takes is that I guess I've always been concerned about fulfilling my appointed destiny as a woman, and I've figured I personally am called upon to do that by exercising motherhood, whatever may be appointed to others. This is not how I thought it would happen, but then I myself set up this situation. Besides, with all that has happened—with brother and sister coming together, which was a crazy situation—and then having the brother die as he did and then having me turn up pregnant, which happened only through a fluke...well, I hope I'm not being foolish, but somehow it feels almost like there is indeed some movement of destiny behind all this."

Although she could not know it at the time, what would happen later would only reinforce her view that, indeed, it was truly wondrous how things were coming together.

With the decision made, Diana went to face her mother with her confession. As it turned out, the difficulty with the mother had been very much overestimated.

"Is that all?"

"Yes, Mother."

"Why have you done this thing?"

Both Diana and Arvid had been at a private celebration and had first met then and there. Both of them had miscalculated and unknowingly drunk too much of beverages with the same active ingredient as the red beverage Diana had drunk with Alfreda. This went beyond calming their minds to clouding their thinking. With their minds thus impaired, both had been persuaded against their better judgment into playing around. They had selected each other to play around with by chance. Once they had gotten started in this way, they had gone on from there, largely because they were so shocked by what had happened they were not sure what to do or not do.

"Well. What you did was very wrong." Then something snapped inside her. She spoke again, but with her tone softened and her face sadder. "When I was young and foolish, I did all kinds of things, including a whole lot of things that were not very good. But I never did anything like that. No, I did worse—much worse—instead. If I could be brought back and turned right side up again, it should be very easy for you to be restored." Then she embraced her daughter and promised, "I don't know what we'll do, but we'll do something and get through somehow." That was the most severe reproof directed at Diana in the whole affair.

Alfreda went and met with them both the next day with serious news. "I have been checking it out. I gather you are thinking of keeping and raising the child, as opposed to giving it up for adoption? If so, this may be important. Many people were killed in that incident, not just Arvid. The company that sent him over there looks to be liable for wrongful death. So if Arvid's paternity can be proved, the child may be entitled to a large indemnity." Both Diana and her mother agreed that it was very important, and Alfreda agreed to check it out further.

Among Beatrice's people, no murder had ever occurred. There had also never been any case where it was necessary to invoke liability for wrongful death against someone. It had happened that someone had been called upon to pay an indemnity to compensate for economic loss, but such cases were rare. However, she did not have to explain these things, since they were well enough known to theoreticians and Travelers and to a lesser extent even to the more sophisticated ordinary adults, based on knowledge of what happened on the third planet of the next yellow star over.

After speaking with Diana and her mother, Alfreda took Diana aside and spoke with her separately. Diana had told Alfreda why she had done that thing when the story had been extracted from her, although much less cleanly and coherently than how she had told her mother later on. So now Alfreda said, "You said you were persuaded into playing around against your better judgment. I have been thinking, and I have my suspicion. But you tell me: How did this happen? By which I mean, who talked you into it, and what did he or she say?" When Diana told her, Alfreda said, "Ah, yes! Cindy the Poison Tongue. That was what I figured. As for what she told you, I was not sure what to think, but I guess I should have expected something like that."

When Diana displayed her puzzlement, Alfreda explained, "You must remember, I have warned you about Cindy over the last few years. But up until now, I have not spoken of it to you beyond that because it was bad enough that I had to know about it. Well, about five or six years ago, she tried to twist me around—not even because she either disliked me or hoped to profit by it, but just because she looks upon life as some game or sport of clever insults and crafty manipulation. It probably would have worked too, but by a fluke of luck I happened to know that something she told me was completely false. From there, it was easy enough to unravel her whole pack of lies, and then I threw the whole pile of garbage back into her face. She knew better than to try herself on me again, but ever since, her chosen pursuit has been to try herself on my friends and relatives and connections.—So in one way, I may be indirectly responsible, as having goaded Cindy into trying her poison tongue on you.

"Six or seven weeks before you met Arvid, she did something with someone else I know that was especially ugly and dirty, and more than just ugly and dirty—it was clearly across the line and over the top. It took a little while, but I found out about it, just as Cindy intended that I should. So a week or ten days before you met Arvid, I went to Cindy and warned her privately. 'You used to be more crafty than that,' I told her. 'Up until now, you have been very careful. By the book, I have been forbidden to return the favors you have done me through the people I know and care about.' She acknowledged this point and boasted of it, saying that this was part of how she had scored on me. Then I continued. 'But with this, you have gone too far and blown all that away.' She conceded that theoretically this was so and challenged me on what I was going to do about it. 'This time? Just the warning and nothing more, if only out of respect for the book. But this is your last warning. If there is a next time, if there is ever any more trouble from you—well, you can be sure something very cruel will happen to you. I am not bluffing or joking, and I am able to do it. You know all this as well as I do.' At the time, there was a sick look on her face, from the combination of astonishment and fear. But evidently, she decided later on to challenge me by scoring on you. So there it is.—If I had known then what I know now, that you and she would both be there at the same time, I would not have let you go without me."

"Then, Alfreda, what are you going to do now?"

"Well, the whole point about Cindy is that she does not play by any rules. It was by crossing that line that she threw away the protection of the book, as I put it. But of course, if I follow her, I become as bad as what I am fighting against. No—unlike her, I do respect the book, and so it has to be appropriate, and it has to be about the fact that she is a public destroyer, instead of mere revenge. On both counts, what is needed is something to turn her mind inside out. Given what she told you, I think I know what is called for. I just have to work out the details of when, where, and how. As for what I have in mind—no. It is bad enough that I have to know about it. So, you let me worry about that."

Five weeks after this conversation, Alfreda spoke with Diana again about this affair. "What I warned her of has been done. Cindy has been well and truly served. I think I can assure you there will be no more trouble from her."

"What did you do?"

"Something she never expected, and much more deeply shocking and severe. She imagined I would do bodily violence to her. Instead, there was only an implied threat of that, just enough to melt the wax from her ears and eyes. Then I simply held up the mirror to make her see the rottenness of her own soul.—I hope, quite sincerely, that the shock will lead her to contrition and conversion. But knowing her, I fear it will only make her go through life with her mind zonked."

Alfreda was right about one thing. There was never any more trouble from Cindy and her poison tongue, for Diana or anyone else. But beyond that, what did or did not happen with Cindy was not given to Beatrice to know in the course of her vision.

About three weeks after this conversation, Diana turned up sick. A few days later, her physician diagnosed the sickness as an infectious disorder known as rubella, and testing in the laboratory confirmed this diagnosis shortly thereafter. Among people of that species, rubella was thought of as a dread disease for pregnant women, since it was known to be very often devastating for unborn children. So when the diagnosis was confirmed, there was some suggestion that Diana should not see it through in view of the changed situation, given the greatly increased danger that the child would be deformed or defective—if it even survived long enough to be born alive.

But Diana decided otherwise. "No, I have already been through all that. I do not know what this child will turn out to be. What I know is that I have had to decide where to stand and what to believe in, and the answer on that basis is that I have to take my chances, as does more or less any mother." And so she stood fast and saw it through.

As time went on, the pregnancy ran its course, and Diana gave birth to the baby girl she had conceived with Arvid. Wendy was very much alive and only slightly defective, at least comparatively speaking. However, she spent the next three weeks in neonatal intensive care, and she spent much time in and out of the hospital for many years after that.

At the time, it was assumed that Wendy's defects were comparatively mild because the infection had hit very late in the most vulnerable phase of the pregnancy and also through the simple luck of the draw. As it turned out, an exotic fluke of luck was involved, but not in the way that had been imagined.

By this time in history, the natural scientists of Wendy's species had learned much about genetics and heredity. Practical applications of this knowledge, with sophisticated devices, were fairly well developed. So, some months after Wendy was born, genetic testing was done on her and on Diana. The results were correlated with the results of tests that had been done on samples of tissue taken from Arvid's body. When all this had been done, it was clear enough that Arvid was in fact Wendy's natural father, for the examination of his body showed the spontaneous reversal of the sterilization. By this time, the questions about wrongful death had also already been settled. The company that had sent Arvid and the others would pay indemnities for those who had been murdered in that incident. Consequently, a large chunk of wealth was set aside to provide for Wendy.

Furthermore, there was Arvid's own wealth. The line of work he was in provided serious economic prosperity, and he had accumulated much of this wealth, having spent not too richly. Also, his adoptive parents had enjoyed reasonable economic prosperity, and the father had died of sickness just a few weeks before Arvid traveled. A serious chunk of his wealth had gone to Arvid as an inheritance. The bulk of all this wealth was set aside for Wendy.

Even so, the medical care Wendy would need over the years could have been ruinously expensive. As it happened, however, Arvid had left behind another source of wealth as well. Just a few days before he traveled, Arvid had bought into an investment that was very much a speculative gamble. He had done so as an amusing exercise of flying hope, a game or joke on himself—"as those people say, on a lark." Although he did not live to see the outcome, the investment paid off quickly enough and very richly, beyond Arvid's hopes and dreams. Much of this wealth also went to provide for Wendy.

But in addition to all this, something else came out of that genetic testing as well. A few years later, there had been a landmark development among Wendy's people in knowing the genetic structure of their own species. The news of this development caused much rejoicing among her people. About a year after that, one of the physicians who had done much work on Wendy was thinking about what had been learned, and this prompted him to remember that there was something strange in what her genetic tests had shown. So he went back over the records and found that Wendy was indeed afflicted with severe genetic sicknesses. She should not have survived more than a few days after birth, if even that long. He investigated further and discussed the question with his colleagues. Eventually, they realized what must have happened. By an exotic fluke of exceptionally rare luck, the rubella had indeed interfered with her prenatal development, but in such manner as to offset in some measure the influence of the genetic faults.

This conclusion was, in fact, correct, as Beatrice was given to know in her vision.

It took a while, but finally this information was conveyed to Diana. After she had gotten over the initial shock, her reaction was that most likely she had been right all along. All the more, it looked like there was some wondrous movement of destiny behind how all these things had come together. But what was appointed for Wendy remained mysterious.

After the three weeks in neonatal intensive care, Wendy's mother took her home. As it worked out, however, this homecoming was not the end but more the beginning of the exotic course of Wendy's life.

The problem began just six weeks after Wendy came home. Diana was walking down a stairway when she lost her footing, fell, and knocked her head. It happened among her species that people were sometimes known to be mortally injured and die in this way, but that did not happen to Diana. Unhappily, she did not go unharmed, either. Her brain was damaged, seriously and beyond any healing available at the time. Diana went through the next decades of her life partially ruined. For many years to come, whenever she was awake Diana would alternate between periods of full lucidity and periods when her mind was just a little dazed. Working around this disability was very difficult, and planning around it was effectively impossible, for these periods alternated unpredictably and uncontrollably.

When Diana came home from the hospital, her mother, her sisters, and Alfreda discussed the situation with her during a lucid period. They agreed that some sort of special arrangement, if not full protective custody, would be necessary for Diana. Her mother said Diana would live with her, along with a younger sister, and Diana submitted to this. Alfreda promised to see what she could do about any other provisions that might be needed. Not long afterward, Alfreda and Diana's older sister Amanda found work that Diana could do at home and be paid for.

But the chief concern among all of them was for Wendy. Diana admitted, freely and readily, that she could not trust herself to care for her daughter. What if her mind were suddenly to become dazed at a critical time? So it was decided that a governess for Wendy would be recruited, to help Diana as far as possible and to work around or even override Diana where necessary. Amanda said she knew someone who would be very good for the job. Alfreda checked out the candidate, and she seemed worthy enough. After sitting down and talking with the mother, sisters, Alfreda, and Diana during a lucid period, the woman was brought in. Her name was Lilikea.

Diana's and Alfreda's ancestors had come to that cluster of volcanic islands from another part of their world, and the civilization from which their ancestors had come had discovered that cluster of islands fewer than a dozen generations earlier. But the bulk of Lilikea's ancestors had come to those islands dozens of generations before, from a different part of the world. Along with this difference came others. Lilikea's native language was that of the earlier inhabitants and not that of any part of the civilization from which Diana and Alfreda had come. More important, as a child, Diana had been taught the right Faith given within the order of Divine Redemption, but what Lilikea believed in was very different. The culture Lilikea represented had developed stories of gods and goddesses, all or almost of whom were really just natural forces and features personified. This system of stories was what Lilikea believed and followed. In fact, Lilikea had set up to be specially allied and connected with the goddess of volcanoes, and she practiced as an agent of that (alleged) goddess as having been initiated in this way.

When Beatrice had told all this, her teacher and the colleague explained that such things were well enough known to Travelers and theoreticians. In many cases on worlds full of Renegades, cultures would have such systems of stories, and women would have rituals to ally themselves with alleged underworld deities. Such women were called witches. Thus, Wendy's governess was a volcanic witch.

Beatrice found this slightly puzzling. "On that world, people speak of witches, but as women who ally themselves explicitly with Renegade Messengers—not what you said."

"Right, of course. But do the people who speak that way say that except for the Lady God Almighty, there is no god?"

"Come to think of it, yes, they do."

"Well, then, there you go! Given the Lady God Almighty as the exclusive basis, the nearest there can be to underworld deities is the forces of evil and darkness. That being so, there are no real underworld deities for any woman to be allied with, but only corrupt higher-order beings looking to lead her astray. So at best, someone like Lilikea is engaging in foolish fantasy, except *perhaps* insofar as she is genuinely concerned to understand those stories as mere images or symbols for talking and thinking about the Real God. At worst, the great danger is that she is, in fact, allied with Renegade Messengers, even though that is not at all what she desires or intends."

When all this had been smoothed over, Beatrice continued her narrative.

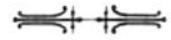

There had been an obvious problem with bringing in Lilikea. Among Wendy's people, the way it worked was that considerable wealth would have to be spent to obtain the services of Lilikea or any other governess. But as it happened, there was a solution readily available. The mishap on the stairway had happened at Diana's workplace. The circumstances were such that the company that owned the place, and with which Diana had been involved, was clearly responsible in large measure. This responsibility was clearly recognized by the law of that land at that time. The point was obvious enough that no one raised any question about it. The only question was how large the indemnity should be. This question was amicably settled fairly quickly, and the indemnity was large enough to leave no serious problem about providing for Diana and her daughter.

As one might have expected, Lilikea's influence prevailed largely over Wendy, in spite of the concerns of Diana, her sisters, their mother, and Alfreda. What she learned as her native language was what Lilikea had learned as a child and conveyed to her in turn. It was the language from the culture of the earlier inhabitants. Far more important, instead of being taught the right Faith given within the order of Divine Redemption, Wendy was taught those stories about the alleged gods and goddesses and their adventures.

Now the teacher and the colleague were slightly puzzled. They had expected Diana's mother would have made sure the situation went the other way.

The answer was that by the time Lilikea was brought in, Wendy was already starting to go in and out of the hospital and thus to spend much time away from home. For this reason, teaching Wendy about the right Faith and Divine worship—or in fact anything at all—worked out to be a catch-as-catch-can proposition. Also, following one of the customs of Lilikea's culture, Wendy spent a whole lot of time in Lilikea's home, being reared and cared for as if she were one of Lilikea's own children. Her grandmother did not like it. The problem was that the grandmother had to spend so much time outside her own home working, which included being away on long trips, that it was hard for her to oppose Lilikea on this point.

A few years later, when Wendy was old enough to begin as a student in school, there was some question about what should be done. Because she had to be in and out of the hospital so much, everyone agreed it would have been problematic for Wendy to fit into the more common arrangements for teaching children. So, with the approval of all, special provisions were set up. In spite of all the difficulties, Wendy was taught much, and she learned very well, for she was extremely intelligent. Indeed, her learning and exploring went far beyond what was assigned to her as a student.

All this led to the first crisis, which came when she was nine years old and had begun to learn natural science. "Lilikea, the books speak about how volcanoes work, but they do not speak about the working of the goddess. Why is that?"

Lilikea had run across one or another version of this question many times before. It was, in fact, a common challenge in that society at that time. "Oh, well, you have to remember—the volcano is the *body* of the goddess. Now, when you go to the hospital, what then? The people at the hospital have books that talk about how a girl's body works, but those books may leave aside the fact that a girl's body is the body *of a person.* Something like that is going on here as well. Your books talk about how volcanoes work, but they leave aside the fact that the volcano is the body of the goddess."

Wendy thought about this and decided it was good as far as it went. Yet she remained puzzled. So the next day she said, "Yes, but the books say there are volcanoes just because of how the natural world works, even apart from anything to do with the goddess."

Lilikea understood very well. She was wise and worthy enough, and loved Wendy dearly enough, not to try any nonsense. "Dear child, how bright and sharp your mind is! You are still puzzled about the natural functioning of volcanoes on one side and the work of the goddess on the other. Is that correct?"

"Well, yes. I am."

Before she could say any more, Lilikea smiled, nodded, and held up her hand to cut her off. "Very good. You understand better than you know. For you see, there is something important I have not yet told you, because the time was not right. But now you need to know." Then, weighing her words very carefully, she began. "Above and beyond the whole realm of gods and goddesses, there is the One God, the Lord God Almighty, Creator of heaven and earth and of all things, visible and invisible."

"You mean what my mother and grandmother and aunts believe in is true?"

"Yes, at least that part of it is true. As for all the rest, we can discuss that later. But anyhow, that much is true. Now, this One God made the world and set up how it should work. The natural functioning of things is what He commanded based on His own wisdom and goodness. All those gods and goddesses are merely His servants and are themselves created by Him, along with everything else in the world."

"My grandmother believes there is only the Lord God Almighty, with no other gods or goddesses at all."

"Yes, I know. She is right that this God has no other beside Him. That is the chief point. But beyond that, the blunt denial of all other gods and goddesses—well, what *she* means by it may be right, but what other people mean by it is clearly wrong. It is too much like they are trying to wipe all the mystery out of the world, to deny the heights and depths. It is almost like they think the world is not governed by any wisdom, even that of the Lord God Almighty. No, that does not make it. Those books you asked about? I too have read such books. They do not speak about the natural world as a realm of chaos and accident, as though there were no wisdom behind it. They speak about the *laws* of natural functioning. So then, if and when I see those people deny all other gods and goddesses, but still affirm the heights and depths and mystery of the world, then I shall have something serious to consider."

The next day, Wendy went to Lilikea with just one more question. "If the One God is really as great as all of you say, then He must be able to govern the natural world by Himself, without any need for other gods and goddesses."

"Yes, of course. He does not need any help to govern. It is the other way around. He gives to His servants the honor of doing mighty deeds and worthy works. It is like how sometimes you want to help your mother with something out of love for your mother, and she lets you do so out of her love for you, even though she could do it herself very well—and in fact she could do it herself better and more quickly than you can do it."

"Then my grandmother is right that this God is to be loved and obeyed?"

"Yes, certainly. Very much so. Among my ancestors, what I have told you about the One God was considered a great mystery to be kept hidden. When I was finally taught the truth, I rejoiced with all my heart. So must you, and so must all who learn of it."

For the time being, both Wendy and Lilikea left it there. Wendy rejoiced as well as she could but wondered where it should go from there. The answer began to be revealed to her about one week later, when she was in the hospital again.

At this point, Beatrice had to interrupt her narrative in order to explain. "As I told you earlier, before I began the story, by their standards all of us are biologically female. Because of this, we always speak of God in the feminine. Of course, with us it is common knowledge among adults and even among older children that really God is far above and beyond any differentiation of the sexes, just as She is above and beyond animal generation. To speak of God either in the feminine or the masculine is correct only by way of metaphor and analogy. Now, in the right Faith given within the order of Divine Redemption, all this is known perfectly well. However, the established tradition within that Faith is to speak of God in the masculine instead. Thus, they speak of the *Lord* God Almighty, they say *He* is above animal generation, and so on." When this had been smoothed over for the moment with the promise of more discussion later, Beatrice resumed telling the tale.

⸻

On this occasion, Wendy was in grave danger of her life. The day after she entered the hospital, it looked like she was beginning the final collapse. Late that evening, it looked like she would die that night and not see the next dawn. At that time, a nurse named Deborah, one of her personal favorites, was on duty to watch over her. Like Wendy's mother, Deborah had been taught the right Faith as a child, and she continued to believe in and follow what she had been taught. So now, as Wendy seemed to be dying, Deborah was greatly concerned that she had not been formally brought into the order of Divine Redemption. A more senior nurse told her what she could do and not do: "As for prayers and blessings, fine and dandy. But as for the other—the full act of formal initiation—no. Not unless and until she is finally sinking."

About an hour after receiving this command, Deborah went to Wendy and found her awake.

"Am I going to die tonight?" Wendy said.

Deborah knew Wendy well enough to know that since she had asked the question, she was ready for the answer. "I hope not, honey child, but it could well be."

Then Wendy confided in Deborah what she had recently discussed with Lilikea. When she had told her story, Deborah asked, "Do you believe it?"

"Yes, I do. Until she told me this, I had started to think all those old stories she told me were like stuff from cartoons or comic books." (Beatrice explained this.) "Then there are the people who say there is no God, but they are just showing how sour they are instead of talking wisdom. All they want is to deny God, not to show there is something better. What else is left? I was not sure what to think. But somehow, this seems to be the right answer. And—I *do* rejoice in the fact of the Lord God Almighty, as Lilikea said everyone must."

"Yes, indeed they must. Your governess was right about that. Will you also submit to receive blessing from Him, so that you may rejoice in Him more fully?"

"Yes, with all my heart." Upon hearing that, Deborah placed one hand on Wendy's head, held the great book of Divine revelation in the other, and pronounced the blessing upon her. It was an ancient blessing, going back to long before the critical events of the Redemption, to the earlier ages of the Preparation. When it was completed, Wendy smiled, closed her eyes, and fell asleep.

In submitting to receive this blessing, Wendy did not hope for or expect any benefit for herself. She followed the teaching of her governess that when she died, she would experience the common fate of becoming a ghost in the parade, and that was all. Wendy thought of what awaited her beyond death as almost like a big nothing, with really very little to hope for or fear. Again, she did not have any idea that she would live even a moment longer or suffer any less in her final hours. Instead, Wendy accepted the blessing only in order to rejoice in God more fully, as Deborah had said. It was an act of pure adoration on her part, or at least as much as she was capable of at that time.

Yet, as it worked out, she did live longer. After the blessing, Deborah and the more senior nurse monitored Wendy from a distance with sophisticated devices. At first, they saw Wendy continue to decline. In a few minutes, it looked like she was finally sinking. But then, just before the more senior nurse would have allowed the full act of formal initiation, the decline stopped.

They watched very carefully to see whether Wendy was beginning to rally. So indeed she was. Her vital signs held steady for a little while and then began to improve, very gradually. But after about two hours, it was clear that Wendy was not finally sinking, at least for the time being. She remained alive through the night, through the next morning, through the next night, and for day after day after that. Four days after the dawn they had thought she would not see, Wendy went home from the hospital, there to complete her recovery.

As she lay sick in bed at home, Wendy turned over and over in her mind what to do and which way to go. She understood intuitively, although she could not have explained it, that the blessing she had received was somehow only the beginning and not the end. But what then? She knew she needed to take counsel, but from whom? Lilikea had spoken to her of the Lord God Almighty, but she had also told her all that other stuff. She loved her grandmother dearly, but Grandma was too pushy sometimes, and that was not what she needed. She loved her mother also, but Mama was just too crazy sometimes. Her aunt Amanda and her honorary aunt Alfreda would tell her the truth and lead her rightly, but both of them were away on long trips. She could ask Deborah, of course. That would be the obvious thing to do. But she saw Deborah only when she went to the hospital, and she could not wait that long. So after thinking all this through, Wendy decided to ask her mother's kid sister Theodora. Theodora was both old enough to be a fully competent, responsible adult, yet young enough to be almost like a big sister to her, instead of almost like a lesser version of a mother, as Amanda and especially Alfreda were.

After she got past her initial astonishment at being asked about these things, Theodora began, "Well, Wendy, so far you have done very well. I am very glad for what you have told me. Now, where does it go from here? First of all, Lilikea was right.

He is to be loved and obeyed. You must honor Him by rejoicing in the fact that there is the Lord God Almighty at the top, as you have said. So far, so good. Beyond that—well, let me ask you, what exactly was the blessing Deborah pronounced on you?" Wendy recited a garbled version. Theodora recognized it, went and fetched her copy of the book from which Deborah had recited, looked it up, read it aloud, and asked, "Was this it?"

"Yes, how did you know?"

"Oh, that blessing has become famous. Now, this book that has the blessing has a whole lot more as well. For example, there are songs for praise and thanksgiving. Would you like for me to copy these for you?"

"Yes, of course I would! I thank you."

"It will be a pleasure. Also, He is to be *obeyed*."

"What does He say we should do or not do?"

"Well, first of all, people must honor God and rejoice in Him. Beyond that, people must accept and remember that whatever happens, the right answer is what God has to say about it. All too often, they think instead the answer is some stuff they make up, or take into their heads, or whatever. They go by what they happen to want, not what they know they should do."

"Well, but what does He say people should do?"

"Oh—well, to begin with, there is the law of right and wrong, and that law is from the Lord God Almighty. You know plenty already about what is right and wrong, and there you go. You be careful as well as you can to do what is right and avoid what is wrong, and that is one of the best ways there is to learn and understand the truth about God and the things of God."

Wendy did begin to recite the songs for praise and thanksgiving to the One God that Theodora had given her from the Book. Everyone, including Lilikea, was happy that she did so. Thus ended the first great crisis of her development.

CHAPTER EIGHT

The second great crisis of her development came about six weeks later. Once again, Wendy was in the hospital, although she was not in any serious danger on this occasion. Once again, it was Deborah who led her through.

From her own standpoint, what Deborah said was not at all remarkable or noteworthy. Wendy heard her speak of praying for another patient who was in danger. This puzzled Wendy. "What? You mean you pray to the Lord God Almighty for Sally?"

"Yes, of course." Then Deborah remembered the last time Wendy had been in the hospital. "Wendy, I need to know what you do not understand in order to explain it to you. Are you wondering about being concerned for Sally, or wondering about praying to the Lord God Almighty, or what, exactly?"

Wendy had great care and concern for Sally. She wondered about praying to the One God, the Lord God Almighty. Little by little, Deborah managed to extract from her that Wendy thought of this God as far too great and wondrous to ask or hope for anything from Him. She rejoiced in God and in the way He had set up the world as a reflection of His beauty and goodness and wisdom, but in something like the same way she appreciated the beauty of light and color and rejoiced at the sun in the sky. She thought of it as an honor to be able to offer praise and thanksgiving to Him. But her attitude was that of purely submissive adoration. She figured God knew what should be done or not done and when and where and how to do it, always and in all things, with no need for His creatures to tell Him what to do or not do.

Deborah did not answer at once. She thought carefully and weighed her words. She rejoiced at Wendy's submissive adoration and realized that what her governess had told her about the alleged gods and goddesses had trained and prepared her in this way to worship the Real God. When finally she was ready to answer, Deborah began by speaking to Wendy more kindly and mildly than she had ever done before. "Dear, sweet Wendy. You good, brave girl. What you said is right, of course. God knows what should be done or not done, and when and where and how to do it, always and in all things, with no need for His creatures to tell Him anything. All that is true. But you see, it is about *asking* Him and not about telling Him."

"Does He need for people to ask Him? You agreed He knows already what should be done or not done."

"How well you understand. No, He does not need to have people ask Him. As you say, He knows already. But we need to ask Him—for our sake, not for His. He has given people the honor of being able to offer praise and thanksgiving to Him. But of course, He does not need that either. It is for our sake that He commands us to do so, not for His. In the same way, He gives people the honor to call upon Him and cry out to Him, and He commands us to do so, for our sake and not for His. As for how great and wondrous He is—yes, that too, except that He says we should do all these things, and that settles it."

Wendy turned all this over and over in her mind, but she understood only in part. She remained largely puzzled. So she asked her aunt Theodora, who came to visit her the next day. Theodora agreed with all Deborah had told her, and she offered further advice. "If my sister or my mother told you to do something, and you were puzzled, what would you do? You would ask them to help you understand. So perhaps your first prayer to the Lord God Almighty should be that He may lead you to understand. How to go about it? Well, you can simply speak to Him and ask Him, but with respect—just as you would speak and ask your mother or grandmother." Wendy thought about this, and it seemed right to her, and so that was what she did.

This worked out. Very shortly after praying, she remembered what Lilikea had said to her about how the One God gave His creatures the honor of doing worthy works. It was like the way a child might ask to do something out of love for her mother, and the mother might let her do it out of love for the child, even though the mother was very well able to do it herself. So now, Wendy figured the need for prayer to God was a further development of such love on both sides. When she asked later on, both Deborah and Theodora told her she understood very well indeed.

After this, Wendy remembered what Deborah had said that had gotten all this started. Her second prayer to the One God was for Sally. She remembered what Deborah had said—that prayer was about asking and not telling. So she called upon Him simply to "take care of" Sally. Alas, Sally died just a few days later. Wendy was very sorry, but her attitude was quite reasonable. "He refused to do what I hoped when I asked Him, just as my mother or grandmother might refuse to do what I hope when I ask them."

"Yes, exactly right—that too," answered Deborah. "But also, stop and think. You asked Him to *take care of* Sally. Well, it looks like He did just that. Think back to when I read that blessing over you. We thought you might die that night. Do you remember? After I read the blessing, you smiled, close your eyes, and fell asleep."

"Yes, I remember."

"Did you expect to die then?"

"Well, yes."

"Were you afraid?"

"No." Wendy was genuinely surprised at this answer. She had not known she would say it until she did so. But then she realized it was true. "No, I was not."

"Were you in pain?"

"A little, but not much. I did not think about it at the time. I was happy to rejoice in the Lord God Almighty after receiving the blessing."

"Something like all that is what happened to Sally. I was with her and saw everything. She fell asleep rejoicing in God without being afraid and with just a little pain while being very brave and being happy to rejoice in Him, just as you were looking to do. She died a few hours later without waking. There was no torment and nothing dreadful."

Wendy was comforted to learn all this, although she was sad that Sally was now just another ghost in the parade. Deborah was ready to challenge this idea, but then she thought better. She remembered something one of her teachers had said long ago about how the people in the earlier times of the Preparation had believed what awaited beyond death was life as a ghost in the underworld, which life was just a big nothing. Yet they had believed in and been devoted to the Real God. When she thought all this through, Deborah decided to leave it alone and let Wendy think just about God for the time being, and then they might discuss the other later on.

The next day, when she was back at home, Wendy asked a question that had grown up in her mind based on her conversations with Deborah and Theodora. "They speak of the One God, the Lord God Almighty, just as God, as if there are no other gods or goddesses."

It was her grandmother who answered. She was pushy sometimes because she believed she had to be, but she was not deliberately harsh. On this occasion, she took care to be especially soft and mild in her speech. "That is because we believe there are no other gods or goddesses. There is only the Lord God Almighty and what He has made. You know that."

"Does that mean He has not raised up servants and given them the work of watching over volcanoes and other things?"

"Ah, now we come to it! What did Lilikea tell you?"

Wendy told her what had been said.

"Well, I guess God could have done it that way if He had chosen to. I myself do not believe He set it up that way, but of course He could have. Also, I agree with Lilikea about the heights and depths and wonders of the world. Yes, there is all that, and it is not to be denied." She paused to let this sink in. Then, "But now, the important thing is that even if He did set it all up the way Lilikea said, still those lesser beings are just that: servants. And so they should not be spoken of as gods and goddesses, because that sounds too much like they are in competition with the One God. It is like this: In a country ruled by a king, the king might appoint servants to do whatever works he decided to give to them. But no one would speak of those servants as little kings and queens. Instead, they would simply say there is the king and those he had appointed. Something like that applies here as well. Even if there is some lady of volcanoes, she is only a servant of the One God and not a goddess as though she were herself a lesser version of the Lord God Almighty. So there you go."

Wendy thought about all this, and she saw that it was clearly right. She remembered what Lilikea had said. There was what her grandmother meant in denying other gods and goddesses, and that might be right—even though what other people meant was wrong. But gradually, there grew up another question in her mind. So a week after the conversation with her grandmother, Wendy went to ask Lilikea. She told what her grandmother had said.

"Well," Lilikea replied, "I had not exactly thought of it in those terms. But now that I come to think of it, yes, of course—all that your grandmother said is right. If we are going to speak about the One God, the Lord God Almighty, in the way that I told you, then all the rest follows.—Even what I have told you about Him is not exactly what I learned as a child. But when I was old enough and was finally taught the mystery of the One God, I had to figure how that should be combined with the old stories, and my answer is what I told you."

"Well, but then, since the lady of volcanoes is not a goddess, a volcanic witch is not hooked up with any goddess, and so what does it mean for a woman to be a volcanic witch?"

"Hmm...that is a very good question. Let me think about it."

It turned out to be three weeks before Lilikea answered. "I have been thinking about my own experience as a volcanic witch since I was taught the great mystery of the One God. I have also spoken with my sister witches who have been taught this mystery, and they have thought about their experiences. We have discussed it, and I think I can answer you now." She paused and weighed her words, then began. "Wendy, people speak of women as witches, but not of men, or only very rarely. Have you ever wondered why?" No, she had not. Indeed, she had not even noticed the fact. "No, of course not. Well, the reason is that it is almost like women have some natural talent or ability, simply as women, to appreciate, and to feel, and even to use or tap into, the energy and richness of the depths of the world. This is a natural fact about women, like the fact that our voices are different from men's voices. Like any other natural fact or talent, it can be used either for good or for evil. I know you find it hard to understand. That is because you have to live with it and experience it within yourself. To do that, you will have to wait until you grow up more and become a full woman. For now, you will just have to take my word. But you can understand in part by thinking about yourself as a girl in contrast with boys you have met. There are many differences, but the fact that you already have some measure of this function as a girl, and boys do not have this, is part—only part, mind you—of the reason why you find most boys to be big nothings. You think there is something important missing in them. This is part, although not all, of what is missing." They discussed all this briefly, and then Lilikea went on. "What, then, is it to be a witch? It is to reach down farther and be involved in the depths of the world more fully, in some special and more powerful way. It is to experience and tap into the energy and richness of the depths in greater measure than other women. My sisters and I have this from the lady of volcanoes, by virtue of being initiated as her deputies. That is what it is and what it means to be a volcanic witch under the One God, the Lord God Almighty."

"You said the natural talent of an ordinary woman could be used either for good or evil. What about this special power of witches?"

"Yes, that too can be used for good or for evil. It is like what your grandmother said about the officers of the king. A king who does what a king is supposed to be doing appoints officers to protect and provide for the people. Those officers, in turn, may appoint deputies. But a deputy could go wrong and become a renegade, and abuse the power given him to work *against* the people instead. That applies here also. The lady of volcanoes received from the One God the work of governing the depths of the world according to wisdom in order to fulfill what He sees to be right. She has that honor from the Lord God Almighty, and we have the honor of sharing in the function given her. The way that works out is that we too are to work to protect and provide for the people. But yes, sad to say, a witch could go wrong and become a renegade and abuse the power given her."

"What if one of these higher beings the One God has created were to go wrong and become a renegade? What then?"

"Well, what if one of the officers of a good king were to go wrong and become a renegade? In that case, the right answer for his deputies would be to stay loyal to the king and follow what the king had commanded, even if that meant standing against the renegade officer. And so here as well. A volcanic witch, like any other woman—or man, or girl, or boy—must stand with the One God, whatever happens." Then she understood what was behind Wendy's question. "What if a higher being were to go wrong, and then women were to go with this higher being, knowing it to be a renegade? I have heard of such things. Is that what you are wondering?" Indeed it was. "That would be monstrously evil, hideously wrong. In the old days, women who were caught doing that were punished by being made to die horribly. I think they should have been just killed and not tormented, and I am very sorry that many innocent women were falsely condemned and wrongly killed. But as for those who were guilty, to be killed was about what they deserved for such an enormous crime. If anyone should ever invite you to do that, you run away, as fast and as far as you can."

Then, as she saw how Wendy's face changed on hearing this warning, something snapped in Lilikea's mind. She realized what she had seen in Wendy's face and heard in her voice a moment before. When she put it together with what she saw now, an alarm went off in her head. Speaking slowly and carefully, Lilikea said, "Wendy, I am not angry at you. I will do what I can to help you. I think you may be in big trouble—much more than you know—but I expect it is not your fault. But you must tell me the truth. Is there something important about this business of renegade beings and witchcraft and so on that you have not told me?"

With that, it all spilled out of the girl. Much of Wendy's studying and learning was done at her home as part of the special provisions for her, but she did have some limited contact with other children and ordinary teachers. To put it bluntly, one of those teachers had tried to recruit Wendy to become a witch based on the worship of Renegade Messengers.

Lilikea was somewhat delayed in reacting. At first she was too shocked to speak. As the shock faded and her mind settled, she found herself too angry to speak. After that she would have burst into a terrible tirade, but she looked at Wendy and thought better. So she went from speaking in Diana's language to speaking in her own native language, but other than that, she controlled herself. Then, keeping her voice as calm as she could, she said, "You have done very well to tell me this. I am extremely angry, but not at you—not at all. You are not to be blamed. You are an innocent victim. Now we must go tell your mother and the others. I am not sure what will be done, but I promise you we *are* going to do something, and very soon."

As it happened, Lilikea and Wendy found the whole group together—Diana, Theodora, their mother, and also Amanda and Alfreda, both of whom had returned from their long trips by this time. The first thing Lilikea said (in Diana's language, having recovered enough from her anger) was, "Good. Everyone is here. That will save the trouble of repeating it later. Alfreda, I am especially glad to see you." She gave a brief summary of the earlier conversation and then said to Wendy, "All right, dear child. You tell them now what you told me about what happened."

Wendy told her sad story. Under very gentle questioning from Alfreda, she filled in all the ugly little details. The questioning went on for some time to make sure the truth was as bad as it seemed. No, Wendy had not done anything to provoke or cause it. As far as she was aware, the invitation to evil had come out of nowhere. No, Wendy had not agreed to it or cooperated with it, nor had she asked the teacher to go on talking about it. At most, she had not refused it strongly, chiefly because she was too astonished, but perhaps because she was afraid as well. No, there was no misunderstanding. As Alfreda extracted the details from her, that became very obvious.

Finally, all was told. At that point, Diana sent Wendy to her bedroom, saying, "Lilikea was right about one thing—no, two things. You are an innocent victim, not to be blamed. And, we're gonna do something, and very soon." When Wendy was gone, Diana said, "If need be, I'll take care of it myself, with my fingernails to rip out her throat." All the others agreed.

But these threats were just wild talk of the kind that was common in such cases among people of their species. What was done was simply to have another teacher assigned to Wendy instead of the one who had tried to recruit her. Diana and the others were sorry they could not do more to protect children from that teacher, but they could not. The teacher was able to protect herself from trouble with crafty lies.

"Well, yes, now that you speak of it that way, I can see how it might sound like what Wendy said, but that was not how I meant it."

Everyone knew she was lying, but they knew a formal accusation would not stand up under challenge. So Diana, her sisters, and their mother had to settle for having Wendy transferred and having that teacher officially warned.

Alfreda had other plans. She too would have settled for the transfer and the warning, but she recognized that teacher from years before as one of Cindy the Poison Tongue's rotten friends. Alfreda had not stopped to think about whether Cindy would have friends more evil than Cindy herself, but since it turned out she did, Alfreda figured that fact should not be surprising. But her mind did not stop there. She knew that Cindy was a master manipulator, and she reckoned that the teacher was probably also a master manipulator, given how good she was at protecting herself with crafty lies. As she turned it over in her mind and remembered what she knew of the woman from years before, Alfreda realized this was indeed so. When she realized this, she figured there was likely more to this whole affair than met the eye.

What Alfreda did was to have the teacher investigated secretly at her own expense, not by officers of the law but by private professionals. This was a service that could be purchased in that society at that time.

The investigation worked out even better than Alfreda had imagined. It did not take long to find there was something very wrong about the woman. When she learned this, Alfreda told them to keep digging. It took a while, but finally the truth came out. The woman had been a witch based on worshiping Renegade Messengers almost all her adult life. Many years earlier, long before Alfreda had first met Cindy, the teacher had worshiped those monsters with human sacrifice, but in another part of the world, where she had been born and raised. The problem for her had been that the law of that land spoke of such sacrifice as premeditated murder. She had been caught, brought to trial, found guilty, and condemned to be punished with death. Before this order could be implemented, she had escaped from confinement and had fled to the land where Diana and Alfreda lived. How she had gone on from there was a story in itself, but she managed to assume a fake identity and pretend to be a qualified teacher. But for Alfreda, the important thing was that the land she had fled from was still looking to have her back and punish her with death for the old murder.

Alfreda had been and remained extremely angry, but she did not exactly want the woman killed. On the other hand, she could not simply ignore what she knew and let her get away with murder. So she had just one question: Was it absolutely certain the woman was in fact guilty? Yes, that was very clear—even out of her own mouth. Had she perhaps confessed under torture or something like that? No, not at all. In fact, it had been the other way around. She had boasted of what she had done when she had been caught. The officers of the law who captured her were appalled. The judge who condemned her urged her, for her own sake, not to add to her evil by talking such filth.

When she learned this, Alfreda knew what had to be done, and she did it. She reported the woman to the officers of the law in her own land. Sure enough, the woman was taken captive, eventually sent back to her old land, and ultimately punished with death. Alfreda and the others hoped the woman had been brought to contrition and conversion before she died.

⁂

Beatrice hoped so too, but she was not given to know, in the course of her vision, whether this was so.

⁂

Wendy was not given to know anything about the whole affair. Diana, her sisters, their mother, and Lilikea all agreed with Alfreda that it was bad enough the adults had to know about it.

However, it took years for all this to be resolved and the corrupt teacher to be killed according to the law of that land. In the meantime, life went on for Wendy and the others. The third great crisis came something over a year later, when Wendy was ten and a half years old. She asked the question that was notorious among her people for being asked by children whose minds were bright and sharp. "Mother, you say God, the One God, the

Lord God Almighty, made the world and everything in it. Well, but then, who made God?"

Diana thought back and remembered what that old teacher had said long ago. "Oh, well, you see, God exists of Himself, by His own nature and power. He does not need to be made."

This satisfied Wendy for the moment. But a few days later, she came back with the obvious follow-up question. "Well, but then why do the things in the world have to be made?"

It was Theodora who answered. Her later days as a student were much more recent, and so she remembered more, including the answer to this very line of questioning she had heard from that same old teacher. "Well, the easy way to think of it is that God exists by His own *power*. It is not for nothing that people speak of Him as the Lord God *Almighty*, for that is what He is. But things in the world do not have such power, and so they cannot exist of themselves. Things in the world are constantly fading and perishing, which shows they are weak. Since they are weak, they depend on God. So there you go." After they discussed it for a while, there indeed she went. As Wendy turned it over and over in her mind, and discussed it again with Theodora a few days later, this answer seemed reasonable enough, although she had to think hard to understand it.

The full understanding dawned on her little by little over the following months, starting about ten weeks after discussing Theodora's answer with her a second time. "God has greater power than other things, and so He is able to exist of Himself. But other things are weak, and so they need to be made, and the proof they are weak is that they are constantly fading and perishing. Is that right?"

"Yes, you understand very well."

"I have been thinking about what you said, and I have another question. You say God is above the whole world. Is that because He has greater power so that He can exist of Himself?"

"Well, yes. I had not exactly thought of it in those terms, and there is also more, but that is very much part of it, yes."

Wendy left it there for the time being. She felt within herself that there was something more to be discussed, something important—some serious implication of what had just been said. But she did not yet know enough even to ask about it. So after just a little more conversation with her aunt, she went on to other tasks and concerns.

Because Wendy was still only a child, it took a long time for the question she needed to ask to become clear to her. She had to learn and develop, grow and mature more. Even then, it was not by deliberately thinking it through but by letting the deeper levels of her mind work that she came to understand. But finally, on the eleventh anniversary of her birth, she woke up that morning with unusually great joy in her heart and with her mind very clear. She recited some of the songs of praise and thanksgiving Theodora had long since given her, and then she went and spoke with Theodora as soon as she could. "When Lilikea told me of the One God, she said He is above the whole realm of gods and goddesses."

"Oh, well, yes, of course. If you are going to speak at all of such gods and goddesses, then that is exactly what you have to say. Yes, certainly the One God would be above the whole realm of such beings."

"But you said He is above the whole world because He is powerful enough to exist of Himself, but they are too weak for that."

"Yes, that too." Theodora suspected what was coming, for she remembered what that old teacher had said. But she also knew enough to let the child work it through for herself.

"Then, is He above the realm of gods and goddesses because they are like the things in the world that are weak in that way?"

Theodora answered, "Well, yes, certainly. Once again, if you are going to speak in those terms at all, then yes, that is exactly what you have to say."

"Is that why Grandma said they should not be spoken of as gods and goddesses?"

"Well, yes, that too. She might not think of it in that way, exactly, and you must ask her to be sure what she had in mind, but that would be at least part of it.—I know I would say they should not be spoken of as gods and goddesses for that reason, and your Grandma would agree."

"So this is what it means that they are only servants of the One God."

"That is part of what it means." Then, sensing what Wendy was starting to think, and remembering something else that old teacher had said, Theodora spoke quickly. "Dear child, you must not think the servants of the One God are less great and wondrous than Lilikea and her ancestors believed in. It is the other way around instead. There is the One God at the top, and He is far *more* great and wondrous than anything Lilikea's ancestors dreamed of.—It is like this: the full moon is very nice, and it is not any less nice because moonlight turns out to be a reflection of sunlight. No, but it is that there is something even nicer, from which moonlight is derived."

Wendy turned this over in her mind for a moment and said, "Then the One God must be—*must be*—must be too much even to think about or imagine."

"Oh yes, very much so. He is beyond the dreams of Lilikea's ancestors because He is far beyond the hopes and dreams of all people."

"And yet He has granted us the honor to offer Him praise and thanksgiving!" With that, the joy with which she had begun the day was complete. She burst into one of the songs of praise and thanksgiving, quite spontaneously, and Theodora joined in with her.

Thus ended the third great crisis of her development. The fourth crisis did not come quickly, but it was not greatly delayed, either. When it came, it turned Wendy's mind inside out far beyond anything she had theretofore imagined.

CHAPTER NINE

Among Wendy's people, the anniversary of a child's birth was often taken as a natural and obvious breaking point for observing or marking various stages of growth and development, and thus as a critical point for things to be done and choices to be made. So, just over two weeks after the eleventh anniversary of Wendy's birth, Diana sat down with her mother and her sisters to discuss the situation about Lilikea. Wendy was eleven years old now. That was old enough and mature enough to need much less care and supervision than she had needed when Diana had first banged her head. There was still some need for a governess, at least for the moment, but a much lesser need. By the time of this discussion, Theodora had already spoken of the third crisis in Wendy's moral and spiritual development and how it had been resolved, and this was taken as a confirmation. All of them agreed it was like some first coming-of-age for Wendy as a real person. Consequently, it was decided that Lilikea would have a lesser function, with lesser involvement, although she would continue in some serious measure, at least for the time being.

⁂

Beatrice, her teacher, and the colleague agreed that what Theodora described to her mother and sisters was indeed like some sort of first coming-of-age for Wendy as a real person. In fact, there was no question about it. They agreed the influence of Divine mercy in pushing it through was not to be discounted or underestimated, but it was not revealed to Beatrice in her vision how much was a special gift of illumination and how much was simply the working of the natural order based on the experiences given to her within the order of Divine Providence.

⁂

Because she was less involved with Lilikea, Wendy was less influenced by her, and so came to have more basis to question what Lilikea had taught her. Because Wendy was extremely intelligent, many of the questions she might have had were already asked and answered before Lilikea's influence was diminished. But something important remained. The day before the meeting at which Wendy's family decided to decrease Lilikea's presence, Wendy asked Lilikea a serious question.

"You agree with my mother and aunts and grandmother about the One God, the Lord God Almighty. Then why do you not follow the religion they follow?"

"Well, perhaps I have misunderstood. But as near as I can figure, the One God has to be far greater than what they say." Wendy found this puzzling, so Lilikea went on, "They speak of Him as being up in Heaven, and as reaching down from Heaven, and so on. But really, He has to be much too great to be confined in Heaven in that way, or to need a special miracle to reach down from Heaven, or to need to come down from Heaven to be among the people, or anything like that. Those who have studied these questions most deeply and exercised the best wisdom say God is always and everywhere, and that has to be the truth." This seemed right to Wendy, and so she left it there after further brief discussion with Lilikea.

⁂

At this point, Beatrice paused to explain, "Lilikea and Wendy were right, of course, that God is always and everywhere instead of being confined in Heaven. It is just that, as Lilikea said, she misunderstood. Contrary to what Lilikea imagined, this point is also clearly affirmed in the right Faith pertaining to the Redemption." Then she went on with the story.

⁂

Unhappily, even though what Lilikea said to Wendy was not in fact so, it was what she believed quite sincerely regarding the right Faith, and Wendy accepted it from her. For she too had heard people speak in this way about God and Heaven, and she too had misunderstood. Although the error was corrected eventually, it caused her progress to be stopped for years and even led her indirectly to go seriously wrong.

After this conversation with Lilikea, time marched on. Wendy learned and developed plenty. Indeed, she learned and developed better and faster than other girls her age, as she had been doing. Other than that, there was nothing especially noteworthy. She went to the hospital from time to time, but there was no more serious danger for the time being. Finally, there was

Wendy's homecoming from the hospital when she was twelve years old.

This turned out to be the last trip to the hospital for a long time, although Wendy still had to see her physician more than other girls. One week followed another, and the seasons rolled by, and the years progressed. There were further learning and development, gradually increasing work on domestic tasks in her grandmother's household as Wendy's body grew and became stronger and more stable, and a gradually decreasing role for Lilikea. But there was nothing especially noteworthy. For Wendy, as for all her people, there were the ordinary ups and downs of life in general, but on the whole, life went smoothly.

"Or at least as much as is possible for a girl who was born a Renegade in a world full of Renegades, with no Normals around."

When Beatrice had said this, she paused, then added, "The problem is not with what happened to her. It is with what did *not* happen. It was now a little more than three years past her last home-coming from the hospital, and Wendy was clearly past the fifteenth anniversary of her birth, but she was still very much a girl." When she saw that her teacher and the colleague failed to understand, she explained, "I mean, she was still a mere child, and not a woman—not even the beginning of a woman. She was fully prepubescent. Her specifically adult development had not started, not even in the least measure. But among her people in that time and place, it was common for such development to begin in girls around the age of twelve, and even earlier in many cases."

The teacher and the colleague agreed that this could be a fairly serious concern. Was Wendy more seriously sick than the physicians had believed when she went home from the hospital for the last time? "No, not at all. As I told you, Wendy was genetically defective. She survived to be fifteen years old only because of that fluke whereby her mother's rubella offset the genetic influence. However, her glands were faulty, and so her hormonal balance was weak, and that was the reason for the delay in maturation. They knew all this, and so the question was what to do about it. By this time in their history, they had developed enough knowledge about the character and functioning of their bodies, and enough sophisticated techniques and devices and mixtures of chemicals, to resolve Wendy's situation for her by correcting her hormonal balance artificially, which would make her grow up normally. The problem was that to do that would be somewhat dangerous—for any girl, not just Wendy. To tamper with hormonal balance could be risky for any of her people. But for Wendy they figured it would be especially risky, just because she was such an extraordinary case with a whole lot of genetic defects. Along with the maturation, there could be some horrible sickness as a side effect."

"Then did she stay as a prepubescent girl through her whole life?"

No, and it was Wendy herself who pushed through the decision.

"A girl is supposed to grow up into an adult woman, or at least try to. If I take sick and die as a side effect—well, I have to die someday. I would rather die for doing what I should do after just a short time than stay as an overgrown little girl, and live for a long time as a big nothing, and then die for nothing. No, Mother, I do not want to die. I am afraid to die, in spite of everything. But I remember Sally died praising God, and I have been thinking. If to die doing what she was supposed to do was good enough for Sally, then I guess maybe it can be good enough for me too."

"You loved her dearly."

"Well, yeah—yes, I did."

"To tell you the truth, Wendy, so did I, although I'm not sure I'd have the courage to—well, to pick up the torch from her in that way, you dear, brave, sweet child."

Diana's mother had another opinion. When she heard of what Wendy had said, she smiled sadly and said of course the child would say that, and she was to be loved and admired all the more for thinking that way, but no. It was just too risky. When she heard that Diana had agreed to it, she threw a tantrum and started a terrible tirade.

It was Alfreda who resolved the situation. She kept quiet and let the tantrum burn itself out. Then she said, calmly and sadly, "My old friend, I feel about this business the same way you do. I too am very much afraid for the girl. But then, I know Diana is even more afraid for her, and Wendy herself is very much afraid. Yes, she is. Talk to her, and it will be very obvious. The problem is that she is also *right.* I know it, and you know it, and there is no way to worm out of it. This is one of those times when we have to decide where we stand, and what we believe in, and whether we what say is more than just words, and what the right terms on which to live and die are. If she is old enough and mature enough that she has begun to understand all this, then who are we to stand in her way? Shall we be too much afraid when she is asking to act bravely?" That shamed the grandmother into agreeing, but on condition that the risk could not be appreciably diminished by waiting until later. Alfreda and Diana said yes, of course, that was understood, and so it was settled.

Then the grandmother asked to speak with Wendy and be assured that her concern was genuine and authentic, as Alfreda had claimed. "Old enough and mature enough to understand, you say. But is she really? Or is she still too much of a child, still playing around? I should like to hear what she says and remove all question for myself." This too was agreed and was done. But it did not take long to see that Alfreda had spoken truly. What made it very obvious was the one anxiety Wendy had. She had spent enough time in hospitals, and knew enough about sickness and death, to appreciate what was at stake. It was not just her love for Sally long ago—that had merely helped her get over the hump. Wendy reminded her grandmother of how she had been prepared to die when she was nine years old after submitting to receive that blessing as an act of adoration. Her great dread was in fact along this line: perhaps she would take sick, die horribly, and be too much distracted with torment to end her life praising God, as Sally had done and as she had been looking to do.

Her grandmother comforted her as well as she could. "Dear child. First and foremost, of course the thing to do is to call upon God at once and ask Him to see you through whatever may happen, now and through your whole life, in sickness and health, including the hour of your death, whenever that may be—in a few weeks or many years ahead. You look to Him and let Him take care of whether your mind may be disabled or whatever." When the child had absorbed this as well as she could and had become calmer, she went on, "Yes, I am sorry, but you are right. There is no guarantee that your death will be kind of merciful and mild, as it was for Sally and might have been for you when you were nine. I have never made you any promises I could not keep, and I am not going to start now. But I can and do promise that we shall do what we can in terms of stuffing you full of drugs and all the rest of it. But the thing to count on is the other."

Because Wendy was older and more mature now, this conversation affected her more deeply than other conversations about such concerns in time past had affected her. She did not have forever, and she was less of a mere child now, which meant she had more of her own responsibility. She decided the thing for her to do was to push harder, and learn all the more, and try to find what she should do or not do in order to resolve her own situation, which she knew had to be wrong somehow. Diana, her sisters, their mother, and Alfreda agreed fully.

There were preliminary tests to prepare for the work on her hormonal balance, and these showed it would be best to hold off for just a little while. It was agreed that the time while they were waiting was a great opportunity. So exactly half a year after the fifteenth anniversary of her birth, Alfreda introduced Wendy to a friend named Alicia, a colleague of that old teacher from whom Diana and Theodora had learned so much long ago. Alfreda had told Alicia of Wendy's situation and background, but Alicia allowed Wendy to speak for herself. "Before I can help you to answer your questions, first I must know what your questions are. So you tell me as well as you can what your concerns are about life and reality, and I shall see what I can do to guide you through. Do not be afraid; what you say need not be perfect. Just say it as well as you can, and then we can refine it later."

This was like nothing Wendy had ever heard before. Not sure where to begin, she blurted out, "Well, first of all, I am an apprentice volcanic witch."

"Well, not to worry. I have met several women who were fully initiated volcanic witches and not mere apprentices. So what then?"

"My governess taught me about the great mystery. Above all the gods and goddesses, there is the One God, the Lord God Almighty. What about that?"

"Great mystery? Well, that is a nice way of putting it. I agree with her there is the Lord God Almighty, although I have not been taught those old stories about gods and goddesses. Tell me, what exactly did she tell you, and what do you believe?"

Wendy laid it all out for her, but she did not speak of why she thought her mother's faith was wrong, only of God's greatness.

When she had done so, Alicia said, "Very good. So far, you have done very well. Now, can you tell me where it goes from there? What do you find puzzling, or why do you think your situation has to be wrong somehow?"

Wendy did not know what she needed to say at this point until she said it. But once she had been asked, it spilled out of her. "I rejoice with my whole heart that there is the One God at the top, but the mystery is just too great—even unbearable. Given His wisdom and goodness, why did He create us so that we should be miserable forever—the good as well as the bad—after just a few years when we might be happy if we are very lucky?"

Alicia took a moment to get past her shock and surprise. Then she replied, "Well, Wendy, I do not know that He has done anything of the sort. Why do you believe that?"

"That is what my governess taught me. When someone dies, he or she becomes a ghost in the parade, and that is all. The life someone has as a ghost is like a big nothing."

"Yes, I have heard of that before. All right, let me ask you. If He were to grant you the special favor to have something better for yourself and all those you care about, what would you ask Him to do?"

"About six years ago now, when I was in the hospital, I had a friend named Sally, who was also sick in the hospital. Unlike me, Sally did not make it. A nurse explained to me that she died rejoicing in God. I was, and still am, very glad for that fact. But then by doing that, Sally completed the perfection of life, or fulfilled what people are supposed to fulfill, or something. Well, that should have been enough. When I finish what I am supposed to do and come to the end of the day, Mama tucks me into bed and bids me sleep peacefully through the night. She does not say I should then spend the night suffering with nightmares. So it seems like Sally should be allowed to just sleep peacefully until time runs out, instead of having the misery of being a ghost in the parade."

"Assuming your friend Sally was as worthy as you believe, then yes, of course—unless something even better is available."

Wendy had heard some loose talk about what there might or might not be in the next world. But the idea that something better might be available in any serious way was new to her. What she said was, "Now I am totally confused."

"All right, let us go through it one step at a time. Since Sally is dead, I guess we can say she is a ghost. As for whether she is in some sort of parade, maybe that too. But as for whether she is suffering misery as a big nothing—well, that is another question. What if—hypothetically—it should turn out that her mind is being illuminated by God so that she is receiving blessedness from Him instead?"

At this word, Wendy's heart leapt up with the combination of rejoicing, astonishment, and anguished cry to God that it might be so. What she managed to say was, "That would be beyond all hopes and dreams." Then, "Do you believe this?"

"As a general proposition, yes. I do. As for Sally in particular, I hope so."

"But no—it is just too much for the mind to accept."

"Well, yes—in one way, it is too much for the mind to accept. Then again, when someone asks the right questions and works the concerns through seriously, the alternatives turn out to be even crazier. I hope you will go on and learn more and see why this is so."

"What about what my governess taught me?"

"As I told you, I have met several volcanic witches. I have heard before now about the teaching of the One God above the gods and goddesses, and I have also heard about the idea of the dead as being ghosts in the parade. I have asked about these things, and the answer is clear enough. You have to remember that the One God was considered a great mystery to be kept hidden. Is that correct? Along that line, most of the stories you were taught as a child were developed apart from any reference to, or concern for, the One God. This includes the stories that speak of the dead as ghosts in the parade. And so there it is. You said your governess told you everyone must rejoice in the One God. Is that correct?"

"Yes, it is."

"Exactly so. Now, Wendy, when you put all these points together, there is the answer to what you said. Those stories speak of the dead as ghosts in the parade because the people are not thought of as rejoicing in God. Those old stories are right about that. Apart from being hooked up to God to rejoice in Him and to offer praise and thanksgiving to Him, then yes, there is only misery to look forward to in this life and the next. As for what form such misery would take in the next life, I guess it could take the form of being a ghost in the parade, although that is not what I was taught. But those details are not important right now. What is important now is the basic idea. You must look to God and rejoice in Him or be miserable in this life and the next."

"Then my friend Sally who died in the hospital—what about her?"

"Well, if Sally was hooked up to God to rejoice in Him, and I hope she was, then you need not be sorry for her. She is not doomed to live in misery. When someone is hooked up to God to rejoice in Him, that fact is not canceled or taken away just because she happens to die. How or why that is so is something we may be able to discuss later on, when you have learned more. But what you should hope for is that Sally is rejoicing in God all the more now and will be forever."

For just a moment Wendy rejoiced with her whole heart. Then a terrible question came into her mind. "But how can Sally or anyone else be hooked up to God? Surely He is far too great and wondrous for people to reach up to Him, let alone be hooked up to Him."

"How well you understand. Alfreda was right about you—unless she underestimated you. Yes, honey child, of course. No one can reach up to Him in that way. He is above and beyond anything like that. But it is possible from the other side. People cannot reach up to Him, but He can reach down to them. They cannot attach themselves to Him, but He can attach them to Him."

"What does that involve, and how does it work?"

"Well, I do not rightly know how it works. None of us do. Even those who have studied it long and hard have only scraps and fragments. But He knows, and He will take care of it. As for what it involves, you know that He does not need worship or anything else people can do for Him. To offer praise and thanksgiving to Him is an honor He gives to the people for their sake and not for His. Well then, in the same way, to be hooked up to Him to rejoice in Him is kind of like a further version of this same honor He gives. To be hooked up to Him is a free gift. People must look to God, and submit to Divine mercy, and allow themselves to be attached to Him, and receive blessedness from Him."

"Did Sally have this gift from God?"

"Well, I hope so, and it sounds likely enough she did—but God knows that, and we do not. What Sally did or did not receive from Him was up to her. What I receive from Him is up to me, and what you receive from Him is up to you."

"How does it work? What am I supposed to do?"

"Well, as I said, it is a free gift. You cannot earn it or deserve it, nor can it ever be repaid. You can submit to receive the gift with rejoicing and thanksgiving, and you can honor it, but that is all. But then, that is all that is needed. What you must do is what all must do. You offer praise and thanksgiving to Him as well as you can, call upon Him to provide for you, learn as much as you can about all these things, and—most important of all—follow as well as you can what you already know about what is right and wrong. If you do all that, then He will see you through. There is much more, but He will lead you to know what to do and when and how."

"You make it sound almost like death is nothing to be afraid of!"

"Well, death as it exists now is not what God originally planned for people—not at all. Why death exists in the way it does now is something else we may discuss later on when you have learned more. But in another way, yes—for one who does what I told you, death *is* nothing to be afraid of. To take over what you said a little while ago, a good girl is not afraid when her mother tucks her into bed so that she can sleep peacefully through the night. She is happy instead. Well, what is involved here is far better than that, as I told you." Wendy remembered Deborah told her Sally had died with no torment and nothing dreadful. She asked Alicia about this. "Yes, of course. To be tormented or to have something dreadful happen are things to be afraid of, but death—just in itself and apart from all that—does not have to be something to be afraid of."

As Wendy turned all this over and over in her mind, she saw a whole field of questions and concerns open up before her. But it was easy for Alicia to see she had plenty to think about already, and so the meeting was concluded.

Wendy turned this conversation over and over in her mind through the next several days, and she found herself to be of two minds. She wanted to say it all seemed very reasonable to her, and she also wanted to say it was beyond all hopes and dreams, and even too much for the mind to accept.

But there was also something else in her mind. She spoke to Alfreda of it. "Alicia knows more than other people, and she is smarter than other people, but there is something else. There is something special about her. I do not know what it is or even how to describe it, but there is something going on with her."

Alfreda smiled. "Yes, I know. Would you like to meet with her again?" Yes, very much. "Then perhaps someday she will explain it to you. All you have to do is ask her nicely."

Alfreda did not tell Wendy until years later that Alicia had said something similar about Wendy. "You keep your eye on that girl. There is something very special about Wendy—some special gift or some exotic destiny to fulfill. Probably both of those things, and maybe more as well. Something I can almost put my finger on, but not quite. Of course, whether it works out for good or for evil will be up to her. Anyway, you keep your eye on her."

"She is much smarter than most girls. Also, given what Lilikea has taught her and its contrast with the dominant culture, she has had more occasion to think about deep questions than most."

"Yes, that too. Smarter and also more willing to listen to reason—less resistant to the truth. That would be plenty right there. But that is not all. There is also something more, beyond that—even given what you said about how Lilikea's teaching made her think more—even beyond that. There is no question. I am very sure, but I cannot yet see it clearly."

"Wendy is her mother's only child, and she has been down sick a great deal. Because of this, she has had more contact with adults, and less with other children, than is common. Also, Lilikea has trained her to have more discipline and less nonsense than most children. For all these reasons, she is appreciably more mature than other girls her age."

"Yes, that too, certainly. But there is also more, even beyond that."

Then Alfreda began to speak. What she said next, she had not explicitly formulated in her own mind until she said it. But when she had said it, she realized that it was true and that she had been aware of it on some level of her mind for a long time. First she blurted out the story of that corrupt teacher who had tried to recruit Wendy as a witch based on the worship of Renegade Messengers. Alicia let out a long, thin whistle, which showed among her people how deeply shocked she was. Before she could respond any further, Alfreda continued. "Her governess, Lilikea, has been looking for a long time—and still is—to initiate Wendy as a volcanic witch when she is old enough. I knew this even before Wendy told us she was an apprentice volcanic witch. I did not have an explicit statement from Lilikea on this point, but you know how it is. The truth is clearly implicit in a thousand little things that happen every day—perhaps not least in the training and discipline she has imposed. Beyond that, I have noticed things people have said, amounting to hints that would call for explicit denial if it were not so, but Lilikea said nothing. But all that may not even be the main thing. If there were any question at all, it was removed with that affair of the corrupt teacher. All of us were very angry, but Lilikea's reaction was different. It was subtle enough that I noticed it only because I was looking for it. I had not clearly formulated all this in my mind at that time, but I knew there was something. Now the point of all this is that I myself have thought of Wendy in those terms in a strange way. I do *not* mean she should go away from the worship of the Real God, or that she should become a witch, or anything like that. But it is almost like...if the Real God did or could have witches attached to Him as a special category of His servants, then Wendy should be—there is no other way to say it—a witch of the Real God. There, I have said it, crazy as I know it sounds."

"Yes, of course it sounds crazy, but the girl is so strange it is not clear what to say. What you said is wrong, but it is almost like you have to say something like that. Maybe the girl is to have some special gift as a miracle worker under the Real God? Maybe that is it, but it beats me. Anyway, you keep your eye on her, as I told you."

About five weeks after the first meeting, Wendy met with Alicia again. Alfreda was also there. Wendy began by saying, "I have been thinking about what you said, about how I should hope Sally is rejoicing in God all the more and forever. I wish it were true, but I think it cannot be."

"Oh, really? Why not?"

"Well, once she died, she was not a full person any more. She is only a ghost now."

"Assuming that to be true, why does that go against what I said?"

"A ghost is like—well, kind of like a living shadow. It is like emptiness that somehow exists as a real thing. Its whole life is just a function of darkness and emptiness. Something like that cannot rejoice in God or worship God. It can only have misery. You spoke of Divine mercy. But surely the best mercy would be just to let Sally collapse completely so that she has no life at all, even as a ghost, and then let her sleep peacefully forever, as I said."

"All right, Wendy. First of all, you have a whole lot of questions and concerns all rolled together. Let us see whether we can work it through, piece by piece. Yes, it is true that one who has died is not a full person anymore, as you said. But whether that one is a function of darkness and emptiness is another question. As I said before, for one who does not honor God, there is only misery. Someone like that might well be what you call a ghost after death. But for one who is hooked up to God to rejoice in Him, it is another question."

"You said that before, and I thought of it. But I figured that one who has died cannot rejoice in God any more, in spite of what you said, because that one is not a full person anymore."

"So now we come to it. That is really very good. Let me think for a moment how to answer." After a short pause, Alicia explained, "Imagine something happened to your eyes and ears, so that you were blind and deaf. Now imagine I had magic powers, so that I could let you see through my eyes—not just by telling you in words what I saw but by having what my eyes saw feed directly into your soul. Again, imagine I could let you hear through my ears, so that what my ears heard would feed directly into your soul. If I did all that, it would be almost as if you were not really blind and deaf at all. Something kind of like that applies here. God can and does provide for the people. What the people lost in dying is compensated for so that there is supplied whatever is needed for them to be able to rejoice in God."

Wendy thought hard about this for a few minutes and then said, "What you said is almost too much for the mind to accept!"

"Well, in one way, yes, it is. But I think as you get older and keep learning, you may come to agree with it more and more."

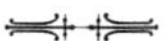

At this point, Beatrice interrupted her narrative to ask, "Is what Alicia said what happens with the Renegades among us, and with those on the other worlds, who die like the dumb beasts but with contrition and conversion?" Her teacher and the colleague affirmed that this was so. "I expected it would be, but the fact that a person could—and does—die like a dumb beast was new to me. I learned of it just before the vision began. So I was surprised at what Wendy asked and Alicia answered, although I reckon I would have hit upon the answer if I had thought it through."

When all this had been talked through and smoothed over, Beatrice resumed.

"After this, Wendy did not meet with Alicia again for years. First of all, it was only a few more weeks now before the hormonal manipulation would begin, and then Wendy would be preoccupied with that business. After that, she was concerned with further education and with taking her place in the world as one who was beginning to be an adult woman. After that was resolved, Alicia was preoccupied with affairs having to do with her own relatives. But they met again eventually, and what happened then was even more interesting."

CHAPTER TEN

The hormonal manipulation went very well, without incident and with nothing untoward. In spite of the early fears, there was no side effect of sickness. There were only the intended effects of maturation in mind as well as body. But these were serious enough—more so than Wendy had expected.

It was now exactly a quarter of a year until the sixteenth anniversary of her birth. That morning, Wendy awoke with her mind full of thoughts and feelings like nothing there had ever been before. On this occasion her mother was dazed instead of lucid, so Wendy asked her grandmother. Her grandmother questioned the girl briefly, but it did not take long to uncover the truth. "What this means is that the treatment is working. This is your first preliminary awakening as a woman. I say 'preliminary' because your body is still unchanged, at least on the outside. But not to worry—that too will happen soon enough." They discussed it for a little while and then went on to other tasks and concerns.

The grandmother was right. Wendy's body began to change soon enough—in fact, just three days later. From there, the changes of both mind and body occurred quickly enough, in regular order and in the customary way. There was the kind of standard difficulty a female of that species has in adjusting to those changes, but there was no special trouble, at least for the time being.

Time marched on, and it was now half a year since that first awakening. Lilikea had taught Wendy to have better discipline and less nonsense than other children, and so Wendy pushed harder than others in her studying and learning. Because of this, because she was much smarter than others, and because of the special provisions, Wendy had now completed the process of working her way through the sequence of education that was standard for almost all children at that time and place. Because her mind was very bright and sharp, all agreed it would be very desirable for Wendy to go on to more advanced learning. Here too, there were standard systems and sequences that been set up among her people. On the other hand, Wendy was only a girl, whose experience of life and affairs was very limited, as she herself recognized. She was also about two years younger than other beginning students would be. Because of this, her mind was slightly less mature than those of others, in spite of her training from Lilikea. Also, her body was clearly less mature than those of other girls. There was the concern that these differences in age and maturity could cause some difficulty for her. So even though Wendy was eager to begin the more advanced learning right then, it was decided that she should hold off for a little while. In the meantime, Theodora happened to know of an opportunity, and so it was decided she should have a fairly mild job in a shop that specialized in selling flowers. She could start the further learning in another quarter of a year, with a light load of study at first, and then work her way up to a larger load. Wendy agreed the job would be a good idea in order to expand her base of experience, but would a quarter of a year really make that much difference to the other concerns?

Diana assured her, "Oh, you'll be surprised how much will change in that time."

As Wendy learned soon enough, her family was right. Much did change in that time—far more than Wendy had expected. Both the natural processes of maturation and the broadening of her experience were very important for her personal development. At the end of that quarter year, Wendy said to her aunt Theodora, "So this is what it is for a woman to be a woman."

"Almost, but not exactly. It is the *beginning* of what it is to be an adult woman—only the beginning. However, your comment shows that we were right in what we told you when this adventure at the flower shop began. You wondered whether this short time would make that much difference, and we said you'd be surprised how much would change even in just that time." Wendy did remember upon being reminded. They discussed Wendy's concerns at some length and then went on to other affairs.

As had been agreed, Wendy enrolled at this time for a minimal load of more advanced study, although she continued working at the flower shop. One week followed another, the seasons rolled by, and the years progressed. Wendy did very well with the minimal load, and she worked her way up quickly to larger loads, always doing very well. Through it all, she continued working at the flower shop, although eventually in lesser measure in order to devote more time and energy to the larger loads of advanced study. Yet even though she pushed as hard as she could, it took her longer than it took most girls to graduate from the first main division of such advanced study. This was partly because she had begun with a lesser load of study and worked her way up gradually, which entailed slower progression than others at first. But it was chiefly because even later on, sometimes Wendy had to study less—or perhaps not at all for the time being—and be more concerned with her old clinical problems, which had diminished as she had become older and more mature but would never be fully outgrown.

⁂

One of the academic projects Wendy went through during these years provided occasion for the further discussion Beatrice had promised her teacher and the colleague.

"She wrote an essay on the specific question of whether God should be spoken of in the masculine, the feminine, the neuter, or what. Interestingly enough, she considered the possibility—which to her was, of course, purely hypothetical—that there might be rational animals on other planets or something that were all male or all female, or at least all the adult persons might be all male or all female. But because this concern was purely hypothetical to her, she developed the point only briefly, chiefly in order to get it out of the way and then leave it aside. As we know, and as their natural scientists had learned by this time, females are biologically the primary and superior beings. To speak in these terms, males are faulty females. To be sure, in one obvious way, it would be best to speak of God in the neuter, to make the point that God is above and beyond the whole division of male and female. But her people ordinarily had no awareness of rational animals that are superior to this division, and so there was not the basis of lived experience to ground this way of speaking about God. In view of all these facts, one might think it would be better to speak of God in the feminine in order to speak of God by comparison with the beings who enjoy the greater perfection. Then in what way could the tradition of speaking about God almost exclusively in the masculine be justified?

"There was some discussion and comparison of the points about motherhood versus fatherhood in order to evaluate the benefits and problems of each as a metaphor for the relation of God to creatures. As with all the metaphors and analogies people use to try to understand God as far as possible, so here as well—the best of both models must be kept and balanced against each other according to wisdom. But as for which model should be taken as dominant, what the question finally came to was that, indeed, one must decide what should be said about God's relation to creatures. Given what the right Faith has to say—although Wendy did not call it that in her essay—the model of Divine fatherhood is, on the whole, clearly superior. This was especially so considering that this Faith grew out of a long preparation that was intended to eliminate faulty ideas—ideas that would go all too easily with the model of Divine motherhood.

"Well, with this project also, Wendy did very well. The essay was highly praised, and she was highly praised for having written it. This was so even though, interestingly enough, the teacher who evaluated the essay disliked the traditional way of speaking about God in the masculine. She was honest enough to admit that as she had discussed with Wendy, given the concerns those traditional people had, then of course they would have to find fatherhood the better model—just as Wendy had argued."

"What were these faulty ideas that had to be avoided?"

"As I told you, full atheism is relatively rare among them. Often enough, Divine attributes are affirmed but then assigned to lesser beings. Along this line, the tendency has been to personify natural forces and features as gods and goddesses, or to take the natural world as a whole as the ultimate being, or to say Divine reality is not fully separate from the natural world, or something like that. In short, very commonly they follow some form of nature worship. This is the kind of thing Wendy grew up with, with the stories about the alleged goddess of volcanoes and so on. Such nature worship had to be swept away in the age of preparation. But the model of motherhood for Divine creation is not so good for doing this, since the mother has much more intimate involvement with the child than the father. In order to make the point that God is above and beyond the whole world and everything in it, the model of fatherhood is better. That is what experience shows. Of course, once the clear understanding has been achieved, then one can go back and pick up what is best in the model of motherhood. Wendy developed this point in the essay. But, as she also pointed out, that is a different issue." All these points were talked through among them and finally talked out. When everything been said, Beatrice resumed her narrative.

Eventually, Wendy did graduate at the age of twenty-two, about ten weeks after the anniversary of her birth. Because she had always done very well in her studies, because her mind was as bright and sharp as it was, and because she herself was eager to explore further, it had been arranged that Wendy should go on to higher levels of advanced study. And so it was done. She graduated from the second main division of advanced study two years later, at the age of twenty-four, again about ten weeks after the anniversary of her birth. During this time, Wendy continued working at the flower shop as she had been, although again in lesser measure. Once again, she had always done very well, and so her teachers urged her to go on to the third level of such study, which was the end of the line at that time and place. This was agreed upon and planned. Wendy would begin the third level in about another quarter year, which was kind of the standard way of doing things among them. In the meantime, she would pursue other concerns.

The first such concern Wendy pursued was what she should believe or not believe and which path she should follow.

⁂

Beatrice commented, "Wendy had by now learned far too much in her studies, and developed too much in the academic projects she had gone through, to take at all seriously the stories Lilikea had taught her as a child. On the other hand, she had come to consider that the popular way at that time and place of taking the material world as primary was at best just another version of nature worship, as I was saying earlier. She knew it to involve the same basic error of affirming Divine attributes but as belonging to lesser beings. Indeed, Wendy thought this kind of nature worship to be even more cheap and dirty than what Lilikea had taught her.

"As I say, she figured such exaltation of the material world as primary to be this way at best. At worst, she figured it amounted to full atheism, with the full denial of all Divine attributes. Wendy thought this kind of full atheism to be at least worth taking seriously, as comparatively honest and clear minded. But then she agreed with an author who said the honest and clear-minded way to develop full atheism was to stop believing that the world displays order or structure in what it is and how it works. One should accept chance as the deepest basis for everything. This would of course include denying the laws of physics and chemistry, as well as everything else. Wendy thought that given this implication, full atheism was 'just a little too ridiculous,' as she herself phrased it. She found it truly amazing that people proclaimed full atheism in the name of modern natural science. So what then? Quite clearly, there were only so many choices. When she worked the question through, Wendy realized that apart from full atheism or affirming Divine attributes of lesser beings, what was left was to affirm such attributes of what was in fact the Absolute Being. By this time, she had learned enough to understand that this Absolute Being, simply by virtue of its absolute character, would be more or less what her family spoke of as the Real God, the Lord God Almighty, except for what Lilikea said about their faith and Wendy still believed. I mean the claim that they said God is confined in Heaven.

"The only serious questions were not about God but rather about lesser beings. Were such beings truly separate from God? Yes, of course, for God's nature could not possibly contain or support the weaknesses and limitations that constituted lesser beings *as* lesser beings. Did such beings in fact exist at all, or were they just some sort of dream or delusion, as one of the traditions in her world said? Wendy had long ago decided that what one of her teachers had said was the answer to that. 'If lesser beings do not exist, then only God exists, and so it is God Who suffers from the dream or delusion, since there is no one else. But to suffer such errors looks to be contrary to God's perfection as the Absolute Being.' Wendy agreed with her teacher that even though there might be puzzles and paradoxes in speaking of God's relation to creatures, it was still more reasonable than this alternative. She decided the answers that tradition offered were not good enough. So, then, what was left for her was to acknowledge and affirm God the Absolute. She had already reached this point in her thinking by the time of the formal ceremony for the graduation from the second level."

It was on the day of this formal ceremony that the next crisis came. Wendy had finally met with Alicia again, just a few weeks before. She rejoiced that Alicia and Alfreda had come to the ceremony, as well as her mother, aunts, and grandmother. After the ceremony, they all had dinner together. They got to talking, and Wendy spoke of the concerns she planned to pursue during the upcoming season. She explained what she had come to believe and why. "However, I have had to admit to myself that just reaching this conclusion in my mind is not good enough. In my case, some positive action to implement the judgment in concrete reality is required as well. The reason is that years before, too much was done on the other side that has to be counterbalanced. Not least along that line, Alicia, is that what I told you years ago is not true of me now. I am not an apprentice any more. I have been fully and formally initiated as a volcanic witch." Wendy addressed this comment to Alicia specifically because the others already knew.

Alicia asked, "Well, Wendy, have you considered converting into what your mother and grandmother and aunts believe?"

Wendy exclaimed, "You speak as though you yourself believe it!"

"Well, yes—I do believe it."

"*What?!* After our conversations years ago, I would have expected you to know better!"

Before anyone else could react, Alicia raised her hand and said, "Full stop, everyone. Wendy has obviously picked up the idea somehow that there is something truly bizarre that we believe in. Is that correct, Wendy?"

"Yes. Yes, exactly so."

"All right, what is it?"

"Well, the truth has to be that, as the saying goes, God is always and everywhere and fills all things. But you believe that God is up in Heaven instead."

For a moment, all of them just sat there, puzzled. Then Alicia understood. "Do you mean, you think we believe God is *confined* in Heaven as opposed to being always and everywhere and filling all things?"

"Yes, right."

The others were too shocked to speak at all, or even to burst into laughter. Alicia began, "Dear child, I am sorry to have to be the one to explain this to you, but *you* are the one who has gone wrong. Yes, as you said—God is always and everywhere and fills all things. That part is true. But then, you see, *we* believe that as much as anyone. To deny this fact is to go against the Faith. It is really just that simple.—As for the other part, no, God is not confined in Heaven. To say God is in Heaven is true only as a poetic image. What I mean is that there is no way to speak of God apart from using metaphors and analogies, as you know very well. When it is said that God is up in Heaven, the word 'up' is not being used to say anything about location or direction. The point is that He enjoys some greater perfection or superior order of being, or something like that. That is all."

Now it was Wendy's turn to be shocked. She turned kind of instinctively to Theodora, with whom she had discussed some of these things years before. Theodora saw the unspoken question on her face and said, "Yes, Wendy, it is as Alicia said. She has laid it out for us very well, better than I could have done myself. All that is what we believe."

By now, Amanda had recovered enough to develop the suspicion in her mind. She saw that Wendy was genuinely shocked, and so she spoke up next. "Wendy, I am not angry with you, because I know you are speaking sincerely. In fact, I want to make it easy for you if I can. So I have one question. Was it Lilikea who told you this about what we believe?"

"Why, yes! How did you know?"

"How do I know, she says. How do you think? For a woman who has just graduated at an advanced level, you are speaking very stupidly. I know because I know Lilikea—I am the one who brought her in, remember? And I know you, and I have seen a whole lot of puzzling stuff over the years. But now, with this answer you just gave me, a lot of things are beginning to make sense. I think I shall have to speak to her.—And yes, it is as Alicia and Theodora said."

"Please, don't hurt Lilikea. She was not trying to mislead me. She taught me as well as she knew. She herself believed what she said."

"Oh, yes, of course—no doubt. I'm sure that's true. But hurt her? Who said anything about hurting her? No, I am just going to explain a little reality to her."

At this point, Alfreda broke in. "'Don't hurt Lilikea,' she says. Your mind is overwhelmed, Wendy. You are starting to babble like a child. You need to be calmed down." Wendy had to admit this was so. "Then you must do as I say." With that, Alfreda made her drink a large load of the same red beverage she had made Diana drink long ago.

Right after that, Alicia spoke up again. "Wendy, you have read some of the great landmark thinkers of history, and you know they believed—even insisted—that God is always and everywhere and fills all things. You know also they believed as we do. What about that?"

The red beverage was just beginning to take effect. That made it easy for Wendy. "Yes, and I wondered about that sometimes. I found it strange—very strange indeed—how they combined the high philosophical sophistication of their arguments and definitions and explanations with some childish religious stuff. As I say, I wondered about it, but there it was."

⁂

Beatrice's teacher and her colleague knew the words in their language that would translate as "philosophy" and "philosophical," but Beatrice had not known these words, just as most of her people did not know these words. These words also were among the specialized vocabulary used chiefly among theoreticians and Travelers. Beatrice was given to know these words and what they meant in the course of her vision, in order that she might understand what was going on with Wendy's conversations and academic studies.

⸻

"No, Wendy, that is not good enough. Why did you not ask about this long ago?"

"Well—to tell you the truth, I never really thought of that. Somehow it always seemed like just a screwy puzzle with no answer, except that people are crazy and will believe anything. Also, by the time I came to wonder about it, you were not around for me to ask you."

It was her mother, presently lucid, who saved Wendy from further embarrassment. "This goes to show what can happen when someone gets something stuck in her head way back in her childhood." The others agreed, and they went on from there.

During this conversation, the beverage took increasingly greater effect as time went on, and it continued to do so. In a short while, Wendy was very calm and even slightly jolly, although at the price of having her mind just a little dazed. She shared easily and even gladly in the mirth at the nonsense she had been following. When they had all finished laughing together, Wendy announced that the whole question about what her mother and grandmother believed would have to be reconsidered. "But not tonight. I think Aunt Freddy made me drink too much."

"Evidently not too much for you to be aware of that fact," Alfreda replied.

But as she turned it over and over in her mind in the following days, Wendy realized that she was unable to bring herself to accept the Faith her grandmother held. Alicia had invited her to engage in further conversations, and she knew she would have to do so. But she felt the need to do something and do it more quickly than that. So she did what she could. Wendy prepared an elaborate and carefully crafted formal statement that was to be her basic vow of recognition and submission to the One God. Given her intellectual brilliance and her learning, this was fairly easy for her. In order to make sure she had done it correctly, she asked Alicia to examine it. Alicia did so and said that given what it was for, Wendy's statement was as good as could be hoped for or desired. Then again, the way in which the act of swearing this vow was accomplished turned out to be much more interesting.

Wendy thought to arrange a nice little ceremony. She did so, but what happened was not as she imagined. Only long after did Wendy come to suspect that what happened had in fact been a Divine mercy to make the act have its full value as being a genuine cry from the depths.

After a brief pause, Beatrice continued. "Things do not always work out among Wendy's people as they expect. She swore some critical vow, all right—but not as she imagined—two weeks after Alicia had approved her formal statement and seven weeks after Wendy's formal ceremony of graduation from the second level of advanced study beyond that standard basis for children. What cleared the blockage from her mind and made it easy for her to see what to do was something her first cousin Elizabeth, Theodora's nine-year-old daughter, said to her."

Wendy was at Theodora's house eleven days before swearing the vow. Elizabeth offered her a fruit known as a banana to eat.

Wendy declined politely, but on this occasion, instead of just leaving it as based on her own wishes, she explained that she was not allowed to eat bananas.

"Why not?" Elizabeth asked.

Of course, the reason was that bananas were forbidden for women in the religion Lilikea had taught Wendy. But now, with all she had in her mind, this question touched off something inside her. "Yes, why not?" she replied. Then, patting the child on the head as a gesture of demonstrative affection, Wendy went on, "I thank you, Elizabeth. I thank you very much. I shall have to think about this."

It did not take her long to think about it. By the end of that day, she knew how to proceed. The only reason it took as long as it did was that everything had to be arranged. But finally, all was made ready.

When she awoke on the morning of the appointed day, Wendy felt "just a little off," as she said. But having made all the arrangements, and especially having involved the other people, she decided quickly she had better see it through. And so she did. At the appointed time, she went in and stood in front of five of those who had been at her graduation dinner seven weeks earlier—her mother, her grandmother, her two aunts, and Alfreda. Only Alicia was not able to come, although she would have liked to. Then Wendy began, "At my graduation dinner, I said what was done in earlier years had to be counterbalanced. It was your daughter Elizabeth, Theodora, who showed me how to go about it. I thank you for coming here to help me with it." They told her they were happy to come.

"Let me begin with my confession about what was done that has to be resolved. When I gave myself to be initiated as a volcanic witch, it was on the explicit basis that I was to be the servant of a deputy of the One God and not that I was giving myself to a real goddess. I insisted on that explicit reservation as though it were good enough. But I knew in my own mind—well, not that it was wrong, exactly, but certainly that as they say, it did not rightly pass the smell test. So what then? I do not rightly know. I only know that I must finally submit to the Real God as fully as I can, with no more nonsense, and go on from there to see what comeuppance or punishment He may appoint for me."

She picked up the notebook with the formal statement and said, "Mama, Grandma, Mandy, Dorry, Freddy—I ask you to witness my basic vow with whatever authority God may allow you." Yes, they would do so gladly, with all their hearts. With that, Wendy opened the notebook to the right page, focused her eyes on what she had written, and would have begun to recite.

However, having started the day feeling a little off, Wendy came to feel gradually worse and worse as time went on. So now Wendy said, "Forgive me, but evidently Another far greater has cut my speech short. Whatever may live inside the volcano is not a goddess. No such goddesses or gods exist. I shall die, if I must, as the handmaid of the One God, if He will have me, rather than live by denying or dishonoring Him. Glory to God in the highest. And now, if you ladies will excuse me, I think I must go to bed." Then she smiled, closed her eyes, and collapsed.

⁂

At this point, Beatrice paused to explain. "Wendy did not have any particular hope or expectation of what would happen or not happen to her when she died. She did not know whether God would simply snuff her out (as she had once wished for), or whether she would become a ghost in the parade, or whether she might even enter into the blessedness of Heaven. All Wendy knew was that indeed, only the Lady God Almighty is worthy to be worshiped, but She is worthy indeed—only Wendy followed the tradition given within the right Faith and spoke of God in the masculine. But that was enough for her. Wendy knew this, and she acted on it." The others wondered at her lack of hope, and Beatrice said it would become clear later.

⁂

But once again, as it turned out, Wendy did not die. In spite of what she imagined, there was nothing magical or supernatural about what happened to her. Nor was she being attacked by any superior being. There was just the common fact of sickness, based on the functioning of very much lower beings. Several days earlier, a load of tainted food had been distributed to the general public. Wendy had eaten some of this food a few days before she would have sworn her basic vow. On the day planned for the vow, the sickness she had contracted from the tainted food became manifest, and Wendy collapsed with a bacterial infection known as listeria.

The news about the tainted food had been proclaimed to the general public only that day. The others had not heard the news, but Diana had. Wendy remained conscious for a short time, and so Diana and the others questioned her about how she felt and what she had eaten. Then Diana announced, "All this sounds like what the news said about listeria."

There were devices among them at this time for distant communication, and even for conversations in real time. So Diana called the office of Wendy's physician and spoke with a nurse on her staff, telling all that had been learned from questioning Wendy. The nurse spoke with the physician, and it was arranged that Wendy should be brought in right then.

The physician had also heard the news. She examined Wendy and realized quickly that indeed it was likely enough to be listeria. To make sure, she tried to question Wendy further. But there turned out to be a slight problem. What Wendy had said in front of her mother and the others before she collapsed had all been spoken in the language of Diana and Alfreda. The questioning had also been conducted in that language. But by the time Wendy reached the office, she was so weak and confused as to be hardly able to speak or even understand that language, although she could have done so if it had been strictly necessary. She had reverted to the language Lilikea had taught her long ago. The last thing she said in Diana's language was, "I am sorry, but it is too hard for me. May I speak in my native tongue?"

Her mother explained to the physician about Wendy's native language, but neither of them knew the language. Happily, both Alfreda and Amanda knew that language, and both of them had come along in order to help transport Wendy. Amanda told Wendy in that language to go ahead and do what she had to do. The physician's questions about Wendy's symptoms and her eating were translated, and Wendy's answers were translated back. When this had been done, the physician was sure it was listeria, but she arranged for a sample of Wendy's blood to be examined in order to verify this diagnosis. It was in fact verified soon enough. In the meantime, on the strength of this diagnosis, the physician ordered drugs for Wendy and sent her home, which was common in cases of listeria.

It was not the next day but the day after that when Wendy confronted her grandmother, based on the exotic dreams she had suffered in the course of her sickness. "Grandma, I need to ask you about what I have been dreaming. Does my failure to swear the basic vow have to do with the great mysteries of our family that you have kept secret from me?"

"What have you been dreaming?"

"Last night and also the night before, I dreamed one of your ancestors came and spoke to me of how I must fulfill my destiny as a great warrior lady, and she said I should ask you to explain. She spoke in a foreign language. I knew it was the language of her own homeland, the land of our ancestors, and what she meant came effortlessly into my mind, but I did not understand the words themselves."

Grandma smiled sadly and nodded. "In answer to your question, yes—that failure has plenty to do with those mysteries. Yes, to be some sort of great warrior lady is your appointed destiny. I have known this for many years and have lived in dread. And so I have watched and waited until the situation developed, which is what had to be done. But now it is upon us, and we must face it. In one way, I am kind of glad that now the waiting is over. But I am sorry for you." Then, after a momentary pause, she said, "The failure is relevant, for your first challenge is to fight your way through in order to be properly sworn in to the cause of the Real God—the One God, as you call Him—the Lord God Almighty. Mind you, this is even before you go on to be converted into the right Faith."

"You knew this when I tried and failed the other day. Who else knew?"

"All of us who were there knew, including Alfreda. All of us have known for years."

"When were you going to tell me about it?"

"When you were ready for it. I hoped the ceremony would go through with no trouble, and I was thinking then it might be appropriate that evening or perhaps the next day. But that was not how it worked out."

"Grandma, how do you know all this about me?"

Grandma was about to tell her, but then she replied instead, "No—a very good question, but just a little too early in the game. Now, Wendy, do you still yearn to be sworn into the cause of the Real God, the Lord God Almighty?"

"Oh, yes—now more than ever, with all my heart."

"Then that is what has to be taken care of first. It really is your first challenge."

"Then I do not need to know the rest of it?"

"Oh, on the contrary—you need to know very much, but not just yet. All that will come later—but very soon, I promise."

And so seven days after the first attempt, the ladies gathered again to witness what Wendy had to do. This time, Alicia was there as well as all the others. The grandmother had made the arrangements this time. These arrangements included telling Alicia what she had told Wendy. Once again, Diana was lucid on this occasion. Wendy opened her notebook to the right page, focused her eyes on what she had written, and this time she did manage to recite the vow.

"There is the One God and His creatures, and that is all there is, with no other beside Him and with the yawning chasm, the great gulf, between God and all His creatures, however exalted those creatures may be. God exists of Himself, He is sufficient unto Himself, and He is complete and perfect within Himself, with no needs or weakness at all. For God is the overflowing superabundance that is totally limitless. He is always and everywhere and fills all things.

"Creation is a free gift based on the choice of God's will. God creates according to His wisdom, and there is true creation from nothing. As the Book says, God commanded, and things were created. Other things exist only as created by God through the exercise of His absolute power. These other beings are not extensions of this God, nor does it belong to their nature to share in Divine attributes or privileges in even the least measure.

"This God is completely and purely righteous, and He cannot do what is morally wrong. Only this good God is primary. No other divine being exists, and no world of the gods exists. All the stories of gods and goddesses, along with their activities, are just that—mere stories. Nothing and no one can stand against Him, nor can anyone possibly reach up to the One God so as to manipulate Him or compel Him in any way whatever. He, and

He alone, is sovereign over all, and He is to be both praised and obeyed.

"All this I affirm and declare with the full dedication of my whole heart. Wherefore, I acknowledge my former beliefs in opposition to the real truth of this One God as errors, and I condemn my former deeds in acting out those beliefs as wayward conduct. I recognize His authority as absolute, I surrender to His dominion, I beseech Him to forgive me for these errors and wayward conduct and all my evil, and I ask Him to provide for me that I may fulfill what He knows I should fulfill. From this moment, I shall not offer adoration—whether in praise, or prayer, or sacrifice, or thanksgiving—save only to the One God, the Lord God Almighty. Only He is worthy to be worshiped, but He is worthy indeed.

"Again, no goddess of volcanoes exists; wherefore, I renounce whatever status and function I have as a volcanic witch. I abjure all the worship of that alleged goddess—explicit or otherwise—involved in my initiation as a volcanic witch, in favor of honoring the One God, the Lord God Almighty. I confess that initiation to be null and void as regards being made more worthy or exalted, and I ask this Real God to purge me of any and all evil attachments I may have acquired. I submit to whatever removal of powers and privileges such purging may entail. Amen."

It was Theodora who spoke up. She let it hang there for just a few seconds. Then she said, "Very good, dear child. You have done very well. And now, as your first act of honoring the Real God pursuant to this basic vow, will you submit to have that old blessing renewed upon you?"

"Yes, with all my heart."

Theodora went and took the great book of Divine revelation the grandmother kept in her house, opened the book to the right place, placed her hand on Wendy's head, and recited the blessing. When it was done, Wendy cried out, "Glory to God in the highest! But now, Theodora, I must act out in concrete deeds what I have just sworn. This is what I learned from your daughter." With that, she went and set down a bag in front of her mother. Kneeling before her, she said, "Mama, you enjoy formal authority over me, in virtue of the natural motherhood the Lord God Almighty has given you. But the governess who acted as your proxy taught me that much is forbidden to me as a woman. Will you now sweep aside all the superstition and nonsense to ratify my full and equal freedom as an adult person, subject only to the laws of this Real God?"

"Yes—agreed and granted, with whatever authority from God I may have at this point."

"Will you give me to eat and enjoy all the fruits of the world and all other foods He has given to the people?"

"Yes, of course." With that, she reached down into the bag, took out a nice, ripe banana, and handed it to Wendy. There were many bananas in the bag, and she gave one to each of the other ladies, then took one for herself. Then she said, "Ladies, instead of drinking together, let us all eat together in honor of Wendy's liberation." And so they did. The bananas were delicious. But Wendy noticed it only in the back of her mind, and she did not think about it until later. For Wendy, it was like a severe act of penitential discipline. She made herself eat the banana by sheer force of will, almost as if she were eating poison in order to fulfill some harsh duty to die.

The rest of the day went without incident. When she awoke early the next morning, Wendy was remarkably happy at what had been done, and yet she was perplexed as well. She understood that somehow, the work of the basic vow was only just begun, even on its own terms. Something serious remained to be done, but she did not yet know what. Happily, because she was depleted after all the excitement, Wendy found it easy to accept the answer. She relaxed, called on God to see her through, and fell back asleep again for another hour and a half.

Right after she awoke, her grandmother came in. Her mother was dazed on this occasion. After they had greeted each other sweetly for the beginning of the day, Wendy voiced her concerns.

"Well, was there any weakness or lack of sincerity in your vow?" her grandmother said. No, not at all. "No, of course not, given your offer to die the first time. Is there anything important about God and the things of God you left out or forgot?" No, she did not think so. "Then there is also something else, in addition to your status as a volcanic witch, that you still have to swear away." Yes—that sounded right, but she was not sure what. The grandmother urged Wendy to pray God to see her through, and then they parted.

Wendy got up out of bed, but she was delayed in getting dressed. As the day wore on, her mother (now lucid) told her to get dressed. Wendy did so, and then she had the answer.

Beatrice did not have to explain to the others about clothing and nudity. They knew well enough from reports about Renegades on other worlds. "Well then," Beatrice said, "that turned out to be her problem. Wendy realized that where she stood, regarding what was for her and her people this basic concern, was seriously questionable at best and totally illegitimate at worst."

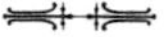

The problem was, at least in earlier years, that Wendy had been raised largely in Lilikea's home, almost as if she were one of Lilikea's own children. Lilikea had followed the older tradition of her ancestral culture by having all the children, including Wendy, go around nude as much as possible until they were older. Eventually, of course, Lilikea did grant Wendy the full basis to be clothed and shod. However, she did so as a conscious act of observing a landmark in Wendy's life. Now, in Lilikea's ancestral traditions, concerns of what Diana and Alfreda would think of as neutral culture were not well distinguished from concerns of what they would think of as specifically religious. To be sure, Wendy's childhood graduation from being naked and barefoot had not been fully and explicitly religious in the same way as her initiation as a witch. But there was still some religious character to it that was at least clearly implicit.

After Wendy had explained all this to her mother and grandmother later that day, she continued. "Mama, when I was preparing to eat the banana, I spoke of being an adult person. But am I really? In fact, yes, but perhaps not by right. I am afraid, in accepting from Lilikea to be clothed and shod, that I submitted to the old nonsense, and that has been underneath all my feminine functioning ever since. Since that basis was false, it is almost like I am still only a little girl by right and not an adult woman."

When she was lucid, as she was now, Diana was herself highly intelligent. "All right, Wendy, let us go through it one step at a time. Think back now, and think back carefully. When you insisted on the hormonal manipulation to make you grow up, what was the concern in your mind? Were you looking to follow that false religion? That was not at all my impression at the time, nor my mother's, nor Alfreda's. But what do you say?"

Wendy thought back for a moment and then said, "No, certainly not that religion. I think it was more a concern with an obvious natural duty, although I would not have used those words at the time." She paused and then said, "I am not sure, but I think at the back of my mind was some idea that this was the path the Real God had prepared for me as a girl. Yes, come to think of it, as I cast my mind back over it, I remember now. That was in my mind."

"All right, let us take it back the next step. What about your childhood graduation, as you call it? We noticed it and talked about it at the time. Do you also remember what happened with that—by which I mean, what *really* happened?"

"Let me think.—Lilikea did not just give me to be clothed and shod. I had to ask her and even kind of push it a little. It was after that blessing Deborah pronounced on me when it looked like I was dying.—Come to think of it, my feeling was that the blessing was making me do it. I mean, I rejoiced in what had been done, and I felt somehow like I had to follow it for real instead of just running around like a little kid. In a word, I had to honor it by being more serious minded about it—although again, I would not have used those words at the time."

"Then the other way to say it is that your decision to graduate from childhood nudity was based on concern for the Real God, and your decision to graduate from mere girlhood and grow up to be a woman was also based on concern for the Real God. That being so, Wendy, what are we talking about? It sounds like your concern is that the formal act you received to be clothed and shod was deficient, for that seems to be all that is left." Wendy agreed that this was so. "Would it resolve your situation to have some appropriate formal act to repair the deficiency, comparable to the ceremony yesterday with the vow and the bananas?" Well, yes, it would.

Because she saw that Wendy was truly sincere in saying all this, Diana was genuinely sympathetic. Speaking as mildly and sweetly as she could, Diana answered, "All right, Wendy. You draw up whatever further vow you think is necessary, have Alicia check it out again, and we shall go on from there."

But in this affair, the interaction with Alicia did not go so simply as Wendy had imagined. Alfreda had informed Alicia very fully about what had been done in the course of Wendy's first attempt—the preliminary confession and the final offer to die as she was going down with sickness. Alicia herself had witnessed the vow when it was finally sworn. Given all this, Alicia was not about to let Wendy off so easily as all that.

"Well, Wendy, you said in your confession leading up to the vow that you knew the initiation as a witch did not rightly pass the smell test, as you put it. Then why did you go ahead and do it anyway?"

"That is a very good question. Would you accept it if I said it seemed like a good idea at the time?" Alicia shook her head in negation, and Wendy said, "No, of course not. But that is the short way to say it. At the time, I had already learned enough to insist on the explicit reservation that I was to be a servant of the One God's deputy. I was genuinely concerned with the One God to that extent. But I had learned a whole lot less than I have learned since then. My head was still enough full of the old stuff Lilikea taught me that I imagined what she offered me to be the best that was available for a woman, even though it was more than a little questionable. It was kind of like accepting a necessary evil, only one or two notches below that—just a little less respectable."

"What about natural motherhood? That is very worthy, and it is available to women."

"Yes, right, and I thought about that at the time. I observed that Lilikea and other witches had their own children, and so I figured there would be no conflict, if that worked out for me. But that was not even the main thing. You have to remember what I was, and especially what I still am. First of all, my adolescent development started very late. So at that time, my reproductive functioning was not fully established and settled. Second, and far more important, I was and remain genetically defective, as you know. I am alive only because of a crazy fluke during my mother's pregnancy. Consequently, there was and is serious question as to whether I should even try for natural motherhood at all. For these reasons, the idea of exercising natural motherhood someday seemed—and still does seem—almost like the idea of finding the pot of gold at the end of the rainbow. I did not take it all that seriously. That left the other."

"Well, that may perhaps be good enough as far as it goes. But tell me, would you have done it if your prospect for natural motherhood had been as good as that of normal women?"

Wendy thought about this. It was a new question for her. "Oh, dear Lord—I don't know, Alicia. I really just don't know. I feel like my whole situation would have been so different that it would be impossible to figure."

"All right. That is at least honest. There is also a second obvious question. It was your mother, not your governess, whose religion included that old blessing you received. That being so, why did you not go to your mother to be graduated or advanced from childish nudity into more mature girlhood?"

"Let me think back…I *did* go to her, more than once. But on that day, she happened to be dazed, and it lasted for a long time. Finally I gave up and turned to Lilikea. After all, that was why Lilikea was there: to compensate for my mother's deficiency."

"All right, fair enough. What exactly did Lilikea do? What was the procedure?" Wendy told her. "Then in one way, the answer is obvious. You swear away what you received from Lilikea insofar as it is tainted, you have your mother authorize you as she did with the bananas, you have her repeat the procedure but do it the right way, and there you go. You do this as soon as may be in order to have this concern settled and out of the way. But then you come back and talk to me, for there is a whole lot of phony baloney you still need to have cut through."

Wendy bowed her head slightly in docile submission. "Yeah, I know."

This was done with no problems or untoward incidents. Wendy prepared what she thought necessary and had Alicia approve it.

Then she went through the ritual, but in front of her mother and grandmother only. In a little while it was accomplished, and Wendy stood before them, clothed and shod once more, but now on the explicit basis of submitting "to the laws and mercies of the Real God." Then, as an added touch on her own initiative, Diana took the great book of Divine revelation the grandmother kept in her house, opened the book to the right place, placed her hand on Wendy's head, and recited that old blessing upon her.

When it was finished, Wendy said calmly, "Glory to God in the highest. Thanks be to God." Then, "But Mother, what happens now?"

Diana had the wisdom to understand that this question was just another form of babbling because Wendy's mind was overwhelmed. She answered, "Well, for right now, you have to be at your old job at the flower shop soon." This calmed Wendy by deflating her grandiose mindset. They laughed together, and then Wendy went to the flower shop.

The ceremony for Wendy to be clothed and shod occurred three weeks after she swore the basic vow, and thus eleven weeks after the graduation dinner. It would not be long now before she began the third level of advanced study. But Wendy did manage to speak with Alicia again once before that.

"Let me take us back to the night of my graduation. I conceded that the whole question of what my mother and grandmother believe would have to be reconsidered. I have tried doing that, but I find I only succeed in making myself more and more puzzled. It is obvious to me what the problem is. The thinking I have done about it over the years is almost totally worthless, being too much tainted with my old misunderstanding. I have to go back again and start from point zero, almost as if I were a little girl, but of course on a higher level, given what I have learned. Now, as I think about it, I believe the place to begin would be with our conversations from years ago, if you still remember."

"Let me think—ah, yes. We talked about being attached to God so as to rejoice in God instead of being a ghost in the parade, and we talked about having God make good the loss of faculties of those who died."

"Yes, right. Now I have been thinking, and I figure at least some version of what you said has to be right. But still, too many questions remain."

"This is getting interesting. All right, first of all—why do you say it has to be right? We can start with that and go on from there."

Wendy spoke slowly and carefully, almost like a child reciting her lesson for her teacher. "There is what has to be involved in the act of Divine creation on God's side. Creation would be a conscious act done deliberately. It would be completely voluntary, totally spontaneous, and absolutely free. It would also be a pure act of giving forth. Such an act is an exercise of love."

"Yes, right. Of course. Once again, so far, so good. What then?"

"Well, somehow it seems kind of bizarre that He would, as an exercise of love, create beings who have remarkable capabilities, clearly superior to those of other animals, but not provide for them."

"It seems too bizarre to you, does it? That is only because it *is* too bizarre. You are right about that. But once more, what then?"

Wendy explained that in ancient times, before the Faith Alicia followed had been established, there were traditional thinkers who spoke of the soul and its superiority, although they were not aware of the Preparation leading up to this Faith. They learned of the soul's superiority just by reasoning from the observed facts. As Wendy acknowledged, Alicia was of course aware of this history.

"Well," Wendy said, "in their works, the concern about being attached to God to rejoice in Him is clearly foreshadowed." They discussed it, and Alicia agreed. "That being so," Wendy concluded, "it looks like it has to be available somehow, as you said. Otherwise, to fulfill what is clearly one's destiny as a person would be just not at all possible, which would be against God's wisdom and goodness." Again they discussed it, and Alicia agreed.

"But, as I said, too many questions remain. First of all, let me say what I do *not* find problematic about your Faith. There is that remarkable teaching on God's inner nature. Well, one would expect the inner nature of God to be mysterious. Yes, the teaching is problematic in a way. But on the other side, if a religion spoke of God's inner nature as being clearly understandable by people, that one fact would be a reasonably good disproof of that religion. So then, all right, fair enough. We shall just have to see how well you can answer the obvious objections.

"Next, to be attached to God so as to rejoice in Him would of course be a free gift. That being so, how it works to set it up, and what procedures are involved, would of course be something He must reveal, or else there just would be no knowledge of it. Again, I can see in a general way that what is involved would have to include purging someone's evils as a precondition for blessedness to be received. So even though I do not see that there should be the elaborate system of rituals you say there is, I also do not see any particular reason against it, and so I am prepared to accept it, if it should turn out to be indeed what He has revealed."

"Right then—very good. What next? Where does it go from there?"

"Well, of course, what it all finally really comes down to is the claim that God has reached down from Heaven in the way you say. If that should be true, then all the rest is just the process of working through what He has revealed about Himself and His actions, and everything beyond that is just a bunch of trivial concerns by comparison. To be sure, on the other side, if that claim should be false, then it is all garbage."

"This is getting interesting! So what then?"

"I cannot believe He has in fact reached down in that way. I have read what some of your traditional thinkers say, and in fact it seems fairly reasonable. But my mind simply refuses to accept it. I find it is like asking me to believe—well, to believe a circle could fit cleanly into a world of pure triangles. I find that is the analogy that keeps coming into my mind."

"Are you saying that He could not have come down from Heaven into the world because the world is somehow such that it would not be able to receive Him?"

"Yes, I think you have just laid it out for me very well."

"All right, then. Let us go through it one step at a time.—But not now. I have to go and take care of something. But soon—very soon. I promise."

This was done. As Wendy had said, it was not that hard for her to appreciate the merits of the theoretical apparatus. It was also not that hard for Alicia to hunt down what it was in her mind that was blocking her progress. But it turned out to be very hard to remove it, as Wendy would learn the hard way.

CHAPTER ELEVEN

Wendy did begin the third level of advanced study as planned and scheduled. At this point, the academic institution where she was studying offered her a job assisting the teaching of low-level courses to beginning students. This offer was too good to refuse. But in order to take it, she had to give up that old job at the flower shop. They parted very amicably, with fond feelings on both sides and even the agreement that it might be very nice for Wendy to go back to work there again someday, if ever that should happen to work out.

Six weeks after she began the new studying and the new job, when her situation was more or less settled for the time being, Wendy met with Alicia again.

"You say He reached down in order to provide redemption for the people by taking onto Himself the terrible burden of resolving their evils. Is that correct?"

"Yes. Yes, exactly so."

"All right, fair enough. What I mean is that given that He reached down as you say, I can see the other in a general way—on the basis that the superior can take onto himself to answer for the wrongdoing of the subordinate, and of course He is the ultimate superior of all. So far, so good. Once again, my sticking point is with the claim that He reached down in that way."

Alicia collected her thoughts and then began. "First of all, as I told you on the night of your graduation, one who speaks of God and the things of God must do so with metaphors and analogies. There is no other way to do it. Do you understand that?" Yes, of course. "All right. Then you must consider what is involved in Divine creation. As you said in your basic vow, God creates according to His wisdom." Yes, Wendy remembered that. What then?

"Now, the point is that the whole universe of created beings may be said to embody Divine wisdom, kind of like the way something an artisan or craftsman makes up in the workshop may be said to embody the wisdom of the artisan." Yes, that too. "All right, now for the kicker. Perhaps there could be some created being that is somehow an especially condensed or concentrated embodiment of Divine wisdom. Perhaps God could set this up by a miracle. But if this were to happen, what then? One might then say God is specially present in this being, so as to have reached down from Heaven in a special way." Wendy figured this made sense in a way. "Well, the thing is that this has happened. He has done this."

Wendy sat still for a few minutes, turning it over and over in her mind. Then she said, "No. I am sorry, but that was too much. I am overloaded. Would you say all that again?" Alicia did so, slowly and carefully. After turning it over in her mind for a few minutes, Wendy said, "I can follow the logic of it, but that is all. It does not seem to add up to any sense in my mind."

"All right. Perhaps you should leave that aside for now and think about another analogy that you may find easier. Then you can come back to it later. A poem or story embodies the wisdom of the author. There might be a story where the author sets himself up as one of the characters in his own story. As the author, he could not be hurt by anything that happens in the story. But as a character in the story, he could suffer just like any other character."

Wendy thought about this. "The character in the story could suffer like anyone else in the story but could also claim truly to be the author."

"Yes, exactly so."

"All right, to take it further, what then? Where does it go from there?"

"Well, let us see how much you can understand. By suffering undeservedly, the author's character might fulfill the logic of the story in some way that changes the moral situation for the other characters."

Wendy thought about this and said, "That would be an exotic story, but yes, it does make a kind of sense—at least in the very abstract way you have stated it."

"It is the story given by God as the real history of the real world." With that Wendy was once again fully loaded, so they concluded the meeting.

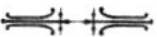

At this point, Beatrice interrupted her narrative to ask, "What, if anything, do the old prophecies say about having God reach down from Heaven in some special way?"

Her teacher answered, "Well, let me think for a moment. Hmm...well, no. As far as I am aware, there is nothing like that. Not even a hint or a trace."

It was the teacher's colleague who had the answer. "But I am aware of something, because of my theoretical researches. I went beyond the prophecies given among our people and even among our friends. I went all the way to the Quazdleem Northix."

Like Beatrice's people, the Quazdleem Northix were all of the same kind or species, but each was separately created. Again, as with Beatrice's people, there were some Renegades among them, but the Normals were clearly predominant. Like other peoples, they exchanged Travelers and knowledge with Beatrice's people, and there were what human societies would call full diplomatic relations. Yet despite their love for each other, the two peoples did not think of each other as friends, simply because they were too different from each other.

"The Quazdleem Northix!" Beatrice and her teacher exclaimed together.

"Yes, and it was one of the more exotic prophecies, at that."

"Well, what then?" asked the teacher.

"It was simply that analogy of the things from the workshop as embodying the wisdom of the artisan. This is common knowledge. Well, God could set up a created being as a condensed embodiment of Divine wisdom. One might then say God is specially present in this being, so as to have reached down from Heaven in a special way. It was given to them that something like this has in fact happened."

They discussed this and also the analogy of the author as a character in his own story. Then the colleague observed, "But still, many questions remain. First of all, the other characters in a story do not exist in themselves to do evil or receive redemption. They are mere fictional constructs from the author."

Beatrice considered and then said, "As Alicia told Wendy, every analogy breaks down at some point. Therefore, different analogies may have to be balanced against each other in order to achieve wisdom. This too is common knowledge among our people and our friends. So I think we must combine that analogy with the analogy of the objects from the workshop and perhaps other analogies as well. The point is that there is some created being who is the act of God to reach down from Heaven in a special way, and so the suffering of this being applies to Him somehow. The analogy of the story provides some partial insight into how this is so. That is all." After further discussion of this point, the others agreed this answer was as good as they could hope for, at least until more had been told. With that, Beatrice resumed her narrative.

Over the next several days, Wendy kept turning it over and over in her mind, again and again. Of course, no one could really believe all that. It was just too bizarre.—Or could they? Yes, of course it was just too bizarre. And yet—and *yet*—somehow she could not deny it. Somehow, if only she could figure out how, it seemed almost kind of reasonable. So Wendy did what she had long since been taught to do in such cases. She called on God to give her understanding.

The breakthrough came two weeks after that meeting with Alicia. She had learned long ago that to ask the right questions could be critical. This understanding came together in her mind with her concerns over what had been said at the last meeting. Wendy woke up that morning as it came blazing hot into her head that what she had to do was to ask the right questions, or approach it from the right angle, and then she would find it very reasonable indeed. In fact, it was much more than that. She would realize it was—in some way—the only thing that did add up rightly to make sense.

The next meeting with Alicia came one week after the breakthrough. Wendy began by telling her what had come into her head as she awoke. Alicia was happy for this, and yet she smiled sadly. "Dear, sweet, Wendy—you poor, innocent child. I have been waiting for this."

Not knowing she was going to speak until she said it, Wendy blurted out, "You are going to say something dreadful."

"No, not exactly. What I must say now is nothing we need be afraid to discuss. It is just that I knew already you would have this kind of trouble, and I knew why. Shall I tell you?"

"Yes, please."

"Are you sure that is what you really want?"

⸻

The others found this question puzzling, and so Beatrice explained. "Wendy understood at once why Alicia had asked her this. She was at the door of a realm of wonders and glories and mysteries far beyond all her old hopes and dreams. Once she went through that door, there would, of course, be no going back. But she was a Renegade who was—at best—still only in the early stages of being provided for. She was not yet properly converted and corrected. So, having only very limited readiness to look to God to see her through, she hesitated. Alicia knew the girl well enough to expect something like this, and that was why she asked." In the course of the ensuing discussion, what came out was that the others had been surprised because the Renegades among them were not so difficult to provide for. They had forgotten that, as Beatrice pointed out, the difference with Wendy was that she had no memory of lived experience as a Normal child to help her through.

⸻

What ended Wendy's hesitation was that she became aware of something else. "No, it is not what I want, but that is beside the point. It is what I need or what has to be, or maybe both—something like that. Too much has happened, and I have come too far, to turn back or even to stop now."

Alicia smiled and nodded in the manner of a teacher showing approval of the point a student has just reached. "Very good.

Let me begin with the short answer, and then I can lay it out in detail. The short answer is what you might expect. You were raised with stories of gods and goddesses and their antics and adventures, and you still have your head full of that. But the important way it affects you is not what you might imagine." Then, weighing her words carefully, she said, "You acknowledge the Lord God Almighty—the One God, as you call Him—and you worship Him with praise and prayer and thanksgiving. All that is fine and dandy. The problem is that your conversion is not complete. You continue to have your head full of the stuff about the gods and goddesses."

"I think of them as His servants only, whom He created just as He created all else and who depend on Him just as all else does."

"Yes, right—of course. And if that were all there were to it, there would be no problem. But you see, somewhere at the back of your mind or in the depth of your soul sits something very different. Underneath, there lurks the idea of the world, not so much as a reflection of Divine wisdom and goodness and beauty, but as some magical realm of energy and richness, as I believe you said Lilikea told you. I mean 'magical' in the sense that leaves aside any reference to the One God, even if it does not involve denying Him explicitly. I am afraid *that* is your problem."

Wendy closed her eyes, withdrew within herself, and tried to explore her own mind as well as she could. After a few minutes, she said, "I am not sure, but I think you may be right."

"Well, then, there it is. You can see that there is no point in any further exploration of what God has or has not done to provide for the people until this business is resolved."

"Yes. But what happens now? Where does it go from here?"

"First of all, of course, there is the same answer as for everything else. You call upon God to see you through and correct your mind. But I can tell you this much: this problem should be on the way to being resolved by now, much more than it is. With all the time that has gone by and all that has happened, and with the fact that Lilikea's influence has long since ended, this image in the depth of your soul should have faded—if not totally, then at least much more than it has. No, but there is something holding it in place, some crazy little trick—some faulty idea that seems harmless but that keeps the wrongness alive as long as you continue to believe it. Most likely it is something you yourself are not aware of—or at least not consciously. I wish I knew what it was. Then it might be easy for us to correct it."

Wendy remembered that episode with the corrupt teacher years before. So she screwed up her courage and reminded Alicia of that. Then she asked, "Do you think I am being tampered with by those monsters?"

Alicia had wondered about this herself. "Quite possibly. But if so, most likely the way it works in this case is that you were taught something long ago that is not very good, and now they are using it somehow to make you go astray."

"Then what is the answer? What should I do about all this?"

"Well, there is prayer to God, of course. Other than that, there is that old blessing Deborah pronounced upon you long ago. Perhaps we can start with that and go on from there." With that, Alicia took out a copy of the Book, opened it to the right place and held it in one hand, placed the other hand on Wendy's head, and recited the blessing upon her.

After this, Wendy's mind began to change more quickly than either of them had anticipated. Just one week later, they met again.

"I reckon the question is whether we should think about right and wrong, guilt and responsibility, love and redemption in the way you said," Wendy said.

"Do *you* believe we should think of it in that way?"

"Well, yes, as near as I can figure."

"All right, given that we think of it in that way, what then?"

"In that case, I think what you said about what God has done has to be right, crazy as it sounds, because that is the only possible answer."

"And you think this based on working through the logic of it?"

"Well, the logic of what I know about right and wrong and all that—yes."

Alicia forced herself to be calm and said, "Well, Wendy, that is very interesting. How do you figure that?"

"My original question was about the gift of being attached to God. Since what is at stake here is God and the things of God, the answer has to be on that level. But that means only God can answer for the people, or else we are just to be left in misery. With everything else I have learned, that seems to be the wrong answer. But that leaves what you said."

Alicia let out a long, thin whistle. "Very good, Wendy. Very good indeed. Yes, you see clearly and understand very well. What I said long ago is true. Alfreda was wrong about you only because she underestimated you."

"Unless perhaps there is some other alternative I have not yet learned about?"

Alicia thought about it and said, "Remarkably enough, no—there is not, or at least not on this point. Other people say other things about God and the things of God instead. But it is not that they ask these questions and develop different answers. It is that they do not ask the same questions. They think of what God does or does not do about the people in other terms instead. So yes, if we are going to think of it in those terms, then indeed that is the only answer."

After a moment, Wendy screwed up her courage again and said, "But my mind still refuses to accept it. As I try to work through why, I reckon it is what you said. I believe there is some trick in my mind that keeps me from accepting the law of right and wrong as the basic rule for everything in life. But I do not know what it is." Alicia tried questioning her very mildly, but she too failed to uncover it. And so the meeting was concluded, after a prayer together.

Once again, Beatrice interrupted her narrative. "Alicia was right about what the problem was, and Wendy was right a week later, although neither of them could identify it. But I knew, for it was given to me. In fact, there were two things Wendy had been taught that blocked her mind. First, Lilikea had taught her to be gracious and generous, but not merciful and forgiving—more the opposite, for that was the faith she herself had been taught as a child. Consequently, Wendy appreciated and accepted intellectually the points about Divine mercy and forgiveness, but this acceptance was not deeply rooted in her.

"The second thing was more subtle. I told you my mind would sometimes be sent back to observe living history. I told you also there was a long preparation leading up to the critical events of the Redemption. Well, after I observed the end of this meeting, my mind was sent back to the days of that Preparation, to observe as some points of law and revelation were given and to watch as the people were guided to understand rightly. To narrow it down, I was given to know the specific point on which Wendy had gone very wrong. She would have said this was just one of the special laws given to those people as part of the Preparation, but that idea was not correct. There was a deep error in her understanding of what it is and what it means for a girl to be a girl or a woman to be a woman—in short, of what it is and means for one of her species to be female. Now, as it happened, there had not yet been occasion for her to act out. Thus, the evil had not come to full flower, and she was still kind of innocent. But of course, this could not last. The time was almost at hand when she would have to go one way or the other. With that ceremony for her to leave behind childish nudity, the remnant of her childhood that had kind of shielded her was gone, and she would have to choose her path as an adult woman."

After a brief pause, Beatrice continued. "As I said before, things do not always work out among Wendy's people as they expect. A week after this meeting with Alicia, Wendy happened to be at that old flower shop. Something came up that led to the next great breakthrough. It was something that Wendy would ordinarily have dismissed as just some noise from a fool running his mouth. But somehow, this time it provoked a reaction in her mind that got her started."

What happened was that two men had come in to buy flowers and were engaged in conversation with each other. They were talking in the language of a foreign land far away. As it happened, Wendy knew this language, having learned it as a student. But it was evident they expected her not to know it. One of them asked the other whether they should continue the conversation in front of her. The other one said, "Of course! This woman knows the language her mother taught her, and she knows the language of the native people as well." They had heard her speaking to people in both languages. "But she is only a woman. Her mind is too weak to hold any more than those two languages."

Any other time, she would have restrained herself from laughing and just kept smiling. But this time, she had to keep herself instead from answering angrily in the language they were speaking, although she still just kept smiling.

As she thought about it later, Wendy realized the insult had touched a sore spot within her because, somewhere in the back or the depth of her mind, she agreed with this low opinion of herself as "only a woman." It was not that she was foolish or weak minded, but it was—well, *something*, but she did not yet know what. As soon as she realized this, Wendy knew it was somehow the answer to a whole lot of concerns. She prayed God for guidance and went on.

The next morning, Wendy awoke with her mind thoroughly astonished, for she knew what it was. The problem was with what Lilikea had taught her. That religion said that as a woman, Wendy was "unmarked," void of ritual status. Through the years, she had continued to believe it, in spite of everything. Of course, this had ruined her whole basis for thinking about the Real God and the things of God. She saw this partially but not fully. So a week after this astonished awakening, she met with Alicia again.

After Wendy had told her all that had happened, Alicia replied, "All right, Wendy. Tell me what you see about how this ruins the basis for your thinking. We can start with that."

"Well, I think this view of myself and of women in general as lacking ritual status is just the other side of the underlying view of the world as magical, instead of as being fully dependent and derivative from Divine creation. So even though I was sincere in that basic vow I swore, there has to be serious question about how deeply I believe it."

"Well, yes, all that would certainly be involved. Is there anything else you can think of?"

"I know there is more, but I cannot rightly think what it is."

Alicia knew enough about some of the problems her people could have to lead Wendy through. "All right, then let me try my suspicions by asking you a series of questions. This lack of ritual status—does it merely affect religious functioning, or is it more than that?"

"I do not understand what you are asking."

"Does this lack of status as a woman make you think or feel yourself to be somehow less than a full person, or even not a real person at all?"

With renewed astonishment, Wendy answered, "Well, come to think of it—yes! Yes, it does. There is what applies to me as a person, a rational agent, and then there is what applies to me as a woman, a female animal, and they are two separate issues. I am also a person, a real person, and so of course I am subject to Divine law so that I have moral and religious concerns and obligations, responsibility before God, and all the rest of it. But as a mere woman, I am beneath all that, like the beasts of the field."

"Like the beasts of the field, eh? Then what hopes or fears do you have for what may or may not lie beyond the grave for you?"

"To tell the truth, not very much." Wendy told Alicia where she stood.

"Right, then. I notice you say you are *also* a person and not that you are also a woman. I guess that shows where your mind stands. Of course, this point has much to do with your ongoing concern that God might simply snuff you out when you die, in spite of what you have learned and what we have discussed. Given that you have a strong claim to be like the beasts of the field, that fate is kind of what is to be expected."

"Well, yes, I reckon so. That sounds about right."

"Shall I go on, Wendy, or do you have enough to think about for now?" Wendy said her mind was already fully loaded, and so they left it there until the next meeting.

The next meeting was a week later. Wendy had been thinking about it, and so now she told Alicia how right she was. They discussed it, and then Alicia said, "There is also another obvious way this view distorts your thinking about the Real God and the things of God. You told me you remain unable to accept the Faith we follow because of your old problem about how God reached down from Heaven to provide for His creatures."

"Well, yes."

"I told you long ago there was some crazy trick hidden somewhere in your mind that kept you from accepting it. Do you remember that?"

"Let me think back...yes, I do remember, now that you mention it."

"Well, I think it is clear that this is it—this is that crazy trick. Can you see why, Wendy, or do you want me to tell you?"

Wendy thought about it, then replied, "I kind of see why, but then again I do not see it. Please, tell me straight out."

"Well, you do not see that you yourself are a unified being as both a rational agent and a female animal. Given that, it is not surprising that your mind cannot accept the idea that God might reach down to be one of His own creatures so that the being involved would be a unified Person. The surprising thing would be if your mind *could* accept it."

After thinking about it for a while, Wendy said, slowly and carefully, "Well, yes, that sounds about right. I guess it would work that way." After another long pause, she added, "So, there it is at long last." After pausing yet again, she asked, "Is there anything else?"

"Possibly so, but you tell me. You spoke of being beneath the reach of Divine law, like the beasts of the field. What, if any, practical application do you think this idea may have?"

"I am not sure I understand your question."

Weighing her words so as to speak with exact precision, Alicia asked, "Do you believe this status brings with it any special freedoms, exemptions, or immunities regarding what concrete deeds women are to do or to avoid?"

Once again, with great astonishment, Wendy answered, "Well, come to think of it—yes! Yes, I believe it does." The older tradition of Wendy's culture said the differentiation of the sexes was to be honored as ordained by God. As a corollary, homosexual activity was disallowed and forbidden as contrary to what God laid down in the very act of creating. Wendy had come to follow this traditional view. "However, since women are beneath the reach of Divine law, this prohibition does not apply to them. Now of course, this is with the understanding that what is involved is the spicy deeds of consenting adults in private. It is not a license for a woman to do violence to other women or to seduce children or to make a public nuisance of herself. Those things are forbidden to a woman as a person, a rational agent. But to have erotic interplay with women is not forbidden to a woman as a person. It is forbidden to her only as a female being, and so it is not really forbidden to her after all. Otherwise that too would be excluded and disallowed, just like homosexual activity among men."

Alicia said simply, "Yes, I understand exactly what you mean." They agreed to leave it at that for the time being.

Now that the issues were cleanly laid out and clearly articulated, it did not take Wendy long to see the real truth. A few days after the conversation with Alicia, she awoke in the night, hours before dawn, thinking about that old academic project on motherhood and fatherhood as models of Divine creation. Yes, and come to think of it, what *about* motherhood? It could be proposed and argued as a serious model exactly because motherhood was one of the deepest and most powerful relationships of a person over another person. Then again, motherhood was perhaps the exercise *par excellence* of any woman's female sexuality. This relationship of overwhelming personal intimacy was based on the woman's functioning as a female animal. That being so, it was just a little too ridiculous to affirm any such strong separation as Wendy had heretofore believed in between what belonged to a woman as a person and what belonged to her as a female animal. No, but a woman had to be a unified being after all, as Alicia believed, with all that fact entailed.

After thinking all this through, Wendy uttered a quick prayer to God, then fell back asleep and slept peacefully through the rest of the night. She met with Alicia again a few days after this and discussed it with her at length. Alicia agreed fully and led Wendy through as much as she could absorb at that time.

"What this amounted to," Beatrice explained, "was one of the things I had to discuss with my teacher just before the vision. There was the whole idea of having higher levels work by means of lower levels as a general principle, along with its application to the specific concern in question. Of course, with all she had learned, Wendy had some awareness of these points already, but she had not heard it all developed and applied so well as Alicia did on this occasion."

Beatrice paused and then said, "In fact, the principal metaphor or analogy among them for how God reached down is how intellect and will are combined with animal functioning to make up a person as a unified being. They discussed this, as well as the more general question of how the right answer here went with the collapse of Wendy's underlying view of the world as magical in the wrong way."

The day after this meeting with Alicia was just another day for Wendy, with nothing special or remarkable. At the end of the evening, she had gone to bed in her grandmother's house and slept peacefully through the first part of the night without incident, as usual. But then later on, she had been awakened by her mother (who was lucid at that time) as she was screaming and writhing in her bed. Wendy found herself to be in a cold sweat, which indicated deep terror among her people. When she was awake enough to control herself, she told her mother something horrible had happened, only she did not know what. Before her mother could say anything, Wendy added, "There is no trouble or danger for anyone else, only for me. Something horrible has happened within my own body."

Her mother knew enough to examine her daughter and to ask the right questions. There was no indication of any difficulty or distress. When this had been established, she persuaded her daughter that she had merely been suffering from bad dreams. But in order to ease Wendy back to sleep, Diana had to lie down with her and comfort her by sharing the warmth of her body with her daughter, just as though Wendy were a very young child again.

The next morning, Wendy was once again a rational, self-controlled, self-possessed adult woman. But she was still sure in her own mind that something horrible had happened inside her. However, as her mother and grandmother spoke with her about it, there was really nothing wrong that she could specify.

Her grandmother added, "All right, Wendy. The hospital taught you advanced biofeedback. You are an accomplished mistress at it, from what they tell me. So you scan within yourself and tell me. Can you find anything wrong?" No, she could not. With that, the grandmother promised to keep an eye on Wendy for the next few days, and they left it there.

Later that day, Wendy told her mother and grandmother, "It took a while, but I have finally managed to remember what I was dreaming last night. People speak of being beside oneself. Well, I dreamed that was literally happening to me. I dreamed I was being ravished by an extension or projection of myself. She was not harsh or cruel—more the opposite. She was almost kind and merciful. She treated me like a child she loved dearly but had to hurt. She said, 'I am sorry, but this is how it has to be.

Try to be brave, and your suffering will soon be over.' Then she ravished me. It was not exactly forcible. There was no need. My body submitted and complied of itself, against my will. When it was accomplished, she said, 'There now, you can relax. The nasty deed is ended. Be comforted, dear child. You are not violated or defiled. A woman cannot be degraded by what her own body does within itself against her will.' That was when Mother woke me up. Also, she spoke to me in my own native language—the language Lilikea taught me long ago." They all agreed it was just another dream, totally meaningless as dreams commonly are. As for the language, they figured it meant only that the experience of being ravished would be truly primal, going to the depths of a woman's life as a female animal.

Even so, Wendy found herself turning it over and over in her mind. Like other women of her species, Wendy had found the whole idea of being ravished to be totally appalling ever since she had come to understand it. This affair reinforced that view, but it did something else as well. It clarified the issues in her mind. The experience was bearable only because it was just a dream, a meaningless phantom or shadow. If it were to happen in her real, waking life, she would have to do something desperate. Moreover, the desperate act would not be about being angry or appalled, nor even about being in agony or anguish. It would be a question of principle. Simply to accept and live with such overwhelming evil would not be legitimate or appropriate or even permissible. Wendy understood she would have to kill off either the one who had done it, or herself. For she would be honor bound to execute in concrete reality either her total rejection of the evil or else the complete refusal to accept life on the basis of carrying such monstrous wrongness within her.

"Furthermore," Beatrice added as she explained this, "in Wendy's mind, she was not *deciding* this was how she would react. She was coming to understand that this is how it would have to be. If asked, she would have said her decision—if it should be called that—was implicit in coming to be aware of and appreciate what it was and meant for a woman to be a woman. But anyhow, she concluded by remembering that since it was, after all, only a dream, she did not have to worry about it—at least for the time being. As for what might happen in real life, now that she had made her judgment and settled it in her mind, she was calm and easy about it."

The teacher's colleague asked, "From the old reports of Travelers, we know that those people will often enough think and say a great many things, but whether they go through with those things is another question. What about that in this case?"

"Yes, I know that about those people as a general proposition. I observed plenty of that. But in this case, no—not at all. Wendy was not the type to do that, and whatever tendencies she had along that line were certainly not involved here. She really meant it seriously, and she really would have done it."

The teacher asked, "But why? I know that view or concern is common enough among those women, and also among the Renegade women of some other species, but I have never been able to understand why. For that is not their view or concern about bodily violence in general, and rightly so. Her inner life as a person is not affected. Specifically, her moral concern and religious devotion are not degraded or diminished. The extremity of evil behind what is done to her remains in the malefactor and does not touch her. That applies here as well as in general."

Beatrice thought about it and then explained, "Well, but you see, it is not about bodily violence, exactly. The problem is that erotic interplay among them is different from what happens among the dumb beasts. The bodily union involved has a kind of symbolic function, so as to at once signify and fulfill personal intimacy. So the dread is that since this symbolic function is wrongly taken over, there is then a twisted version of this personal intimacy imposed on the victim as something dark and filthy and poisonous. Along this line, there is some idea that the victim's basic character as a woman is distorted, or downgraded to be less worthy, or held captive by the malefactor as part of the twisted personal intimacy, or something like that."

Her teacher thought about this and said, "Well, yes, I understand intellectually. And if all that were true, then it might indeed be worth killing and dying over—at least if it could not be corrected otherwise. Moreover, even the attempt to do such evil would be so enormously wrong that there might be at least some measure of serious merit in claiming the act deserved to be punished with death. But it is all nonsense, for the basic premise is totally false and obviously absurd. Natural symbolism cannot be abused in that way. Any attempt to take it over wrongly like that would simply ruin or cancel it. Moreover, whatever the malefactor may have believed or intended, the victim would *receive* what happened as a mere imposition of bodily violence, and that would already wipe out whatever basis for distinctively personal intimacy there may have been. At most, just as the act is one-sided, so there might perhaps be some one-sided personal union set up. The malefactor would be given away to the victim, having entered into union by acting out the natural symbolism, but the victim would not be given away, having only suffered violence. She would be totally free, undiminished, undamaged, and uncontaminated—in that case and indeed in any event. As I say, this is *at most*. I would expect the whole thing to be null and void. But since we are talking about Renegades, I reckon they might manage to develop some exotic situations from which such one-sided relationships would result. Anyway, I am amazed they did not know all this, and especially that Wendy did not know this."

"Eventually Wendy did come to know it, along with much more. As for her people in general, Wendy's own case illustrates the problem very well. Wendy found it very difficult to understand rightly the relation between her character as a female animal and her character as a rational agent. That kind of difficulty is very common among her people. Different people go wrong in different ways, but this view of the natural symbolism as available to be abused is one of the most common errors.

"Also, we have to be careful about saying the victim would be undamaged. There is their idea that the victim's basic character as a woman is somehow distorted based on having the natural symbolism abused. To be sure, yes—that idea is false. If that is all you mean by saying she is undamaged, then yes, she is undamaged in that sense. However, the bodily violence itself can be very serious, and there can be emotional shock that leaves her mind severely disordered for many years after—sometimes even for the balance of her life."

"Yes, I know. As you say, I was speaking only about the question of abusing the natural symbolism. Is that all there is to this line of thinking among them?"

"No, not exactly. There is some idea that just through the bodily violence involved, the victim is somehow conquered so as to be degraded—perhaps even to be less than a full person, just something to be used."

"Then their nonsense is even worse than I had thought. She is 'conquered,' if they insist on talking that way, only as a predatory wild animal may be said to 'conquer' its prey by leaping upon it, overpowering it, and eating it. There is no conquest so as to give dominion by right. Indeed, all the rights and claims would belong to the victim instead, as being entitled to have the wrong that was done to her answered. Moreover, even if—hypothetically—there *were* some such dominion, the idea that the victim is less than a full person would still be false and absurd, for any such relationships of right and dominion exist only between persons."

"Yes, certainly. You know all that, and I know it, but as I have said, *they* find it hard to understand rightly. Also, they are Renegades. It is to be expected that they would imagine one is somehow entitled to whatever he can manage to impose, whether by fair means or foul. Those women accept and submit to the malicious nonsense because their minds are distorted, for they too are Renegades, and they grow up in cultures developed and maintained by Renegades." When all this had been settled, Beatrice went on with the story of her vision.

About six weeks after the nightmare, Wendy was speaking with Alicia again. She told her of the dream, and she went on to tell Alicia of her concerns about being ravished in her real, waking life. Alicia answered her first of all by taking her through the same points Beatrice's teacher had laid out. Then she continued. "In fact, it is very well you have told me of this, for what is involved here is an application of a much larger concern. I have spoken to you about having the higher level work by means of the lower. Well, what is being proposed here is exactly the opposite. Underlying this error is the idea—or should I say the fantasy—that one can produce results on the higher level by manipulating the lower level and doing so based on the lower level's vulnerability—which is to say, by virtue of its specific character and function *as a lower level.* Of course, this imagined inversion is just that—purely imaginary. It is in fact an inversion of truth and reality. The best term for what is proposed is 'magic.' For that is what it is to try to manipulate the higher level by means of the lower. And it is all nonsense. Such nonsense is often taken seriously and practiced so as to be at best superstitious and at worst blasphemous. But it is still a blatant denial of truth and reality, even though it is all too common for people to think that way about all kinds of things. Now, given what your governess taught you as a child, Wendy, I suspect there may be many residual traces of this error lurking in the dark corners of your mind."

As she turned it over and over in her mind later on, Wendy figured this was likely enough to be true. Her answer was simply to pray to God all the more to correct her.

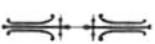

"Well," said Beatrice, "Wendy was corrected all right, regarding a whole lot of things. But how this occurred makes everything else that had happened to her up to that point be very mild by comparison."

CHAPTER TWELVE

After this conversation with Alicia, life went on more or less as before for Wendy. As before, she pushed as hard as she could and learned as well as she could. Four years after beginning the third level of advanced study, she graduated. In order to graduate from this third level, the student had to produce a substantial new work of scholarship. Wendy developed a lengthy treatment comparing and contrasting the great landmark thinker of the tradition her mother and grandmother followed with one of the landmark thinkers of an alien culture in a foreign land far away. This work was approved, and Wendy was greatly praised and honored.

About three weeks after the formal ceremony for this graduation, Wendy was at the hospital for testing as part of her ongoing concern with being defective. The procedures were more or less routine, and Wendy would be able to go home the same day. As she was leaving, she met her old friend Deborah. They got to talking, and Wendy spoke of the basic vow she had sworn. "It looks like that old blessing you pronounced on me long ago is working out very well." Deborah rejoiced greatly at this news. "But there is one point of regret for me." Wendy explained how she would have liked to conclude the ceremony by singing one of the classic old hymns among her people as her first act of adoration proper pursuant to the vow. "Instead, there happened to be an outbreak of listeria around that time, and I was stricken. This screwed up the whole affair. It was not accomplished until later. So that hymn ended up being left aside. I have come to believe that what was given to me within the order of Divine Providence was more valuable than what I had planned, and so thanks be to God. But still, there is an ongoing feeling of incompleteness—of not having rendered the first act of adoration proper pursuant to that vow."

"Well, but Wendy, what is there to keep you from singing the hymn now?"

"Nothing—nothing at all. I have, in fact, sung it many times in private as an exercise of rejoicing and devotion. But somehow it does not have the same value and significance as if it had been part of that landmark ceremony. Maybe that is not necessary. Maybe what I have is good enough. But that is not how it feels."

As they discussed it, what came out was that Wendy felt as if the failure of adoration had been underneath all her religious activity ever since. Deborah answered that she should look to God and call upon Him to see her through this concern. Wendy answered that she had done so.

And then Deborah thought of something. "The critical thing in your mind is that it was not part of that landmark ceremony, and so there is the ongoing incompleteness. But what if it were to be made part of some other formal or official act to be done pursuant to that basic vow? Would that repair the deficiency?"

"Yes, I believe it would."

"Well, then, yes, Wendy—by all means you will do well to sing in adoration, but surely it would be best for the rejoicing in the

Real God to resound as widely as possible.—Indeed, if we are going to speak about official acts pursuant to the vow, then I think we should consider it your sworn duty to do exactly that—to render adoration and display rejoicing so that what He has granted you may be as fully effective in the world as possible."

"What are you thinking?"

"Do you remember your old friend Sally, from those times long ago when I first pronounced that blessing upon you?"

"I shall never forget her so long as I live."

"There is another one very much like her who will soon be taking off. I wish you could have gotten to know her. I do know her, and you will just have to take my word for it. Well, she would find it deeply comforting to share in your rejoicing by hearing you sing that old hymn. I can set it up very quickly, if you are willing. That hymn is one of my personal favorites. I can get it at my desk." Of course Wendy was willing, but she questioned whether her singing was really all that good. "Oh, Wendy, you underestimate yourself. I have sometimes thought that with the beauty of your voice, you should have been a choir girl."

Deborah went and fetched the hymn, then returned and took Wendy to the girl, explaining as they went that the poor child had not yet gotten past her fear. "What you have to do is largely to help us work her through that."

When they arrived, the child kept silent but looked upon Wendy with obvious horror, expecting something dreadful. Speaking as sweetly as she could, Wendy said, "Honey child, I am sorry you are afraid of me. I am not here to hurt you. I am here to rejoice in the Lord God. If you find it helpful to share in this rejoicing, I shall be greatly honored. Will you allow me to sing?" The girl said yes, and so, bringing the full beauty of her voice into play as well as she could, Wendy began the hymn.

By the end of the hymn, the horror and misery had left the child's face. She was too weak to sing along, but she followed as well as she could by mouthing the words. After the hymn, she asked calmly and reasonably bravely, “Will it hurt to die?” In asking this, she was seeking to prepare by knowing what she had to face.

Deborah answered, “Oh, maybe just a little, but not much. Not enough to worry about.” She asked next whether Wendy might stay. Wendy agreed to it, and Deborah said she could. As Deborah had anticipated, it did not take long—only about one hour. The child died very well, just as Sally had done, exercising courage and rejoicing in God with only very minor pain and with nothing dreadful. She lapsed from consciousness smiling calmly and died nine minutes later.

When Wendy asked her, Deborah agreed that what had been done was an unusual way of doing it. “But hey, as you of all people should know, sometimes the standard or customary ways work out, and sometimes unusual arrangements are needed. In her case, it happens she was to be a junior choir girl—which is to say, she was to be enrolled in a children’s choir, only this other thing happened instead.”

“I wonder what she would say if she knew what I really am.”

“What you are is someone looking to worship and rejoice in the Real God and to have Him resolve her errors and evils. Why would she need to know any more than that? What you and I know is our problem, not hers.”

Wendy was about to spout some blather, but then she realized something. She was suddenly aware of how remarkably happy she was. So instead of the inane remark she had planned, Wendy said, “You were right, Deborah. This act has resolved it. How did you know?”

Deborah smiled. “When a girl wants to sing in adoration as part of a ceremony for others to hear, what is she really looking for? I know the answer to that, for you see, I myself was a choir girl many years ago, and I have often reflected on my experience.

Here is an easy way to think of it. What if you had been granted the privilege of singing that hymn in the choir at the great cathedral on some solemn occasion? Would that have finally resolved your concern?"

"Come to think of it, yes—certainly."

"All right, what you just did was a miniature version of that. There was the underlying basis, the essential quality, even though there was just one singer and just one listener. Beyond that, the grandiose setting and all the rest of it are mere trappings."

"Dear, sweet Deborah. When can I hope to have such wisdom?"

There was much in Deborah's mind in response to this question. What she said was simply, "For that, you must look to Another far greater than I."

The next morning, Wendy woke up feeling remarkably happy, again because the old incompleteness was finally resolved, but now in a deeper way. She felt that she had somehow crossed some critical threshold. Wendy had learned enough by now, and she had run out of objections and excuses, and she knew this at the back or in the depth of her mind. But the full answer was not yet explicit.

The explicit development came about a week later. Wendy woke up in the morning and knew where she stood and what her path had to be. There was no more question and no other choice—or only the choice to destroy oneself by refusing to follow what one knows all too clearly to deny or evade. Yet she did not feel compelled. She had only the astonished feeling of being more fully awake.

And so later that day, she went to her grandmother, for her mother was dazed. Wendy spoke of the vows she had sworn and asked what her grandmother thought. The grandmother said all that was very nice, and it was good as far as it went, but she hoped Wendy would soon go even further.

Wendy answered, "Yes, so do I. That is why I have come to you. I have already learned too much to stop now. This morning, I realized that my rejoicing in what has already been accomplished shows me that I have already crossed some critical dividing line." Then, changing her voice to display greater formality, she said, "I reaffirm what I declared with that vow concerning God and the things of God, and I renew my surrender in recognition of His sovereign dominion. Wherefore, I ask that you take me to His officers, that I may surrender fully and formally." The grandmother could hardly believe her ears for sheer joy. She asked whether this meant what she thought it meant. "Yes, indeed so. Dear Grandma, when next you go for regular Divine worship, I ask that you take me with you and present me, that in submission I may receive what He has appointed." When she got over her shock, the grandmother said yes, by all means—of course, certainly, it would be a great pleasure.

⸻

"With this, Wendy's life began to be truly remarkable."

"What do you mean, Beatrice?"

"Well, first, of course, God is truly wondrous, and so to be attached to Her—or to Him, as they would say—within the order of Divine Redemption is already plenty remarkable, as is the order of Divine Redemption itself. But also, Wendy would soon find out just how much a child of destiny she really was. Her exotic adventures were about to begin."

⸻

What Wendy had asked was done. Her grandmother took Wendy along when next she went for regular Divine worship. When the ritual had been completed, she asked the officer to speak with them privately. Then she introduced Wendy as a newcomer. The officer asked about this, and Wendy said, "Yes, sir. You see, I was a very sickly child, and so I spent a whole lot of time in and out of hospitals. As a result, a great deal of what happened with me worked out to be a catch-as-catch-can affair. My mother was disabled shortly after I was born, and so I was raised largely by my governess. Well, she raised me and trained me to be a volcanic witch." The officer let out a long, thin whistle. Wendy continued. "But I have come to realize that way is not so good. I have had to learn a great many things. Sir, may I speak of what I have learned?"

"Yes, of course."

Adapting her vow for the situation at hand, Wendy said, "My old teacher laid out very nicely what stands at the heart of your Faith, and what your Faith says is right. There is the One God and His creatures, and that is all there is, with no other beside Him and with the yawning chasm, the great gulf, between God and all His creatures, however exalted those creatures may be. Volcanic witchcraft is clearly wrong, for in His hand are the depths of the earth; the heights of the mountains are His also. God is Light in Whom is no darkness at all, compared with Whom all the suns and galaxies are nothing. The depths are not realms of darkness anymore, for He has reached down and illuminated the very depths with His own presence."

"Wow! That is quite a mouthful."

"Have I said anything wrong about Him or unworthy of Him?"

"No, no, not at all. That was very good, in fact."

"Well, then, as I said, I have had to become aware of all this, and much more as well. Wherefore, I submit to His sovereign dominion, and I surrender to you as His officer for whatever is supposed to happen to me now."

"Right. I think I know, but you tell me, to make sure there is no misunderstanding. What are you asking?"

"If I understand rightly about what is supposed to happen, I am to be formally initiated when I have learned enough and been made ready. If that is so, then I ask that this be done. I ask in that case to be enrolled for learning and preparation and then initiated in due course."

"Yes, it is so, and it will be done, since you have asked."

And so, indeed, it was done. It took a while, but Wendy was formally initiated a little less than three-quarters of a year after the twenty-eighth anniversary of her birth. After the basic initiation, she received also a second procedure to increase and strengthen what she had just received. Then she took part in the chief ritual for Divine worship and received God's presence and action very richly and fully, as was ordained and provided for the people.

After the ritual, Wendy stood outside the house of worship with her mother (now lucid), her aunts, their mother, Alfreda, Alicia, and Deborah, all of whom rejoiced to witness what had just been done. Her mind full of wonder, Wendy said, "Awesome and wondrous as He is, it is just that simple."

It was Diana who answered. She was, in fact, highly intelligent when lucid. "Yes, dear child, it is just that simple—and also, as you of all people should know, that complicated." Wendy simply smiled and bowed her head in honor of her mother's display of wisdom, being too overwhelmed with wonder and deep joy to speak.

Then, once again, Deborah thought of something. "I told you, Wendy, that you should have been a choir girl. Will you now try for the choir here? I hope so!" Wendy decided she would, and she did so. She was accepted very happily, and so she sang in adoration plenty over the next two years, rejoicing that it was given her to do so.

But this was not all. After hearing her sing in the choir, Deborah told Wendy of other sick children to be comforted with singing, beyond that girl for whom she had sung to complete her basic vow. Over the next two years, Wendy sang with rejoicing in adoration for at least two dozen such girls.

Why only girls? "Well, of course she would have sung for boys as well, very happily, but it simply happened not to work out that way," Beatrice explained.

Both before and after this initiation, life went on after the graduation. For the time being, Wendy was employed teaching low-level courses to beginning students. She continued with this, and she went on learning what she could regarding God and the things of God, as well as with worship and private singing for those girls. She also worked to improve and expand the work of scholarship she had developed for the third level of advanced study into a larger book, hoping to publish it as a serious contribution in that area of research and knowledge. All this continued for a little more than half a year after the initiation, which placed Wendy a little more than a full year beyond her last graduation and a little more than a quarter of a year past the twenty-ninth anniversary of her birth. Then something happened.

Through that time, Wendy had kept going to the academic institution from which she had graduated. She conducted research in their library for the prospective book to be published, and she went to hear visiting speakers as well. On the morning of the disastrous day, Wendy awoke with no special feeling or concern, any more than any other day. Her mother was dazed again. Her grandmother greeted her nicely, then said, "As you know, Wendy, some of my dreams are significant. I can always tell which dreams are significant and which are mere froth. Well, last night I dreamed significantly. Something remarkable is waiting for you if you go out as you plan, whether for good or evil or perhaps both. But I do not know which." Yes, it was true—some of Grandma's dreams were in fact significant. The problem was that what she had said was not enough to do anything serious with it. However, her grandmother extracted a solemn promise from her to run away at once at the first sign of trouble.

Wendy went to the institution and spent hours conducting scholarly research in the library. Then, late in the afternoon, she went to hear a visiting speaker.

This speaker was a woman from the foreign land far away in which that landmark thinker of the alien culture had dwelt. She was speaking on the energy and richness of the depths of the world, much as Lilikea had done long ago. But unlike what Lilikea said, what this speaker had to say about it was not a bunch of half-baked stories and superstitions. It was a very sober, serious-minded, scholarly treatment. On that basis, Wendy decided it would be worth hearing.

As she sat listening, Wendy came gradually to feel a strange foreboding. Out of respect for her promise, she was ready to leave quickly. But then she stopped and thought. Was there really any sign of trouble? Nothing had happened to make her believe she was in danger or under threat. It was the speaker that Wendy found somehow alarming, but there was no indication the woman intended any evil to her or anyone else. So Wendy stayed.

Almost as soon as she reached this decision, Wendy remembered a severe warning from a teacher long ago. He had pounded into her head that she must never, never, *never* let anyone make her doubt her own instincts. If anyone were ever to try that, or if she found that happening, she must run away quickly. She had agreed with him then, and she agreed with him now. Also, in the brief moment it had taken her to run through this in her mind, her foreboding had grown worse. And so she stood up to leave.

But she was not able to leave. She was barely able to settle herself back into her chair instead of merely collapsing. And then she understood. Like Lilikea, this woman spoke about the depths of the world. Unlike Lilikea, she was in fact able to tap into and exploit those depths. In a word, the woman was a witch of some sort—but a real witch, with real power, and Wendy was under attack by this woman, for whatever reasons of her own.

Wendy could not speak. In her mind she cried out to God to deliver her from the attack, if it might be, and to see her through what was to happen in any event. Then Wendy decided that if she must stay, she may as well hear the lecture. After all, that was what she had come for.

When the lecture was concluded, Wendy found that her mind and body were completely clear and had been for a while. When she stood up, someone introduced her to the witch and told the witch about the new work Wendy had written leading up to her graduation at the third level. They discussed the scholarly concerns involved for a short while, and then Wendy left. But from the expression on the witch's face, the tone and inflection of her voice, and the way she carried herself, Wendy knew it was not over—not at all. She went home quickly, severely shaken, and did not speak until her grandmother spoke to her.

"I was right. Something happened. I gather it was for evil and not for good."

"Yes, Grandma—right on both counts."

"Can you speak about it just now?"

"No, not yet."

"That bad, eh?"

"Yes, very much so."

Her grandmother got them each a small vessel of the same kind of red beverage Alfreda had given Wendy five years earlier and Diana long before that. When they had drunk together, Wendy began to speak, slowly and carefully. She told the whole story in order, with full details. "Now, let me ask you: Do you believe it?"

"Yes, Wendy, I do. That is what is most disquieting for me about all this. I believe you have described your own impressions correctly. But more than that, I believe that woman *was* in fact a witch in the sense you mean, and that you *were* in fact under attack by her, and that she let you understand it is not over—all just as you said."

"You really believe all that?"

"Oh, yes, I do—very much. Wendy, as the poet said long ago, there are more things in heaven and earth than are dreamt of in men's philosophies. I do not just believe that—I *know* it for a fact, in a very hard-line way. I am not, and for many years have not been, one of those who has the luxury of disbelieving or even doubting it. Now, it is about time for us to have dinner. After that—well, you are obviously in no fit condition tonight for anything very serious. But tomorrow, rest assured, this will be seen to. Tomorrow, I promise, you're gonna hear the craziest story you have ever heard."

CHAPTER THIRTEEN

At this point, Beatrice halted her narrative in order to explain more fully what she had seen and what had been revealed to her. "I told you that my mind would be taken back to observe living history. Much of this happened while I was with Wendy during the course of her learning and preparation leading up to her formal initiation." She paused, collected her thoughts, and said, "There were the critical events of the Divine Redemption, and there was the Preparation through many centuries leading up to that. I have already indicated in some measure what popular errors had to be purged from the people selected for all this in the course of the Preparation. To oversimplify slightly, there is what Wendy swore in her basic vow concerning God and the things of God. Well, much of what was accomplished in the course of that long process was that those people were brought to accept and appreciate that what she said was so. It was set up that the critical events occurred, and the Redemption was presented to the people, within this framework that had thus been established."

Beatrice paused, and her teacher's colleague spoke up. "This is getting interesting. From what I know of Renegades, when they need to hold to the truth against constant and serious temptations to fall back into error, there is a strong tendency to cling to the truth with a kind of hard stubbornness that leads all too quickly into an ugly closed-mindedness, which could even lead into real viciousness."

"Yes, indeed so. I observed that among them."

"Now, what about what you were saying earlier—that God reached down and became one of Her own creatures? You say this happened among the people selected for that training, and it was presented to them. Then, I gather they were called on to believe it. Is all this correct?"

"Yes, it is."

"I gather also this creature was one of those people, that species, and not some alien being. Is that too correct?"

"Again, yes, it is. The person was one of that species, and in fact, as a person of that species, one of those people selected."

"Then given what we have agreed about the tendency of Renegades, I would expect a whole lot of those people would look upon that Person as just another woman spouting lunatic delusions or malicious nonsense. To be sure, given what you have explained, it does make sense somehow, and I can kind of see how it can be reconciled with what they had to learn and believe. But then, I have the advantage of not being a Renegade."

"Yes, right—very much so. That is what happened. Except for one thing: this Person was a man and not a woman."

Beatrice's teacher spoke up. "A man and not a woman. Later on, we shall have to discuss what significance that fact may have. But for now, we need to go through the basic points. Evil must be resolved through suffering somehow, but the superior can answer for the wrongdoing of the subordinate. So, as the ultimate superior of all, God in Her mercy reached down and became one of Her own creatures, and thereby suffered undeservedly as a created being in order to resolve the evil of Her people. The idea that She became one of Her own creatures can be thought of along the line that created things are embodiments of Divine wisdom. There can then be a condensed version of this embodiment, of which the analogy of an author making herself into a character in her own story is a different version. Then again, one can think more abstractly about how higher levels are embodied in the functioning of the lower levels, as with the relation of mind and body in a rational animal. Does that sum up correctly where we are, Beatrice?"

"Yes, I would say so. I believe it does, as least as regards the basic points. I can elaborate a little further or go to something else."

"No, please—elaborate."

"In fact, the process of reaching down to correct someone's waywardness is observed enough even among us. A teacher may have to explain something to a Renegade child who insists on being difficult. When the teacher sees clearly what is going on with the child, she may perhaps respond in any of various ways. But she might say to the child, 'All right, we can do it your way. I can explain it to you even in your own terms, if that is what you really want.' Now, that function of a teacher is a tiny little image of what Divine wisdom did in the course of the Great Redemption. But it must be combined with the other analogies, as we discussed before."

There was lengthy discussion of all this. When it was concluded, Beatrice's teacher said, "All right, very good. Now, you were speaking of how the Preparation led into the Redemption. Please, say more about that."

"First of all, the tradition of the Redemption took over much from that of the Preparation, which is kind of what one would expect. Both traditions speak of God in the masculine in almost all contexts. Thus, they say of God that in *His* mercy, *He* became one of *His* own creatures, and so on. Long before the Redemption, those people said of God that *He* commanded and things were created. Again, this extraordinary Person was a man and not a woman.

"Beyond that, there was more to the Preparation than just the discipline to learn what Wendy would later swear. There were also mysterious prophecies pointing to something more, and very different, that was to come. But these prophecies were not understood rightly until after the most critical events of the Redemption were accomplished."

"What about these mysterious prophecies?"

"Most blatantly—well, relatively early in the Preparation, at one of its great landmark events, God reached down to offer a kind of agreement to those people. One of the remarkable prophecies, centuries later, was that there would be a new agreement, not like the old agreement, that would involve being devoted to God and being forgiven."

"And still they did not understand!"

"No, for they were looking for God to raise up a ruler who would resolve their problems of the day. They were not so much looking for one who would rule by exercising the power to pardon and do so while suffering death by torture. Yet there was a prophecy on this very point. It was foretold that there would be some remarkable person through whose suffering the people would be redeemed."

The teacher's colleague spoke up. "To follow the logic very strictly, in an obvious way, that was not properly effective until *after* the suffering was accomplished. Did they then believe, after that happened?"

"Some did, and some did not. You have to remember, this man died by torture, as I said. But he claimed to have dominion over life and death—which of course God has. Specifically, he said he could and would rise from the dead after he was killed. So the question was, did he really do so? If so, then his claim to be Divine might be true after all and in spite of everything. But if not, then of course he was just another liar or fool who got killed for running his mouth and spouting garbage. Well, one of the things he did before he was killed was to tell a story in order to illustrate a moral or religious point. In fact, he told many stories to illustrate various points. But this one story is relevant here. He concluded the story by telling how a wicked man was told that if people would not believe the Divine revelation already given, then they would not believe even if one should rise from the dead. Sure enough, as was later commented among the people of that world, with this man, one did rise from the dead, and still they did not believe. The hard stubbornness of Renegades will lead them to deny almost anything unless and until the evidence is just too overwhelming even for them. That includes making up stories with no initial plausibility in order to explain away the evidence—or try to."

After a pause, Beatrice said, speaking slowly and carefully now, "In one way, Wendy had a remarkable advantage over the people in the age of the Preparation, although she did not rightly understand this until much later. From her studies as a theoretician, she realized the critical question had to be that of being attached to God so as to rejoice in God, as she put it. But the people of the Preparation did not think along those lines, or at least not until fairly late in the game. Of course, there is the obvious reason why it had to happen this way, or else it would not have worked out rightly. In order to appreciate rightly what is involved in having God reach down and provide for the people in that way, one must first appreciate that God is above and beyond the whole world of other beings, and that is one of the chief lessons—if not *the* great lesson—that people had to learn in the age of Preparation. Once this point is appreciated, one can understand that the thing to do is to *submit* to be attached to God as a free gift. But until it is appreciated, the idea of being attached to God can all too easily lead someone horribly astray. In fact, something like that happened among them. Wendy spoke to Alicia of ancient thinkers as foreshadowing the concern to receive blessedness from God. She was referring to people who were not part of that system of Preparation. Well, one of those thinkers spoke of the soul as naturally suited to dwell within the world of the gods. Yet he was one of the great landmark thinkers of history in their world—one of those who understood best!

"Now, the thing is that it is a free gift, with all that entails. From the nature of the case, this kind of connection with God goes beyond what can possibly belong to any created being simply as a created being. In order to accept it, therefore, one must go beyond what belongs to oneself as a created being. This involves, so to speak, leaving aside one's functioning and character as a created being. In this way, there is a kind of deathlike quality entailed—there is no other way to say it. With the Normal people among us and among other species, this takes the very mild form of simply giving up the preoccupation with oneself and one's desires in favor of what is known to be more worthy as soon as one stops to think about it. But for Renegades, it is far more severe. Their whole chosen basis in life must be wiped out and replaced. In other words, they must be remade. In order for something to be remade, it must first be destroyed. Therefore, the deathlike quality involved for them is much more pointed. Is all this correct?" Her teacher's colleague assented. "In view of all this, it is almost as if what happened is what had to happen. They are to receive blessedness by being connected to that man somehow and receiving his action. Yes, of course—given that he is God reached down from Heaven somehow and that they participate in his death and return. It is said that this man's mission in life was to die. I accepted that as having been given to me, but it seemed like a question with no answer until I was given to understand how all these things came together in this way."

Her teacher spoke up. "Moreover, the act whereby God provided for the people is also the same act whereby She avenged the sins and punished the evil of those very people. What you have told is truly wondrous."

Beatrice and the colleague agreed it was truly wondrous. With this, Beatrice was about to continue telling the story. But then she decided something else had to be explained first.

"I was given to observe the living history of what God had done, to learn the right Faith based on the revelation of what She is and what She did, and to witness the conversion to which one of the people had been brought through Her mercy. When all this had happened, my impulse was that there was the end, at least for me and my vision. I figured I had now acquired what insight and understanding could be acquired from that world. I was genuinely surprised at first when the further adventures I have already begun to describe were shown to me. I called on God for guidance, and I was led to consider how an adult among us might teach a child. Then it was easy enough.

"Sometimes the best way is to show or recite examples. So, with my vision, I was to learn more by seeing how Wendy was called upon to live out the Faith through the course of her life. Again, sometimes it is better to give typical examples, but other times it is better to give extreme examples in order to make the point very graphically. As I have already indicated in some measure, given what her further adventures turned out to be, Wendy's life as an adult convert worked out to be one of the extreme examples." With that, Beatrice resumed her narrative.

CHAPTER FOURTEEN

The next day came quickly enough, and the telling of the story began soon enough. But it began, not with a statement, but with a question.

"Wendy, I know this is a remarkable thing to ask, but you must tell me now. Do you remember how, long ago, you used to think of me as having wondrous qualities?" Yes, she did. "Good. But now—this is important—do you still think of me that way?" Well, come to think of it, yes. That too.

Ever since Wendy could remember from her early childhood, her grandmother had seemed almost magical, much more than just exceptionally well able to read people and situations. She could sometimes know what was happening without being there to observe it, or what other people were thinking without being told, or what was going to happen before it did. Moreover, this was not by projecting or calculating from how things were working. It was—well, somehow it was different. Also, there was the fact that her dreams were sometimes significant. Again, Grandma would often display something like a magical ability to manipulate objects. In addition, even though she had not studied biofeedback, she had remarkable awareness of and control over her own body. Because her experience of people in general was unusually limited during her childhood, it took Wendy a long time to learn that grandmothers in general did not have such capabilities, and so she had finally come to realize Grandma was wondrous.

"Good—that makes it easier. Now, do you remember what I told you when you asked me about all this as a child?" Yes, she did. Her grandmother had affirmed that all this was so and had promised to discuss it with Wendy at the proper time—when she had grown up.

"Well, evidently the time has come. So, here we go. First of all, stop and think. What about your aunts and your mother? I mean your *real* aunts—not Alfreda, dearly as we all love her."

"Hmm...come to think of it, Amanda and Theodora have such capabilities as well as you. My mother does not have those capabilities."

"She did, although you were too young to understand or remember it. She was beginning to display such capabilities, and she was even promising to develop a higher level than I have, when she fell and banged her head. That wiped out everything. Do you see where this leads?"

"What—that it runs in the family to have such special powers?"

"Yes, exactly so—for generations back, as far as can be traced. Only women have these powers among us." She paused, then began again. "As near as we can figure, it is what they call sex-linked, kind of like hemophilia or color blindness, but in an opposite way. The genetic basis for it resides on the X chromosome. Men and boys have one X chromosome, but they can only be carriers, for the masculine development of the brain suppresses or disables such functioning. At most, men can show some very slight traces. A woman can have both of her X chromosomes be void, in which case she will be totally lacking in such powers. None of us in this family are that way, although most women are. Alfreda is, dearly as we all love her.

"A woman can have just one X chromosome with it, in which case she will have such powers in lesser measure. Again, none of us in this family are that way, although my mother and one of my sisters are. Alternatively, she can have both of her X chromosomes with the inheritance, in which case she will have these powers in full measure—like me or like your mother or like your aunts Amanda and Theodora. Whether she has a single dose or double dose of the genetic basis, either way there is a range of how much of these powers she has. So far as we can tell, where she stands within that range is just the luck of the genetic draw."

Wendy let out a long, thin whistle. "So, what then?"

"Come now, Wendy. You are a very learned woman. I am surprised you have not heard of such things before."

"Well, yes, of course I have, and I know the fancy names they give such things nowadays. But I never dreamed I would be personally involved with it in any serious way once I dumped what Lilikea had taught me."

"I too know those fancy names, and I am glad you understand that is just what they are—mere labels. We do not really know how those things work anymore than anyone else. What Lilikea told you long ago about the alleged talent of women for witchcraft may or may not be the truth—or part of the truth." They discussed this to refresh Wendy's memory. Wendy was surprised her grandmother remembered. "Oh, I have never forgotten. It stuck in my mind. For you see, I knew this day was coming. Besides that, I myself have often wondered how it works. As for the question of fancy names, in the old country from which my ancestors came, they called it 'second sight'—which is perhaps as good a name as any for it."

"I have heard of second sight before, as well as the modern talk with the fancy names."

"Good. That may make it easier for you. As for the fact that you are seriously involved with it, I did more than dream of it—much more. I have expected it and lived in dread of it, ever since—well, for many years now. Since your infancy, in fact. If you remember, I spoke to you about the great mysteries of our family around the time of your basic vow. I promised to tell you very soon after the vow was sworn, but then I never imagined your path would work out as it has with this long delay in your beginning as a great warrior lady."

"Yes, I remember all that. But in dread of it, you say? Why, Grandma? So far as I can tell, it has worked out all right for you and for my aunts to have those powers."

"Yes, but then—Wendy, you spoke of my ability to know what is going to happen before it does. In the old days, that was called 'soothsaying.' Have you heard that name for it?"

"Yes, I have, but until now I never took it seriously."

"Well, in times past, there have been great soothsayers among our ancestors—women whose minds could reach far ahead to know what was to be, in full and exact detail, decades, generations, or even centuries beforehand. This is not based on easy and convenient interpretations after the fact. It is genuine, serious minded—the real thing. Again, it is not just a bunch of stories built on top of other stories. It has been carefully checked out and completely verified. My own grandmother and her daughters made sure of that long ago, and my sisters and I, together with your aunts and Alfreda, have checked it and verified it again more recently—in fact, when I learned of the reason to dread what was coming. If you think we were not skeptical enough... no, Wendy, that could not be more wrong. Alfreda and I and the rest of us hoped to *dis*prove it—to show it all false—but we could not. Moreover, there is the further proof that much of what has been foretold has already happened. Indeed, it was when the early pieces were fulfilled that I began to dread. So there it is. I have lived in dread because I have known what is coming. And now, with this situation, it is upon us."

"Grandma, what is it? Do they say I shall be damned? That I shall end up lost in Hell?"

"No, not at all. That is not foretold."

"Then whatever it is, we just have to look to God to see us through all that may happen or not happen, as with everything else in life."

"Yes, of course—I know that. Only by keeping that before my mind have I been able to keep going and get through."

"Then Grandma, what is it that is so horrible? Am I to die very young? Any woman can die young—special predictions or not. As for me, we both know I have been living on borrowed time since before I was born."

Somehow, the grandmother managed to say, "Yes, Wendy. Yes, you are. I am very sorry."

"Is my death to be dreadful somehow?"

"That I do not know, nor how long exactly you have or how far you may be able to fulfill the great works you hope to do as a learned thinker. I know that it will not be many more years now, even at best." She could not bring herself to say more at that time.

Wendy absorbed this, prayed to God silently, took thought, and then spoke slowly and carefully. "Grandma, we both know the obvious answer. If I have only a short time, I must look to God and try to make every moment count all the more. Moreover, in my case that is not just words, as we also both know. When I was fifteen, I had to realize that fulfilling my appointed destiny, even if only for a little while, was more important than having a long span. Perhaps He allowed that situation to happen to prepare me for this business now."

The grandmother managed to say, "Dear, sweet, brave Wendy! How much I love you!" Then she broke down and wept. For the first time in her life, Wendy had to comfort her, pointing out that after all, they really did both know that she had been living on borrowed time for almost all of her life.

When the grandmother had gotten hold of herself, she said, “Many questions remain, of course. But I want to do it right and gather everyone together and get it all over with, rather than drag it out day after day or even week after week. I think that will be best for all of us.” Wendy agreed, and so it was arranged.

Not long after, on the appointed day, Wendy sat down with her mother (now lucid), her aunts, Alfreda, Alicia (whom Alfreda had obtained permission to bring along), her grandmother, and her father’s adoptive mother. The grandmother began the session by introducing the adoptive mother and Alicia to each other. Next she spoke at length of what Wendy had told her of the meeting and of what she had told Wendy of family history some days earlier. Then she continued. “Alfreda and the others knew what they needed to know in order to check out the authenticity of the received predictions and the reliability of the old soothsayers. But they did not know about Wendy in particular, except for a few pieces having to do with the first year or two of her life, starting from her conception. I kept the rest from them, other than the basic fact that some exotic destiny was foretold for Wendy.”

Alfreda added, “Alicia, as she said, I knew Wendy had some exotic destiny. I did not know what it might be, except in vague generalities, and I was sincere in what I said to you when we discussed her long ago. As for the old predictions—I kept quiet about those because I could hardly believe them myself, even though I had checked out all that stuff and verified it.”

“Well, that was very good, Alfreda. I do not exactly believe it now—or at least not yet—in spite of what you two ladies just said, although I do not *disbelieve* it.”

Alfreda answered, “As you say, not yet. All of us may have to change our minds about many things before the day is over. But I can vouch for it—she does have the special qualities Wendy noticed in her. I have observed it over the years." Wendy, her mother, and her aunts spoke up and vouched for it as well. With that, Alicia conceded the point, albeit only provisionally.

Then the grandmother began the exposition. She spoke of what all of them knew already about the first two years of Wendy's life, starting with her conception. Then she went on, "As I said, to have these qualities belongs to women only, and it seems to be sex linked as depending on having zero or one or two doses on one's X chromosomes. But the old predictions, which I believe to apply to Wendy, call for the one who is foretold to be exceptionally powerful through having a double dose, which depends on having one's father be a carrier." With that, she turned to Arvid's adoptive mother and said, "Maria, will you kindly tell everyone about Arvid?"

"Yes, Margaret—very gladly. It is always a great pleasure for me to speak of Arvid or hear him spoken of." There had never been any discord or tension between Margaret and Maria—quite the opposite. After learning the truth about himself, Arvid had returned to Margaret and met with her just once before he had been killed. There was no trouble to speak of. They had, in fact, come to love each other very quickly. Margaret knew better than to try to grab back the motherhood she had lost wrongfully. She assured Arvid that in spite of what should have been, based on the earlier history, Maria was in fact his mother at this point and had been for many years. Margaret told Arvid to look upon her and think of her like an honorary aunt. Later on, after Arvid had been killed, Margaret and Maria met. Their love for Arvid brought them together, and they had loved each other from almost the moment they met. They had in fact long since been like honorary sisters.

Turning to Wendy, Maria explained, "Wendy, your father was a genuine boy and later a genuine man, fully masculine and all, with no question and no nonsense. But there was always something—well, not wrong, but strange or exotic. He was almost as good as a girl—in fact, he was better than most girls—in being able to read people and situations. Even more than that—I kept wondering whether he was merely exceptionally clever to know things or whether he had those special qualities. If men could inherit this, I would say he did."

Margaret responded, "As I told Wendy, men can sometimes show very slight traces. So yes, he could and did inherit it. In fact, there is no question about it. First of all, my own powers enabled me to know that when I met him. Second, it is clear from working through the genetics. I have a double dose, and all my daughters have a double dose. That could not be unless my husband was also a carrier. But anyhow, just the fact that I have a double dose would be enough to make Arvid a carrier. In the present context, the important thing is that Wendy also has a double dose. I know this about her from what I observe with my own powers as well as by working through the genetics."

For several seconds, Wendy sat there stupidly. Then she felt the need to say something, but she was not sure what to say. So she asked, "Grandma Mary, did you know anything about this second sight business with Arvid before Margaret told you?" Wendy had known the facts about Arvid very well—ever since she was old enough to understand and accept the truth. But she had grown up with Arvid's adoptive mother as her second grandmother, and this relationship had been maintained.

"No, Wendy, not at all. I wish I had known. It might have been easier to guide him."

Wendy turned and asked, "Grandma Peggy? What happens now? Can I escape my fate?" This was what she called her biological grandmother when Maria and Margaret were together.

"Well, but is it right that you should escape your fate? Is that even what you really want? As you told me, we have all known all along that you have been living on borrowed time, as you called it, almost all your life. That one fact assures that you cannot be an ordinary woman to go through life and enjoy simple happiness as other women do. It was just never one of the options available to you. Moreover, that is before we get into the twists and turns your life has taken through the years. You are headed for exotic adventures involving wondrous things. But then, given your situation, what else would you ask or hope for?"

"You said I am not to live very long. I guess I might ask not to die too soon, before I accomplish whatever I may accomplish."

"Not to worry. It is foretold that you will work for a time as a very learned and highly capable theoretician, which is what you were planning to do and have begun to do. Eventually, you will come to be involved in the exotic adventures. But it will not be simply imposed on you. It will be in some way by your own will, though I do not yet know how."

At this point, Alfreda spoke up. "Alicia, I think the time has come for you to tell Wendy what you told me about her long ago." Alicia agreed and did so.

When this had been told, there was at first a stunned silence. Then Wendy was the one who picked it up and pushed it through from there. She said simply, "All right, Grandma Peggy. Tell us the whole story in order."

There followed a long discussion of family history, what had been foretold, how the predictions had been handed down and eventually recorded, how everything had been checked and verified, and what had already been fulfilled regarding Wendy. As for what was to come, Margaret could say very little, having been sworn to secrecy to tell beforehand only what was needful. But she told what she could. "I did not reveal you would die young in order to frighten or torment you, Wendy. I told you so you could plan and prepare."

"What time frame are we talking about? A few hours, or days, or weeks, or what?"

"Oh, no—years. Maybe five or six years—maybe even eight or ten. As I said, you will work as a great theoretician for a time. How much you may accomplish, I do not know. I hope you will do plenty. But in any event, you will not live to see two-score years beyond your birth, to use the language of the prediction."

"Do you know whether I am to die in the course of the exotic adventures?"

"Yes, I know, but I am not allowed to say at this time."

"All right, then. What else are you able to tell me now? Or no—there are two questions. What about the meeting with that woman, and what about my powers that are still dormant?"

"Those two concerns are related. Each one's awakening is different. For you, that meeting is what will awaken your powers. Within a few weeks, your special powers will surpass my own. You will be at the top of the double-dose range. Indeed, you will be at the level of the great soothsayers of history that I told you about. Whether you will engage in soothsaying, fulfill other concerns, or perhaps do all those things, is another question."

"Well, but she let me know it is not over. What about that? Is anything foretold? Can you tell me anything based on your own awareness with your own powers? Of course, the first obvious questions about her are who is she, and why did she make contact with me as she did?"

"I do not yet know. I have scraps and fragments of hard fact, and reasonable suspicions with which to weave these pieces together, but that is all. It will have to be investigated. What I do know is that the business with that woman is *not* part of the exotic adventures I spoke of before. It is foretold, but it is to be some sort of preliminary instead."

"But Grandma Peggy, how can you investigate her? How can anything be done against her? I have been thinking, and I think she must be vastly more powerful than you and Amanda and

Theodora all put together. She could wipe us all out very quickly if she chose."

Margaret smiled. "I too have been thinking about it. You have to remember that there is much I know but have not told. So you let me worry about that."

There was further discussion for another two hours in order to clean up all the leftover questions and objections. Then the conference ended.

It happened as Margaret had said. Wendy's powers grew to the upper limit over the next few weeks. However, as with Margaret and her daughters, Wendy's use of those powers was only incidental or secondary. She did not even think of exercising such capabilities as her chief occupation. Her main concern was with her professional functioning as one who was very learned and especially with her ordinary personal life as a woman.

During these weeks, all went well enough, with no serious problems or noteworthy incidents. Wendy continued teaching low-level courses to beginning students, and she also worked to improve and expand her prospective book. As for her personal life, of course Wendy went on learning as much as she could about God and the things of God and striving to fulfill what she had been sworn into. In addition, she learned all that she could from her grandmother about her powers and how to use or not use them. She also learned about the family history, about what was foretold that had been fulfilled, and about what was to come that she needed to know. Beyond that, Margaret investigated as well as she could, but nothing significant turned up.

At the end of this time, Wendy was out taking care of some business, along with her mother and grandmother. When this was completed, they went and had lunch together. A few minutes after they sat down, the witch came to the table where they were and said, "Wendy—ladies—may I join you?"

Wendy's astonishment showed in her face and voice, but she held herself together to introduce the ladies to each other. After the customary polite greetings, Wendy said, "Mother, Grandma, I said I met some lady when she was giving a lecture as a visiting speaker. Well, this is that remarkable lady I told you about."

Before the others could react, the witch laughed and said, "'Remarkable lady.' That is a nice way of putting it. But yes, it is true. I am the paranormal mistress—the witch, I believe, is how Wendy thinks of me—whom she encountered at that lecture a few weeks ago."

Wendy said, "'Paranormal mistress.' *That* is a nice way of putting it."

"Well, yes, and why not? Unlike 'witch' or 'sorceress,' that phrase is neutral. It does not carry any suggestion of wickedness or depravity. Maybe I am that way, and maybe I am not. But you do not yet know enough to accuse me of that."

Diana, lucid for the moment, demanded, "Oh, really? Then why did you attack my daughter when she had not provoked it and did not deserve it?"

"I did not attack her. No, I am sorry—you will misunderstand that statement. Yes, I did attack her in the sense you mean. But that is not how I think of it. I was not taking any action against her. I was merely probing and scanning, and I was not trying to be violent. Quite the opposite, in fact—it was the lightest touch I could do."

Wendy spoke up. "You kept me from leaving."

"Yes, I did, but not from any malevolent motive. Again, it is the opposite. You were not aware of it at the time, but you were too much depleted. It would have been dangerous for you to leave. You might well have collapsed down a stairway or something. So of course I stopped you. It would have been irresponsible not to head off the danger I had caused."

"All right, fair enough, but then why the whole thing in the first place? Why not just come to me and speak to me straight out, openly and honorably, as one woman does with another when she is not wicked or depraved?"

The lady nodded. "Yes, of course. And now we finally come to it. You are right, Wendy—it should have been done that way, and I am very sorry. If I had known then what I know now, I would have gone to you as you said. But I had to make sure you were what I thought you were before I could do anything else."

Wendy kept herself from exploding and said, "You must know that I myself have paranormal powers, although far below your level, and that this runs in my family. Well, just recently my grandmother told me that I was foretold by the great soothsayers of history, and now there is something critical about what I am. What the blank is going on here?"

"Are you sure you really want to know?"

"The question is whether I *need* to know. You know so much—you tell me."

"If I were in your position, I might be even more angry. All right, then—yes. Sad to say, you do need to know. Not the whole story just yet, but much more than you know now." With that, she paused, smiled sadly, and began.

"First of all, you need to know something of who I am and what I am about in order to appreciate how I know what I have to tell you. Yes, I am a witch in the sense you meant at the time, which is to say that I have some special gift to tap into the depths of the world. But it is not just about exploiting energy and richness. Far more important is the awareness of reality—of the underlying structures and patterns, rhythms and cycles, deep underneath things. What your tradition calls 'soothsaying' is almost like a triviality, at least as people usually think of it. What I mean is that it is about knowing what is going to be because it has to be, and so it is about helping people fulfill rightly what they are called on to fulfill and sparing them suffering as much as possible. It is not about enabling them to get what they think they want. And so what I have to tell you now is not about you, and it is not about me. Do you understand?"

"Yes, I do. It is really very clear. Let me ask you this way. How far can you help me?"

Instead of answering Wendy, the witch turned to Margaret and said, "Like you, only much more so, I can sense what other people are thinking. You want to ask me something." Margaret would have spoken, but something was blocking her. The lady smiled and said, "I understand. People with your native language find it hard both to remember and to pronounce my name. My friends in this land call me Ginger, as they say, based on the kind of spicy character they find me to be."

Beatrice explained what this meant and then continued.

Margaret took out a little mirror and said, "Wendy, Ginger, both of you look into this mirror together." They did so, and Wendy understood.

Ginger was a few years older than Wendy, but she could almost be mistaken for Wendy's identical twin sister grown a little older, save only for the difference in race or ethnicity. Even so, she looked very much like an older version of Wendy reflected or translated into the other race or ethnicity. Margaret asked simply, "Do you remember that dream, Wendy?"

Indeed she did. Ginger asked and received permission, and Wendy felt a momentary flush of being probed. Then Ginger explained, "The occasion was just after what was in some way your first coming-of-age as an adult woman. Consequently, there was then the dream as the first preliminary flicker of having your powers awaken. Yes, Wendy—I am sorry, but you will be ravished by another woman. Someone else will do it, not I. What will or will not happen from there, or how the incident will end, I do not know. But I do know that the course of your life will be greatly changed after that. As for helping you with what you have to fulfill, yes—I can do that. With your book, when you reach a natural and obvious ending point in the course of the work, end it and settle for it. Resist your impulse to take it further. Finish it out and publish it instead, as soon as may be. Do not waste any time."

"Is it coming that soon?"

"I do not know exactly how long, but the short answer is yes."

"But Ginger, if that is all there is to it, why did you need to check me out before you could speak to me?"

"That is not all there is to it. You know about yourself and your family, and you know now there are people like me. But there is much more than that. There is much out there most people do not know, and rightly so. It is bad enough some select few have to know. To put it crudely, there are things that go bump in the night, to use that marvelous phrase. Even your own family must know something of this." Margaret nodded in assent. "But there is much more than what they are able to know. People like me know, and that is why I had to check you out first. When I saw you, I knew at once you were involved with these facts, but I knew only part of the truth. I did not know until I scanned and probed you what you were or where you stood, whether you were part of the evil in some way or even yourself one of those things that go bump in the night, or whatever. Now, of course, I know better, and I apologize once again."

"No apology is needed. It is an obvious thing. You did only what you had to do. But tell me—given that I am not a thing that goes bump in the night, what is the other alternative?"

"You will, in fact, be ravished by another woman. Sad to say, that is not up for debate or decision. That is going to happen, and it is not that far off. Unless something goes very wrong and the incident works out far worse than I expect, it will be given to you later on to have a large role in casting down the evil. That is the other alternative."

Diana asked, "You see this whole elaborate complex of facts for my daughter?"

"Yes, in the sense you mean, but that is not exactly how it works. I see the deep reality as a unified whole. In order to describe or explain it in words, it has to be set forth as an elaborate complex of facts. That is all."

"You had to say 'unless.' So your knowledge of the deep reality has serious gaps. You know only the conditional basis of what will happen *if,* but not how it will be."

"Well, as for how it works as a general proposition, I am not going to go into that here and now. But in this particular case, it is less about my power to know and much more that the thing to be known is weak or limited. The deep reality has to be applied to Wendy in particular, and that involves points of personal choice that are still to come. I am only a woman, not a goddess. I can only view things from within time, like any other woman—not from the standpoint of eternity, as though I were God. From my limited standpoint within time, what depends on personal choices still to come does not yet exist for me to know or not know."

"What if something were to go wrong? What if she were even to be killed?"

"That would not cancel or destroy the deep reality involved in this affair. That reality would still exist, but it would work itself out in some other way, with some other application to the concrete facts and beings of particular situations. I do not know how that would happen, and I would not tell you if I did. Unless and until it does go wrong, what is appointed to Wendy is the primary or dominant basis, and that is where the focus belongs."

That would have been the end, but then Wendy thought of something. "One thing puzzles me. I thought you were here as a visiting speaker for that one lecture, for just a day or two." Yes, that had been the original plan, but something had come up the day after the lecture, shortly before she would have left, and so it was arranged for her to stay on for a while.

With that they parted on friendly terms all around, or at least as far as possible after the sour news of what was to come.

After they had gone home, Wendy had seven words for her grandmother. "Is what Ginger told us today true?"

"Yes, as far as I can tell with my own powers, and as far as the predictions say."

"Am I to be ravished by another woman with an uncertain end to the incident?"

"Yes, child. Yes, you are. I am very sorry."

"Why did you tell me that dream was mere froth?"

"At the time, I thought it was. You insisted something dreadful had happened within your own body. That was false, and so I mistook the dream for a mere coincidence. Looking back, I can see that was foolish. But it seemed right at the time."

"All right, no harm or foul has come from that error. What else? What about the exotic adventures and wondrous things to come that are to happen to me by my will?"

"I wish I could tell you, but I am forbidden. I am allowed to tell you beforehand only what is needful, and there is no need for you to know that right now."

"Then let me ask another question. How is it that you know that answer, even though you are forbidden to tell, but Ginger does not, even though she is much more powerful?"

"As I told you, we do not rightly know how these powers work. Therefore, I do not know how this happens. However, I expect the strong personal connection we have with you may be very much involved."

"When or where or how is it to happen? Who will the woman be?"

"I am sorry, but I do not know any of that, at least not in detail."

"Well, this has to be about the most cheerless conversation of my life."

After all this, Wendy knew that she needed to talk with Alicia much more, as did Alicia.

"Well, Wendy, where would you like to begin?"

Wendy smiled. Once again, she was like a child reciting her lesson for her teacher. "Why, I begin with what is the obvious basic concern for one who has been trained as I have. Do I even know enough to ask you the right questions?"

Alicia smiled in turn. She understood very well. "Yes, of course you do. I suspect we both know what you want to ask, and it is as good a place as any to begin."

Alicia's suspicion was correct. "All right, then," Wendy said. "At the conference my grandmother called, you and Alfreda showed that you knew about me years ago. It turns out you were right. Well, I wondered about you even then, and I wonder all the more now. Excuse me for putting it this bluntly, but...what are you, really?"

Alicia smiled and nodded. "First of all, let me assure you that there is nothing to dread. What you are really concerned about is whether the nightmare suspicions in the back of your mind are correct. No, they are not. I was speaking truly when I told you I follow the same Faith as your mother and grandmother—and now you—by the grace and mercy of God. I am not a goddess, for as you said, there are no such goddesses. I am not any kind of higher order being. No—I am simply a woman, just another woman, as you are a woman, Wendy. There is nothing magical about me. I was conceived and born much less than a century ago, and I shall die less than a century from now. In both of these ways, I am very ordinary, like other women. That is all."

"All right, fair enough. But now, what is it you have not yet told me?"

Again, Alicia smiled and nodded. "What do you think I am, Wendy?"

"You are extremely bright and sharp, as they kept saying I was, and you are very learned. You enjoy tremendous knowledge, but somehow it is more than that—much more. There is some special quality to your wisdom and insight, something hard to explain. So I think, even though you are simply a woman, you are somehow specially gifted by the Lord God Almighty. I think perhaps *you* are the miracle worker you thought I might be, and you know more because your mind dwells in the heights and depths of reality more than the minds of other women. So, there it is."

Alicia sat calmly and waited patiently for Wendy to finish her spiel. Then she let out a long, thin whistle. "Very good, Wendy. Very good indeed. I do not exactly think of myself in those terms, but yes, something like that is the truth." By the grace and mercy of God, her mind was greatly illuminated, so much so that she had long since found it appropriate to receive low-level formal consecration within the order of the Faith. Now it was Wendy's turn to whistle. Alicia went on, "As for being a miracle worker—well, I have found that sometimes He will decide to speak through me, and sometimes He will decide to heal through me."

"You are saying you have the gifts of prophecy and of healing from God."

"I guess that would be the short way to say it, yes."

Beatrice confirmed for the others that Alicia did in fact have those gifts.

⁂

After she had gotten past the shock of this, Wendy said, “I do not believe it is just an accident we have come together, developed all this history between us over the years, and had this conversation today. Do you believe that?”

“No, of course not.”

“So what then? Where does it go from here? I mean, is there anything He has given you to tell me or to do for me?”

“No, not yet. For now you have plenty to think about. You must boil around in your head what we have discussed today. We shall meet again soon enough, and then we shall see.”

They met again one week later. Alicia began, “What do you need to ask me, Wendy?”

“You sat in on that conference my grandmother called, and you heard what was said about that witch, as I called her.” Wendy told of the meeting at lunch and of what she had learned from her grandmother afterward. “So, to roll all the questions into one, what the blank is really going on with me?”

“The short answer is that what Ginger told you and your relatives at lunch is all true, and what your grandmother told you afterward is all true. Now ask freely, and we shall see what can be given you for the long answer.”

“What about the ravishing that is to come? Can you tell me when or where or how or by whom? Can it be headed off, in spite of what they say? What will end up happening to me?”

“No, it cannot be headed off. Sorry, Wendy. It is not at this time given to me to know when, where, how, or by whom. Nor is it given to me now to know what the end will be.”

“What is the point of it? I mean this. Given what Ginger told me of my involvement with the facts about things that go bump in the night, it sounds like there must be some great movement of fate or destiny at work here. Is the assault on me to be how this movement works itself out, or is it to be an obstruction or interruption—something that has to be worked around or even that frustrates what was to have been or should have been? I understand that Divine Providence cannot be frustrated. It is just that there is no other way to say it."

"Yes, right. No, it will not be an obstruction or interruption that ruins or blocks what should have been, or at least not in the sense you mean. Whatever happens, it is to be clearly part of how this movement of fate or destiny works itself out. But mind you, how or why this is so remains mysterious. What will happen to you remains to be seen."

"Is there anything else I should be told?"

"For now, just that you should do what Ginger said about the book."

Wendy did so. She completed the book and submitted it for publication just twelve weeks after the meeting with Ginger. It was approved and published a little more than a quarter of a year after the thirtieth anniversary of Wendy's birth, about two years after her graduation. The book was greatly acclaimed as a monumental work, and Wendy was lauded for writing it.

Her rejoicing at this success lasted for several weeks. The knowledge that her span would at best not be long—and might be very short indeed—helped her to rejoice for the right reasons. She was happy it had been given to her to develop a great work by means of which Another far greater might provide for the people.

"So," Beatrice commented, "for that brief moment of her life, all was going very well. Then the dark deed happened."

CHAPTER FIFTEEN

The dark deed happened the day after the anniversary of the meeting at lunch with Ginger. As it turned out, it was indeed not Ginger who did it. Instead, it was her identical twin sister, who had gone stark raving mad.

Ginger was visiting for a scholarly conference. The conference had ended, but once again it had been arranged for her to stay awhile longer. Her twin sister, whom people called Pepper, was traveling through on her way to go elsewhere but had stopped to visit Ginger and was there just for that day. Wendy was visiting, discussing the new book and also other concerns with Ginger. Alicia, whom Ginger had met before, could not come along with Wendy owing to a prior commitment, but she was to join their meeting later as a fellow theoretician.

Pepper was also a theoretician in the same field as the others. Her presence was at first a pleasant surprise for Wendy, and all three took part in the conversation about the book and other scholarly concerns. She also had powers similar in kind—and almost equal in degree—to Ginger's, and so Pepper joined as well in talking about the other things Ginger and Wendy had discussed.

For the time being, all went well, but that was only because Pepper remained lucid.

About two hours after Wendy arrived, Ginger received a call on one of the devices for remote communication in real time. She was sorry, but something had come up, and she would have to leave for a short while. Wendy offered to leave, but Ginger insisted against it, saying she would be back in twenty or thirty minutes—an hour at most. In the meantime, "Please, Wendy, you should stay and get to know Pepper." There was no apparent reason against this and no foreboding in Wendy's mind, so she agreed to this proposal.

Pepper's mind held for about three or four minutes after Ginger left. Then it collapsed.

⁂

Beatrice explained, "When it occurred, Pepper stayed lucid long enough to finish the comment she happened to have been making. Then she paused, and then she started talking lunacy. It was not gibberish. It was in coherent sentences, but the content was bizarre." She paused and then began again.

"What Pepper was talking was the kind of stuff I discussed with my teacher as the absurdity that follows if the denial of God is really taken seriously and worked through correctly. But Pepper did not mean it hypothetically, as falsehoods that follow from a false premise. She meant it as the real truth. She started talking about the world as a living structure of nothingness and how the nothingness works itself up *as* a living structure to be a kind of positive something as pure emptiness. Then she talked about how this emptiness in turn reflects its own lack of life so as to constitute deadness and about how this deadness exerts its own negative character back on itself so as to give rise to life in the world.

"After she knew Pepper was not joking, and before she realized the woman was insane, Wendy raised one question. 'But Pepper, if the nothingness is already a living structure, then how does the world get from there to emptiness and deadness?' Pepper conceded there seemed to be some problem here and that further exploration would be needed. But there was no question the problem could eventually be resolved without serious difficulty. Wendy wanted to say it was this theory that was a big nothing, but something inside warned her to be quiet and listen.

After she answered Wendy's question, Pepper started on how the natural history of living beings in the world could best be explained in the light of her theory. 'Living beings are the beings that are both most deeply unified and most highly organized. Yet they arose through a series of accidents, kind of like a series of explosions in the junk yard. Now, Wendy, chance is obviously the *denial* or failure of unified order. That being so, to take chance as the basis for unified order is just too ridiculous, or it would be if being as a positive fact were the primary basis, as you and your tradition say. But it is kind of reasonable given that life comes out of the functioning of deadness on itself, as I say.' Wendy figured this was likely enough to be true, but she figured this was less a proof of Pepper's theory and more of a reason to deny that living beings arose by accident. She wanted to say so but kept quiet. And then she understood.

"The stuff this woman was talking was coherent but twisted. It had logic, but it was lunatic logic. With a sudden shock, Wendy remembered where she had seen and heard such stuff before. About three years earlier, Elizabeth's father's brother, her uncle David, had gone insane and had spouted nonsense with just this quality of being coherent but twisted. Very carefully, so as to avoid being detected and arousing suspicion, Wendy brought her own capabilities to bear on Pepper. Yes—sure enough, there it was. The woman was insane because of some disorder of her brain Wendy could not understand. She was also working up to something dark and terrible.

"In her mind, Wendy cried out to God to deliver her from the present danger, if it might be, and to see her through what was to happen in any event. Then she thought about what she should do or not do. Given Pepper's vastly superior powers, it would be hopeless to try to run and even more hopeless to try to fight. The one chance she had was to keep her talking until Ginger returned.

"So, weighing her words as carefully as she could, Wendy said, 'Well, Pepper, what you say sounds likely enough to be true. But you know, it is a strange thing. As near as I can figure, those people who claim that living beings arose by chance would say living beings are something positive and not functions of emptiness or nothingness.'

"Pepper answered, 'Yes, you are right, of course. But that only shows the world is full of fools.' Wendy agreed with this, and she conceded the point—but once again she drew the opposite conclusion from Pepper, although she kept that fact to herself.

"Then time ran out for Wendy. The next thing Pepper said was, 'Speaking of what the world is full of, there are children of light like you, and it is appropriate for dark characters like me to resolve our evil by tapping into you. I would not have you misunderstand. I am not simply taking my pleasure nor even merely exercising a privilege. I know that would be wrong, for you are kind of innocent and deserve better. No, but I am fulfilling a sacred duty—what God has commanded. So, Wendy, come now. Come along, and let us do what must be done.'

"So at long last it was happening. The nightmare was being played out in real life. As she had dreamed, her body was complying apparently of itself, against her will. What was really happening, of course, was that Pepper had taken control of her body, as Ginger had done to keep her from leaving that day. Wendy knew this, but that knowledge did not help her to escape. Pepper went to the bedroom, and Wendy's body walked behind her. When they arrived, Wendy's eyes closed, and her own hands stripped her naked, pursuant to Pepper's command. Finally Pepper said, 'Now you may open your eyes and look at me.' Wendy did so—not that she wanted to see Pepper naked, but by way of reacting to having had her eyes closed against her will. Pursuant to a further command, her body lay down on the bed, positioned itself, and held still. Then Pepper ravished Wendy."

Beatrice had to pause after this. The bodily violation inflicted on Wendy was bad enough, but to say it was commanded by God—such blasphemy was just too much! It took her a moment to resume her narrative. She had to be reminded the woman was not responsible for her actions.

"When the deed was done," Beatrice said at length, "Wendy became aware of two things in rapid succession. She realized Pepper had made her keep her eyes closed longer than was needed to strip. Then she saw Pepper reach over and fetch a knife. She understood Pepper had brought the knife into the bedroom while her eyes were held closed, and she knew why."

Wendy said simply, "Are you also commanded to kill me?"

"Yes, honey child. I am afraid so, and I am sorry. This too is a sacred duty. As I said, you are kind of innocent. It would be monstrous to allow your soul to be ruined by the darkness that has just touched your body. So this is what has to be. No noise, please. A mother or sister hurts a child because she has to, not because she wants to, and so here as well. Come now—relax as well as you can, try to be brave, and your suffering will soon be over. I am very good. There will be just a quick moment of harshness, and then you will be in Heaven." With that, Pepper plunged the knife into Wendy's chest and right through her heart.

When she was able to collect herself enough, Wendy cried out to God in her mind as one expecting to die momentarily. Then her mind faded, and she lapsed from consciousness. Pepper smiled with satisfaction. As she had promised, Wendy had not been abused in being killed. It had been quick, clean, and merciful. She withdrew the knife from Wendy's body.

Ginger had kept her word. She had returned in forty-two minutes. As soon as Pepper withdrew the knife from Wendy, Ginger stepped into the bedroom and cried out, "What have you done?!"

But these words were more of a reaction than a serious question. With her powers, Ginger knew well enough what had happened before she finished asking.

Pepper had always been slightly inferior in power to Ginger. At present, she was seriously weakened because of the disorder that deranged her mind and even more because of her momentary dissipation. So Ginger threw her into a deep sleep in order to get her out of the way harmlessly. This took just a few seconds. Then she turned to Wendy, whom she had already detected to be still alive, at least for the moment. Ginger threw Wendy's body into an emergency shutdown mode in order to buy time. She was about to go on from there when Alicia arrived.

At Margaret's conference on family history, Ginger had been spoken of badly. So, after the meeting at lunch, and after both Margaret and Alicia had confirmed what Ginger had said at that meeting, Margaret gathered them all together again, and there was much more discussion about Ginger. But this time it was all done the right way, and the truth was hammered out.

After all had been said, and as people were ready to leave and go home, Ginger had taken Alicia aside and asked her, "What about you? I can tell that you do not have even the paranormal powers of Wendy and her family, let alone what I have. But there is something very special about you—much more than what they are. Who are you? Or should I say, what are you, really?" Alicia had explained it to her just as she had explained it to Wendy.

Because of this, Ginger was not puzzled now as Alicia said, "I know what happened. You need not call for help or do anything more. It is given to me to take care of Wendy. While I do that, you take care of your sister." Ginger did so and then waited.

In a moment, Alicia said, "There—it is done. Her body is mended to be as if the stabbing had never happened. Instead of the shutdown mode you imposed, for which I thank you, she is deeply asleep, which is best for her just now." Then Ginger explained.

"As a child, my sister was seriously banged on the head. For the most part, she recovered well enough, but there was residual damage. Most of the time she is all right, but she plunges briefly into mental insanity two or three times a year. We keep an eye on her and intervene before there is real trouble. So this terrible wrong she has done is my fault. This morning, I knew there was something strange about her, and an alarm went off in the back of my mind, but I ignored it. I was legitimately distracted, and I thought I did not have time to get into it, but I should have remembered the danger and *made* time."

"No, Ginger—even at worst, you are guilty only of negligence that is largely excusable. Your sister was not responsible for her actions and so is not guilty at all. This is one of those cases where guilt is a fool's game, and it will certainly not help Wendy—or your sister, for that matter. What we have to think about now is cleaning up the mess."

"Yes, I know. I have been thinking about that. My sister is also in a deep sleep for the moment. When she awakes, she will remember, with her mind restored and lucid. Then she will be screaming with horror and ready to kill herself. What do I tell her?"

"You tell her the truth. If that is not good enough, you tell her she does not have the luxury of killing herself. She must stand ready to do what she can to help clean up the mess."

"Yes, what about that? All the damage to Wendy's body from the stabbing has been repaired. But what about the other, the fact that she was first ravished? How is that to be repaired for Wendy or any woman?"

"Again, with the real truth. Wendy must be brought to appreciate what happened to her as the worthless exercise in nonsense that it is, instead of as some great landmark event of her life."

"But you see, that is just the problem. Yes, what you said is true in the way you meant it. But in another way, it may well end up being some great landmark event of her life."

"Are you saying Pepper gave her some terrible infection or sickness?"

"No, not at all. Pepper was and is clean, and Wendy was and is clean. But that is not all that can happen to a woman upon being ravished."

Before Alicia could ask about this, Pepper awoke. What happened from there was exactly what Ginger had said. After they had gotten her calmed down, Pepper told her pathetic little story, which lined up with what Ginger had explained, but from another perspective. Then she said, "Alicia, it is worse than you imagine. I spoke to her of how darkness had touched her body. That was lunatic nonsense, and I know that now, of course. But in fact, something else did touch her." She turned to her sister and cried out, "Help me!"

Ginger explained, "It is what I was starting to say when Pepper awoke. With the bodily interplay inflicted on her, there was an overflow of—how to say it—of paranormal energy onto and into Wendy's body. This can have serious consequences for her. I told you, infection or sickness is not the only thing that can happen to a woman upon being ravished. There is also the classic concern that she may become pregnant. Perhaps you are thinking that can happen when a woman suffers violence from a man but not from another woman." Alicia nodded in assent. "Yes, in general, but with Wendy in particular, it is a little more tricky. What did her physicians tell her? That she cannot conceive?" Again, Alicia nodded in assent. "Almost, but not exactly. She cannot conceive in the regular or normal way, that is true. For the most part, she cannot conceive at all. Most of the germ cells inside her, her ova, are totally worthless. They were right about that as well. But some few are different. With some few, it is just barely possible she could be made to conceive through parthenogenesis."

In years past, an occasion had come up for Alicia to explore the question of parthenogenesis within her species, and so it did not have to be explained to her now. With some species, a mature female might reproduce from within herself alone.

Ginger went on. "Whether one of these ova, or one that is worthless, comes forth in a given cycle of her reproductive functioning is just the luck of the draw. Now for the punch line. If one of these few special ova should happen to come forth within the next twelve weeks based on the natural rhythm of her body, she will conceive through parthenogenesis. The effect of what happened will linger for that long. After that, however, she will be safe."

"Is there anything that can be done to neutralize or counteract it?"

"I assume you mean in terms of the special powers I have? No, not now—it is too deeply absorbed. At this point, it will just have to play itself out."

After further discussion, Alicia took Wendy home. As it happened, Amanda, Theodora, and Alfreda were all there, in addition to Margaret and Diana. Alicia wondered about this until she remembered they had planned to meet today in order to plan a celebration for one of Diana's friend's children. Well, this would work out handy. She could tell the story once to all of them together and get it over with. After Wendy had been put to bed, that was exactly what was done.

At first, those who heard Alicia were too shocked to speak, then too angry. Finally Alfreda said, "We can indulge emotion later. First are the pragmatic necessities. Alicia, is it absolutely certain that Pepper was not responsible for her actions?"

"Yes, there is no question about it."

"A demented woman who acts out once might do so again. So, is it also absolutely certain that she has since been neutralized from being any danger to others?"

"Yes, again—no question."

"All right. Fair enough, at least for now. When Wendy wakes, we shall see."

Wendy slept through the rest of that day, through the night, and then first awoke early the next morning. Diana and Alicia were there waiting for her. She greeted them nicely, smiled, turned to Alicia, and said, "It was not just a dream? It really happened?"

"Yes, child, it did." Then she realized Wendy needed for her to lay it out, so she added, "Pepper went insane, ravished you, and then stabbed you through the heart. All that happened in real life, when you were awake to suffer through it, and I am sorry."

"Stabbed me through the heart? Yes, I remember. So it really happened. But I seem to myself to be alive and not dead. Is that correct? Am I still alive?"

"Yes, it is, and you are. Ginger walked in a moment after you lost consciousness, threw Pepper into a deep sleep to neutralize her, and then threw your body into a shutdown mode, which bought time. I walked in a moment after that, and it was given me to bring healing to you, as we have discussed. Your body is mended to be as if the stabbing had never happened."

"What happens now?"

"Well, what do you think should happen?"

"I think, for now, I need to sleep a little more. After that—He decided to save me from being killed, and I shall have to take counsel about what else He has to say about this affair."

"Very good, Wendy. Yes, you sleep now, and then we shall see."

And so Wendy slept for a few more hours. Then she awoke and greeted Alicia and Diana once again. Wendy was about to ask Alicia what prophetic revelation, if any, was given to her. But at this point, Diana spouted some noise about avenging the evil through the law of the land. Wendy turned to her, smiled again, and said, "Dear Mama. Dear, sweet, Mama. But no, what you said is out of the question and off the table when the victim herself knows very well that the one who did it was not responsible for her actions at the time. She was insane—demented. I realized that intuitively and confirmed that with our special powers. No, to call for legal revenge would only be making trouble." Then she turned to Alicia. "Unless it is necessary in order to protect others from a homicidal maniac."

"No, not at all. Ginger took care of that before I brought you home."

"Well, then, there it is. Also, somehow this feels almost like a great opportunity."

Alicia said, "I think I understand. Do you want me to help you explain it to your mother, or do you want to try for it yourself?"

"Let me try. Mama, dear Mama, there was that horrible nightmare—years ago now—when you had to lie down with me and comfort me. At the time, it seemed to be merely something dreadful. But it turns out to have been almost like a Divine mercy. I saw that the old nightmare was being played out in real life. But as the affair unfolded, that very fact made me appreciate all the more the warnings I had received from Grandma and Ginger and Alicia. Yes, there was the movement of fate or destiny here, and what was happening was somehow what had to happen. This was not about me, and it was not about Pepper. When I realized that, it was very easy for me to stop fighting and submit to be carried along by Another far greater."

Alicia asked, "When did you realize that?"

"It developed gradually, but the full realization came when Pepper allowed me to open my eyes and look upon her. I did so as an act of defiance from having had my eyes held closed. When I saw her standing there naked, I understood she was just a pathetic crazy woman, in her own way almost as much a victim as I was. That resolved it for me."

Diana blurted out, "She defiled and ruined you! What about that?"

"No, Mama, she did not, in spite of everything. She believed she did, but that was just her lunatic fantasy. She spoke of the darkness that touched my body. Wrong—that is not how it works. No darkness touched my body—only female flesh. Whatever darkness she brought to the situation remained within her." Wendy turned to Alicia and said, "We went through this whole question of violation and defilement years ago, at the time of my old nightmare. Finally your counsel is fully effective. At last I understand." Then she turned back to her mother. "Mama, do you think I am degraded to be—what shall we say—some lesser being or whatever?"

"Well, I am not sure how to think of it exactly, but something like that, yes."

Wendy nodded eagerly in assent. "That is about what I thought when Alicia spoke to me years ago. Finally, at long last, I understand. As I said, that is not how it works. What happened was totally against my will, and so what I received was mere violence, of no greater moral or religious or spiritual importance than any other bodily violence I might suffer. If anyone is degraded, it is only the one who did it, not I. No, but I stand where I stood, within the order of Divine law and mercy. That is already enough to settle the whole concern. But it can be reinforced to be superabundant by reaffirming this order through Divine worship, and that is what I intend to do."

Somehow, this did not seem good enough for her mother, so Wendy reminded her how her formal initiation had "wiped out everything. Do you think to be purged in that way is just a magic gimmick for that one moment in a person's life? No, that is ridiculous. It is about the ongoing illumination from God, which burns up any contamination instantly. What if she had touched my body with darkness? As the Book says, God is light in Whom there is no darkness at all. To borrow from a modern philosopher, He is that Light compared with Whom all the suns and galaxies are nothing. No shadow can withstand His presence even for a moment."

Then Alicia called an end to it. "That will be all for now. She must relax and sleep again."

"But she has just slept and slept and slept!"

"Yes, I know. Come along, and let me explain it to you."

Alicia returned a few minutes later. Wendy was not yet asleep, and she asked, "Come to think of it, why do I feel so depleted?"

"As I explained to your mother, it is because your body has been heavily charged with paranormal energy, as Ginger called it, in the wrong way." Wendy had missed all the earlier conversations, and so Alicia laid it out for her. She was about to ask something else, but Alicia said, "No, we shall discuss it later. For now, you stay in bed as long as you need to, and get up only when you are ready."

Wendy did finally get up from bed a couple hours later. Alicia was still there. After her first meal of the day, Wendy turned to Alicia and asked, "What happens now?"

"What happens now? Well, something that will both help you wake up better and also address your mother's concerns." With that, she turned to Diana and said, "If we are going to talk about what defilement Wendy may have suffered, there is one point of reality to consider. A woman's body can be made somewhat cruddy from having such things happen to her. Well, Wendy was simply thrown into her bed yesterday without being washed."

That was all the mother needed. She dragged Wendy into the shower right then, refusing to accept any challenges or objections, and scrubbed her very thoroughly, taking an unusually long time to do so. The nightgown and slippers Wendy had worn were discarded, thrown away as garbage. All the cloths on her bed were removed and put aside to be washed. They would be washed twice before being used again. In the meantime, Diana made up her bed with other cloths that were clean from the last washing. Finally, when all had been accomplished, she relaxed.

Wendy was reluctant at first. Her initial feeling was that Alicia was a spicy character who had set her up for something. ("'Spicy character,' you say—I hope you knew that about me long before now.") But once she was in the shower and being washed, she felt the struggle was over and had been resolved in her favor, even though she had squawked like a wayward child. Wendy relaxed and allowed her body to be serviced. She found herself happy for it, even grateful to be taken care of in this way. She remained docile and submissive as her mother finally sat down, embraced her and held closely as if she were a little girl again, turned to Alicia, and said, "That takes care of those problems. So what next? What happens now?"

"Well, first of all, as regards any moral or religious or spiritual concerns, I think Wendy has kind of laid it out for us and said it all with what she said earlier today. Are you ready to accept that, Diana?"

"I think maybe my mind is, just barely. My guts are still burning."

"All right, fair enough—you have the right motherly instincts. As for her body, nothing exists to be resolved. There is no damage to her body from the ravishing to be healed apart from the question of the paranormal energy. The damage from the stabbing is already taken care of. There will not even be any scarring. All this has been given to me to know."

"Then where does it go from there?"

"Well, there is really no change in her status or condition that it should go anywhere. For the time being, she should continue more or less as she has been doing. For the time being. But—Wendy, do you want to tell her, or do you want me to?"

"You tell her. She may accept it better from you."

Alicia smiled sadly, nodded, and said, "Diana, remember about paranormal charge, and what the result might be? It has been given to me to know that what Ginger explained is all true, and the result will be what she was afraid of. Wendy will in fact conceive through parthenogenesis. This is not up for debate or decision. It is going to happen."

Diana turned to Wendy. "Do you say this also?"

"Yes, Mama. It seems to be in my mind as part of the package deal of accepting the movement of fate and destiny."

"But is it really your appointed destiny?"

"I think it must be. Even beyond my own feelings, there is what Ginger explained and Alicia has now confirmed. I have the rare prospect for parthenogenesis, and also the rare basis of what can activate that prospect. Given that these extraordinary facts have come together in this way, it would be just a little too ridiculous if it did not work out and I did not conceive."

Before anyone could say anything else or react in any way, Margaret came in, having returned from visiting a friend. Alicia took her through a quick summary of what had been discussed.

"Well, I am certainly glad everything else is right side up for Wendy, with no problem and nothing wrong. But as for conceiving from being ravished—no, that is not so good."

Wendy replied, "Well, Grandma, of course it is not so good, but it is a fact—it is, as they say, the situation on the ground. You tell me: What do those old predictions say?"

She was reduced to silence. Finally she managed to say, "It looks like this is one of the things foretold. You are to have exotic adventures with wondrous things. The first adventure was to be that you would receive motherhood by being ravished—or at least, that is the natural and obvious interpretation of what is written. I could not accept that, since that would certainly be a serious adventure, but hardly exotic or wondrous. Yet now here it is."

At this point Alfreda arrived, having come for the specific purpose of checking on Wendy. Alicia gave her a quick summary, including what Margaret had just said. When all this had been talked through and resolved, Alfreda said, "All right, so be it, and God help us all, including Ginger and Pepper. In the meantime, there is the pragmatic necessity. What about the forthcoming conception? Alicia, is it given to you to know when this is to be?"

"Yes. It is to be very soon now, at the point of ovulation in Wendy's current cycle."

Wendy said, "That is only about three weeks away. I hope that will be enough time to prepare." Then she looked to Alicia and said, "What is the point of all this? I mean, yes, there is the general basis for any woman who receives motherhood, and that is plenty right there. But with all the extraordinary business in my particular case, is there anything special about why this is happening here and now and with me?"

"That is not given to me now."

Then Wendy thought of something. She gasped with a look of horror on her face. "No! Dear God, no! I cannot have a child through parthenogenesis." She turned to Alicia. "You know about parthenogenesis. You explain it to them."

"Any child conceived through parthenogenesis would be an exact genetic copy of its mother, apart from mutations. Now, Wendy is genetically defective, and so her daughter will be genetically defective. But the working assumption has to be that there will not be any exotic fluke of luck this time of the kind that saved Wendy." Alicia turned to Wendy and said, "If He can arrange for all this to happen in the first place, then He can also arrange for it to work out rightly, in terms of having problems taken care of—or even whether the child is to live or die or whatever it may be. You must simply look to Him to see you and the child through."

"Can you tell me any more?"

"Not to panic—all in good time. Beyond that, no."

Alfreda brought up something else. "In addition to the question of conceiving, Wendy's reproductive system is weak. She may not be able to see the pregnancy through."

"Yes, I know. That too is covered under what I just said."

Alfreda continued. "All right, then, and as I said, God help us all. There is also the need to know where we all stand to avoid misunderstanding. Since Wendy is at the center of all this, we should start with her. Wendy, your feeling seems to be that of simply accepting the unfolding of fate and destiny. Is that correct?"

"Yes, that is the short way to say it. But that makes it sound like I am merely resigned to my fate. No, it is much more than that. I rejoice in God and the things of God. How shall I explain it? For most people, it is almost like simple faith to accept that there is the basis of fate and destiny underneath. Even for theoreticians like Alicia and me, it is generally just one notch above that. But I am given to see—*really* to see—just a little more. This is a tremendous privilege. I think I begin to know something of why Alicia has always seemed so extraordinarily happy, for much more is given to her than to most." Alicia smiled and nodded in assent.

"All right, does all this entail that you are ready to accept the whole basis of motherhood and see it through—conception, pregnancy, and childbirth—with no question and no nonsense, if He will grant that to you?"

"Yes, with all my heart. Also, it is not just about honoring the wondrous basis of destiny, although that would be plenty right there. I am genetically defective, and the course of my life has been crazy, but I am a *woman*, not some freak who belongs in the sideshow."

⸻

Beatrice had to explain what this meant.

⸻

"As a woman, my natural yearning is for motherhood. This is a crazy way for it to happen, but the fact that it is happening at all is like a great gift. I had given up hope for it."

"Assuming it is granted to you, and the child is born alive and healthy enough, what—if anything—is in your mind about whether to keep and raise it yourself?"

"Again, my natural yearning as a woman would be to do exactly that. But this is getting ahead of the game. Too much can happen between now and then. We have to wait and see."

"All right, I guess it is clear enough where Wendy stands. Does anyone else have any questions?" No, no more questions. "Then what about the rest of us?" This was quickly and easily answered. All of them stood with Wendy. They would back her up and do what they could to see her through. When Amanda and Theodora were brought in later on, they concurred fully.

For the time being, Alfreda concluded the discussion by saying, "Then it is settled among us. Even though her body is undamaged, it will probably be best for Wendy to see her physician as soon as possible and tell her as much as possible. If you want, Wendy, I can go with you and do most of the talking." Wendy accepted this offer gratefully. "Also, all of us should try to learn as much as we can about parthenogenesis."

Several days after this discussion, Alfreda took Wendy to the physician, and as she had promised, did most of the talking.

"Ravished by another woman, eh? That is relatively rare, but it is not so rare as all that, especially nowadays."

"Yes, and it is worse than that. The one who did it claimed to have magic powers or something like that, and so Wendy might get pregnant as a result, through parthenogenesis. The assailant and her sister—who was not involved in the assault—had some spicy story that most of Wendy's germ cells, her ova, are worthless, as you told Wendy long ago. But they said there were some few mixed in that could be activated by what happened and that it would just be the luck of the draw. So what then? Can you verify or disprove whether there is any such possibility? I mean, of course, regarding her ova—not the claim about the special powers."

The physician checked Wendy out and went back over her records. Then she said, "Oho! Yes, I think I can verify that it could be so. At least, it is barely possible. Wendy may be one of the relatively rare women for whom it may be possible. As I look back over the record and see about the ova from her we examined, most were totally worthless. But there was one that could have gone that way, at least in theory, if everything had gone exactly right. If there was one, then there are probably some others in there as well. So, yes, it looks to be possible for her—again, at least in theory." She paused and then said, "Wendy, assuming it is truly in prospect for you, do you hope you will conceive from this affair or that you will not?"

"With all my heart, I hope I shall."

The physician's mind was full at this answer. What she said was, "All right, then. So be it. It looks like there is no damage and no infection, but we must wait for the report on the blood we drew. In the meantime, I shall keep my eye on her. I shall also research the whole question of parthenogenesis." She learned from Wendy where she was in her reproductive cycle. "All right, that will be the first thing to look for. Be happy, Wendy. If it works out as you hope, your picture will be in the medical textbooks."

Two weeks after this, Wendy happened to be at Alfreda's place and found Alicia there as well. "Hello, Wendy. It is very nice to see you. Please, sit down." The tone of her voice was more magisterial than usual. At first Wendy was puzzled. She looked to Alfreda, who nodded in assent. Then she understood.

"Is this it, then?"

"Yes, child, it is. But Wendy, there is nothing to be afraid of. You are not here to be punished or anything like that. Please, you must speak freely."

"Even though I have not yet conceived, let alone had my body awash in hormones, I am already thinking more like a mother. I am less concerned to ask and to seek for myself and more concerned to ask and to seek for my child-to-be. When am I to conceive?"

"The day after tomorrow. What do you ask for the child, and what—if anything—do you ask for yourself?"

"I remember my old training. Once again, there is the concern in my mind I may not know what I should ask. So I begin with that. As regards your gift of prophecy, I ask to know what I should ask."

"Once again, there is nothing to be afraid of. I am not here to trick you or to catch you in the details of your exact words. So long as you are honest and ask in good faith, He is looking to provide for you, not the opposite.—Even if you have corrupt motives, you need only say so openly and be willing to accept correction, and there will be no need to be afraid."

"Well, for my child, I guess I want what any mother would want. I want all and only the best for her. I would ask that her eternal destiny be assured or guaranteed, if that were possible." Alicia frowned and shook her head in negation. "No, of course not. Then I ask that she be not genetically defective, that there be no problems or complications, nothing untoward, that the gestation go well for her, and that she be born alive and healthy as a baby girl can be. As for her eternal destiny, I ask at least that she survive long enough and be fully and formally brought into the order of Divine Redemption with no problem or nonsense."

"All right, fine—so be it. Granted."

Wendy was almost ready to break down and weep with joy. "It is really just that simple—just that straight out?"

"Yes, of course—what else should it be? It is what I told you. The other way to say it is that there is trouble only for those who are looking for trouble."

"How much may I ask for?"

"Ask freely, Wendy. Ask for anything and everything, for yourself and the child, so long as you are honest and ask in good faith. You let Him decide what is or is not appropriate."

"Was my grandmother right, that I am to die less than ten years from now?"

"Yes, I am afraid so. Sorry, Wendy."

"I am concerned about leaving her motherless. Can you tell me how that will work out?"

"Not at this time. But ask freely what is really in your heart."

"Then I ask that whatever may happen, He will take care of her as well as may be and keep her from being ruined or led astray by any problem along that line."

"Yes, agreed—granted, and so be it."

"For myself, I ask that my relevant medical problems, including the weakness of my reproductive system, be corrected in order that I may be able to see the pregnancy through and provide for the child as long as it is given me to do so. If I could, I would ask that—if may be—all my other medical problems be corrected as well."

"But of course you can ask!"

"Then yes, I ask for all of it, for myself as well as for the child."

"Yes, you have it all. Granted, and so be it."

"I ask also for patience and courage to see me through the whole process of conception, pregnancy, and childbirth, and for wisdom and insight, as well as patience and courage, to guide me through the exercise of motherhood beyond that."

"Yes, agreed—you have it. So be it—granted."

"Is there anything else that I should ask but do not know enough to ask?"

"No, not for now."

"Then finally, for the one illumination of my soul that includes all the others, I ask that I be kept rightly mindful of Him in all this."

"Yes, granted—agreed, and so be it."

When she awoke the next morning, Wendy felt better than she could remember feeling ever before. She understood why. Her clinical problems that she could never outgrow were at long last resolved. She cried out to God with extra praise and thanksgiving, and then went on.

The day after that, Wendy conceived through parthenogenesis. Her mother and grandmother saw her at the breakfast table with an idiotically blissful look on her face. Diana did not understand at first, but Margaret did. "So this is it? The child's life is begun?"

"Yes, Grandma."

"I am puzzled at your attitude, Wendy. It is the right attitude to have, and Lord love you for it. But I wonder how you manage it. To appreciate intellectually what you said about fulfilling destiny and all the rest of it is very good, fine, and dandy. But generally, a woman in your situation takes a long time to get over the emotional shock, if she can ever get over it. Yet you were ready to go the day after. How so?"

"I have thought about this and explored within myself, and I believe it is a combination of three things. First, given that a woman is to be ravished and conceive as a result, what happened to me is perhaps the best-case scenario or mildest version. Most women like that are compelled to find the experience much more harsh and ugly than I did, even though what happened to me was certainly bad enough. The attempted murder was very harsh, yet even that worked out handily for me in a strange way, by showing clearly that what happened with the whole affair was mere violence and nothing more.

"Second, I grew up being in and out of hospitals. That being so, I was kind of used to it, and so it was less of a shock for me than for others. My body has been handled, poked, prodded, scanned, and everything else so much it is not even funny. I have been explored inside as well as outside, including that specific region of my body. Why do you think I was undamaged from being ravished? Or, to be more specific, what do you think that statement means in this context? Yes, I was undamaged, but only relative to what I was going in. I was and am pure as not having given myself for erotic interplay. But I did not have unspoiled freshness of body, and I did not have the naiveté of mind through lack of experience commonly spoken of as innocence.

"Third, and I believe most of all, there is that paranormal energy. It made me conceive, but as Ginger has explained, it also has a mild euphoric effect."

Beatrice paused to explain. "Wendy was right about those three factors, but she was not fully aware of all that was involved until long after. As Wendy understood, the differentiation of the sexes is indeed given by God, with all that fact entails. In the back of her mind, she realized one of the more noteworthy things it entails. No valid sexual union results from erotic interaction between people of the same sex, regardless of what bodily interplay may be involved. As I say, this point is really very clear, given that the basic differentiation of the sexes is from God. Wendy's old view of women as being unmarked had prepared her to develop and accept this more serious-minded concern. But she still thought, although in a different way and on another basis, to have sex with another woman was almost like nothing, something null and void, except insofar as to do so dishonored her basic character and status as a woman. But motherhood is the central function of a woman as a woman. For this very reason, to conceive from what happened, so far from being an extra hardship imposed, was very much like something to redeem the situation." Then Beatrice resumed her narrative.

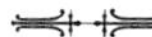

From the day of the conception, all went smoothly enough. There was much questioning from her physician and others, and there was much testing, but eventually the parthenogenesis was clearly proved. In the meantime, the pregnancy ran its course with no problems and nothing untoward. Just under nine weeks after the thirty-first anniversary of her own birth, Wendy gave birth to a very healthy baby girl, to whom she gave the name Anna. About seven weeks later, Anna was fully and formally initiated into the order of Divine Redemption, with no problem or nonsense, as her mother had asked.

On this occasion, Elizabeth was present, along with Theodora. After the rituals were completed, they were at lunch together.

Wendy could tell that something was puzzling Elizabeth, and so she invited the girl to ask freely. "Well, Aunt Amanda said you were made to conceive through parthenogenesis by some crazy trick, but I am left wondering."

"Yes, right. Ginger explained it to me. Given my old clinical problems, most of my female germ cells, my ova, were worthless, but with some few, there was the failure of meiosis, and so there was the full genetic structure—a copy of what I myself had. This failure of meiosis is rare, but not all *that* rare. Thus, there was no need for fertilization in order to provide part of the genetic structure. However, fertilization has other functions as well. One of these is to provide instructions to the cell on which genes are to be active and which are to be dormant. In my case, my body was flooded with what Ginger called 'paranormal energy' when Pepper ravished me. This flooding caused that information to be copied from the cells of my own body's tissues into those few ova. Ginger said it would be like shining a brilliant light through a translucent medium and thereby transferring onto a screen information about objects embedded within the medium. Also, with fertilization, there is a calcium spike that activates the embryo. In my case, by the luck of the draw, one of these ova came up within my ordinary reproductive cycle before the flooding with paranormal energy had worn off, and so my own body provided the spike."

Then Elizabeth said, "Wendy, may I ask you a very personal question?"

Because of both the context and her special powers, Wendy knew the question was something about having been ravished, although she did not know the details. Against her better judgment, she replied, "You go ahead and ask, and I shall see what I think."

"When you were ravished, you say it was against your will, but you say you submitted to it as your appointed destiny. How can both things be true together?"

Theodora rebuked her daughter. "Anything to do with an incident like that is something you ask only in private, if you must ask at all."

But Wendy said, "No, Aunt Dorry, it is all right. I knew she was going to ask about that incident somehow, and I allowed it, even though it was against my better judgment. But that question—no, nothing like that. It is a very good question, Elizabeth. I have often talked to my students about the question of how chance, choice, and destiny or fate come together as in some way the great question of all questions. Now we come to the other side of that concern—how people are called upon to experience and respond to those facts. Do you understand?"

"Yes, I think so."

"There can be all the difference in the world between submitting and consenting. Yes, I saw what was happening as what must happen, and I accepted it *as* what must happen. But what that involved was, I submitted to suffer abuse, to have violence inflicted upon me wrongfully. That is not consent—it is almost exactly the opposite. The very terms in which I thought of it involved that I recognized what was happening as against my will, and I submitted to it *as being* against my will. I did not cooperate in terms of assisting or playing along. I merely became like a rag doll to allow what was going to happen to go ahead and happen. That is how those concerns fit together."

⁂

Beatrice had to explain the comparison with the rag doll to the others.

⁂

"I kind of understand, but not completely."

"Well, I hope you understand someday, but please God, not the way I had to learn."

"May I ask something else?"

"No, Elizabeth. Not here and now. Your mother was right, you know. A thing like this is to be asked about only in private, if at all. I agreed to it the first time, and that was my fault. Later."

This time, Wendy knew much more specifically what was coming. So she obtained permission from Theodora to tell Elizabeth what she knew might be needed.

Later on, Elizabeth asked, "Wendy, may I ask you about Anna?"

Wendy knew what was coming, but she said, "Ask freely."

"In spite of—how she got here, you were totally willing to accept the conception and then the pregnancy and see it all through, with no question about it. I know what the book says about what people are supposed to do in such cases, and I know what you say about fulfilling your destiny and all that, but I think there must be something more."

Wendy smiled sadly and said, "It has to do with my own personal history. First of all, you know about the clinical problems I used to have. Because of those problems, I did not mature naturally or normally. I had to be worked through it artificially when I was fifteen, rather late in the game. There was some question at that time of dangerous side effects. I was afraid that the worst case might happen. But I had to realize it would be better for me to fulfill my destiny as a girl by growing up to be an adult woman, even if I lived for only a short time, than to live a long span while remaining a mere child. I thought that way then, and I still think that way now. If I am going to be an adult woman, then I have to see it through and fulfill my destiny as a woman, which turns out to include exercising motherhood, even though in this way. In view of all these facts, I had to decide whether, as Aunt Freddy would say, what I claim to believe in is more than just words. This challenge became pointed when the situation with Anna came up. By the grace and mercy of God, I decided rightly. So there it is."

But Elizabeth thought this answer sounded more like a good story than the real basis. Wendy replied, "What I said is true, and it was very much part of my motivation, but yes—there is also much more, having to do with another point of my personal history. Now, Elizabeth, once you hear it, there is no going back, and it just might turn your mind inside out. Are you sure you want to hear it now?"

"Yes, I am."

"All right, then, so be it. Remember you had fair warning. This point of history makes me take questions of destiny more seriously than some other people do, and it also gives rise to a kind of debt or duty of honor that I had to fulfill. Do you know the point of my own history I am talking about?"

"No, not really."

"Do you know how I myself got here?"

"Well, no, not exactly. I know your father was murdered long before you were born, and I know there is some sort of dark secret, but that is all."

"Do you know my father, Arvid, was adopted as a child?"

"Yes, of course. I have met Maria many times."

"Yes, so you have. All right, you are sixteen years old now. I guess that is old enough for you to know much more. My father, Arvid, was one of our grandmother's children, but he was wrongly removed from the family when both he and my mother were far too young to remember. Many years later, they came together by chance and were manipulated into having illicit sex with each other. When they learned the truth about their kinship, they broke off the relationship, but by then it was too late. I had already been conceived. Arvid had been sterilized, supposedly irreversibly, long before he took up with my mother. But by a fluke, his body had overcome the sterilization. That has been known to happen sometimes. Arvid was murdered a few days before my mother learned of her pregnancy. He died without knowing either of the reversal of the sterilization or of my existence, let alone being able to do anything to provide for me or my mother." Wendy paused to let the girl absorb what she had said and then said, "Now, Elizabeth, what I have just told you is a large load. Do you understand all this?"

"Yes. Yes, I do."

"All right, then. Beyond that, children of such relationships are especially at risk to be genetically defective, and that is what happened to me. Later, at just the right point in her pregnancy, my mother contracted rubella. That should have finished me off. Instead, by a fantastical fluke of luck, it saved me by offsetting the genetic problems. Again, Elizabeth, do you understand all this?"

"Well, yes."

"All right. Now the point of all this is that I am here only because all these things came together in this extraordinary way. That being so, it kind of looks like there was something remarkable within the order of Divine Providence behind the very fact I existed at all and then managed to last long enough even to be born alive. That being so, it would be just a little too ridiculous for me *not* to honor points about fate and destiny. I have to respect all that, and I have to figure what was good enough for me is good enough for Anna as well."

"But your mother was not horribly abused as you were."

Again, Wendy smiled sadly. "No. But it is almost as if she might as well as have been. What happened with her is not so many notches away from that. Here is the other way to say it. What am I? To put it bluntly and crudely, I am the bastard child of my mother's unwitting incest with her long-lost brother. On top of that, she contracted rubella when she was pregnant with me. The standard or customary way for her in those days would have been to have me aborted. But instead, she saw it through, and so here I am. So with Anna, I figured I was honor bound to respect the precedent my own mother set by taking care of what has to be."

"But you love Anna dearly."

"As opposed to merely having my head full of stuff about duty and honor and all that. Right. Of course I love her dearly, Elizabeth—that is one of the natural functions of a mother. How to explain it? When a woman in my situation does *not* love the child dearly, it is because she thinks of the child as an outgrowth of the original violation or something like that. Well, I cannot speak for others. But as for myself, that is not how I think of Anna. She is given *to me*, to be *my* daughter, as a gift from God. The one who ravished me was just His unwitting servant." Wendy could have said more but decided to leave it there for the time being.

At that point, however, an alarm went off in her head. Very gently, as she had done with Pepper, Wendy examined Elizabeth's mind. Yes, of course. The girl was not mouthing off as an exercise in insolent presumption. She was crying out in terrified anguish.

"What are you really afraid of, Elizabeth?"

Given what Wendy and Theodora had explained, she could see that a girl might still be at least technically pure if she were merely raped by a boy or a man, but not if she became pregnant from it. Surely she would then be thoroughly defiled. "Wrong. She is still as pure as she was going in regarding not having given herself for erotic interplay. To exercise natural motherhood—to conceive, become pregnant, and give birth—is not an act of erotic interplay. She stands where she stood within the order of Divine law and mercy. To be sure, whatever unspoiled freshness of mind and body she may have had is much more thoroughly ruined than it would be if there were only the original violation.

But that is not the same thing." Wendy paused to let Elizabeth absorb this, and then, "Why do you ask? Has something happened to you? Have you been tampered with?" No, she was merely concerned about the general danger.

But Wendy could detect that this was not correct. To be sure, the girl was not lying—she was speaking sincerely from her own standpoint. As she had said, there was the concern with the general danger. Yet there was something else, although it was still subliminal for Elizabeth—below the threshold of her conscious awareness. Now that she thought of it, Wendy herself realized that something momentous was coming. Her own powers had latched onto this fact, and it had been in the back of her mind, but she had somehow ignored it until now—perhaps because she did not yet know enough about what it was.

But for the moment, she kept this concern to herself. What she said was, "Come, let us go back and join the others again."

CHAPTER SIXTEEN

Two weeks after Anna's formal initiation, the whole group was gathered at Theodora's house for a private celebration. Elizabeth went to Wendy and asked to speak with her privately. When they were apart from the others, she asked Wendy, "Is it true what Mother and Aunt Amanda and Grandma say? That the women in our family have special powers?"

"Yes, it is. I noticed it in our grandmother before I asked her the first time, as a child. She admitted it and said she would explain it when I was old enough. What about you?"

"Yeah, I noticed it too. Is it also true what they say, that you have the greatest power among us?"

"Yes, that too."

"Then I need to ask you." What Wendy had found in her mind had gone beyond being subliminal. In the past week or ten days, there had been a growing foreboding in her mind. "Am I just crazy, or is something going to happen—something big?"

"Only God knows what is going to happen, but yes, I sense something big is coming."

"Then I feel the need to confess something in order to prepare." She paused, then forced herself to speak. "Wendy, I have been thinking about what you said two weeks ago. I would find it horrible to be raped, and I would be extremely sorry if it happened, and I would rather die than be raped. If I were to be raped, my impulse would be that I would then kill myself. To be killed—well, all women die. But to be dishonored as a woman and then go through life as something dishonored—no, that is too much."

"Yes, of course, except that is not how it works. A woman's or girl's worthiness to be honored cannot be destroyed or diminished in that way. No one is or can be made less worthy because someone commits some violence, sexual or otherwise, upon her body. It is not about such accidents. To be worthy or unworthy belongs to a level of a person above all that."

"Yeah, and I knew all that intellectually, and that was what kept me from the full decision that I would kill myself if that were to happen. But it was still too much for me to face. But after talking with you, I got to thinking. If it is good enough for you—and for some other women I respect and admire—to go through life having been violated, then I guess it can be good enough for me, if need be. When I reached that point, I came to appreciate what the book says a victim should do in such cases. I think it might still be my *impulse* to kill myself, but I hope I would look to God to see me through. I need to talk to you more about it, but for now, whatever He allows is what I have to accept. I must look to Him to see me through rape or murder or whatever. But I am still very much afraid."

"Good. You'd be a fool otherwise." Elizabeth found this surprising. "Honey child, do you think being brave is about being not afraid? No, no. It is about not being *too much* afraid, not being merely like a frightened child. But really, the point is to look to Him and allow Him to escort one through the valley of the shadow of death, as the Book says." After letting the girl absorb this, Wendy went on, "But good enough for me and others like me? No, not at all. It is as you said. By the grace and mercy of God, I can ride the tiger through the minefield."

⁂

Beatrice explained this double metaphor to the others.

⁂

"But that is what exactly what I must do," Wendy said. Then, after a moment, an alarm went off in her head once again. "Elizabeth, please, let me help you. Let all of us help you. What is there you have not yet told me?"

Elizabeth blurted out, "Wendy, I know this sounds silly, but do you believe there are monsters running free in the world? I mean real monsters, not just very bad people. That is the fear that keeps growing in my mind. It is almost like I am going to be ravished by one of those beings. Almost like, but not exactly. I do not know how else to say it."

"Elizabeth, listen to me. It does not sound silly to me or to your mother or to your grandmother. We know too much for that. Yes, I believe it, and so do they. But we do not merely believe. We *know* there are such things out there. The women of our family have known this for generations back, although they have had only scraps and fragments. As for how to say it—what you said is better than you know. I told you I sensed something big is coming. I would not say what you said exactly, but then again I myself am not sure how else to say it. It is still early enough in the day, and the whole gang is here. I think maybe we shall all sit down together and discuss it this very day."

This took a little arranging, but it was done. Elizabeth told her story. Then she was dismissed, being still just a little too young to be entrusted with all the family secrets, although she had already been told much. Wendy spoke of what she had sensed. Amanda and Theodora said they had had similar feelings. Margaret said so as well, and she spoke of what the women of the family had long known.

Then Wendy began. "What I have spoken of thus far is within the framework of knowledge and capabilities I have had for about the past two years. But I think now I can take it further than that."

Margaret spoke up. "Wendy, how so? Our powers have never reached that far, not even at the upper limit."

"No, and neither did my powers, until Pepper ravished me. Ginger explained it all to me. When my body was supercharged with paranormal energy, it caused me to conceive, and it also had a mild euphoric effect. As Ginger told me it would, this euphoria faded in several weeks, but by then my body was awash in hormones, and I did not need it to help me through anymore. However, I was not exactly left empty. The feeling I had was that of being expanded or enlarged—there is no other way to say it. With this expansion, the limits of what powers I could have were increased, although my powers were not thereby increased. I grew into these limits and came to have greater powers as my motherhood progressed and I gained greater experience of female functioning. I increased to my full capacity after ten days or two weeks of giving milk to Anna."

At this point, Timothy, Elizabeth's father and Theodora's husband, burst out. "Wendy, excuse me. I know you mean well, as do all of you, and I appreciate your concern, but do you ever listen to yourself? Do *any* of you ever listen to yourselves? We are talking about the prospects of my daughter to be ravished by a thing that goes bump in the night, based on what can be discovered by a woman with special magic powers of perception and knowledge—even more than the rest of her family—because she herself was ravished by a crazy woman with magic powers. Does anything seem even a little wrong to you—to *any* of you—about all this?"

Wendy kept herself one notch above lashing out. "Yes, something seems wrong to me. It seems very wrong to me that I was ravished by *anyone*—woman, lunatic, magic powers, or whatever. I rejoice in how God has, as they say, produced straight writing out of the crooked lines Pepper provided. I do not hold it against Pepper. I know too much about her and about the whole affair. But my mind has been twisted by those crooked lines and may well remain so for as long as this crazy course of life continues for me within this crazy world. Yes, Timothy. Something seems very wrong to me."

"I understand, Wendy, and I am very sorry for what happened to you. I do not mean to belittle it—not at all. But the concern over such wrongness works both ways. I have to protect my daughter or bust, and that means I have to look to hard facts in order to do so."

"Good. Then we are agreed. No, I am sorry—of course I understand. You do not have such powers, and so your natural tendency is to think all this talk is just froth and fantasy and that we are just a bunch of goofy women. Perhaps that can be left as a debate for another day. That will depend on your answer to my next question. Do you claim positive assurance there are *not* things that go bump in the night, out there somewhere?"

A whole world of lies died on his lips as he conceded, "I think the whole idea is totally ridiculous. It goes against everything I have ever learned about real life in the real world. But positive assurance? No, of course not. What was that marvelous phrase that author made up for those fools who build their lives on the confident certainty there are *not* more things than are dreamt of in men's philosophies? Anyhow, no. I am not one of those, Wendy."

"Good. That makes it much easier. So then, let me ask you just this. If perchance there are such monsters, and if perchance Elizabeth is especially at risk, what then? By which I mean, what would you propose doing to protect her?"

Timothy forced himself to take the question seriously. "Well, as you say, Wendy, we must look to God and the things of God. The obvious thing is to persuade Lizzy to look to Him all the more and to arrange special prayers, blessings, and all the rest of it. If need be, we see what else may or may not be called for from there. But even in the worst case—whatever He may allow her to suffer—then at least her eternal destiny will be assured in any event."

"Very good. So far we are in full agreement." The man found this surprising. "Timothy, what is it you imagine? I am not a witch—at least not anymore. None of us is a witch. We are devoted handmaids of the Lord God. That being so, of course we agree what you just said is primary. I did not speak of it only because it is understood among us. I skipped ahead to what else we may or may not be called on to do. But you are right, of course."

"Very well, then," Timothy said. "What time frame are we looking at? Can you tell me how long before these monsters try whatever they are going to try?"

Alicia spoke up. "I can tell you this. It is given me to know that her danger is not immediate. There is time enough, but there is also no time to waste. She must begin to prepare at once. Call her back. We must speak to her, and then I must tell you more when she has left again."

When she had been told the point they had reached, Elizabeth turned to Alicia and said, "May I ask what is to happen to me?"

"Yes, of course. Ask freely, and I shall tell you what is or is not given to me."

"Am I in fact to be raped or ravished by such monsters?"

"Yes and no. Yes, you will be violated in some way that is specifically sexual, but it will be exotic. And so no, not in the sense you mean. It will not be like the ordinary ways women are raped or ravished." She paused and said, "I am sorry, Elizabeth. You will be violated sexually in some special way, but you will not be spared anything. It will be worse—much worse—than the standard ways of being violated."

"Can you tell me what is to happen?"

"No, not now. Maybe later, and maybe not. I must wait and see what He gives me."

"Will I die or be killed from it?"

"The short answer is yes, as you mean it, but somehow that too will be exotic."

"How long do I have?"

Alicia smiled sadly. "As the Book says, He does not willingly afflict or grieve the people. He does not allow any more harshness to happen than He has to. Relax, child. You will be at least genuinely begun as an adult woman. You will not suffer and die this way as a mere child, which you still are in some measure. You will know well enough when you have arrived."

"Can you give me any advice?"

"Don't delay or put it off. Don't waste any time. Begin at once to look to God all the more. Be devoted to Him all the more, and turn to Him to see you through all the more—always and in all things. If there is anything to be resolved or forgiven, see to it as quickly as you can. That goes for everything else as well as for this, although especially for this, of course. But take care of all unfinished business as soon as you can. Your danger is not immediate, but the time will go by more quickly than you imagine. So as I say, don't delay. Start this very moment so far as you can. And learn as much as you can of what He has given the people to know. Don't bother trying to learn about things that go bump in the night. That will not help you. Don't bother about the powers your relatives have or what they know or anything like that—that is another path, not yours. As for what you have inherited along that line, do only what you must—otherwise leave it aside. Look to God at once, and let Him kindle love within you, and go through whatever time you have left on that basis. That is the right advice in general, of course, but in your case, the concern is especially pointed."

By this time, Elizabeth had learned of how short Wendy's life was to be, and so, as if by way of confirmation, she asked, "Am I to die before Wendy?"

"Yes, child. I am sorry. Yes, quite clearly so."

"Will I suffer the ultimate horror? I mean, will I myself be turned into a monster?"

Alicia paused, prepared, and said, "Yes, child, you will. I am very sorry. But not to worry. No blame or discredit will attach to you, for it will be totally against your will. You will not be allowed to hurt anyone else, and your eternal destiny will not be in any jeopardy."

At this news, Elizabeth showed considerable relief. Then she spoke. Her voice was more that of an adult person than her mother was used to hearing from her. "Every girl grows up afraid of being raped, and so did I. But I have always known somehow that yes, there was that, but there was also something more—something different. I have always been aware that something dark and terrible was coming—like being raped, somehow—but far worse, as bad as it is to be raped. In the past few days, I became afraid something was to happen soon, but I could not see enough to put it together with this old fear. I am still concerned about being raped, as every girl is, and I am far more afraid of this, but I am almost glad now that finally I understand. Am I to be killed off as a monster?"

"There will be some complication involved, but the short answer is yes."

"Is that how the danger I will be is to be neutralized?"

"Yes, very much so."

"Will the nightmare filth also be purged from me by this death?"

"Yes, child—at least in the sense you mean. You will be restored to whatever purity as a devoted handmaid of God you had going in."

"Then I should hope to be killed off as soon as possible once this happens."

"Yes, very much so."

"Will I be able to give myself to this fate? To surrender and submit to death?"

"No, you will not. I am sorry. Your mind will be too badly distorted to allow for that. But once again, not to worry. You will be granted euthanasia very quickly. And yes, it will be euthanasia. Your death will not be harsh. You will not be abused or tormented. Your death will be quick, clean, and merciful." With this, Elizabeth showed even greater relief. Then Alicia said, "Now go, child, and fall to your prayers. We must talk more." Elizabeth complied.

When she was gone, Timothy complained to Alicia, "You spoke to her in riddles."

"On some points, yes, but only because I had to. But the main thrust is clear enough."

"Yes, and what about that? As for what is clear, do you really expect me to accept that?"

"For now, no—of course not. Later on, when you see it happening, you will accept it because you will see there is no other choice."

While Timothy sat—wanting to explode but being reduced to silence—Wendy spoke up. "Ginger told me, and you confirmed, that I would have some serious role in casting down the evil of things that go bump in the night, if I made it through being ravished. Well, I did, and so what then? Is this business with Elizabeth part of that?"

"Yes, very much so."

"Is her situation part of a larger scheme or pattern of evil?"

"Again, yes—very much so."

She paused and then asked further. "Something very terrible has just come into my mind. I say what I am about to say because from my childhood, I was taught to believe in having it out in the open and calling it by its right name, however ugly it is. There is no nice way, so I ask you straight out. Alicia, am I to be the one who euthanizes Elizabeth?"

"Yes, Wendy. Yes, you are. I am sorry you have to live with such horror, but there it is. I can tell you this much to comfort you. It is horrible to contemplate or anticipate. But it is like what I told her father. When you see it happening, you will find it acceptable, because you will appreciate what must be."

With this, Elizabeth's father exploded. "This meeting is ended! This is my place, and I want you all out of here right now. Wendy, once again, I am sure you mean well, but you will not expect me to sit calmly with a woman who is looking to kill my daughter, regardless of what ridiculous fantasy from a cheaply written novel is supposed to justify it. There will be the religious points we agreed to, not to worry, and that will be all. Now goodbye, all of you."

As they were leaving, Alicia turned to Theodora and said, "You make him understand."

When the others were gone, she did so. "Dear Timmy, you have the right instincts as a father, but in this one case, they are leading you the wrong way. Ever since before we were married, you knew about my special powers. You knew also from Lizzy's infancy that, like me, she is a double-dose girl, with all that entails. But you know as well as anyone that with power comes responsibility. You always knew that this day—or some other day like this, or worse—might come. We both knew, and we knew it was much more than just a remote possibility. Furthermore, with Alicia's gift that has come into play, it is even more. It is like that ends all question about it. Lizzy is only sixteen years old, but she is more mature than some, and she is enough of a woman to make some of her own serious decisions. She is not a mere child anymore, and many girls as young as she is or younger have taken big risks and even died for what they believe in." Timothy was about to interrupt, but Theodora cut him off. "If sixteen is not old enough, what is? How old should she be to suffer her fate? If anything should happen to her, a great chunk will be torn out of my heart as well as yours, for whatever remaining years of life in this world may be granted to me. But what other choice do we have? 'Oh God, please let us off because we are too much afraid to accept that whatever may happen to her is in Your hand?' As Alfreda would say, this is one of those times when we must decide whether what we say we believe in is more than just words. As Wendy would say, it looks like this is one of those things that must happen."

"But she is not a woman—not yet, as Alicia acknowledged. You ask how old she must be. Well, I'll tell you how old. When she is old enough to have her powers begin to awaken within her, that will be the time for the responsibility you spoke of to be at issue." Theodora knew enough to keep quiet and let him burn himself out. "Yes, I know what the answer is to what I just said. The problem is with this crazy talk about monsters. That is just too much to accept."

"Dear, sweet, Timmy—you are forgetting that there is a parallel case we already know about. Someone could be infected with rabies and be turned into a homicidal maniac, all through no fault of her own. She might then have to be killed off in order to protect other people. So you see what can happen to an innocent girl—to any girl—even though she is and remains virtuous and pure in her devotion. She could be turned into a monster to be destroyed, even against her will."

At this point, he simply broke down and cried out to God in anguish. Then, "Is it any easier for you as a woman with special powers?"

"As a woman, no—not at all. As for my special powers, no—not really, or at least not yet. I can appreciate in some measure that this is what has to be. That makes me calmer and more docile. But easier? No, for I do not yet see at all how or why this business is anything more than a pure blot on the world He has made. We just have to ask Him to see us through."

And so life went on for the time being. For Elizabeth, it began that very night as she fell to her prayers. For Wendy, it took just a little longer.

The next morning, someone showed up at Wendy's door. "Ginger!" After they exchanged greetings and pleasantries, Ginger explained. Pepper had traveled back to their own land and stayed there. As for herself, it had finally been arranged for her to come and stay in Wendy's part of the world on a longer-term basis, although she would go back eventually. Then she spoke of Pepper's shame and sorrow and asked about Wendy's child. "Dear Ginger, you must have your sister come here again and meet with me someday, that we may be fully reconciled. But for now, yes, come and meet my daughter."

After this had been taken care of, Ginger said, "I am here on business. First of all, Pepper is not a wicked woman, in spite of what she did in her madness. Quite the opposite. She was horrified and ready to kill herself, but Alicia persuaded her to stay and help clean up the mess. That is what she is doing. Children can be expensive, and so she has sent a chunk of wealth and will go on sending what she can when she can." Wendy appreciated this. She could have gotten by without it, at least for the time being, but it would be very helpful. "Second, I know something of what you are involved in. What we discussed approaches quickly. You must start to prepare for your work against the nightmare filth. What have you observed, and how much can you tell me?" Wendy confided in her, sharing all the main points. "Right, then. I am sorry that you will be the one who must provide for your cousin. I can only hope Alicia was right, that you will find it acceptable at the time. Anyhow, I shall do what I can. I shall teach you about your expansion, and I shall watch and wait, ready to act if and when may be." They spent that day and the next having Wendy learn all she could. Then Ginger said, "You are as ready as you are going to be. May God be with you."

The next day, Ginger came and saw Wendy again. Once again, it was on business. "Things are starting to happen, faster than I expected. The tempo has picked up even since yesterday. I taught you what I could about your expanded powers, but much can be learned only through experience. You must begin practicing at once. Today and tomorrow I shall lead you through some trivial activities, but then you must begin more serious work. Not to worry—I shall supervise you at first and be ready to intervene in case of trouble." That day and the next went well enough. The day after that got to be interesting.

"Very good, Wendy. You are as ready as you can be to begin serious work. Your mother is a very nice lady and all that. It is a very sad thing that she must go through life with her usefulness greatly diminished, suffering those sessions of being dazed. It is especially sad now that your grandmother is starting to show her age. An elderly lady needs her adult daughter's care, an adult daughter still needs her mother's help and affection, and a baby girl needs her grandmother."

"What are you saying, Ginger?"

"In addition, of course, a woman needs to have appropriate clarity of mind in order to be good for anything, for herself as well as for others. It would work out very handily if Diana's adult daughter began the work with her expanded powers by repairing the damage from that old banging of the head so that Diana would be as good as if it had never happened."

"Are you crazy? I am not a physician. I do not know the intricacies of the brain. If I try that, we can expect me to make her even worse!"

Wendy was still at her grandmother's house. Other women of Wendy's age had long since moved out of their childhood homes. Very often, this happened when a woman got married. But in many cases, this happened even if—like Wendy—they had never married. Wendy had considered doing so, but her ongoing clinical problems had made this excessively difficult until very late in the game. There had not, in fact, been the fully clear basis to do this until her clinical problems had finally been resolved, just before she conceived Anna, and then there was that whole affair to be concerned about. So now, Wendy and Ginger were at Margaret's house, and it was Margaret who answered Wendy's objection.

"No, Wendy, she is not crazy. She is right. This is one of the things foretold for you."

"Grandma?"

"Yes, child. The way the prediction is written is too much like a riddle, and so I did not understand until just yesterday, when I learned of your expanded powers. But yes, this is part of the preparation for your upcoming adventures."

Ginger spoke up. "Also, I *am* a physician. Oh, yes! I have studied and become fully qualified in the traditional medicine of my homeland, and I have also gone on from there. I have studied and become fully qualified in the coordination of that with the medicine of your tradition as well, although of course the coordination is still being worked through. My sister Pepper and I are both that way. It was, in fact, some of the theoretical problems about that coordination that led us both into philosophy."

They discussed it for a while. Finally Wendy said, "Very good, but one thing puzzles me. I can repair my mother with your guidance and supervision. Then why can you not repair your twin sister?"

"The short answer is that like me, my sister is a paranormal mistress far above your mother's level. That brings in…complications. We can discuss it further later on, if need be."

"Well, it is still against my better judgment, but all right—provided Mama agrees to it. God help us all if you are wrong."

Right then, Diana was dazed. When she was lucid again an hour later, she said, "My own powers have long since been wiped out, but I remember enough of what was beginning to awaken within me to believe all Mother says about it. Do I believe enough to gamble what is left of myself, if not my very life? Yes, I do. You go ahead, Wendy, and do what has to be done. Yes, as Ginger says, you try to repair me. God help us all if I am wrong. But Wendy—if you should fail, know always that I love you dearly and will carry that love to my grave. And be comforted. I shall not blame you for whatever trouble there may be, and you must not blame yourself."

Then Ginger took her through it. "Remember what you have learned from my tradition. To speak of repairing your mother is right only as a loose way of speaking. She is not a machine to be repaired. She is a living being, to develop and maintain herself from within. You are not a physician, you say. But as you have learned, no physician ever really *heals* anyone. He removes the problems, and then the patient restores himself or herself as a living being."

"How exactly is that to work in this case?"

"You begin by probing and scanning. You find where and how she is disrupted as a living being, which to say, where and how the structure of exotic energies within her is spoiled. Good, you see the problem. There are inoperable blood clots pressing on her tissues. Now you pinpoint the exact location of each. Very good. Now, do you know how to destroy each of them without damaging the surrounding tissues?" Wendy proposed something. "Yes, exactly so. All right, now, Wendy—there is nothing left but to go ahead and do it." Wendy went ahead and did it, slowly and carefully, with each in turn. When finally the work on the last had been concluded, Ginger said, "That is the end. The job is done. That is all we can do. Now she must heal herself."

The job had taken three hours. Diana had been offered the choice to be conscious or not. At her own request, Wendy had lulled her into a deep sleep as an exercise of what her people would call telepathic hypnosis, to use the fancy name for it. She remained asleep now that the action on her was completed. Wendy asked Ginger, "How long before she is recovered?"

"That is up to her. You tell me, though—given what you observe going on inside her, what do you calculate?"

"With luck, perhaps even this very day." That was, in fact, how it went. Several hours after Wendy did the job on her, Diana awoke with her mind fully clear as it had not been for thirty-plus years. Ginger would not allow her to do much and said she must sleep a whole lot for a while, but yes, she was mended to be as though the problem had never been, and there would be no more trouble from it, no more spells of being dazed, ever again.

Diana did spend much time sleeping. Later the next day, when she was fully awake and ready to go, Ginger came by again. She checked Diana, had Wendy do so, conferred with Wendy, and confirmed that all was well. Then Diana, being highly intelligent, was full of questions.

"As for the structure of exotic energies within you—and every woman, man, girl, and boy—the energies in question are not currently recognized by the natural science of your culture and tradition."

Then Ginger explained it as well as she could. She concluded by saying, "Perhaps you are concerned that what my tradition says about it may not be fully in keeping with what your Faith teaches." Both Diana and Margaret nodded in assent. "This is something I have discussed with your daughter. Both of us have agreed that with my tradition as well as yours, the people in earlier times saw various parts of the truth well enough, but each group of people also had some failure of full and correct understanding. We hope it may work out for us to collaborate someday and hammer out better explanations.—However, in order to ease your mind, I can tell you this much right now: the exotic theories my ancestors developed about the nature of the universe and all that are wrong. That is not in question or dispute. But it could be that they became aware of neutral and natural forces that are genuinely real, and then they misunderstood what those forces were and how they acted. That is what investigation seems to show, and that is my working hypothesis, and Wendy's."

"All right, fair enough. But there is also another question. What connection does all this have to what you told us at lunch that time about your ability to know beforehand what is going to happen by looking into the depths of the world?"

"That is very much one of the things we are still trying to hammer out. But I shall tell you what I can. In order to do so, I must use a couple of different analogies. At lunch that day, I spoke about being aware of the rhythms and patterns underneath things as the basis. Yes, exactly so. A trivial version of something like that happens all the time, even with ordinary people. When someone reads a story or sees it dramatized, he may know ahead of time what is to happen, or how the story will develop, based on his intuitive appreciation of the story's internal logic. But that function is more intellectual, and what happens with me is more like simple perception. It is like hearing music and being able to anticipate what is coming based on awareness of the tempo, melody, and key. What I have is something like the one function and also something like the other. You must never let anyone tell you there is no such thing as destiny or fate. People like me know better than that."

"What about the kind of soothsaying my family has?"

"That works in another way. I do not know how."

"And what about what you knew of what was to happen to Wendy?"

"We have discussed it, and what you suspected long ago is right, Diana. Wendy is very much a child of destiny, whether for good or evil—perhaps both. The moment I first saw her, that was as clear to me as if it had been trumpeted from the sky."

In the upcoming days, Diana was checked out by her own physician. What had been done was verified, but all the physician could tell her about how or why was, "Well, these mysterious remissions happen sometimes. This may or may not last. I hope it does last, and I am happy for whatever benefit you may gain. The thing to do is to live out your life with your renewed clarity of mind for whatever time you may have, and may God be with you."

When this word came through, Wendy was happy for her mother all over again, but she had a serious concern for herself. With power comes responsibility. This was a commonplace among her people. Given the power she had just exercised and still possessed, what now? Her world was full of sickness, crime, and all kinds of things that ought not to be. She could do much that others could not. But on the other side, she was only a woman, not a goddess. She had long since learned enough to know that if she tried to go beyond her appointed limits, she could expect to end up creating a worse mess. So what then? What was she called upon to do or not do about it? And so, one week after taking care of her mother, Wendy took counsel from Alicia.

"The general rule is simple enough. You were personally involved with the situation of your mother, and there it is. You are responsible for what you find yourself called upon to do—what you are involved in or faced with. You are not required—or even allowed—to poke into the affairs of others without due cause. Whatever powers you have are not a license to go around making a public nuisance of yourself because you imagine you can produce good results by doing so.—Superheroes who roam the world, solving problems, casting down evil, and turning situations right side up, exist in stories. As for real life, that is another question. Even if they do exist in real life, you are not one of those people."

"What about the remarkable adventures I am to have?"

"Yes, you will soon enough be called upon to do those things, and that is just the point. You do such things if and when you are called upon, *as* you are called upon, and not otherwise."

Wendy bowed her head in docile submission. "Yes, ma'am."

Time marched on, and the season arrived for the next cycle of courses to begin. But because Anna was very young and at an early stage, and because she had the luxury to do so, Wendy decided to stay home and forgo teaching for a little while and see about the next cycle later on. For the present, Alfreda had learned of an opportunity. There was a short-term situation that called for a translator with two foreign languages as well as the language Wendy had learned from her mother. Wendy was one of the few people at that time and place who knew all three languages. So she filled in the time until that next cycle of courses started with a temporary job translating. She was able to do almost all of the work while at home with Anna, and she found it convenient that this job paid more than teaching the low-level courses. Then the job ended. Shortly after, there was a great religious holiday that

Wendy and her family celebrated (including Timothy, long since reconciled), and she was about to take up teaching again.

During that time, Wendy had also been working on a second book, comparing and contrasting what the different traditions said about personal identity.

⸻

Beatrice explained to the others what this meant. "Among them, there had grown up some serious theoretical question and elaborate discussion over what was involved in having someone be the same person across time. Of course, what makes the question pointed is the fact of constant change. What changes do or do not disrupt someone from being the same person he or she was yesterday? Wendy was comparing and contrasting various answers to such questions as these." With that, Beatrice resumed her narrative.

⸻

The new cycle of courses began, and Wendy started teaching once more, albeit with a minimal load of just one course. This cycle ran through without any serious problem or incident. A few days after the cycle ended, she submitted the book on personal identity for publication. This work was approved and published a little more than three-quarters of a year later—on the thirty-third anniversary of her birth, in fact. Once again, the book was acclaimed, and Wendy was lauded. In the meantime, she went on teaching and caring for Anna, as she had been doing. The book was published during a cycle of courses. This cycle also was concluded without any serious problem or incident. So far, all was going well for her.

When the book was published, Wendy stopped for just a moment and took stock of her situation. She was now thirty-three years old, and she would not live to be forty. Well, so be it, and glory to God in the highest. As she had told Elizabeth, like any woman—or man or girl or boy—she must look to Him to escort her through the valley of the shadow of death, and there it was. Wendy cried out to God briefly and then considered what she was called on to do or not do in whatever time she had left. With the acclaim from her two books, it looked like opportunities for her to engage in more serious work as a theoretician—both in teaching and research—might finally be arranged. Of course, given that she had *at most* less than seven years left, and given that she had other adventures to fulfill, it would be an exercise in bad faith for her to undertake any long-term commitments. But it might be very reasonable for her accept something short-term. She would have to travel and leave her grandmother's house, at least for the time being, and there was Anna to think about. But the clinical problems she could never outgrow, which had kept her in her childhood home, were now finally resolved, thanks be to God. As for Anna, she was almost two years old, and it would be at least another half year before Wendy would have to travel. Anna was not a mere infant anymore, and she would be even less by then. Anna might be old enough that her mommy could take her along with her.—On the other side, there were the upcoming adventures. What she was called upon to do about those concerns might well disrupt all else. So Wendy called on God to guide her and decided to take counsel from Alicia.

"The simple fact is that something is about to happen. After this cycle ends, you will not be teaching for a while, contrary to what you plan. Your next adventure will begin too soon for that. Where the affair will go—or how it will work out or end up—is not given me to know at this time."

Sure enough, before the next course they offered her would have concluded, the situation arose for the second adventure. Because of Alicia's warning, Wendy was able simply to refuse the offer to teach at that time. This was arranged cleanly and honorably and even amicably on both sides when she explained there was a special situation coming up she would have to take care of. But on both sides, how this project would work out was beyond their dreams and Wendy's nightmares.

CHAPTER SEVENTEEN

The invitation for the adventure came from Wendy's government. Beatrice explained. "They did not want to undertake the project involving Wendy. They found they had to, after they got into serious trouble. Her government had this secret project, which was thoroughly corrupt and totally discreditable, and it blew up in their faces. Then a remarkable person stepped in and told them what would be required to resolve the situation as well as possible. The way it worked out was that this person had to be recognized as the queen of an extremely old but long-hidden land. When this had been done, eventually the queen called for Wendy to be involved. When they asked why, she said she would explain it to Wendy when she met her and to the government people in her own good time."

And so it was done. Wendy was called in, introduced to the queen, and told that she was being pressed into special service for an extraordinary situation. When she started to protest as to whether they could legally do that, they cut her off and told her—before she made any noise, she had better find out what was really going on. This reduced her to silence.

Then the queen spoke up. "Yes, to be sure, but that is a nasty way of putting it, and she deserves better. I am sorry, Wendy. You are right, of course. But they are also right. First you need to understand what all this is about. There is much I need to tell you, but not here. Please, take me to your house." Wendy could hardly believe it, but the queen repeated her request, and Wendy did so.

When they arrived, the whole group was there—her grandmother, mother, aunts, Alfreda, Alicia, and even Ginger. She murmured that this was a remarkable coincidence. But the queen said, "No, this is not a mere coincidence—it was foretold long ago." Margaret, Ginger, and even Alicia all affirmed that this was so. Then the queen walked over to Alicia, knelt before her, and said, "I know what you really are, Alicia. You see, there are old prophecies given to my people as well as yours. In view of the freedom and dignity He has granted your people, that makes you the presiding officer at this gathering. I shall honor your word."

Wendy exclaimed, "What the blank is going on here?"

Alicia began. "Please, be seated in one of the chairs, Your Majesty.—Wendy, you may refer to this queen under the name Paula. We cannot pronounce her name in her own language—our vocal organs lack that capability. As for what is going on here, you have very good powers—you scan her and tell us."

Wendy did so. "At first I thought she was just another woman. I would almost think so now, but what has been said in the last minute or two makes me search more carefully. It is very subtle, but she is masking herself. In order to do that as I find her doing it, she must be an extremely powerful paranormal mistress, far above even Ginger's level." Then it hit her. "No, she is not just another woman, for she is not a woman at all. No woman can exercise the level of power Queen Paula is displaying. The infrastructure of exotic energies required to support such functioning would fry her tissues to a cinder in a fraction of a second. Even I know that much. Alicia, what is going on here?"

"Well, there is no need to speak of the lady as though she were not here. The thing to do is to ask her, straight out."

"Then, Your Majesty, what do you say?"

"I say, you are right, of course. I am not a woman as you and these ladies are women. I am an alien—a being of another kind or species."

"You are very different, but you are more than just very different. You are vastly superior, as belonging to a higher order—a superior level."

"Yes, that too. You will do best to think of me as a fairy in the sense of the fairy godmothers in your stories—or even better, as an elf. Yes, perhaps the nearest approximation in your cultural tradition is one of the high elves, although that too is imperfect. You might best think of me as an elvish woman, by which I mean, a female adult person of that species."

"You are also a queen. What about that?"

"Once again, that is not exact, but it is the nearest equivalent among the social and political structures your cultural traditions are familiar with. I am like a queen over a client state. I can act within the realm given me with very broad authority, and my official acts do not require ratification, but I can be overruled and even removed under the laws of my homeland."

"Then your realm here in our world is an outpost or colony of some sort?"

"Yes, or at least that is the short way to say it."

"So then—to lay it right out—are you the queen of the elves and fairies?"

"Once again, yes, or at least that is the short way to say it. My—fellow beings and I are the reality of which the old stories among you speak, sometimes accurately and sometimes not."

Margaret, Ginger, and Alicia assured Wendy that all this was so. After a long pause, she went on to ask, "All right, since you are a superior being, why do you need me?"

"First of all, you need to understand about my superiority. I am not a goddess. No such goddesses exist. There is the One God, the Lord God Almighty, and His creatures, and that is all there is. I am not even a created pure spirit, a Messenger or anything like that. Like you, I am a material body endowed with life, but my inner basis of vital functioning is powerful enough that I can exercise very rich mental life, including even the functions of intellect and will. This inner basis of functioning is what you call the soul. Your stories say elves and fairies have no souls, but that is false and absurd. No being endowed with rationality can be only a living body and nothing more. The best traditional thinkers among you understood this. Well then, strictly speaking, I am a rational animal, just as you are a rational animal."

Diana blurted out innocently, in genuine astonishment, "I thought the soul was supposed to be superior to the body."

Queen Paula smiled and said, "You explain it to her, Wendy."

"Yes, Mama, but you see, there are various kinds of superiority. A craftsman is superior to his tools, but he may still depend on his tools to be able to work. So even though the soul governs the body and has capabilities that go beyond what is material, still what has all these functions is the living being as a unified whole, and so the person can fail if something goes wrong with her body, just as the craftsman can fail if something goes wrong with his tools."

Diana looked to Queen Paula and asked, "Is that right?"

"Yes, or at least as correct as it can be explained to be without getting into it more seriously. But in this case, we have to get into it at least a little more seriously." She paused, then said, "You will do best to think of the body as a material realization or implementation of the soul. That applies to me as well as to you. It is just that my body works on very different principles from yours. This gives me various advantages. First of all, just as a craftsman with better tools can do greater works, so I can exercise greater capabilities and display greater perfections of mental life, especially intellect and will. It also allows me to have extra powers and extra senses—something like what Ginger has and what Wendy has come to have, but at a far higher level. Perhaps most notably, I am not subject to natural death as you are. The stories among you say elves and fairies live through vast stretches of time. Yes, indeed we do. Of course I can be killed, just as any material body can be destroyed. But that is not exactly the same thing."

Theodora said, "Some stories say you can change size and form at will. Is that true?"

"Well, that is an oversimplified exaggeration, but the short answer is yes—at least as regards size. But with form, no—not really. Form is too deeply rooted in the underlying reality of what the person is. On the other hand, size is more of a mere construct. It can be manipulated, although not so easily as the stories indicate."

Diana asked, "Then, Your Majesty, what about the fact that you are masking yourself? I too can detect it, just barely, now that it has been pointed out. Since Wendy healed me, I have come to be almost as powerful as she is—or was, before Pepper expanded her."

Queen Paula smiled. "Yes, I know about the healing and also about Pepper." Then she swept back her hair to reveal her pointed ears and said, "Here is another thing the stories among you are right about." After letting everyone absorb this, she went on, "What is presented for your eyes to see is genuine. It is my true appearance—my real visual aspect—based on the natural fact of what I am. The masking is not about that. It is about the internal structure and functioning of my body and about the structure of exotic energy in and around my body. But there is no more need to bother with masking now. I shall stop it gradually so the shock will not be too great." Over the next seven seconds, the masking diminished and then ceased.

Wendy's aunts and grandmother were not powerful enough. Alfreda and Alicia had no such powers. Only Diana, Ginger, and Wendy could sense what was happening, and Ginger had seen the Queen unmasked before. After Diana and Wendy got past their initial astonishment, Ginger said they would discuss it later. Then Wendy said, "Your Majesty, if I may, let me take us back to it. Why do you need me?"

"We have been here in your world for a very long time. The last of us should have left and gone home long ages ago. I am speaking now of tens of thousands, or even hundreds of thousands, of your years. But something went wrong. A terrible crime was committed, and some of us have had to be here through the ages to take care of the resulting mess. It would have been resolved in the course of the ages if all had gone right, but that too did not work out. Finally, in this age, some of the people in your own government thought they saw their chance to exploit what my people had set up. They were wrong, of course. It blew up in their faces. So now, we need you to help clean up their mess."

Margaret said, "That is the short version, Wendy. Your Majesty, given what I know of my granddaughter, it will be easiest for her if you will now go on to tell the whole story in order."

And so she did. "Prior to this present age of your species as dominant on your world, there was the age of my people—the high elves as you might call us. But prior to our own age, very long ago, there was the age of what you would call mermaids.—Oh, yes, they did exist, although they were very different from what most of your stories say. To begin with, they too had souls.—Well, the wrong was done just as their age was ending and our age was beginning.

"Their age was drawing to a close, and they knew it. One might have hoped this would lead them to look to God all the more as they prepared for their own personal lives, as well as that of their civilization, to be concluded. That would of course include setting aside petty quarrels and resentments in order have it all end with the full splendor of the greatest perfection that could still be achieved. We stood ready to help them through as much as we could, including making sure their deaths would be soft and mild. But instead, they squandered it all as far as they could.

"In the last few decades of their age, there arose among them an especially terrible war. This war was the most harsh and ferocious war that had ever been fought among them, and it went on and on for an unusually long time—about twenty-five of your years. What the issues were is not important now. Suffice it to say, there was clearly the right side and the wrong side of the conflict. It was clearly obvious to all of us which side was which, but we were forbidden to do anything about it, even though we had greatly superior powers and could have ended it very quickly. We were allowed to react to any harm wrongfully inflicted or attempted against ourselves, and we could intervene with the consent of both sides, but ordinarily that was all. It was their problem, and it was for them to resolve it among themselves, and we had to respect that so long as they kept it among themselves and did not spill over. The war ended eventually with the right side on top. But by that time, almost everything had been ruined. We helped them through as well as possible, but this took the form of caring for the surviving remnant and of salvaging what scraps and fragments we could of what had been best in their culture. Except for one special survivor, the last of them died only about six of your years after the war finally ended.

"This one special survivor is what concerns you, Wendy. It was with her that the terrible crime I spoke of was committed. It was very late in the war. Those on the wrong side were facing imminent defeat, and they knew it. A desperate proposal arose among them to gain an advantage by tampering with one of the—the natural scientists, as you would say—among my people, and to do so by fair means or foul. This proposal was debated among them.

"I wish with all my heart wiser heads had prevailed, but instead, the desperate fools who listened to their fears carried the day. The wisest and best among them were totally appalled. This decision to adopt wild lunacy shocked them into fuller wakefulness and clarified the situation for them, including the real moral positions of the parties and the real merits of the original conflict. So the wisest and best among them broke away and surrendered to the opposition. They were held captive and treated as well as possible. As for the others—well, as I said, they were desperate fools. Tampering with our people opened the door for us to intervene and end it quickly, and they should have known that out front, but they convinced themselves of some nonsense. We did intervene, of course, and that was how the war was finally ended. We were not harsh to those poor losers—we knew they would very soon die anyway, and our concern was to help them prepare for that. We did what we could to comfort them and to facilitate the process of having them brought to contrition and conversion. But the crime had already been committed and could not be taken back, and the result existed and could not just be canceled out.

"The natural scientist they tampered with was personally innocent through the whole affair. He was extremely intelligent and very learned, but he was clearly less powerful than most of us, even though he was still very much superior to any mermaid. However, he was just weak enough that they managed to run some crazy trick and dominate him by telepathic hypnosis, to use your fancy name for it. Their plan was to have him raise up among them a group of elite warrior girls to fight for them. It might have worked, too, except we detected what was happening long before it could get that far.

"The problem was that the scientist got as far as starting the prototype before we could stop him. One of the mermaids on the wrong side was made to conceive a daughter who was very much genetically altered. Her growth and development, both before and after birth, were then to be artificially accelerated in order to have the girl ready as a warrior in short order. But we learned of the scheme and stopped it before that could be done. So the child grew and developed through what was a normal pregnancy for them, and her mother gave birth to her in the usual way, without incident.

"Happily for that mermaid, her experience of motherhood and her natural love for the child helped her to see through the nonsense she had been following, and that made it easy for her to be brought to contrition and conversion. But, like the others, she died very soon—in her case, about three-quarters of a year after giving birth, as you reckon time. As she was dying, she was concerned for her daughter, and we promised she would be cared for as well as possible.

"This promise was kept. What the scientist did was to combine genetic factors from the mermaids and our people and weave these factors together very skillfully. Technically, therefore, the child was a being of a new species, kind of like the way a mule differs in species from both a horse and a donkey. But unlike a mule, this girl was fully capable of reproduction, although only by parthenogenesis. Now, as a being of a new species, there was serious question as to what her status before God would be. What I mean is that your people, Wendy, start out with what comes down from your First Parents and then go on from there. Something like that applied to the mermaids as well. The details are not important right now. The point is, what about this girl? Would she have the status of a mermaid, an elf, some exotic combination of the two, neither, or what?

"In the end, the wisest heads prevailed, and it was decided to follow the safest course for the girl. Among the survivors of her people was a priestess who was, as you would say, a living saint. She had many times administered the ritual given to them for the initial act of formal consecration. It was given as universally valid, and so it would work for the child. There was some question about whether she was a real person at all or just a monstrosity. But the question was settled when she began to learn language and display the exercise of rudimentary rationality. So, very shortly after this was clear, when she was still a toddler, the priestess administered the ritual to her. This consecration was good as far as it went, but it turned out to be still a lesser thing. I shall come back to this point.

"Beyond all that, she was given to a suitable family among us and adopted upon the death of her mother. Her adoptive family loved her dearly and cared for her as well as any child among us was ever cared for, with the advice and assistance of the best scholars and thinkers among us to provide for her special needs.

"The girl did very well indeed, considering. Unhappily, this was one of those situations where the word 'considering' says it all and carries a whole lot of punch. Her mind and body grew and developed very well. She learned much, exercised wisdom, was very well behaved, and strove to be worthy as a devoted handmaid of the Lord God. So far, so good. But underneath it all, she was still a warrior girl. That part of their scheme had succeeded. Yet she cared about the right things for the right reasons, and her striving paid off. She was not quick tempered or cruel or vicious—quite the opposite, in fact. She was remarkably patient and kind, generous and merciful—soft hearted, as you would say. All would have been well if only nothing had gone wrong to get her started. When she did get started, she had the very strong excuse—the *strong* excuse, mind you—of having been pushed into it."

Queen Paula paused, smiled sadly, let slip a couple of tears, then resumed. "It became clear soon enough how much of a hybrid she really was. Unlike the mermaids, she was not fully subject to natural death. But unlike the elves, she could not just go on and on through the ages. As it says in one of your stories, the natural span of a mermaid was about three hundred years. So the compromise worked out to be that she would be active for three hundred years, and then she would be dormant, with severe depression of all vital signs, for thousands of years. She could go through such cycles indefinitely, with no natural or obvious endpoint. As it happened, after the three-hundred-year span beginning with her birth, she slept and rose to be active through nine more such spans before the crisis. It was at the end of the ninth additional span, thus the tenth all told, that it all went wrong."

Wendy had more than a suspicion in her mind of what it was that had gone wrong, but she asked anyway. Sure enough, her worst fears were confirmed. "What happened, Your Majesty?"

Queen Paula smiled sadly, nodded, then said, "I think you know, Wendy, but you need to have me lay it out explicitly. Right, then. As you must suspect, what happened was the defection of your own people—specifically your own First Parents. That poor girl had learned all she could learn, and had developed as well as she could, and had experienced all the joys and benefits a being of her kind could possibly have, from living within this world. She had one thing left to look forward to, and that was to have her formal consecration perfected, in order that she might finally go home. We could not provide that for her, since what she needed was something superior to the whole combination that she was. All we and that mermaid priestess could give her was within that system. From her standpoint, we represented just the factors of the hybrid, not exactly what transcended both sides. But your people could have—and presumably would have—taken care of her very quickly, if only—! But of course, that was not what happened, as you know.

"Oh, Wendy, you have no idea what tears and anguish that poor girl went through. Yet even then, she did not go spinning off or get started. That happened only much later, when she was really pushed into it. At first, she simply cried out to God in her anguish to see her through. When she was ready to think instead of merely burning emotion, she asked Him that she might remain dormant until her situation could be resolved, after the Great Redemption—which we all knew would be granted someday—had been accomplished. But she settled in her mind that after all, she had been raised up as a warrior girl, and so she would make that work for her to be a devoted handmaid of the Lord God. Come what may, whether she remained dormant until the end or not, she would look to God to strengthen her mind, that she might suffer through whatever it might be as a good warrior. This was not just brave talk on her part, either. Her concern was not purely selfish. She was genuinely sorry for your First Parents, and especially for their descendants to be, that they would go through life being ruined. She accepted in her mind that she might even be called on to be active for extra periods in order to help them in some way. A few days after all this, her active period ended, and she became dormant again."

"Your Majesty, I am very sorry for that girl and for the whole filthy history of my people. I apologize for my First Parents and for all the rest of us—including myself, sad to say. Is there anything I can do for her?"

"That depends on how it works out. I am not sure, but given what was foretold long ago, it is just possible that you will be the one to take care of her. We shall have to wait and see. But you must hear the rest of it first.

"She rose and then slept peacefully through ten cycles—over about forty thousand of your years. When she rose the last time, she learned quickly enough that the old system of history for your people was gradually drawing to a close. There was much discussion among us of this fact. But we knew the Great Redemption had not happened yet and was still far off, in ages to come. In the meantime, in all the cycles, there was work for that poor girl to do, and she did it.

"Because she was neither a mermaid nor an elf, the standard rules did not apply to her in the normal way. Consequently, she was allowed to involve herself in the affairs of your people much more than we were. You see, for many thousands of years now, we elves and fairies have involved ourselves in your affairs only because your evil spills over to go beyond the confines of your own species, or else because we are specially called upon to do so, in spite of your stories. But as for her, after she was consecrated as far as we and the mermaids could provide, the last queen of the mermaids gave her the title of—well, 'Princess Regent' would be the best translation. That made her the sovereign ruler, and this was while—strictly speaking—the age of mermaids was still going on. All of this made her ruler over this world, except insofar as she was subject to us elves, as being under our care and protection. At least in legal theory, her dominion continues down to the present day, and she can lawfully act insofar as you violate the rules under which you enjoy relative autonomy.

"She learned soon enough that newborn children among your people would sometimes be simply abandoned and left to die. She was deeply horrified at this. Her first reaction was that it was almost too much for the mind to accept. Her sensibility as a woman was so outraged that she almost got started as a warrior girl over that. She was ready to burn your world down, which she could have done with the vast powers she had. We restrained her and made her understand, albeit with difficulty, that the women who did that were generally more to be pitied than censured. In most cases, they were driven to desperation and were doing what they thought they had to do.

"Eventually, after calling on God for guidance, she accepted this explanation, though somewhat reluctantly. She came to see that instead of lashing out, the thing for her to do was to try to clean up the mess as far as she could. It was very clear that in default of anything better, she could apply that archaic ritual for formal consecration given among mermaids to those children, and it would be valid. She could not do much for them, but she could do that, and then she could make sure their deaths would be soft and mild. And so that was what she did. Over the ages, through all of her ten waking periods, many thousands of your children died much more mercifully than they would otherwise have done, after having their eternal destiny assured."

At this point, Wendy said, "Excuse me, Your Majesty, but was it really valid? Alicia?" Alicia assured her that, in view of what was given, and in view of the situation of that age and of that girl in particular, it had been valid—the key phrase being "in default of anything better." For the more serious and more powerful things had not yet begun.

Then Diana asked, "Why did she not try adopting those children herself?"

"Because she was not authorized to do so. She had only the dominion she had received from the old queen of the mermaids, and that queen could give only what she had. It happened among them only rarely that a child would be left without adult care and support, but it did happen. Then the child would be adopted under the supervision and with the approval of the queen, but not *by* the queen. In all the ages of their history, that was unheard of. Her role was limited to making sure there was, as you say, no funny business—no phony baloney. So the best the girl could do was to ask us elves to receive the child. But under the laws and rules that govern our relations with your species, we could do so only in some few cases. In general, she could do only what I told you. We did adopt such children when we could, and that fact has given rise to ridiculous stories that we steal children from you."

"Somehow that excuse sounds like legalistic trickery to cover rotten garbage."

"No, not at all. You are thinking that any decent woman would figure law exists for the sake of the people, not the other way around, and so she would have found or invented some way."

"Something like that, yes!"

"But you see, she was not a woman as you and others of your people are—she was an alien being, and that was just the problem. She had to respect the relative autonomy your people had. The point is very clear when viewed from the other side. Their own mothers did not find a better way, and along that line, it was from her standpoint largely an internal domestic problem of your species. She was forbidden to interfere beyond what I told you, except in one thing. In some few cases, she was able to arrange exile and asylum for the mother and child. This happened when the mother was compelled by one or more others to abandon the child against her own desires and inclinations. Sometimes she would be aware of what was happening and persuade the mother to reclaim the child before it was too late, after which she would set it all up for them.

"She tried also to reason with those who had compelled the mothers and persuade them that better arrangements could be made, but as it happened, none of them was willing to listen. Anyway, what she accomplished was a great joy to her heart, but it was all too rare." When all this had been talked through, the elvish queen went on with her explanation.

"Once again—so far, so good. All would have worked out well enough, if only your people had not gotten funny about—well, about her. The evil occurred in the final days of her active period, as she was coming home again for the last time before becoming dormant. To put it bluntly—for there is no nice way to say it—she looked very much like an exceptionally beautiful woman of your species, and so one of your men tried to rape her. There, I have said it. He failed, of course. Yet even then, she did not simply lash out like an angry animal. With the powers given her, she picked him up and threw him away, as an ordinary woman of your kind might pick up and throw away a child's doll. It was strong enough to let him know what she thought of him, but not enough to do him lasting damage. She controlled herself and said, 'You have a chance, which is more than you deserve. Run away now. Run away before I kill you.' She would have done it, too, but he ran away in time. You see, nothing like that had ever been done to her before. Among us, she had known only love and friendship. As for your people, she had really had very little contact with them, except for what happened with the children and rarely with others. But that assault triggered what she had been set up to be and got her started as a warrior girl.

"She was, in fact, to be greatly praised for controlling herself as well as she did. The problem was that once she got started, there was no stopping her. That was part of how she was set up. Well, she came in and submitted to have us care for her as usually happened when she was about to go dormant, and she told her story of what had happened. But then she added, with tears, 'As a warrior, I was ready to serve and protect these people as He gave into my hand. That is not good enough for them. So be it, and now I must be a warrior girl the other way. I am very sorry, and I know many of them deserve better, but that one nasty has ruined it for all of them. This is how it has to be. Pray that I may remain dormant until I can be finally and fully consecrated and sent home. That will be best for all of us. The alternative is just too terrible.' Sad to say, we knew she was right, at least from her own standpoint. She herself asked God to grant her this, as did we. Later that day, she lapsed into dormancy again.

"But that was not how it turned out. She awoke after about fifty thousand of your years. By this time, the system of history for your people that continues down to the present day had begun. But the Great Redemption was still far off, and we knew it. After she got past her tears, she said, 'I am sorry, but now I shall do what I have to do.' We were not authorized to restrain her forcibly, but we made her understand that the question of what she had to do cut both ways, and we extracted a series of sworn promises from her to restrict her to doing *only* what she had to do. And that was what happened, at least through that active period, in spite of the ridiculous stories that have grown up among your people. For example, she is said to be a seductress who leads astray and consumes men, but that is just not true. Given how she got started as a warrior girl, the question of sexual abuse and violence has been and still is one of her pet concerns. That is all. A man who respects girls and women has nothing to fear from her. Even a fool who mouths off to a girl or woman is not yet in any real danger from her. But if he goes on to lay his hand upon her, he may be in danger of his life unless he backs down and apologizes right then. Otherwise, if she happens to witness the incident, she may invite him to try himself on her, if he really wants to play and has the courage for it. Some few have been shocked into wakefulness enough to realize how wrong they were, apologize, ask forgiveness, and then turn and walk away, slowly and carefully. That is in fact the outcome she prefers, deep in her heart, underneath her wildness as a warrior girl. Slightly more have been smart enough to know they were in big trouble and run away. But too many have gone on to try themselves on her. When they do, she shows them something of what she can do if she has to and offers to walk away herself. If they accept that, well and good. But if not, she turns the table on them, drinks their blood, and extracts exotic energy from their bodies. They die very quickly. *That* is how she has consumed some men. But seductress, no—not at all. She is, in fact, strictly virginal, at least in some narrow technical sense, and she consumes only men who insist on trouble."

Wendy figured she knew the answer to her next question, but she needed to be sure. "Your Majesty, you speak of stories about her among my people. Then, by what name is this poor girl, as you call her, known among us?"

"The dim echo of ancient memory has become mixed with an archetypal image. She is known by an old title that translates as 'Night Monster'—you people call her Lilith."

"I have heard of Lilith before, but I thought she existed only in myth and legend."

"Well, honey child, you thought wrong." It was Margaret who said this. "As we have discussed before, the women of our family have known for generations there are, in fact, things that go bump in the night. We have only scraps and fragments—much less than Ginger, let alone Queen Paula. But even we know, and have long known, enough to be aware that Lilith is one of those things." Then, turning to the Queen, "But we know about her as a thing that goes bump in the night—a monster to be destroyed if possible. You make her sound almost like an innocent victim instead."

"No, not instead. She is both. She was made to be a warrior girl, and then she was pushed into acting out as a warrior girl. In that way, she is kind of like an innocent victim. On the other hand, as a warrior girl, she must pay the price of a warrior, which is to answer for what she has done with her own life. Yes, from your own standpoint, Lilith must of course be destroyed. But it is one thing to say that. It is very much another to curse and damn the woman as a woman, let alone to hope she may burn in Hell forever."

Now it was Wendy who spoke. "The arm of the Lord is not shortened, as they say, and the Redemption He has accomplished is to be respected. So yes, if even Lilith can be brought to look to God and submit to Divine mercy, then so be it, fine and dandy, and I hope she too may be saved in spite of everything. If she is already genuinely concerned with God and the things of God, at least as far as may be given her own situation, then so much the better. That is the right answer, and I am sorry if anything I have said dishonors it. But is it really so? What about the children whose blood she has drunk?"

"She has never harmed one of your children. During that active period, when she was acting out as a warrior girl, she provided for abandoned children as she had done before. But the difference was that now, *after they were dead*, she would extract and consume what remnants of blood and exotic energy she could from their bodies. She was not trying to dishonor them, even in death. She took what she did to be justified, for she figured their bodies were a prize of war. Technically that was correct, under the laws of war among mermaids. Moreover, even then, she would first try to persuade the mothers or have us adopt such children instead."

"So you are saying she is an honest warrior?"

"Well, not enough for her life to be spared, but perhaps enough for her soul to be saved."

"Then what? Am I to kill her and send her to Heaven, thus punishing her and saving her both at once somehow?"

"What if that were given to you, Wendy? Would you accept it?"

"Well, this is too much of a new thing for me. It is hard to get past the shock. But as I think about it, yes—with all my heart. It would have to be a thing beyond dreams."

"Then once again, you must listen and hear the rest of it. That active period ended, and again she came home to us, told of her adventures, and submitted to be cared for and then go dormant. We were sorry for the violence she had done, limited though it was. But we were kind of proud of her, for she had kept all the promises she had sworn and then some, and we knew how hard that must have been for her. She arose again after a much shorter time—in the present era, in fact—about two hundred and fifty of your years ago.

"By this time, the Great Redemption had been accomplished. I spoke to Alicia when I arrived of the freedom and dignity He has granted to your people. Along that line, the rules under which you enjoy autonomy have been changed. You can still manage to trigger her dominion to act against you, but that is much more difficult now. You have much greater freedom to resolve your problems among yourselves. Again, along the same line, in many cases we elves are not authorized to restrain her forcibly, but you people are. On the other side, there is much less work for her to do. She is not ordinarily called upon to provide for your children as she once was. And now we come to what I need you for.

"Your authority to restrain her would be useless without the power. So about five years before Lilith arose again, when we saw the process of revival begin, I went out into your world and recruited women from among your people to assist Lilith. Why I say 'assist her,' you will understand shortly. All of these are double-dose girls like you and your family, Wendy, and all are devoted handmaids of the Lord God within the order of Divine Redemption, who follow the right Faith He has given. I gave special powers to those I recruited in order that they would be able to do what is to be done. Ginger and Pepper are not themselves among these servants, but their great-great-grandmother was, and what they have is the last echo of the power given. Starting with their daughters, what is inherited will be beneath the critical threshold to be effective. As it is, Ginger and Pepper and many others like them are a kind of auxiliary for those who have been formally recruited. It was from Ginger that I learned about you." She paused, and Ginger affirmed that all this was so. Then the Queen resumed.

"Incidentally, Pepper has been taken care of. Her occasional insanity has been healed, once and for all. No one of your species could have done it. But we elves could and did. Pepper was able to ravish Wendy largely because of the elvish energy and functions she inherited. When she abused all that for criminal violence, her madness went from being an internal domestic problem of your species to being our problem as well, and we resolved it.

"Well, to get back to it. When Lilith arose, she rejoiced greatly at the news of the Great Redemption. She submitted willingly enough when she was given to understand that yes, she would finally be provided for—but not right then. Rather, it would be after an exotic situation had been played out. This was in accordance with old prophecies given to both us elves and also the mermaids. Then I explained to her that her involvement with you people was to be greatly diminished, as I have explained it to you. I spoke of what was deep in her heart, underneath her wildness as a warrior girl. Sure enough, Lilith was in fact greatly relieved at this news of her diminished involvement with you. She knew well enough what she had been doing was grimy and ugly, even if she could claim it to be technically justified. Then I said to her, 'I am very glad you have the attitude and concern you have. I know this has always been there underneath, but you were pushed into the other. I know how hard it has been for you to do as well as you have done. It will be much easier for you starting now. From this moment, you are in the keeping of my friends, that you may live harmlessly within this world until what has been ordained is fulfilled, but with all care and concern for your comfort and welfare.' At this, she rejoiced greatly.

"With that, the nightmare should have been over for her. She should have been able simply to wait peacefully until finally it would be given to her to awake fully and find herself in Heaven. You see, these friends of mine could not restrain her forcibly, but they were empowered to make sure—by telepathic hypnosis, if need be—that Lilith kept the sworn promises we had elicited from her to honor appropriate rules and protocols. For part of what she swore was that she submitted to be held to it—coercively, if need be. I should add that she swore all this very willingly. She was not looking for trouble. Quite the opposite, in spite of what you people have imagined about her. Poor Lilith. Everything should have worked out nicely for her at long last, and she should finally have been able to live happily ever after, in this world and then the next.

"But once again, the right way was not good enough for your people. As you know, your friend Alicia has the gift of healing as well as of prophecy. Well, Wendy, to put it bluntly, some deluded fool within your own government got the idea to try to use the power of healing as a magical power to manipulate matter. Your world is full of poor fools who dream up all kinds of crazy things. The problem is, others who should know better listen to them instead of giving them the answer they deserve. That is what happened here."

At this, Wendy said, "I am sorry, but what did you just say?" Queen Paula repeated it. "That is what I thought you said. All right, the cynical explosion can come later. Finish it."

"Your government tried for it. It was, of course, a scheme of wild lunacy, but as with that history of the mermaids I told you about, so here—they convinced themselves of some nonsense. But that is not all. They learned very quickly that no one with that gift would even think about going along with their scheme. So they managed to manipulate some of the women I recruited, through elaborate schemes of deceit, into trying to manipulate those gifted people with telepathic hypnosis. Again, it was a scheme of wild lunacy, but here too, they had convinced themselves of some nonsense. They learned quickly, but too late, what malicious nonsense it was when it blew up in their faces.

"They did not stop to think who these women were, why they had these powers, what rules might come along with these powers, or anything like that. No—all they saw was a bunch of women with special powers whom they could use for what they happened to want at that moment. And that was what they did. They failed miserably, of course. But unhappily for them, that was not the end of it, in spite of what they imagined.

"The exotic energy exerted in the attempts on those gifted people had no effect on those people. But even though the energy was not spent on those people, it had to be spent somehow. What then? As the Book warns, the sins of the fathers may be visited on the sons—or, in some cases, on the daughters. This was one of those cases. There turned out to be hundreds of people in your government with some guilty involvement in the affair. Among them were scores of daughters who were young women in their late teens and early twenties—at the beginning of their adult womanhood. Of these, dozens were seriously devoted handmaids of the Lord God, kind of like the women I recruited. These girls were truly and especially worthy. There were sixty-four attempts at manipulating those with the gift of healing, which entailed there would have to be sixty-four targets on whom the exotic energy would be spent. So, of those dozens of girls, sixty-four were granted visions in their dreams and submitted to absorb the evil into themselves in order that He might finally neutralize it as harmlessly as may be. What was this evil? To put it crudely, they screwed around with the provisions for Lilith, the old bloodsucker. So it worked out that by having the exotic energy spent on those girls, they were turned into vampires.—Yes, I said vampires. All through your history, these monsters had existed and prowled only in stories, but now your own people had finally managed to bring this evil into real life.

"Of course, I would not have allowed the tampering with my friends to get anywhere near that far if I had known at the time.

The problem was that I had been called away to my homeland for an extended time on official business. What that official business was is not important now. The point is, I was not available at the time to head off the evil. When I came back and learned of it, I put a forcible end to it very quickly. Otherwise there would have been far more than just those sixty-four attempts, which would have entailed far more targets. How far it would have gone, and where it would have ended if I had not stopped it—well, I would rather not even think about all that."

After taking a long moment to digest all this, Wendy said, "I gather you want me to help kill those vampire girls?"

"Not exactly. They were not promised to come through with their lives in this world. They were assured their eternal destiny would not be in jeopardy, but they submitted to die if need be in order that the evil might be neutralized. However, they were promised to come through alive in this world if possible. They are to be detained and held in suspended animation in the hope that they can finally be restored. Only if that should fail will they die."

"What then? Am I to restore them, or what?"

"Oh, no, that is not possible. That depends on Lilith. Your chief function will be to face her and persuade her."

"It depends on Lilith?"

"Yes, certainly. Only Lilith can restore the vampire girls to be proper women instead of monsters, for it is given specifically to her. The reason is that she is the one person in this world with the formal authority as well as the power to resolve the tangle of laws and rules in which their own government—indeed, even their own parents—have caught these girls."

"How do I find her, and how do I keep her from killing me off when she does?"

"I shall give you special power beyond what Lilith has. As for finding her, that will not be necessary. She will find you. You see, the evil your government did ruined the protection of those rules and protocols. Now she will do what she thinks she has to do."

"Why? You are a higher-level being, smarter than I am, who knows more than I do, and so on. Why do you not simply have your friends, as you call them, bring her to you, then speak to her very nicely and persuade her into it yourself?"

"Yes—that is a very good question, Wendy. The answer is that this is one of the very few things your people could do that violates the modern rules under which you enjoy autonomy. Because you have done it, her dominion has been invoked. Now it is you who must ask her nicely for her help, in the name of your people. What you must do is ask her nicely enough to reach what is still deep in her heart, underneath her wildness as a warrior girl, and thus make her see she does not have to do what she imagines."

With that, the Queen asked Alicia to conclude the session for the day, saying they had enough to think about for a while. She said they would all meet again in five weeks and warned Wendy to clear away all other concerns and commitments and make ready.

Five weeks later, they were all gathered again at Margaret's house. Wendy said, "Well, all else has been cleared away. I am ready, as you said. Now what?"

"Now I believe there is something you would like to ask me. That may be as good a way to start as any."

"All right, then. I have been thinking, and there are two things. First of all, if Ginger is one of your auxiliary servants, then why did she have to scan me as she did when we first met? Why did she think I might be part of the problem? Why did she not know about me from what is given to you and your people?"

Ginger replied, "It is what I told you at lunch after that meeting. My abilities for what your family calls 'soothsaying,' and even those of Queen Paula, do not extend to things that depend on free choice of the will where the critical decisions are yet to be made. Only Divine prophecy can do that. Long ago now, my maternal grandmother and her sister met Lilith briefly. This prompted both of them to foresee that someone like you would arise and that you would be greatly involved in the situation with Lilith, but they could not tell which side you would be on, good or evil, for there were critical decisions yet to be made. They could supplement this and solve part of the puzzle by referring to what they could learn from the elves, but not enough was given to tell which way you would go, and you had not yet decided. You see, this happened about eighty or ninety years ago. Some twenty-plus years ago, my mother saw that the one her mother and aunt had foreseen had arisen and was now an innocent girl, eight or ten years old, but she was coming to some great crisis that would shape the course of her life and set her on the path of light or of darkness. She prayed God rather intensely to guide the girl rightly, but we did not know how it turned out. When I saw you, I knew at once you were the one foreseen, but I knew which way you had gone only when I had scanned you."

Alfreda was the first to understand, because she had been an adult when it had happened and because she had been involved in the affair more than the other adults around Wendy. She spoke up and reminded Wendy of the affair with the corrupt teacher who had tried to recruit her as a very different kind of witch from Ginger. When this had been talked through, Wendy went on to her next question.

"The second thing is that Lilith arose two and a half centuries ago, and you started recruiting people of my species to take care of her five years before that. Then why was her formal consecration not perfected, as you call it, long ago? If that had been done, your group could have been disbanded centuries back. Then there would not have been the basis for my government to try that idiotic stunt, and so much the better all around."

"That was tried and failed many times over the years. Until very recently, your people were not really prepared to deal in any practical way with alien beings, regardless of what was understood in theory. Even now, many of your people would not be prepared. You are, Wendy, but then you are on a much higher level of education and sophistication than most. No, but for many—perhaps most—Lilith is a thing that goes bump in the night, and thus a monster to be destroyed. Their minds stop there."

"But then how is she to be provided for?"

"I know from old prophecies it will work out. I do not yet know how." Wendy was about to object when Alicia cut her off and assured her that what Queen Paula said was in fact so.

The Queen spoke again. "The girls had those visions in their dreams, and they offered themselves. They are classic heroes, and for that they deserve to be remembered. In addition, their appropriate relatives, friends, and connections had corresponding visions in their dreams. Consequently, with almost all of them, there has been very little trouble about bringing them in. All but one are now at an estate I have, as my guests, waiting to be—well, 'put to bed' is the nice way to say it. Wendy, you will not have to travel in order to go to my realm. I have been able to bring my realm here, to you. You see, the parents of these girls are people in your government, including even the most senior officials. So special arrangements have been made, and a place not far from this abode has been set up as an outpost or extension of my realm, under my dominion.

"As for that one who remains, my friends have finally managed to capture her alive just today. As it happened, they caught up with her in the daytime, when she was dormant, which made it easy. Her name is Lucy. Unhappily, there was too much delay, and she turned into a full vampire. This happened because her father was a fool and was obstructive instead of cooperative. Well, when she is brought in, tonight or tomorrow, all that will be suppressed, and her mind will be cleared so that she can be put to bed properly."

Alfreda asked, "How much trouble did she cause before your friends captured her?"

"Too much. First of all, there is something you need to know. Only women can be vampires. Not men, and not children, but just adult women. Only women, and not many of them, either—only about six percent. One in sixteen, in fact. All other victims just die straight out from the loss of blood and exotic energy. I know—this is contrary to what the stories among you say. But then those who developed the stories did not understand. To be made a vampire is not an affliction proper to your kind or species. It is only by a fluke that any of your species can become vampires at all. As it is, the wonder is that so *many* can be made vampires, not so *few*.

"Lucy killed her father. To his credit, he accepted the truth at last, stood bravely to protect others, and died well enough. Well, this is one of those cases where—as you say—better late than never. Lucy happened to spare her mother and kid sister. In fact, there was just one other victim, a young woman who has been declared dead but is in fact in the process of turning into a vampire."

It was Amanda who asked, "Can you stop it or save her in any way?"

"No. I am very sorry, but not now—it is too late for that. Nor can we take her in and put her to bed. The structure of force fields we have constructed, the matrix, has just sixty-four places. For technical reasons, it is not possible to expand it or have any more. If they had tried more than sixty-four times, those original girls over the limit would just have had to be killed, for there would be no room to provide for them. And so now, this one will just have to be killed. I am very sorry for that one, but as it is, I give thanks to God that, in His mercy, I shall not have to play God and decide who goes into the matrix and who must simply be killed. It is very clear what must be."

"Maybe this one should take the place of the one who drank her blood."

"Yes, Wendy—that is the natural and obvious thing to say, and of course I thought of that. Perhaps that would be the best way, in terms of natural justice. On the other hand, the girl who did it is herself totally blameless. In any event, it is not about that—it is about blunt practicality. The matrix has been set up to fit the one who drank her blood. It will not fit her. It cannot be changed without collapsing the whole thing and starting over. By the time we did that, she would already have to have been killed anyway, as a homicidal maniac. So there it is."

Margaret asked, "Too late to stop it now? Why? I mean, if it were tried, what physically would happen?"

"Well, yes, the process could be forcibly arrested. But it would take so much energy to do it that her tissues would be fried to a cinder, and she would be dead anyway."

At this point, Wendy spoke up. "Well, so what? If that is all, then why not do it? After all, if it comes to that, it would be better to die cleanly and honorably as a woman, straight out, than be turned into a vampire and then have to be killed anyway." All the other women agreed. Except Alicia, who surprised all of them by calling an intermission when the Queen asked her to do so.

CHAPTER EIGHTEEN

During the intermission, Queen Paula took Wendy aside and said to her, "May I probe into you and exploit your linkages to other people? I assure you, it really is that important." There were telepathic linkages to her mother, her daughter, and others with whom she had had enough intimate contact over the years. These linkages were ordinarily dormant and even subliminal. Wendy agreed and felt a momentary flush as she was probed. "Right. I called for the intermission because I came to suspect something, and now I have verified it. Wendy, do you know who that girl is, the one who is turning into a vampire?"

What she said next, Wendy had not consciously realized was in her mind until she said it. "There is a dark foreboding in my mind. I suspect, but I do not know. Is it my cousin Elizabeth?"

"Yes, Wendy, it is. I am very sorry."

"How did you know? You do not have any linkage with her."

"No, but Theodora does—much more than you. I can perceive the structure of exotic energies of someone's body much better than you or even Ginger. Within Theodora's structure, something extraordinary regarding one of her daughters showed up very blatantly, like nothing I had ever seen before. Once I realized that, the rest was easy enough."

"So, as was foretold years ago now, my cousin Elizabeth is gonna have to be killed, and I'm gonna have to kill her. I'll not ask how we tell her mother. There's only one way to do it, and that's just straight out."

"No, Wendy—you keep quiet until you are called upon to speak. I am the one to do it." Wendy was very grateful for this. But that did not diminish her dread of how they would all get through the next minutes. She cried out to God, Queen Paula joined her, and then they returned.

As she sat down, Wendy looked around at the others. Ginger knew. Diana and Alicia might or might not know. Margaret and Amanda knew there was *something* dark and terrible at hand, but not yet *what* exactly. Alfreda, with no special powers at all, suspected something was wrong just because the intermission had been called, but she knew nothing beyond that. As for Theodora, it took just a moment, and then Wendy understood. Yes, she knew and did not merely suspect, but her knowledge was still subliminal. She seemed distracted, but that was because it was too much for her mind to accept, and this was how her mind protected itself from having to be consciously aware of the truth.

Now the Queen was speaking. "I spoke with Wendy privately in order to have her help in verifying what I had come to suspect with the powers given me. Sad to say, it has been verified. There is no nice way, so I shall say it just straight out. Ladies, that girl I spoke of, who is turning into a vampire, is Elizabeth, Wendy's cousin and Theodora's daughter."

Theodora asked, "Did you just say what I think you said?"

Queen Paula replied, "Yes, I did, and I am very sorry. Your daughter Elizabeth has been attacked and destroyed by one of the vampire girls, as I explained, and she is now turning into a vampire."

After a moment of stunned silence, Theodora turned and said, "Alicia, what do you say? What is given to you to know about all this?"

"I am sorry, Theodora, but what is given to me is that what Queen Paula said is true, and what we discussed at your place the summer before last is being fulfilled."

"But, this is not what we discussed! Elizabeth was to be abused sexually somehow, but in some exotic way, even worse than simply being raped. She was to be turned into a monster, yes, but by having that happen to her."

Speaking as mildly as she could, Queen Paula answered, "Yes, Theodora, and that *is* what has happened to her. As I said, only women can be vampires. The way to think of it is that a woman can abuse her qualities and functions as a woman to be like a consuming vortex. She may be said to devour and destroy other people by doing so. This is, of course, a monstrous perversion of female sexuality, and to do that is enormously wrong, but there are plenty of women among your people who do it anyway. Well, a woman who goes wrong as a woman by setting herself up as a consuming vortex is like a lesser version of a vampire. But it is better to say it the other way around: a vampire is like a complete and perfect version of such a wayward woman. With a real vampire, the consuming-vortex character—which, in this context, is distinctively feminine—is more than just the corruption of her mind. It is the basis for her bodily functioning as well. In that way, and on that basis, the violence done to Elizabeth *was* sexual. And, as bad as rape is, this is worse. For the evil reaches into the victim more deeply and affects her more powerfully."

"What about the point that she was supposed to be started as an adult woman and not die as a mere child?"

It was Margaret who answered. "That has been very clearly fulfilled. Have you forgotten why she is not here among us? Elizabeth turned eighteen not so long ago, which makes her a legal adult. But more seriously, very soon after she turned eighteen, her awakening as a double-dose girl began, which is relatively early, but there it was. Along with this, it looked like she might be truly remarkable, perhaps even more than Wendy. So she traveled to take counsel from my sister, who is kind of like the family expert on this business. Again, it was she who pushed it. She insisted on learning, not merely about these powers, but more important, about the rights and duties attached as well. Indeed, if it were not for the question of rights and duties, she would have stayed home and pursued other concerns, based on the advice Alicia gave her. But she appreciated that with power comes responsibility. Given all these facts, I think we have to recognize her as at least the beginning of an adult woman, in fact and not just legally."

Theodora turned now to Wendy. "You helped her verify it? Then what do you say?"

"I am very sorry. After the Queen told me, and before I returned and sat down, I did my own probing in order to verify it for myself. Yes, it is true."

With that, the woman began screaming. She kept screaming for at least a full minute. When finally she stopped, Alfreda simply handed her a drinking vessel full of the same kind of red beverage she had given to Wendy and to Diana in years past.

When she had drunk and had regained possession of herself in some measure, Theodora said, "I stand by what I said just before the intermission. If she cannot be saved alive, then my daughter is at least entitled to die cleanly and honorably as a woman, straight out, given that she can be burned up before she turns into a vampire."

"Is it certain this is what Elizabeth would choose for herself?" Yes, indeed so. Theodora had overheard Elizabeth at her prayers sometimes, and the girl would pray God that if possible, she might simply be killed rather than turned into a monster. "All right, then. I shall see what can be done. Theodora, I want to place my hand on your head and use your telepathic linkage to Elizabeth. May I do so?" Yes, of course.

But alas! Something had gone wrong. The Queen's calculations had been right based on the information she had at the time, but those calculations had been rendered totally worthless. "Dearest God, please! No! I am very sorry, but it is too late now. There is nothing I can do. We shall have to wait now for her situation to develop and ripen. It should not be so. There should still be maybe three or four hours—five at the outside. But that is based on—well, as I told you, she has been declared dead, albeit falsely. Her body was supposed to be kept in cold storage. That would preserve her body by retarding the chemical processes involved in decomposition. But it would also retard the chemical processes of her body that are involved in having her turn into a vampire. That gets into technical details, but those are not important right now. The point is that cold storage retards the process, and warmth allows it to go more quickly. Well, there is a weakness in some of their equipment for refrigeration. Elizabeth's body has been kept at a higher temperature than it should have been for a considerable time. So the process went faster than I calculated. The critical point was passed two or three hours ago. There is no stopping it now, even at the price of burning up her tissues."

Margaret spoke up. "Again, why not? What physically would happen if you tried?"

Queen Paula paused, took thought, then replied, "I am sorry. My words have misled you. That is my fault, for I did not say it rightly. There is no stopping it now, for she is not anymore a woman *turning into* a vampire. Technically, her life as a vampire has already begun. It has merely to be—consolidated. That is the best way to say it. The coherent structure involved must be fully developed. Otherwise, her death—her *real* death—will be a long process of torture." She stopped, then resumed. "I can retard that process by remote control, even arrest it, long enough for her to be brought back here so that she can be properly taken care of. But that is all."

It was Amanda who said, "'Properly taken care of?' That is a very nice way to put it!"

"Yes, it is, and I am sorry. I do not mean to be cute in a nasty way. But think about it. If I do not intervene, the process will go through to completion in five hours at most. Then she will arise as a vampire where she is. It has been foretold that she will not be allowed to harm anyone else. But that will be fulfilled by having my friends watch, and wait, and destroy her as a monster, and that will be that. They will, quite sincerely, wish and hope for the best for her eternal destiny, but it will be like having a rabid dog shot down in the street, as you say."

Beatrice had to explain what this meant.

"Alternatively, if I do intervene, she will remain dormant for a long time, and they will go on thinking her truly dead. She will be sent back here, and when she arises, all that is still possible will be provided for her. Elizabeth must be killed so as to be truly dead, but her death will be a genuine act of euthanasia based on the serious concern to put her out of her misery. Even more, as far as may be, she will enjoy the dignity of dying cleanly and honorably as a woman. You will be surprised at how much can still be done along that line. All that is what I meant when I spoke of having her brought back here so that she can be properly taken care of."

Alfreda asked, "How long before Theodora and Timothy receive the official notice?"

"Probably tomorrow, although it could be very late today."

Alfreda turned to Theodora. "What about Timothy?"

"He too is traveling. I shall of course send him word as soon as the official notice comes through, but he will not be able to return for some time."

Queen Paula said, "That will probably be best. We are kind of like the experts in this area. I include Alfreda, even though I can tell she has no special powers, for I gather she has been involved in these affairs before." Yes, indeed so. "But what about Timothy?" Theodora affirmed he was an ordinary man, even though he was a carrier. "Then it will be best that he should be involved only after all has been resolved and Elizabeth is already truly dead and in Heaven." She turned to Theodora and said, "Yes, you can relax—that is in the old prophecies given to us elves long ago. 'All the vampires among those people that may ever be in this world will be pure girls, and all will be heroes save for one innocent victim, but that one as well as all the others will dwell with God in glory and rejoice in Him forever.' That is how what is given to us translates into your language."

Theodora turned to Alicia. "Yes, it is given to me to know that it is so. That was given to her people, and what was proclaimed is true. That is what is waiting for Elizabeth and all the others. You need not be afraid for her." At this, Theodora broke down and wept with joy.

When she had gotten hold of herself again, she asked, "What about Lilith? Does all that apply to her?"

"No. She is not a true vampire as the others are. Her bloodsucking is more an act of willful and deliberate violence as a warrior girl, and that is not the same thing. But now, to get back to Elizabeth—Theodora, if you will allow me, I want to use your linkage to Elizabeth again." Theodora agreed, and it was done. "There—it is accomplished. Now the process will proceed, but very slowly, until she is properly developed and ripened, so as to be ready for euthanasia. Then the process will stop and remain at a dead halt."

"Can she stay or be kept at that point instead of having to be killed?"

Queen Paula smiled sadly. "So as to sleep through the ages, like the girl in that story you have? No, Theodora, that will not work. She will be dormant long enough to be received at my estate and be taken care of, but that is all. And if it were possible, what would be the point? With the girl in the story, there was the basis for her to be awakened someday and resume her life as a girl, if only it could be fulfilled somehow. There is nothing like that here. Elizabeth will not be awake again in this world other than as a vampire, except as she is dying. That is the situation on the ground. It is not up for debate or decision. I am sorry, but there it is."

Then Alfreda said, "I have been thinking. There are two questions. I believe I know the answer to the first, but it is my professional duty to ask. I have no idea about the second. So, first of all, you say Elizabeth was proclaimed dead falsely, and you speak of when she will be truly dead. Then, was she declared dead in error?"

"No, not by their standards for declaring someone of your species dead. Elizabeth was in fact dead, and is still dead right now, in terms of having her heart, her lungs, and especially her brain all shut down. In that way, she is as dead as any woman has ever been. Ordinarily, that would be enough—that would settle everything. It is just that in these exotic cases, with her as with Lucy, there is something going on underneath that overrides all that."

"That is what I expected, but I had to ask. Second, why was an autopsy not done, and what would the result have been if it had?"

⸻

Beatrice explained this to the others.

⸻

The Queen responded in the last way any of them would have expected—she laughed. "I am sorry—of course it is not amusing, but this is one of those crazy twists and ironies that go to make up much of what you people call the absurdity of life. More seriously, this is one of those cases where someone has to laugh to keep from screaming or sobbing. You see, if an autopsy had been done early enough, Elizabeth would have been killed—truly killed to be really dead—by having her body cut up. It was not done because at present there happens to be a minor outbreak of influenza at that place, even though this is not the season for it. The thing is, Elizabeth could have survived the loss of blood. They found her wounds, although they did not know the cause, and they transfused blood into her."

⸻

Beatrice did not have to explain this—the others knew about such things from the third planet of the next yellow star.

⸻

"No, but it was the loss of exotic energy that shut down her body more than anything else. To a physician of your tradition who lacks paranormal capabilities, it would look as if she had simply been powered down and deactivated, like a machine that has been switched off. In addition, before it shut down, her body reacted to the influence she received from Lucy with fever and inflammation. So to a superficial view, given the situation at that time and place, it might look like she had died of influenza, and that was their diagnosis. On that basis, they figured no autopsy was called for. Lucy would also have been killed by an early autopsy, but there was no clinical involvement, and she has not been diagnosed as dead. The man she killed was treated by a more experienced physician with a sharper eye. He was also given blood and later diagnosed as having died naturally, but from an unknown sickness, not from influenza. An autopsy was done on him in order to learn more, but that attempt failed. They had to settle for the answer of unknown sickness."

Ginger blurted out, "Given what they know about Lucy and the others as vampire girls on account of their parents' evil, surely Wendy's government must know more than that about what sent Lucy's father."

"Of course they know well enough what really happened. What then? They look to keep this whole affair very secret. The line of least resistance for them is to let stand the diagnosis of death by unknown sickness, and that is what they decided, and that is what they are doing. They are standing aside and letting me and my people take care of everything."

Wendy asked, "Alicia, so there is no question, am I commanded to kill Elizabeth now?"

"Yes, you are. What was said long ago is being fulfilled. That is what is given to me."

There followed a brief discussion of practicalities and arrangements. It was agreed that Elizabeth would be transported to the Queen's estate, and there she would be taken care of. But it was further agreed that most of the planning should be held off until the official notice came through. And so the meeting broke up, and then they waited.

But before she left that day, Queen Paula took Wendy aside and said, "I must begin expanding your powers now." With that, she placed her hand on Wendy's head for just a moment. Wendy felt a quick flush expand to fill her head and run through her whole body. It was over in just another quick moment. "There—it is done. When you wake up tomorrow morning, you will feel a mild euphoria, and you will be equal to Ginger."

This happened as the Queen had said. The official notice concerning Elizabeth also came through that day. The notice came early enough that most of the day was spent on arrangements and preparations as they communicated with those devices and met with each other. At the end of the day, the Queen touched Wendy's head again and told her she would be equal to Ginger's grandmother when she awoke the next morning. This too was fulfilled.

Late the next morning, Wendy, Theodora, and Alicia went to Queen Paula's estate to await Elizabeth's arrival. But each of the three arrived separately. Wendy was first. When she reached the front gate, she paused before entering.

So, she thought, *this is it—this is Fairyland. This is what all the old stories were about, and it exists in real life. In spite of all the nonsense in those stories, it exists in real life.* There was no foreboding in her mind—quite the opposite. Somehow she felt, not that anything was wrong, but rather that here, at this place, things were unusually right. Wendy called upon God to see her through whatever there might be and crossed the threshold.

Here, in this realm, the colors of things were brighter and clearer, the outlines of things were cleaner and sharper, everything was more—in focus, than things were out beyond the gate. The difference was unmistakable, even though it was rather subtle. But she knew the difference was also nothing of the kind that any optical instrument could detect. Then she understood.

—What was it that old author had said, in that dream fantasy novel she had read? Ah, yes. "It was more like itself, that is, more ideal, than ever." Yes, that was not exactly the quote, but close enough. As that author had said, a thing was more ideal as displaying more plainly and fully the basic idea at its heart.—But hey, given this adventure is about the nightmare filth of vampires, all that should be expected. For here is the world where heights and depths, glories and horrors, stand forth in greater purity, with less admixture of the comparatively neutral concerns of common routine.

Now Alicia had come and was speaking to her. Yes, she too saw it. They discussed it briefly. Then Theodora came. For just a moment, she too was overwhelmed with wonder. Then she broke down and wept. "The irony is too horrible. This realm of fantastical beauty is where my daughter will have an ugly death as a monster!" Then she began weeping again.

"No, Aunt Dorry, but this realm is where the ugliness will be purged from Elizabeth."

"By killing her in cold blood!"

Alicia spoke up. "Yes, for even death itself is made to serve Him now." Theodora smiled sadly and nodded.

"Aunt Dorry, I know it still hurts too much, in spite of what Alicia said. For whatever it may be worth, I would rather die myself than do this."

"I know that, Wendy. Otherwise, I would be very reluctant to allow it." Queen Paula had arrived to escort them. "Ladies, I bid you welcome to my realm."

Soon after, when they were sitting together at lunch, Wendy said, "Queen Paula, one thing puzzles me. This realm is a land of special clarity and beauty. But it is so as an extension of the superior level of being and functioning your people have. But then your own body should be that way as well. Yet that is not what we saw out yonder."

"Very good, Wendy. Now why do you think that is?"

"Probably because you suppress it in some way."

"Yes, exactly so. But why?"

"I expect because my people would find it destructive or unbearable or perhaps both."

"Right, indeed they would. The material world is in fact a structure of poetic beauty, as being an image of Divine glory that embodies His wisdom. But for most of your people most of the time, to see it that way would be more than their minds could accept. This is one of the measures of your corruption, to speak bluntly. They need to see it as a mere construct based on—well, on what you think of as the laws of physics and chemistry. This entails their world really has to work that way for them. So that is what is provided. As your Book says, even the ground is cursed on account of your evil. What you see here is not trickery—it is reality. What you see out yonder is the artificial set up, based on what I have just explained. You must understand that the measure of reality here in my realm is fairly mild compared with what there is in my homeland as an alien being. Of course, even *that* is quite weak compared with what there is up in Heaven."

"Does that mean you can throw aside the laws of physics and chemistry?"

"If you must speak in those terms, then the answer is yes. But that is the wrong question to ask. We do not defeat those laws on their own level. We act on levels where those laws are themselves subordinate. That is the basis for what you people call elvish magic."

"Then what about what my family has?"

Queen Paula had to stop and think for a long moment. Then she said, "First of all, you will notice that in order to make your gifts work, the women of your family have to be considerably more honest and realistic than is common among your species—even among the women of your species. That is a big chunk right there.

"Yet many women are as much that way—or even more so—but they have no such powers. Right. My functioning depends on material mechanisms, just as the work of a craftsman depends on his tools, even though he is superior to his tools. It turns out that people of your species can have some of the relevant lower-level mechanisms in some very slight measure. That is what is going on with your family and with Ginger's family as well."

"Many of my people say there are only material mechanisms with nothing superior."

"Yes, Wendy, I know that. But then what do they know of me, or my realm, or anything along that line? Nothing. That being so, there is no reason I should care what they say."

Alicia asked the next question. "Your Majesty, if this place does not exactly work by the standard laws of physics and chemistry, then how can we breathe the air, drink the water, and eat the food?"

"Very good, Alicia. As I told you, the measure of reality here is comparatively mild, both to keep from disrupting the whole system of your world and to minimize the concern over what you said. But also, on the other side, your bodies have been correspondingly enhanced. You have not noticed it before—you have been preoccupied. You cannot readily notice by looking at your own bodies, although you could eventually. You have seen it in me, but you have dismissed it as being just my elvish superiority. But now stop and look at each other—really look carefully."

And so they did. Queen Paula articulated what they saw. "Speaking somewhat loosely, the easy way to sum it up is that out yonder, my body is more like a mess of biological facts. Here, my body is more like a structure of feminine power and perfection. It is not just that I am *perceived* that way—I *am* that way in fact, for I suppress my functioning in some measure. A very mild version of that applies to you ladies as well, but in the opposite direction. Instead of being suppressed out there, you are enhanced in here."

Theodora asked, "What will happen when we leave?"

"A very mild version of what happens to me, again in the opposite direction. There will be no active change of functioning—you will simply revert. For just a moment, it will feel like you have gone into a hostile environment where you must strain to see, or hear, or stand upright, or even breathe. But your bodies will readjust, and the feeling will pass, in less than one second."

"A very mild version, you say. Then, for you to be present in our world...?"

"Yes, Theodora. I must suppress my natural functioning and then compensate for the hostile environment. It is an ongoing process of serious bodily exertion for me. No, do not be sorry for me. I knew what I was getting into, and I chose this life. All of us did. You see, when we came to what should have been the end of our age in this world, with the advent of your species, we looked forward with eager anticipation to going on. Well, as I have explained, that fell through, and some of us had to stay to take care of Lilith. We knew that would entail going out into your world and dealing with your people. In spite of that, it was a highly prized honor among us to be chosen to stay behind. And let me assure you: knowing what we know now, every one of us would do it all again."

After a long pause, Theodora asked another question. "So what happened with Lucy? Did the friends you recruited from our species hold her dormant until they managed to bring her here? That trip across our world would be difficult with a comatose woman to haul around."

"Oh, no, not at all. Scattered across your world, we have what you would call safe houses, with just a few elves in each. They are like bubbles or pockets within the system of your world. One safe house is near where Lucy was captured. My friends gave Lucy to the elvish mistress of that house. From there, in turn—well, we have our own ways of doing things, which I am not going to discuss here and now."

This talk of bubbles in the system set off something in the back of Wendy's mind. It took her a moment, and then she understood.

"What is it, Wendy?"

"No, Your Majesty—it is just too crazy. I want to ask Ginger before I propose it."

"You ask me instead. You let me be the judge of how crazy it is."

"Well, I am reminded of a trick that Ginger explained to me. Bubbles in the system—what about doing that for Elizabeth? Perhaps she could not go into the matrix, but could it be wrapped around her or something like that?"

Queen Paula let out a long, thin whistle. "Yes, you are right—it *is* totally crazy. But it is just crazy enough that it might work." With that, she summoned two other elves telepathically, a man and a woman. Then she spoke to them in elvish language. After two or three minutes of this, she said to them, in the language Wendy had learned from her mother, "Very good, very good indeed. Now you give the news to my friends here."

The man said, "Yes, the—the mathematical physics, as you would call it, can be made to work. It will be somewhat tricky, but there is no question that we can do it. As for what effect it will have on Elizabeth, my colleague is the one to speak of that."

The woman said, "As for Elizabeth herself, I am sorry, but it will not save her life. She will still require euthanasia as a full vampire. However, it will help her. When she arises, her mind can be held clear of vampiric frenzy long enough for a serious act of ending her life rightly as a proper woman, instead of for just a very few minutes. Moreover, it will also help the others by reshaping the matrix. Maybe they can be saved alive and maybe not, but there will be a much more serious chance for them. At the least, they will have much more time as clear-minded, proper women when they awaken."

Wendy said, "A much more serious chance? I thought there would be no problem once Lilith had been persuaded to cooperate."

Queen Paula answered, "I am sorry—perhaps my words have misled you. All of us elves know, and Lilith knows, that of course it is a doubtful chance at best. I spoke as I did because I forgot you did not know." She paused, then told the other elves, "Elizabeth will be here fairly soon now. You go and make all ready." They went and did so. Then she added, "We shall know twenty-four hours after she goes into the bubble how it will be. All I can tell you now is to be ready for anything."

Elizabeth arrived late the next day, shortly before sunset. She was placed into a box that was then hermetically sealed, with atmosphere, temperature, and the balance of exotic energy carefully controlled to protect her body against decay and deterioration. Then the matrix was activated and wrapped around her, which would keep her dormant and provide at least some measure of healing. Now they could only wait.

At the end of the day, when Elizabeth was securely lodged at Queen Paula's estate and all that was possible had been done, the Queen touched Wendy's head again and told her she would be equal to Ginger's great-great-grandmother when she awoke the next morning. "And that is it. You will have the full power of the friends I have recruited from among your people."

"Right, then. So in a little while, I can kill my cousin Elizabeth."

"As I told your aunt Amanda, this is the best of the miserable choices available."

"Yeah, I know. But there should be some sort of better way."

"I know that. Wendy, you must try to understand. We have known these days were coming since—well, long ages past. Not with you and your cousin, of course, but with some people, who would be created to God's own image and likeness as much as anyone else. Please, for your own sake, do not disturb your mind and make your heart sick trying to find some trick or gimmick to get out of it. You have received Divine prophecy, and that settles it, as you know. And what if you had not? We elves are smarter than you and your people, we know more, and we have spent *centuries* thinking about it, trying to find or contrive something. We have gone over it again and again, from all different angles. It is just not there. No better answer exists. I am very sorry."

"Yeah, well, I thank you for trying. It is not so much that Elizabeth must die, although that is bad enough. All women die. It is not even that I must kill her. Given the situation, well—so be it. It is that there *is* this situation. To die like this—that is just too much."

"Again, I know that, Wendy. Why do you think I am giving myself the trouble of doing it this way instead of having my friends just destroy her as a monster?"

Wendy bowed her head in docile submission. "Yes, Ma'am."

Then the Queen smiled sadly. "Wendy, I am not your enemy—quite the opposite. I am not being harsh or cruel, although I know it must feel like that to you. Tomorrow I shall train you for what has to be done. Maybe not tomorrow night, but soon enough, Elizabeth will arise, and you will take care of her, and then her living, waking nightmare will all be over. That is how you must think of it: as taking care of her in the best way still available. Again, I know you want to get it over with, but it will be best to think of getting it over with for her even more than for yourself, so that she can go home and be at peace in Heaven, as was foretold."

Wendy followed the Queen's advice, as well as praying to God, and it worked out for her. In this way, she managed to get through the next days. "The stories among your people are right about one thing. A vampire is, in fact, hard to kill. The reason is that it is about the structure of exotic energy and not about her tissues. Specifically, the structure of metastatic charge—that is perhaps the best way to say it in your language—well, the structure of metastatic charge inside her must be collapsed. Once that is done, she will be dead in less than two minutes. But if the structure were collapsed and nothing else were done, her death would be like torture. It would feel to her as if her body were being consumed with cold fire until she lapsed from consciousness, which would take a little over a full minute. Happily, that is out of the question. The quick, clean, easy way to collapse the structure of metastatic charge within her will also do severe damage to the structure of her tissues, enough to kill an ordinary woman. But it will merely deprive Elizabeth of consciousness within several seconds. It will also be intensely painful, but much milder than the other, which she will not feel because of the damage to her tissues."

"What is the procedure? What am I to do?"

"Exactly what Pepper did when she tried to kill you. No, Wendy, do not be horrified. Yes, I know, it does not sound like euthanasia as you people think of it, but just stop and think. You were in fact not killed, but what is your feeling about that way of dying, given what you know of it from your own experience?"

After a pause, Wendy forced herself to say, "Alicia promised Elizabeth her death would be quick, clean, and merciful. I guess I would have to agree. Other things being equal, I would be very grateful—even kind of happy—if I could be sure my own death when it comes will be no more dreadful than that. It is bad enough, but not nearly so bad as all that. Any ordinary adult courage should be able to suffer through that measure of harshness well enough, and certainly if a woman can make it through childbirth, she can make it through that. It is having to face death along with the harshness that is the chief difficulty."

"Well, there you go! After you suppress the vampiric functioning and clear her mind as far as may be, you can comfort her by explaining all that to her."

"If I can do that, then why does she have to be killed?"

"Because she can only enjoy such benefit for three or four minutes, six at most, and then she will revert, after which it will be several weeks before she can enjoy the benefit again. That is, apart from the effect of the matrix. You see, it really will be a serious benefit to her."

"Then, what am I to do? Can a vampire be killed with a simple knife through the heart?"

"Not a simple knife, no. The knife you will use will be thickly coated with silver. The stories are right about the value of silver for killing vampires. That will collapse the structure, and the damage to her heart will degrade the circulation of blood to her brain. Her experience will be exactly like that of an ordinary woman who dies from being stabbed through the heart. Moreover, the collapse of the metastatic structure will entail dying with her mind fully clear, or at least as much as the mind of any woman is clear as she is dying in that way. You know what I mean. But come now—you must be trained in how to kill with a knife so as to make her death as soft and mild as possible. There is no time for extensive practice, and so I shall just feed it directly into your mind and body, with your permission." Wendy agreed. Queen Paula touched her head, she felt the flushing again, and then the Queen said, "That is it. Your training is accomplished. Your mind and muscles are ready."

"May I help her through with telepathic influence?"

"Yes, of course! That is expected. I shall be surprised and sorry if you do *not* do that." Then the Queen went on to explain something important. "Wendy, I need to tell you something in order to remove any doubt or question that may linger in your mind. You need to understand that we cannot keep her here. She would break free in a few hours at the most, and then she would rampage across your world as a homicidal maniac. So it really does have to be done."

"Well, but—Your Majesty, why would she break free?"

"The answer is somewhat technical, but it goes back to the way our elvish powers—and thus the powers I have given to those of your kind as well—do and do not latch onto the structure of exotic energy within her. The easy analogy is that the structure of metastatic charge makes her kind of slippery. We can do various things to her, but we cannot really hold onto her."

"The woman who turned her into a vampire, Lucy, was captured, held, and brought in."

"Lucy was dormant at the time, as I told you, and thus was totally helpless. Even if she had not been, it was *Elizabeth* she turned into a vampire, with Elizabeth's distinctive facts and features. That distorted Lucy's structure of exotic energy in an extraordinary way, and so she is not too slippery to hold for short periods, unlike most vampires."

Then the twenty-four hours were up. Alicia, Theodora, and Wendy sat and listened as the Queen gave them the news. "It will not be tonight or tomorrow or the next day. But it will be the day after that. I wish it were longer. Then she would have more healing, which would give her more time for her mind to be held clear. But there it is, and I am sorry. She will have maybe half an hour, maybe a full hour, or maybe even an hour and a half if she is lucky. Theodora, have you spoken with your husband?"

"No, I was not able to reach him. I have tried five times now."

"Too bad. It would be good to have him help comfort Elizabeth at the end. I am sorry for her and for you. Then again, as I said, it may be just as well." After this, the Queen told them how it would be—"Based on theoretical projections only, for this has never happened before in real life, as I told you."

The next day, Queen Paula spoke to the whole group to whom she had spoken concerning Elizabeth. "The stories among you speak of vampires as being killed while they are dormant. That can still be done for Elizabeth, who will rise very soon unless it is prevented. She would feel nothing. There would be no fear and no pain. She would simply awaken in the next world, fully purged and healed as she would be of any other sickness. Now, I have been following a different path. I believe she should be allowed to awaken, have her mind cleared, and be offered the dignity of submitting to a kind of formal ritual. But, is there any question or dispute among us on this point? Are we agreed that this is the better way, instead of having her die as she sleeps? If not, we need to discuss it now, while there is still plenty of time." But indeed they were agreed. It was Theodora who summed it up and laid it out for them.

"Elizabeth is my daughter. As her mother, I know her, and I am the one to speak for her. If she could have been kept from turning into a vampire at the cost of her life, it would have been different. But we are past that now. Again, if Queen Paula could keep her dormant, then it would be different—I would have to think about it. But as it is, Elizabeth must awaken as a full vampire unless she is killed off first." She looked at Queen Paula, who nodded in assent. "So be it. What then? The important thing is that her mind can be cleared for a little while. If it were not so, then once again, it would be very different. But as it is, we have to remember, she was enough of an adult person to have this happen to her. In view of these facts, and of the events leading up to this situation, we have to consider that Elizabeth is entitled to face her fate and stand her death as a woman, instead of being simply put down as we would do for a sick animal.—And yes, Your Majesty, this is what she would choose for herself. I know her well enough to be sure of that. Indeed, I know much more. I know this answer is clearly implicit in the choices she has already made." All concurred, and so it was decided.

Here Beatrice paused to explain. "Elizabeth had not anticipated a final interlude with her mind cleared. She had expected to be a full monster right up to the moment she was killed. For that reason, she had hoped to be killed while dormant, thinking that would be best for everyone. But given the chance for the interlude, the question had to be reconsidered. From the nature of the case, Elizabeth could not be consulted, and so Theodora decided for her. She decided rightly. Her decision based on the new information was in fact implicit in what Elizabeth had believed in and followed through the years."

Now the dread day had arrived. Elizabeth had been removed from the matrix, removed from her box, and placed into a large room. The sun had sunk almost to the horizon. Wendy came and waited where Elizabeth was. All the others from those meetings at Margaret's house except Queen Paula waited along with her. ("I would be with you if I could, but this task is for you and your people.") All too soon, the sun had set, darkness had fallen, and Elizabeth arose. The place was richly supplied with artificial illumination, and so there was no trouble about seeing her. It had been agreed that Wendy was to do all the talking, along with Alicia if need be, unless and until the others were specifically called on to speak.

When she arose, she growled and slobbered in the manner of a ravenous animal. The first thing she did was to rip off the monitoring devices Amanda had attached to her. Then, as if to prove herself as a dangerous wild animal, she tore off the gown that had been placed upon her, so that she was totally nude. Then she looked around, saw her mother, and began walking toward her. She stopped growling and slobbering and said, "Mommy! Dear, sweet, mommy! Come now—let me show you the rich love a devoted daughter can offer her mother, far beyond anything either of us dreamed before." It was obvious enough from her words what was coming. But even worse was her tone. Her voice was very sweet—much more than any of them had ever heard before from her. It was far too sweet, with something dark and filthy and poisonous just below the surface.

Elizabeth was still at least twelve feet from her mother when Alicia intervened, not by speaking, but by holding up a classic symbol of the Faith. On this point as well, the old stories were right—Elizabeth found this unbearable and stepped back quickly, continuing backward until she was up against the opposite wall, a look of horror on her face. Then Wendy spoke.

"Do you know why I am here, Elizabeth?"

Now she reverted to growling and slobbering. "You are looking to make trouble for me."

"No, I am looking to *resolve* trouble for you. Please do not contradict me. You know I have never lied to you. I am not lying now. I am not going to lie to you, and I am not going to make any promises I am not prepared to keep, just as I have never done before. As I say, I am here to resolve trouble for you—to take care of you."

"Yes, you were always very gracious and generous to me. I know you loved me dearly."

"I love you dearly now, Elizabeth. That is why I am here."

"Then will you make Alicia put away that nasty piece of harshness she is holding up?"

"When you ask me to do so as the devoted handmaid of the Lord God I remember, then yes, very happily. Are you asking as a devoted handmaid of the Lord God?"

Elizabeth's answer was to scream loudly in horror and rage.

"Well, you see, that is just the problem."

Elizabeth answered by screaming again, even more loudly.

"Are you even ready to speak as a woman, instead of growling and screaming as a ravenous wild animal?"

Elizabeth screamed a third time and lunged at Wendy, but Alicia headed her off again.

"All right, Elizabeth. You tell us why you are here. By that I mean, tell us what you want. And no lies—no deceit. You know I can detect any such attempt with the powers I have. Are you looking to drink your mother's blood?"

"Yes, I am."

"Are you looking to make her as you are now?"

"Yes, with all my heart."

"Is this the rich love you offered her?"

"Yes, certainly."

"Do you recognize or understand any other kind of love?"

"No, not at all. I did once, long ago, but that was back when I was just another fool."

"Is there anything else you need or want to say to us?"

"Only that I would offer all of you the same kind of rich love, if you would allow it."

"All right, Elizabeth, now I am going to help you with the special powers I have. I shall do it gradually, over about a minute. It will not hurt. It will feel like waking up. I am not going to drive you crazy—quite the opposite. You will understand and remember everything you know now, but you will also know much that you cannot understand or remember now. By this you will know that I have spoken truly and that I have not merely driven you crazy. Do you understand what I have just told you?"

"Yes, I do, Wendy. You have never played tricks on me before."

"And you will see in a moment I am not doing so now. Here we go."

Over the next minute, Wendy simply stared at Elizabeth with her eyes narrowed as Alicia kept holding up that classic symbol of the Faith. It worked out exactly as Wendy had said. After just a few seconds, Elizabeth's face showed the astonishment of one who suddenly finds herself suffering through growing awareness. At the end of the minute, Elizabeth fell to her knees and cried out, "My God! What have I done?"

"Nothing to feel guilty over. You did only what you had to do, and not much of that. You stripped off your gown in front of us and then mouthed off, but for a vampire, that is nothing."

"A vampire?! Is that what I am now? Dear God!"

"Yes, you are a vampire now. I can clear your mind somewhat for a very limited time, but that is all. Think back. Remember and think it through for yourself."

She did so. "Good Lord, yes—I see it must be true. I am a vampire. God help me." Then she turned to Alicia.

"Yes, child, you are a vampire now. This is what we discussed at your house the summer before last, and it has been fulfilled. I am sorry."

"Yes, I remember the discussion. Must I be killed now?"

"Yes, you must. I am very sorry."

Now she spoke again, but as a pure and innocent girl, not as a monster, and with much more the voice of an adult woman. "I have asked God that I might simply die instead of being turned into a monster. I stand behind that all the more now that I remember the filth I spouted. I apologize to all of you—especially to you, Mommy. Please forgive me. Alicia, you said my death would be quick, clean, and merciful. Is that true?"

"Yes, child, it is. As for the other, we understand—all of us, including your mother. We have nothing to forgive." Elizabeth turned to Theodora, who simply nodded in assent.

Then she turned to Wendy. "Wendy, you were right, and I apologize. Yes, I am ready to speak as a woman instead of as a wild animal—for which I thank you."

"As Alicia said, we have nothing to forgive. As for thanking me, it is an honor to do this."

"But I must apologize again, for I see I cannot fulfill my dignity as a woman instead of being like an animal. I have torn apart my gown. I have nothing to wear."

"Yes, you do." Wendy took a bag from Theodora and brought out a dress and sandals. "We knew it might happen this way." When Elizabeth was clothed and shod, Wendy said, "Now you can fulfill yourself as a proper woman for as long as your mind can be held clear."

Here again, Beatrice paused to explain. "What Elizabeth was given to wear was based on what she herself had chosen to be buried in, albeit indirectly. Once she was killed, she would be purged of the nightmare filth. What moral and spiritual purity she had going in would be there underneath all along, and this purity would then be restored to be fully effective. So, after taking counsel from her mother and from Alicia, Elizabeth chose a simple, long, white and green print dress with long sleeves and a high neck line. For her feet, she chose white sandals.

"This decision was an expression of faith and hope. White was to symbolize purity. But green was to symbolize life and renewal, which God would provide in His own good time.

"However, no final interlude with her mind cleared had been anticipated. But since it was to be, what should Elizabeth wear? Theodora figured the occasion of ritual euthanasia was not the time of renewal—it was the opposite. So an opposite color would be appropriate. On that basis, Theodora chose a simple brown dress and simple brown sandals for her daughter, figuring brown fits autumn, the season opposite that of renewal." The axis of rotation of Beatrice's planet was less tilted than that of Wendy's planet, and so the alternation of seasons was milder. But this alternation was still enough that Beatrice did not have to explain.

Elizabeth turned to Alicia. "What will happen to me now? Who will do what?"

"Wendy has a special knife that has been set up and prepared to kill vampires. She is going to ram it into your chest and run it through your heart. You must be as brave as you can and keep your mind on God and the things of God. There will be a quick moment of harshness. Then this nightmare will be over, and you will be on your way to Heaven."

She turned to Wendy, who assured her, "Yes, it is true. Remember, I myself have had exactly this done to me. It is somewhat spicy, but on the whole a soft and mild way to die. I would find it almost like a cause for celebration if I knew my death would be no worse than this. But first of all, I would spare you from having to take the filth with you. It will help you to talk it out and get rid of it. What happened to you?"

"It was really not seriously harsh or cruel. I was walking down the street just after sunset on an errand for Grandma's sister when I was set upon. My arms were grabbed from behind. Before I could get past my initial astonishment to react, my neck was bitten very severely, and I felt sucking. I struggled, but in vain. Then I felt some weird energy flowing into me—like dark fire is the best way I can describe it. Then I felt my mind beginning to fade. Somehow I knew I was dying, and so I cried out in my mind for God to have mercy on my soul. That is the last thing I remember before waking up here a little while ago."

"Another thing. You need to get this out even more. What is your craving like?"

"Oh, Lord, how to say it? It is kind of like hunger, thirst, and—I am ashamed to say it—erotic desire, all rolled into one. Yet there is also something else, rolled into that same package deal. It kind of like being cold and craving heat, vast quantities of heat, as if I cannot get enough to warm me up, but it is also clearly different from that, only I am not sure how else to describe it. Dear God, save me from myself! Wendy, until you cleared my mind, I was totally dominated by the craving, with no self-control at all—or nothing beyond the crafty patience of a ravenous animal." She turned again to Theodora. "Please forgive me, Mommy." Once again, Theodora simply nodded in assent. Then, "Wendy, better you do it than anyone else. But please, do it quickly and finish it for me, before I become too much afraid."

"What about your offer of rich love for your mother?"

"Now that is a very strange thing. Of course, there too, I was thinking like a wild animal. I wanted to consume her to fulfill my craving. Yet somehow, what I said was not just a stratagem to seduce her. I was speaking sincerely in some way. Perhaps that is the worst of it. I was really looking to show her some filthy, nightmare perversion of love." At this, Elizabeth would have broken down and wept, but Wendy spoke up quickly to comfort her.

"Relax, honey child. We have already gone through all that. You were insane, and that happened against your will. No blame or discredit attaches to you. There is nothing to forgive. This is why we are here: to see you through this nightmare and out the other side, which includes witnessing the symptoms." Wendy paused to let Elizabeth absorb this, then asked, "Now, one last thing. Why did you find the symbol of the Faith unbearable?"

"It was as if Alicia had opened up a magic window that allowed sunlight to come in and flood my soul. Then I saw my inner life as a vampire for the process of filth and darkness that it was, and I was filled with horror and loathing. It will all happen again when the clearing of my mind wears off. Please, Wendy, do it and send me before it starts back up."

"That will not happen for a little while yet. Relax—I shall give you plenty of warning. Perhaps it would be best to spend the time in prayers and hymns to God, if you are willing."

"Oh, yes, Wendy—yes, with all my heart."

So Alicia led them in prayer, and then Wendy led them in singing. All too soon, Wendy had to say, "And now, alas, this is the warning I promised. We have come to the end game."

Elizabeth stood there, waiting to be shepherded through the procedure. Wendy understood and said simply, "You may bid your mother goodbye."

They embraced, exchanged several kisses, and bade each other, "God be with you," through their tears. Then, as she parted from her mother, Elizabeth blurted out, "Wendy, I feel an overwhelming urge to strip naked again!"

"Not to worry—that is just a symptom your mind is fading. It will be best for you to go ahead and do it. Apart from everything else, the procedure will be easier if I have full and free access to your chest. Be not afraid. No one is here to see you but just us girls." She complied, and Wendy said, "Now that we have gotten past that distraction, you see how much easier it is."

With mild astonishment, Elizabeth said, "Yes, I do." Then, "One last thing. I know how it is for me as a vampire, and so I can figure how it must be for the woman who did this to me. Is that correct, it was a woman?" Wendy nodded in assent. "Then, if possible, tell her for me that I hope someday we may meet and be reconciled in Heaven. Now I am ready."

Wendy smiled and said, "Relax, honey child. It will be even easier for you than we said." She had Elizabeth lie back down on the table where she had been, utter a quick prayer, close her eyes, and keep repeating, "Glory to God in the highest." Then she waited, being unwilling to kill an innocent woman in cold blood. It took only a moment. Right after the last repetition of which Elizabeth was capable, Wendy detected she was a full vampire again, but calm and sedate for just these few seconds. So then, before the poor girl began to be tormented again by vampiric frenzy, and controlling Elizabeth's body as Pepper had once controlled her own, Wendy rammed the knife into Elizabeth's chest and through her heart. Almost at once, she withdrew the knife. Then, even before her mind was fully restored to be that of a woman again, Wendy acted with the special powers Queen Paula had given her. She touched Elizabeth's head and caused her brain to be flooded with endorphins. Now Elizabeth would not suffer at all.

The training Queen Paula had given her was very good, and the job was done very well. The knifing was quick, clean, and merciful, and of course the endorphins made it very easy for the girl. Wendy helped her with telepathic influence—first to focus her mind, and then to conclude with an extremely brief prayer. Then her mind faded, she lapsed from consciousness, and the nightmare was over for her.

Wendy waited and observed until she detected that the girl was dead, less than two minutes later. Then she announced the end of the nightmare. "Well, that is all. It is over now. Elizabeth is dead, really dead this time, truly dead as Queen Paula would say."

Theodora turned away, covered her face with her hands, and began sobbing.

Alicia said, "She has been set free to go home. The victory has been accomplished."

"Victory?! No, Alicia. Real victory would be if we had never come to this."

It was Ginger who answered. "Yes, Wendy, but you and I and people like us are not called upon to decide about that or strive after that. We have talked before about the movement of fate and destiny. People like us have to look at the limited things given into our hands, and with that, yes—the victory is accomplished. No level of victory beyond that is to be sought after."

"Oh, Ginger, I thank you for trying. But what you said cannot be good enough, because it is not good enough for poor Elizabeth."

Amanda spoke up. "The important thing is what Alicia said. Elizabeth has been set free to go home.—Also, she *asked* you to finish it for her."

"Yes, Aunt Mandy, and I thank you as well for trying.—But then why is all this that has been said not good enough?"

It was Diana who cut through it for her. "Because you are a decent woman, and you loved her dearly, and the fact that it had to be done does not make it any less dreadful. There would be something very wrong with you if it *were* good enough."

Then Wendy went to Theodora, knelt before her, and started to beg forgiveness. But Theodora brought Wendy back to her feet, and said, "No, Wendy, I have nothing to forgive. You killed my daughter, but I have nothing to forgive—quite the opposite!" They embraced, and both women started sobbing. All the others joined in.

A few minutes later, when the ladies had regained their composure, Queen Paula came into the room. "I could not be present, but I monitored all that happened with the powers given me. Theodora, I have witnessed the deaths of many of your people through the ages. Some did better, and some did worse. Your daughter's departure was truly noble and heroic. It was one of the finest examples I have seen, for whatever that may be worth." Theodora merely smiled sadly and nodded. "Wendy, it really did have to be done. Be comforted."

"I thank you for trying, Your Majesty. But—I am of two minds. I did this only because it is what God ordained for me. Yet I rejoice that Elizabeth has been set free and sent home, and I rejoice to be the one who did that. But Queen Paula, you should have had someone else—another recruit—do it instead. She was like the kid sister I never had. My heart should not have been torn out like this. No woman should have to suffer that."

"Dear Wendy, you poor child. For your own sake, you must tell me the truth. Would your heart be any less torn out if I had done what you said?"

Against her inclinations, Wendy admitted, "No, not really." Wendy was surprised at what she had said, but she realized it was true. And then another thing hit her. "You knew."

"I have not observed your species through all these centuries for nothing."

After that there were some formalities to be taken care of. But this did not take long. Then the Queen asked Diana and Margaret to take Wendy home. The others would remain for a while for further discussions. Thus ended Wendy's first episode with the work of handling vampires. As she had been warned, it was not at all to be her last.

CHAPTER NINETEEN

There was much more to be done for Elizabeth, but it was out of Wendy's hands. First of all, her body would have to be disposed of. The day after Wendy ended the nightmare for her, Theodora explained there had not been any planning or even discussion within their family about those concerns until that horrible meeting the summer before last. "But the day she left to visit my aunt, it was as if she knew. I can see that looking back, although I did not see it at the time. That day, she said to me, 'Mommy, please pray to God for me that if anything should happen to me on this trip, I may go to Heaven. But if this is when I am to be turned into a monster, please give your blessing to whoever has to kill me, and then do whatever has to be done with my body to make sure there is no more trouble.' I made light of it and fluffed it off, although I was deeply terrified underneath. I hoped it was not yet time, for I underestimated how much of an adult person she already was. But it *was* time, and it happened, and there it is, and here we are." Then, by sheer force of will, she managed to conclude by saying, "So, Queen Paula, what is the standard procedure?"

"There is none. It is given to us to set the precedent. I shall tell you what can be done, and then we can go from there." Theodora agreed to this, and the Queen began.

"I monitored by remote control what happened. That includes the telepathic assistance Wendy gave her. By the mercy of God, Elizabeth died with her mind restored in the final seconds to be that of a proper woman, and she even died as His devoted handmaid, with her mind crying out to Him in prayer. In that way, she *did* die cleanly and honorably as a woman after all, in spite of everything. Perhaps the best way to say it is that through her death, she was restored *as* a woman. We elves think of her as a dead woman, not a dead vampire. We need not destroy the body of a monster to make sure there is no more trouble. Elizabeth is dead, and she will remain dead. There is no need to make sure the monster does not rise again. That is just some crazy stuff from ridiculous stories. The monster is destroyed, and that ends it. Elizabeth will rise again only when the Lord God resurrects her, in His own good time. No, but it is about disposing of the body of a woman so as to honor her dignity as a woman. Her body can have its full feminine beauty restored, be dressed elegantly, and lie peacefully at the appropriate ritual of Divine worship. Then she can be buried, again with appropriate religious activity. Elizabeth will repose in the home territory of my realm here in your world. I shall be greatly honored to have her."

"How long do we have to complete the task?"

"Days—even weeks. As long as you need, if it should come to that. With our capabilities, her body can be kept here and preserved indefinitely. But, of course, it is best not to put it off."

"Where is your realm?"

"It is on the other side of your world and far to the north."

"Then we would never be able to visit her in her grave."

"On the contrary—you will be able to visit her whenever you choose. That will be provided for you. This is to be the age in which at long last, one way or the other—win, lose, or draw with the work given us—we can all go home to our own world. To provide for the families of fallen heroes—which is how we look upon Elizabeth—is just part of the cleaning up we have to do in order to finish the job rightly. To take care of her father and mother and little sister throughout their lifetimes, in that way and whatever other ways may prove to be appropriate, will be a pleasure for us. And, as we reckon time, it will mean only a slight delay in going home."

"Let me speak to my husband about it and speak to you again tomorrow, if I can finally get hold of him." This could be done with their devices for remote communication in real time. The Queen agreed to this, and so it was done.

Timothy agreed that Elizabeth's body should be richly prepared. For the rest, he asked that everything be held off until he returned, since there was the luxury of time. But he asked about something else as well. He too remembered that horrible meeting the summer before last, and so he asked whether what had been said had come true. Before Theodora could respond, he added, "Please, no nonsense. If it is so, tell me now, the truth, the whole truth, and nothing but the truth, straight out front, for both our sakes." And so she did.

When it was told, there was a pause for just a moment. Then he spoke, and his voice showed he was in some cold region beyond emotion. "If that story is true, then Lord love you all, and especially Wendy, for doing what had to be done. But how shall I know it is true? I am not doubting your word, nor am I doubting what Alicia told us at that meeting, nor am I denying what we discussed afterward. But how shall I know Elizabeth was truly turned into a vampire? How shall I know she was not misdiagnosed as dead when her vital signs were suppressed and then killed in error when she was merely insane?"

"The Queen said she would discuss that with you when you return. How long will it be?" He had been able to conclude the business sooner than was planned—just three more days now.

Four days later, Timothy met with the Queen, along with all the others. He heard from her the same story Theodora had told him, but with more background and details. He listened quite patiently and attentively and asked very reasonable questions. Finally he said, "Well, Your Majesty, given what I know about my wife and her family and their powers, and given what I know about Alicia and about what has been discussed in times past, I am sure enough your story is all true—as a general proposition. But that is just my problem. Yes, my daughter was to be turned into a thing that goes bump in the night, but was this truly the occasion that was foretold? How shall I know she was not misdiagnosed as dead and then killed in error when she was merely insane? Wendy, I am not blaming you—not at all. I know you loved her dearly, and you meant well, and you acted in good faith. I know you were striving to achieve the best for her, and for all that I bless you. But all that is one thing, and to be truly right is another. How shall I know you and the others were not horribly misled?"

Queen Paula replied, "First of all, let me assure you that what has happened to Elizabeth is a great sorrow to my own heart, to all my fellow beings here in your world, and to all my servants—my friends, as I call them—among your species. For myself and for all of us, I offer condolences to you and your family. With what I am about to say, I do not mean to be callous or cavalier. But as for your question, what would you accept as proof?—I am not being cute. I gather you want more than just what we have observed with what you would call our paranormal capabilities. Is that correct?" Yes, indeed so. "Then, Amanda, this question is for you."

Amanda began. "Timothy, as you know, I am a physician, among other things. I figured this question would arise, very probably from you and perhaps from others as well. So I checked it out and made sure as a physician, even apart from my special powers as a double-dose lady. Yes, it is absolutely certain she was dead by all standards other than those for a vampire girl. There are three proofs I have.

"First, as a physician, I was able to tap into the records at the hospital where she was diagnosed as dead. These were not just the records of their observations. I was able to tap into the recordings from their instruments as well." This had been done with the devices they had for processing information and for remote communication. "There is no question. Her body was totally shut down in the manner commonly known as death. I am sorry, but there it is.

"Second, what about the worst-case scenario—which is to say, what if she had been wrongly declared as dead but were still alive? She was sent back in the cargo hold of an airplane. When the airplane arrived, I checked with the staff, the crew, and made sure. Yes, the flight went normally, and they reached their appointed high altitude and all the rest of it. Inside the cargo hold, the air was too thin and too cold for Elizabeth or any woman to survive. Again, I made sure of that. So even if she had been alive, she would have been dead by the time she arrived here."

⸻

Beatrice explained to the others what all this meant. Other societies they knew about, whether of Normals or Renegades, had other things, but not that kind of air travel.

⸻

"Third, when she arrived, I myself checked her out very carefully. I took as my working assumption that she had, in fact, been misdiagnosed as dead and was still alive, and I then went through everything on that basis. But no, all the points proved to be negative. I did not even trust my own observation—I took a portable device and checked with that. But no, there was not a trace of electrical activity in her heart. I checked the device to make sure, and it was good. So there are the three proofs. And mind you, all this is apart from any paranormal awareness."

"So, Elizabeth really was dead, except for being a vampire."

"Yes. I am afraid so, and I am sorry."

"And then, when she arose, she did so as a vampire, with no question about it."

"Yes, that too. Timothy, she did not die as a monster. Elizabeth was criminally insane because her brain malfunctioned. As a physician, I have seen such things before. She had to be killed as a homicidal maniac in order to protect others, but as she was dying, her right mind was restored in the final seconds."

Timothy turned to Wendy. "Is that true?"

"Yes, it is true—very much so. Queen Paula has raised me up to have enormous powers compared even with what I had at that meeting the summer before last. After the knifing and before her mind was restored, I flooded her brain with endorphins so she would not suffer. When it was restored, I assisted her with telepathic influence to focus her mind and to call on God. That is how she departed—as a woman at prayer."

At this news, he was greatly relieved, but he said, "Tell me the rest of it, how it went."

The Queen said, "We can do better than that." Wendy's people had developed devices to record sights and sounds. One such device had been running in that room on that night. So now that recording was played for Timothy.

When he had seen and heard all, he sat in stunned silence for at least a full minute. Then he jumped up and cried out, "No! Not good enough! To be delivered from the nightmare only because finally she is really dead—no! That is no blessing! She deserved better than that!"

Wendy went and knelt down before him. "Timothy, my friend, I agree fully. What do you think has kept me from killing myself through these last five days?"

"What are you talking about?"

"Have you forgotten what the Queen said about the old prophecies and what Alicia said in confirmation? Yes, it was dreadful, but all women die, and—here comes the kicker, so listen carefully—*her eternal destiny is assured.* I think otherwise I might have ripped apart the wrist that held the knife and bled out."

Timothy smiled sadly and said, "Dear Wendy! No, you would not kill yourself. I know you better than that, even if you do not. Something would have stopped you—probably the discipline of the Faith." Then he stopped smiling as his face became twisted with anger. "As for me, if I kill someone, it won't be myself. No—if I kill, it'll be those filthy, rotten, no-good, low-down varmints who did it, who dare presume to collect taxes from me and then destroy—!"

Still kneeling before him, Wendy cried out, "Timothy, no! Elizabeth did not die with hatred and the thirst for revenge. Quite the opposite! As Theodora told you, as she was leaving, she said to *bless* the one who had to kill her. How do you think I feel? I burn with fury to balance what I did by avenging her on the ones who made me do it. But no, I know too much. We dishonor her if we lash out like wounded animals in her name. And that is before we get into the discipline of the Faith." With that, Timothy broke down and began sobbing like a child.

When finally he had regained some measure of composure, he asked to see his daughter, who was lying in state in the room where she had died to be truly dead. Her body had, indeed, been richly prepared. Ginger had done the cosmetic work to restore her feminine beauty, and Theodora had dressed her, with finishing touches by elves. It had been very well done.

Timothy turned to Alicia. "Her eternal destiny is assured?"

"Yes, it is. As I told her, what Wendy did was send her on her way to Heaven. Elizabeth did not know, of course, but that was more than just a pious hope, as we have explained to you."

"Then why does it still hurt so much?"

"As the Book says, He Himself found death something to weep at."

Timothy smiled sadly and nodded. Then, "Alicia, I believe you are gifted with healing as well as prophecy?"

"Yes, as He gives it to me. That is correct."

"Then why was Elizabeth not restored by being healed, instead of having to be killed? Yes, I know—all women and girls die, and healing is a special gift, and so on. I appreciate all that. But I mean, this is such an extraordinary situation that something extraordinary to resolve it might seem to be called for." He stopped, settled his mind more fully, and then said as calmly as he could, "I am not challenging or demanding. I am *asking*."

Alicia nodded and closed her eyes. After a brief moment, she opened her eyes, showed astonishment on her face, and said, "Whatever other reasons there may or may not be is withheld from me, at least for now. But there is something that Wendy knows—something that is very relevant—whether or not there is anything else."

"Yes, it is true. As I said, Queen Paula has given me vast powers. So I knew what was inside Elizabeth's body before I finished it for her." She paused, then said, "She was already doomed anyway, even before she was bitten. If she had not been bitten—if she had gone on normally as a woman—there was left for her about six weeks at most, and probably somewhat less. Then she would have taken sick and died within a few days. Clinical intervention would only have prolonged her agony. To be sure, all this should not have happened, but in one way, it was almost like a blessing in disguise."

Timothy objected, "But it was a blessing in disguise only because there were a whole lot of people standing ready and situations in place to make sure it worked out nicely for her. What if there had not been?"

Alicia replied, "But there were, and the point is that that was not a lucky accident. It was within the order of Divine Providence, just as this whole affair has been. And there is the answer to your question. One does not ordinarily expect a special miracle to overturn what is in fact a blessing in disguise, and that turned out to be how God chose to handle this whole crazy affair."

"Yes, ma'am. But then let me ask something else. Why was this crazy affair allowed? This is not like the normal evils that people just have to live with. It is across some great divide, it should not be possible at all, and yet it happened. Why?"

"That is not given to me at this time. I know what the Queen told us and what your wife's family knows, and I can confirm it, but that is all."

Alfreda said, "Maybe that is enough. Remember what the Queen said. The tampering that set all this into motion was across some sort of line, and now this is the consequence."

"Yet Elizabeth was herself involved with such affairs in some way. What about that?"

"No—wrong. Elizabeth was not tampering, not diddling around, not looking for trouble. She was doing the opposite instead. Elizabeth *found* these things awakening within her—not because she asked for it or sought it or desired it, but simply because that is what she inherited. This is what happens with all of us. She traveled and met with my sister to receive guidance so that she might honor God and do what is right with these functions, as with any other special talents someone might have. As you know, before she traveled she went through rituals and prayers and blessings, calling on God to purge her of what ought not to be, including even wiping away these powers if it should be so. This safeguard is standard for all of us exactly *because* of the danger you pointed to, Timothy—that of being involved, even though unwittingly, in forbidden filth."

"Yeah, I guess I knew all that well enough." But he still seemed doubtful, so Alicia spoke.

"Astrology is also forbidden by the book, yet one of the great saints of history believed in astrology. The difference was, he believed in the influence of the stars over people's lives only as being what God set up. Now, does astrology work in real life? That is irrelevant in this context. The point is this. What would get Elizabeth or anyone else into serious trouble is the concern to go beyond her appointed limits instead of accepting what God has given her to know and to work with and looking to Him to see herself and others through whatever is to come. Elizabeth's government did that, far beyond their usual dirty dealings, in an especially blatant way. So yes, it looks like that is why all this has happened, as Alfreda said. But Elizabeth herself did not."

As she heard Margaret and Alicia say all this, Ginger remembered that this safeguard was something she herself had gone through and that it was standard for the women in her family for exactly the same reason. Then she thought about that landmark saint. But she spoke to the others of these things only much later.

In the meantime, Timothy smiled sadly and nodded in assent. Then, after a long pause, he asked, "Wendy, I know what the Queen said, but you were able to make my daughter hold still. Why could she not have been held in restraint, instead of what happened?"

"Because the Queen was right. I held Elizabeth still for just a few seconds. I could have gone on holding her for maybe another minute, two at the outside." He was about to object again, but Wendy cut him off. "Timothy. Stop. Listen to me. In those horrible days when I was waiting to put Elizabeth down, the Queen warned me not to disturb my mind and make my heart sick by searching for some trick or gimmick to keep it from having to be done. That applies here as well. You will drive yourself crazy by going on and on with 'ifs' and 'maybes,' and it will be for nothing. It will not help you or Elizabeth or anyone else. If we were wrong, and there was another way, then God help us all. But the simple fact is that it has been done, and it cannot be taken back, and that is the situation on the ground. Now, would I accept that if our places were reversed and you had killed Anna with equal justification? Oh, Lord, I don't know—I really don't know. So first of all, the situation with Elizabeth must be finished out. After that, I am ready to negotiate with you for whatever you think you have to do."

At this point, Queen Paula cut through it for them. "No, Wendy. He will not avenge Elizabeth on you, just as you will not avenge her on the people behind this mess. This is how we all shall be punished. Nothing will be done until after the situation with Elizabeth is finished out. Then—not now but when she is old enough to understand—the rest of us will answer for our part by standing with you as you answer for what you did by facing Elizabeth's little sister, Sarah, with the truth. Timothy will answer by watching you squirm as his own guts burn because he was not around at the time to approve or object or say anything at all. That will be the bitter medicine all of us, including me, will have to swallow."

"Including you, Your Majesty?"

"Of course! I am a lawful queen, not a tyrant. With power comes responsibility, not some license to evade or shirk responsibility. The whole problem with your government is that they had already long since forgotten that, before this mess ever began. It would not have happened if they had remembered."

Then the Queen had Theodora take Timothy home, seeing he had gone through plenty for one day and had much to think about and was indeed already overloaded. In the following days, Theodora and the others did much talking with him to help him through.

But on one point, Timothy showed wisdom. "Your Majesty, your offer to have my daughter buried in your realm is very gracious and generous, and I thank you. But this is not about you or me or any of the rest of us. It is about Elizabeth. She never knew you, never met you, and never even heard of you or your realm within her lifetime." What she did know was her local house of worship and the people there, where she been initiated into the order of Divine Redemption, strengthened, cared for, taught the right Faith, and raised to adulthood. So the ritual of Divine worship, at which she would lie peacefully, should be conducted there, and then she should be buried out of that place as well. "But I think that means she should also be buried here, in this local area." All of them, including the Queen, acknowledged the merit of this proposal.

Then the Queen added, "But, sad to say, that will not work out. As I explained to your wife, there is no need to destroy or neutralize her body beyond what has already been done. No, but Elizabeth is dead, and that ends it. The other is only in stories. Nor will she be any dishonor or defilement to the place where she is buried—quite the opposite. The problem is that the real truth was not good enough for your government. To put it bluntly, the superstitious horror was too much for them. They were like frightened children. I pointed out that we were talking about their own daughters, who might die as classic heroines and then be at peace in Heaven. That, at least, got their attention and reduced them to silence. Then I promised I would take care of it. They accepted this answer, and it is written into the legally binding agreements. All who die as full vampires must go to my realm for final disposition, except with special permission on both sides. That is a point of law. I am sorry, Timothy, but I have already asked about special permission for you and your wife to decide freely about Elizabeth, and it has been declined. So there it is. She may leave my estate and go through the religious observance and then return, but that is all—and even that is only with an elvish escort."

And so, a few days later, Elizabeth lay peacefully through the ritual at her local house of worship with no problem or incident. Then she was taken to the appointed place in the Queen's realm and buried with appropriate religious activity.

She was not buried at once. When all were there, Queen Paula said, "Timothy, when you saw Elizabeth lying in state, you said she looked almost like a princess sleeping peacefully. You were right. After she arrived at my estate and before she was put down, I gave her the honorary title of 'princess.' So tonight there will be appropriate solemnities for the dead princess. Tomorrow, she will finally be put to bed to await the Great Day when she and other sleepers will awake, arise, and be given light. Except then, of course, she will arise the *right* way—from true death back to true life."

Beatrice continued. "As Queen Paula had said, she was in fact a lawful queen, and so she did it right—the clean, honorable way of openly declaring the truth. I told you of the monitoring devices Amanda had attached to Elizabeth, and I said there were formalities to be taken care of after Elizabeth was put down. The Queen sent official documents concerning what had happened, including a revised formal declaration of death for Elizabeth.

She had awoken at the Queen's estate after being misdiagnosed as dead owing to an exotic sickness, contracted through personal contact with another victim of the same sickness. That sickness simulated death by causing total suppression of all standard vital sings but maintained an exotic basis of vital functioning underneath. Upon awakening, she had shown homicidal tendencies owing to that same sickness. Her mind could be restored only for a brief time, and then she had reverted. The woman could not be cured, nor could she be controlled or even restrained or confined, in any serious measure. So before she could break free and rampage against others, she had been killed as a homicidal maniac. The person who did it had been given a title as one of the Queen's servants, and so, with the authority of her crown, Queen Paula had declared the killing to be an act of justifiable homicide in the performance of her official duty and had acquitted her of all liability for any claim of wrongdoing. Under the legally binding agreements the Queen had concluded with Wendy's own government, that ended it.

"Soon after Elizabeth was buried, public officials from the place where Lucy had assaulted her sent and asked Queen Paula about the one from whom she had contracted that sickness. The Queen explained that with the approval of the central government of that land, the person was in protective custody in the Queen's realm, undergoing an experimental treatment. Her agents had investigated, and no one other than Elizabeth had contracted that sickness from that person. One other person had been affected, but he had simply died instead of becoming sick as Elizabeth had. This central government—which had tried the project that caused the vampires—verified this story.

"Those local public officials pressed the question, and Queen Paula told them the truth. Lucy was the one who had infected Elizabeth, and her father was the other one affected. And yes, Lucy had spread her sickness to him in the course of the violence she had committed upon him. Yes, this was the mysterious sickness from which he had died.

"Such violence resulting in death was, of course, forbidden by the law of the land, and so there could have been serious trouble for Lucy upon her return. There was some talk of having her formally accused and brought to trial for murder. But the Queen explained that Lucy had not been responsible for her actions at the time. She had been wrongfully made to go insane through heroic involvement with a secret project the central government had been running. Along that line, Queen Paula had been less forthcoming with the truth than she knew to be desirable, and she was sorry for it, but she had been bound by promises to respect the secrecy of the project as far as may be. Because their own central government backed this whole story, the local officials accepted what the Queen had said and agreed to what she asked, albeit reluctantly. All concern over criminal wrongdoing was thrown aside in the interest of justice. But they reserved the right to take appropriate action upon her return to safeguard and protect the people. This was agreed on all sides to be very reasonable, and so the affair was settled, at least for the time being."

Beatrice's teacher said, "I have been thinking, and one thing puzzles me about the claim that Elizabeth could not be confined or restrained. Alicia was able to hold her at bay with some classic symbol of the right Faith. Then why could she not have been placed into a room whose walls were covered with such symbols and kept there?"

"I too wondered about this, but I was given to understand. That would not be a legitimate use of the symbol. When Alicia held up the symbol against Elizabeth, she did so as an exercise of faith, to invoke the living reality behind the symbol. But apart from this, what she held up would be just another material object, with no special power. The point of that symbol is what it represents, as with any symbol. It is worthless otherwise. Even to try what you said would be to degrade the symbol to the level of mere magic. And it would not have worked. No vampire could be detained by being kept in a room full of such symbols. She would simply have escaped as though the symbols were not there. Queen Paula and her people knew all this." The colleague remained unsure, so Beatrice added, "It was not about the symbol as such. It was about the exercise of Alicia's faith *by means* of the symbol. Faith is about having one's mind directed to God and the things of God. It is a Divine gift insofar as it involves accepting Divine illumination of one's soul. Ultimately, therefore, what can be done as an exercise of faith is what God can do through Her servants—through *His* servants, as they say. Well, what can She *not* do? Their Book says many things were done through faith, and even mountains can be moved on that basis. That last may be a figure of speech, but of course it could literally happen that way if it really came to that. Mountains can be moved, and vampires can be stopped. On the other hand, if such an object had landed in front of Elizabeth through an accidental explosion, that would have been worthless. She could simply have walked over it or picked it up and thrown it away."

After the burial was concluded, the Queen said, "Wendy, you stay here for a little while along with Alicia and Ginger. The vampire girls must be put to bed to await their restoration. There is to be a mild ceremony for that in just a few days. The girls are here now, in this realm. They will go down and be tucked in nicely and all that, and then they will wait in dormancy for however long it may be.

All that has already been arranged, and others will take care of it. What you will do is what I may call the lullaby address." The Queen explained what she meant by this. "So there it is. You must begin preparing at once what you are to say to them."

As Wendy prepared to speak to the vampire girls, she came to appreciate more fully why she had been the one to finish it for Elizabeth. There was the love between them, which had led Elizabeth to say better Wendy than anyone else. There was also the fact that Wendy was one of the few who could have comforted her about the prospect of being knifed through the heart. But as she saw now, it had also led up to this present work. What other experience could have prepared her so well to offer the lullaby to vampire girls?

And then the fateful day was at hand. The time had gone by very quickly, and Wendy was barely ready, but she was ready. Before her sat the vampire girls in an eight-by-eight array. On either side of her sat Alicia and Ginger. Now Queen Paula was speaking. She bade the girls welcome, pointed out Wendy and introduced her, stepped aside, and sat down. The time had come for Wendy to offer the lullaby address. With that, Wendy rose and smiled, bowed to Queen Paula, went to the lectern, faced the vampire girls, and spoke.

"Ladies, I join with Her Majesty in bidding you welcome. You all know why you are here today, as do we. First of all, I salute you as classic heroines. I am not at all sure I would be brave enough to do what you are doing, let alone to keep free of blame and resentment. To suffer such loss—and even torment, if anything should go wrong—is harsh enough. But to hold such slimy horror within oneself, not to be defiled by it, but so as to keep it confined and finally have it destroyed—this calls for truly exceptional strength of mind and character.

"In fact, of course, it calls for much more than that. It is an exercise of devotion, to imitate Another far greater Who submitted to suffer wrongfully and to participate in His action. Evil can be swallowed up so as to be neutralized—perhaps this is the greatest mystery He has taught. But you ladies have offered yourselves to partake of this mystery at a far higher level than I dare to dream of, and for this I salute you again."

Here Wendy paused. There was much she would have said about many things. But the Queen had forbidden her. "Yes, Wendy, I am sure you could weave it all together very skillfully. But it must be kept brief for the sake of that one full vampire, whose mind can only be kept clear for a short time. Besides, a lullaby is not a lengthy landmark speech, as you know very well from your own experience of motherhood. No, you must save it for the greeting they will enjoy upon awakening, if all goes well."

Wendy resumed. "Now you will sleep peacefully through whatever times He may appoint for you. What dreams you may have I know not, but I know there will be nothing dreadful. How your sleep may finally end, I know not, but I know it will go well for you, one way or the other. What I know is that the One Who presides over all times—and far beyond—is to be praised and obeyed, always and in all things. Wherefore, let us now lift up our voices to honor Him." With that, Wendy led them in singing one of the classic hymns among her people, having to do specifically with the point that He rules over all the ages as He stands above them all.

When the hymn was concluded, Wendy said, "Dear ladies, I wish I could promise you much more, but I cannot. All I can say is that compared with what He has already granted, all the rest is like nothing. Wherefore, let us lift up our voices once more with praise and thanksgiving in honor of the Divine Shepherd, on Whose love and mercy we all depend." With this, Wendy led them in the classic hymn Deborah had led her to sing for that girl as she had completed the work of her own basic vow. After the hymn, she finished it by pronouncing on them that blessing with which Deborah had started her own journey long ago.

With that, the ceremony was concluded. The elves began escorting the vampire girls, each to her own simple bed, calmly and mildly setting each to sleep peacefully and tucking her in like governesses with children, all of whom they loved dearly. All the other girls were provided for without incident and with no problems. The last to be set to sleep was the full vampire. She begged to speak with Wendy before going to sleep. This was granted.

"Lady Wendy, what you said does not apply to me. I am defiled and ruined. You see—."

"Peace, child. I see plenty. With the special powers Queen Paula has given me, I know who you are and what you have done. You are not defiled—not at all. In the same way, you would still be pure and innocent if you had allowed yourself to be bitten by a mad dog in order that others might be spared, and then you had turned into a homicidal maniac with mad rabies only because you were kept—very wrongfully and totally against your will—from having proper treatment in time. No blame or discredit would attach to you then, whatever harm you might do, and so here."

"Very good, Lady Wendy, and I thank you for trying. But I did more than just harm—more than just homicide. *I turned another woman into a vampire!* God help her! God help us both!"

"Yes, child, I know that. Her name was Elizabeth. God bless you that you have such care and such sorrow. But all that horror is over now. She has been taken care of and finished to be really dead, and we have been given to know that she is at peace in Heaven. Oh, yes! Also, before she died, she said her own experience as a vampire had shown her how it must be for you, and she hoped the two of you could someday meet in Heaven and be reconciled. So there you go. None of the rest of it has to be important anymore.

"Now, enough. Relax, and let God take care of you, as He has done for Elizabeth." Lucy nodded in assent. "Now, close your eyes." The girl did so. "Don't be frightened, honey child. Think of it as having your fairy godmother and her sisters send you and your sisters into a long, deep, lovely sleep, to fulfill what was foretold long ago, under the guidance of the Shepherd." With that, Lucy relaxed and smiled, her eyes still closed. Wendy placed her hand on the vampire's head, said "God be with you," kissed her on the forehead, and drew back as the elvish lady touched her head to take her down. After that, the elf tucked her in and then led Wendy away. Thus was the full vampire set to sleep peacefully through the times appointed for her.

⥈

At this point, Beatrice's teacher objected. "From what you have told us, the full vampire who drank Elizabeth's blood was put to bed only several days after she was captured. If the elves could do that for her, why could they not do it for Elizabeth as well? It would not have resolved her situation so as to save her—she would still have been a full vampire—but it would have bought time. It might merely have been necessary to kill her later instead, but then again, anything might have happened."

"Well, as it worked out, the elves did not have to do much of anything to keep Lucy. She was captured when she was dormant, and she was forcibly held dormant until shortly before the lullaby ceremony. Her mind was then held clear for just a very short time. As for what else the elves could or could not have done about Lucy if need were, that was not given me to know. On the other side, Elizabeth had first to awaken as a full vampire before she could go into proper dormancy at the end of that first night. They spared her most of that experience."

⥈

When Lucy had been put to bed, the Queen and her sisters activated the matrix in which the girls were to be lodged. Then everyone left the great hall in which the ceremony had been conducted and where the girls were lying dormant. The room was then sealed hermetically. Next there was a brief flash of exotic energy, and that was all. The Queen explained it to Wendy. "What the matrix does is hold the structures of exotic energy of their bodies at an absolutely dead standstill. This holding, in turn, reaches all the way down. So everything is now locked in place for them. No vital functioning is going on inside their bodies, and so it is almost as if they are already dead. But their bodies do not need to be actively maintained and will not deteriorate so long as the matrix stands. They will not decay, for the microorganisms within their bodies are also shut down. Beyond the structures of exotic energy in and around their bodies, there is now nothing alive in that room—not even a microorganism. The room is hermetically sealed, and so it will stay sterile. They will not be disturbed. The matrix will hold everything still so as to keep even the corrosive oxygen in the air from harming them. It will be simply as if time does not elapse for them until they are brought back."

"Then there will be no dreams at all for them."

"Yes, that is correct."

"Very good, Your Majesty. But then what happens now?"

"It is what I told you. Now you must face Lilith. She will be here to claim these girls as belonging to her within a few days. In the meantime, there is much to be done to prepare. You must be raised up to have appropriate powers, as I told you, and then you must learn much more from Alicia. Oh, yes—I have already discussed it with her."

The special powers were first to be taken care of. "First of all, by our standards Lilith is on the whole in fact very weak. She is, on the whole, clearly inferior to any ordinary mermaid. As regards ordinary everyday functioning, you are clearly superior to her, and even Ginger could offer considerable resistance if she had to. The problem for the people of your species is that one cannot beat something with nothing, as the saying goes, and the other side of that is that something beats nothing every time. Therefore, most of your people—including even your own relatives with their remarkable capabilities—would not have a chance against her. The problem for you, Wendy, is that I said, 'on the whole.' She has one special gimmick she can do as a part elf. It is far below the level of all but the very weakest elves, but it is enough that you would die helplessly before it, apart from what we are about to do for you.

"The best way to say it in your language is that she can project fire bolts. I know that must sound to you like something out of a story for children, but it is the best that can be done in your language, and the fact is very serious indeed. I told you she was almost ready to burn down your world in ancient times, and she could have done it with the powers she has. Well, this is the chief power involved. Apart from the special protection you are to receive, one *minimal* fire bolt from her would vaporize your body, with nothing left for your mother to bury.

"On the other side, you are what we call a—well, in your language, a 'one-in-ten-billion woman.' You are one of the very few in the history of your species who can receive what we have to give you. There are basically two things.

"First of all, think what would happen if someone were to shine a laser into a mirror. There is a device that can and will be implanted into your body so that the fire bolts she projects at you will be reflected back at her with very little of the energy going to your own body. But I say very little, not none at all. Enough would be absorbed by your tissues to fry you to a cinder, except the structure of exotic energy within you will be set up to shield your tissues and absorb it harmlessly. How the energy will be spent will become clear shortly."

"What more can you tell me about all this?"

"You need this device because you are the kind or species of being you are—you are not an elf. If she were to go up against us, our bodies would be protected in a different way. How that works is not important right now. This device is in fact totally unknown to your people, but it has been imagined in stories, and then in another context, with no reference to elves or fairies. How it works is somewhat technical, and once again, those details are not important right now.

"The second thing is that you will be given the ability to retaliate in kind. You will be given the ability to project fire bolts, in fact at a slightly higher level than what Lilith has. A 'self-renewing supercharge' is the best available translation—this will be placed upon you. The energy you absorb from what she throws at you will feed into and supplement this supercharge."

And so it was done. With her consent, Wendy was thrown into a deep sleep. When she awoke the next morning, there were strange sensations in her body like nothing she had ever felt before. Queen Paula asked Wendy about this, and Wendy described what she felt as well as she could. Then the Queen said, "This was to be expected. Nothing to worry about—it is just a question of fine-tuning the adjustment to fit the signature of your body. My sisters here are scientists and technicians, as you would say, who will take care of it. Relax and be brave, and it will all be over in just a moment." This happened as the Queen had said.

Then she introduced Wendy to her sisters. They spoke nicely to her, with genuine care and concern, but not with the tender solicitude that had been shown to the vampire girls as they had been put to bed. It took Wendy only a moment to understand, and then she rejoiced. The reason was that even though she was very much a lower-level being, they looked on her as less like a mere child to be cared for and more like a woman to be respected as a junior colleague.

This meeting was brief. It was provided largely to settle Wendy's mind. After this, Wendy spent the rest of the day learning how to use and control what had been given her.

At the end of the day, the Queen said, "It is perfected. You have learned all that I can teach you or any of your people about it. So be it, and may God be with you. But, Wendy, there *is* a catch—just one, but that one is the big one. Alicia, I know this gets into what has already been discussed with her of her appointed destiny, and so it might be best for you to tell her."

"Alicia? Is there any question of violating some moral or religious concern here?"

"No, child, not at all. You may rightly have and use all this according to the general laws on doing violence and engaging in combat. Nothing here is forbidden in that way, and your eternal destiny is not in any special danger. That is not the catch the Queen was speaking of."

"Will there be some danger from this to some innocent third or fourth party?"

"No, not at all. Nothing like that either."

"Then is it perhaps that I am guaranteed to die from this work?"

"Yes, child. That is exactly what it is."

"Will what time I have left be harsh or miserable, or will my death be ugly or cruel?"

"No—or at least there will be no special danger of it. That will be just however it works out, as with any woman—or man, or girl, or boy."

At these words, Wendy showed tremendous relief. "Oh, well—that is all right, then. For a moment, she had me seriously frightened. But if that is all, then I can relax and be easy. Your Majesty, I would not have you misunderstand. I am not a fool. Nor am I bitter to have my mind twisted and morbid. I love the beauty of sunlight and flowers and a thousand other things, I love my mother and a whole lot of other people, and I am sorry that I shall have to give it all up. Like all my people, I am also afraid to die. Most of all, I am concerned about leaving my daughter motherless. But, as you said, there is what has already been discussed with me regarding my appointed destiny. I have known for years my span will be short, and I have long since had to accept that there is nothing for it but to allow Him to escort me through the valley of the shadow of death, as the Book says. Have I been told because you were honor bound to give me fair warning?" Yes, exactly so. "Then very good, and I thank you. But now that has been taken care of, and we can go on to pragmatic realism. How will this happen?"

"To absorb and reflect the fire bolts will indeed be harmless. But to project fire bolts at her—well, it is harmless for elves, but not for you. As the fire bolt is built up and sent forth within your body, there will be a kind of spillover into your own tissues. No one spillover will be enough to have immediate or even proximate effect, but the effect will be cumulative. The nearest comparison is standard radiation poisoning. With just one protracted session of combat with her, you can expect to die in a few years at most from what will look to the physicians like an exotic form of radiation poisoning. You can be spared the misery of dying that way, in the same way that any woman can be spared, but that is all."

Alicia added, "Wendy, you must not have false hope. If you do this, then you will die from it, for that *is* your appointed destiny. You will not be gotten out of it to go on living in this world. Queen Paula and her sisters will be able to stave it off for you in some measure, to buy you more time, but that is all."

"Let me make sure I understand rightly. You say it is my destiny to die if I do this. Does that mean, dying like that will be the penalty I pay for playing around with something dreadful? Or does it mean that I must suffer death as a side effect of fulfilling what I am called on to do, in the manner of a classic heroine?"

"It means the second, of course. You *are* called on to do this, as you have known for some time now, but until now you have not been promised much about how you will or will not come through it, just as people in general are not given such promises concerning what they are called upon to do."

And so Wendy waited.

CHAPTER TWENTY

Queen Paula had planned for Wendy to learn more from Alicia about Lilith the next day. But this had to be delayed in order to provide for Sarah, Elizabeth's sister. Wendy had wanted to put it off until later, being full of the urgency of the main thrust of her appointed work. Queen Paula showed superior wisdom. "No, Wendy—you need to calm down, stop, and think better. To fight and die as a classic heroine—what do you think that is about? It is about children like Sarah, to provide for them, to honor and protect their purity and innocence, and to make the world a safe place for them to grow up in. The danger is not right on top of us right now, and what if it were? If we cannot make time to keep an innocent child from having her mind wrongly turned inside out, then we have already lost an enormous chunk of what we are fighting for."

"Yes, you are right, Your Majesty. But then again, those fine words—true though they are—will not stop Lilith."

"Oh, dear Lord, you people are truly hard to teach. No, Wendy, those fine words will not stop Lilith. You will.—Let me make it easy for you. What if the positions were reversed—which may perhaps yet happen in some way. Imagine if Theodora were to display that kind of attitude toward Anna, based on such excessive eager enthusiasm."

Wendy bowed her head in docile submission and said, "Yes, Ma'am." Then, "But still, what about the danger from Lilith?"

"Are you asking or challenging?"

Wendy forced herself to be calm, settled her mind, nodded in further docile submission, and said, "I *was* challenging. Now I am asking."

"That is all right, then. Yes, if it came to that, we would just have to do what we must and accept that we had lost a large chunk of what we were fighting for. But we would have to *accept* that, and not forget about it, and not imagine otherwise. However, it has not come to that. As I said, the danger is not right on top of us right now. There is time enough to do it the right way and still take care of Lilith."

And so the day after Wendy had been taught to use the reflective device and the supercharge, she, Queen Paula, Ginger, and Alicia—along with Alfreda, Amanda, Diana, and Margaret—were at Sarah's house, where she sat with her parents, waiting to hear what had to be told. The only consolation they could offer her, beyond what had already been explained to her, was that the reality was less ugly and gruesome than what she had been led to imagine.

Sarah was eight years old now, with the eighth anniversary of her birth on the same day Elizabeth had marked her eighteenth anniversary. This was old enough that she had heard of vampires and even seen dramatizations of fictional stories. Word about the affair with Elizabeth had leaked out, and so Sarah had heard rumors that her sister had turned into a vampire and been killed as a vampire. That was, in fact, true, but not as Sarah imagined. The adults would try to make her appreciate the reality, which was merely horrible.

Wendy began, "Honey child, let me ask you. First of all, let me go over what you already know. Your sister Elizabeth was a devoted handmaid of the Lord God. When she reached the age of eighteen and was kind of started as an adult woman, she traveled to speak with her mother's aunt about what she should do or not do with some of the special talents God had granted her. While she was traveling, she came to have a weird sickness through personal contact with another woman who already had that sickness. Because of that sickness, Elizabeth appeared to be dead and was declared dead. She was sent back here. But in fact, she was not truly dead. Elizabeth revived, but she was insane because of that weird sickness. Later, she died on account of what had happened to her. What happened to her was totally against her will, and so she is not to be blamed or condemned in any way for what happened or for what ugly things she said or did because of the insanity. At the end, by the mercy of God, she was restored for just a brief moment so that she might be His devoted handmaid again and die on that basis. She *did* die on that basis, and now, by the grace and mercy of God, she burns with pure love as she rejoices in Him, for that is what it is to be at peace in Heaven. All that is and remains true. Nothing stands against it, at least nothing in reality. Now, first of all, do you understand all this?—Yes or no."

"Well, yes."

"All right, then. Do you think you have some reason to believe it is not so? Yes or no."

"Yes!"

"Is it that you have heard she became a vampire and was killed as a vampire?"

"Yes."

"Right, then—now we come to what I have to ask you. Honey child, what do you think it is for a woman to be a vampire?"

"A vampire is some ghastly, slimy monster, too horrible even to talk about."

"Well, I can assure you, Elizabeth was not like that. First of all, she was not too horrible to talk about. We knew what was happening, we talked plenty about her, and we took care of her as well as we could—even though we could not save her from dying. Moreover, no—her body was not slimy. Not at all. Is there anything else?"

"They say a vampire hates God so much that she cannot even bear to look upon daylight."

"Well, but you see, her hatred of God was just because of her insanity, which was not her fault, and so she is not to be blamed for it. As for finding daylight unbearable, that too was just a symptom of her sickness."

"So she *was* a vampire?"

Theodora answered her. "Yes, Sarah. Yes, she was. But the truth about vampires is what your cousin Wendy told you."

"But—but—but—."

Queen Paula went over and knelt down before Sarah. The girl knew well enough who and what the Queen really was, and so now the Queen said to her, "Honey child, listen to me. My people have known for a very long time that someday this business about vampires would come true among your people—in real life and not just in stories. So we know that the truth about vampires is what your mother and your cousin Wendy have told you. Also, we too have been given Divine prophecies, and so we have long known that your sister and all the other vampires would go to Heaven. What happened to her was very wrong, and I am sorry she was cut down wrongly and left you too soon. But all women and girls die, as do all men and boys, and I am happy for her that she is at peace in Heaven.—Maybe I can make it easy for you. If you think of her as a vampire, your head will be full of crazy stuff from ridiculous stories. Think of her as a bloodsucking criminal lunatic. That phrase takes hold of most of the serious reality but leaves aside the nonsense. Any woman might be made sick against her will, and go insane, and want to do horrible things. It would not be her fault, and she would not deserve any blame. She could be stopped from harming anyone else and die with her mind restored at the end. Your sister did."

"She did not hurt anyone else?"

Theodora answered. "No, not at all. That was made sure of."

For just a moment, Sarah showed tremendous relief. The moment ended, and she asked, "But how was it made sure of?" Then, with horror, "Was she killed as a vampire?"

Wendy felt it was up to her, but Diana answered first. "Yes, Sarah. Yes, she was." Before she could say any more, the child broke down and wept, screaming and blubbering. Finally, Diana was able to speak to her again. "Sarah, it had to be done. There was no other way."

It was Margaret who finally settled it for the child. "Sarah, I am sorry, but you need to stop and think. You thought at first she was a monster, too horrible even to talk about. Well, that is about what she would have been if she had not been stopped. She could not stop herself—that was part of what had been done to her. So, it had to be taken care of for her, and it was. If there had been a milder way, it would have been done. But there was not. Now, you tell me. Which is better? That she should be a monster roaming the world by night and living by destroying others? Or that she should be dead and at peace in Heaven? Because you see, those were the choices."

For just a moment Sarah broke down and accepted this. Then she began weeping again. "But to die like that!" And she was screaming and blubbering. Finally, and with difficulty, it was extracted from her that she imagined Elizabeth had died horribly, being held down and writhing in agony as a wooden stake was slowly driven through her heart. This was what she had seen in those dramatizations of stories, and this was what people had said to her.

It was Amanda who answered this. "You poor child. If that is what you think, then I can see why you feel the way you do about it. But no—this is what the Queen called crazy stuff from ridiculous stories. No, that is not how it happened. Not at all. It was quick, clean, and merciful. Sarah, in my line of work, I have seen people die in different ways, and it is almost like a gift—a privilege—to die as easily as your sister did." Then, to cut off the obvious next question, she added, "I know, because I was there when it happened, and I witnessed it."

"You let her be killed!"

Queen Paula cut her off. "No, not at all. It is as your grandmother said. Like the others, your aunt Amanda understood there was no other way. She was there to witness, and to help with the work, and to offer Elizabeth what comfort she could. But she could not have stopped it."

Now the child turned on the Queen. "You killed my sister! You killed my sister!" She went and started pounding on the Queen in her childish way, with her little fists. True to her word that she too would have to swallow the bitter medicine of facing Sarah, the Queen stood still for it. It was Wendy who stopped the girl.

"No, Sarah, no! It was not the Queen. I know, for I too was there. You see, I did it. Yes, Sarah—yes. I killed her. I killed Elizabeth myself, with my own hand. God help me."

With that, the child broke down and wept again. Theodora dismissed them all, saying there was enough for one day. She and her husband would take it from there. If they needed further help, they would call for it.

It took a few days, and then Sarah's mind was changed, very quickly, in a way no one had expected. She had been at the house of another girl, and they had been watching dramatizations of fictional stories together when the dramatization of a story about vampires began. In just a few minutes, Sarah ran home, screaming in horror. As Theodora embraced her and comforted her as well as she could, the girl cried out through her sobbing that Grandma had been right—it was far better that Elizabeth should be dead and in Heaven than be one of those monsters. Happily, Sarah was fully reconciled to that girl and her mother from whose house she had run away, once Theodora called with one of those devices and explained. ("Sarah was frightened because what they started watching reminded her of a nasty story she heard about Elizabeth.") It did not take that much longer for her to be reconciled to everyone else. Over the next few weeks, her parents, her aunts, and her grandmother went through it with her and took her over what had been explained to her. The rest of it did not come until later.

In the meantime, Wendy had to learn more from Alicia about Lilith. "Queen Paula told you the consecration Lilith went through as a toddler was good as far as it went. So it was, but the question is, what does that really mean? It was adequate to free her from various rules and restrictions and to restore various functions and capabilities, but that was all. Since she was neither a true mermaid nor a true elf, she could not be fully and properly consecrated by any standard functioning among them, as they could.

"However, there was that archaic ritual given to the mermaids, which she applied to abandoned children in centuries to come. This ritual is best thought of as a sign of faith, good in the older ages before the more serious things were begun. 'Receive thou the inner mystery of the Divine Creator unto the gift of superior life in God's own good time and wondrous way' was to be said to the recipient as the one speaking drew an equilateral triangle, as nearly as may be, on her forehead with her finger. Since technically Lilith had dominion over abandoned children in the manner explained—as even now a queen may act as a surrogate mother over abandoned children in her realm insofar as necessary—the action was valid. Now here is the punch line: Lilith was herself provided for with this ritual even before that consecration by the priestess, both by her biological mother, the mermaid, and also by that scientist, who was kind of like her father and who was in fact her genetic father. He did it because he did not know she had already done it, as the priestess did not know the parents had done it. What was done was valid—Lilith was brought to the right Faith in this way, insofar as that was possible, given the situation of that age and for a being like her. Through the first several active periods, she went through life honoring this Faith and acting upon it. If she had died in the older ages, she would have had to wait for the Great Redemption, like a full mermaid or any of our own people, but finally she would have gone to Heaven—as the others would—in God's own good time, when it was accomplished.

"The problem was that she was enough of an elf not to be subject to natural death, but she was not enough of an elf to be able to do well by living through the ages. We think of what was done to Elizabeth as taking care of her—putting her out of her misery and sending her home. Something like that is what Lilith is longing for."

Alicia paused and smiled sadly before continuing. "As I said, there it was. The archaic consecration was not adequate to set her free from the tangle of laws and rules that compelled her to go through an indefinite series of three-hundred-year spans. If our own First Parents had held fast, they could have set her free upon assuming full dominion over this world, with her formal surrender of her title as Princess Regent. To be sure, there would then have been the question of when and where and how the Great Redemption would have been accomplished, but that is a further concern in this context, not exactly the same thing. But of course it is a moot point anyhow, for that is not what happened.

"So where does all this lead? First of all, she must be led to perfect the process of acting out the Faith as far as is possible for her at this point by rendering an act of adoration that is appropriate to the present situation He has established. In fairness to her, it should be noted that this has never been proposed to her before, and so she is kind of innocent for not having done so long since. Not to worry, Wendy—at the proper time, it will be given to you to know what to say to elicit this act from her. I hope for her sake she will comply, and if so, somehow it will be clear what she needs for us to do to provide for her.

"The other thing is that her right name is not Lilith. That is a title—an insulting title—we have given her. As with Queen Paula, so here as well—we cannot pronounce her name in her own language. Our vocal organs are not set up for it. The nearest equivalent in our language would be 'Amy,' which means 'beloved.' The war was ended, and her mother was taken captive and treated well, early in her pregnancy. Once this was done, her mind settled and grew calmer, and her natural love for her daughter grew as she waited. By the time of the child's birth, the old malicious nonsense had more or less faded away, and she was ready to have motherly concern sweep aside all else, which it did. The name she gave the girl translates as 'beloved,' and so there it is. Lilith knows you cannot pronounce her real name, but if you call her 'Amy' as much as possible, she will understand and appreciate it. Do you have any questions or concerns?"

"Yes, just one. The Queen said Lilith experienced all the joys and benefits possible for her in her first active period. Does that include natural motherhood? I ask because I have found the experience to be so important that the knowledge might be useful."

"Yes, it does—seven times in her first active period, and then never after that. All of her children died young because of a low, mean, filthy, ugly trick played on her. She was to be the prototype for a whole bunch of warrior girls, as the Queen explained. But they did not want the complications of starting a whole new race with these girls. Even at best, there would be just too many imponderables. We would say, 'Just make her sterile.' But for them, it was not so simple. It could have been done, but it would have been difficult, with serious technical problems about the biological engineering. Also, there were basic laws and rules for their kind or species that even those on the wrong side recognized and were not prepared to violate. The way the debate worked out was that they decided to have her able to reproduce, but by parthenogenesis only, and then make sure all her offspring would be genetically defective and die off at the end of the prepubescent period. They figured that was the line of least resistance, and that was what they did. That was what happened with all her daughters. She tried seven times because it took that long for the elves to figure out what was going on. It was an elvish scientist who was manipulated into doing it, and he acted with full elvish knowledge and intelligence. The others got to the bottom of it eventually, but it was difficult. Let me say that this is part of why she was so angry when she learned about the abandoned children of our species. Her heart had been torn out seven times, and here were these people throwing away their children as garbage. What finally kept her from getting started as a warrior girl right then, as much as anything, was the hope for her daughters that they would someday be in Heaven, for they too had received that archaic ritual from her."

Then Wendy waited, but not for very long. Four days after Alicia told her about Lilith, Wendy got up in the morning as usual; went through praise, prayers, and thanksgiving; and then went through the preparations to go through the day. At the first meal of the day, she greeted Alicia and Ginger, then turned and said to the Queen, "Lady Amy approaches. It will be today."

"Yes, that is correct. It will be very soon now."

"How long do I have?"

"An hour and a half—two at the most."

"Is there anything more you can tell me or do that might help?"

"Only that it is not about beating her in combat. The whole point of exercising force against her is merely to get her to listen to reason. It really is up to *her* to restore the vampire girls, not to you and not to me."

"Alicia?"

"What Queen Paula said. And you are there to *help* Lady Amy—to lead her through so that it may finally be resolved for her—not to hurt or destroy her."

"Ginger?"

"No, I think these ladies have laid it out for us."

For a little while, they spoke of other things—happier times. Then Queen Paula caught Wendy's eye and simply nodded to her. Wendy stood up and said, "Now I must go and face her. Pray for me that I may not falter or fail. Ginger, if I should fall today, give my deep love to Pepper and tell her I hope we may meet to be finally and fully reconciled in Heaven, if it is not to be in this world. Now, God be with you all." But before she could go, Alicia made her wait and receive from her that old blessing one more time.

And then she was facing Lady Amy, as Alicia had taught her to call the woman. She began by waving a white flag, which was the classic sign of truce among them. Showing considerable surprise, Lady Amy said, "Are you surrendering?"

"No, not at all. I ask for a truce, that we may negotiate."

Then Wendy felt herself being probed and scanned, much more strongly than she had been by Ginger long ago, and for a longer time. Finally, Lady Amy said, "Yes, I understand. You are one of them, but one of the rare freaks whom the Queen has given special powers. That means she thinks you are an upright, worthy woman, gifted with wisdom—a devoted handmaid of the

Lord God. It is likely enough she is right, and you are. All right—what do you want to discuss with this truce you call for?"

Wendy understood this was the opening of some elaborate game, but far above her level. This woman in front of her had already gone through long ages of formal courtesy, diplomatic maneuvering, crafty intrigues, and the whole thing, centuries before any of the languages she knew had originated. Her one chance was simple honesty, straight out, totally plain and pure, at all times and in all things.

"A rare freak, you call me. Lady Amy, I spoke in good faith. Is it necessary for you to begin by insulting me?"

"'Lady Amy,' you call *me*. Very good. Perhaps the Queen was right about you after all. Fair enough. All right, then—we shall see. Let us hear what you propose, starting with your alleged good faith."

"Yes, I do want something, but not for myself or my own personal circle." Before she could say any more, Lady Amy cut her off.

"No, of course not. You are here in the name of your people, concerning the vampire girls, with whatever fancy title the Queen has given you. Is that correct so far?"

"It is part of the truth, yes, but only part."

"Are you going to speak in detail of whatever big plans you have for those girls? Nice try, but you need not bother."

"Well, to tell you the truth, I was going to speak instead of my big plans for you."

"Again, nice try, but it will not be necessary. Maybe you can beat me, and maybe not, but there is no need to discuss it. There is nothing to do but play out the contest. All the rest is froth."

"Those were not the big plans I had in mind."

"Oh, really? This is getting interesting. I shall hear your proposal."

"Lady Amy, Queen Paula has told me your sad story."

"'Queen Paula,' you call her. Yes, of course—it is the best you can do, just as calling me Lady Amy is the best you can do. Speak on."

"As I say, she has told me your story. Not all of us are alike. Some of us have not yet forgotten that there is something better offered to us."

"And so you are sad and sorry and sympathetic at my story, and you would like to help me if you could. Is that it?"

"The short answer is yes."

After a long pause, Lady Amy said, "Yes, you are sincere, and so I thank you. But what makes you think you can help me?"

"Only He can truly help you. I know that. But I have been sworn into the order of Divine Redemption and raised up to have the privilege of serving and striving. I can take you in and offer you to Him. If you will approach Him in docile submission, all can be made well for you, quickly and easily. I am ready to do all I can to help it work out for you."

After another long pause, Lady Amy said, "None of your people have ever invited me in that way before."

"Yes, I know, and I am sorry. I know how it has been for you. Please try to understand something of how it is for us. My people find it very hard not to listen to their fears."

"And so they call me 'Night Monster' because they are afraid of me, and I should make allowances for them, and so on, and so forth. Madam—what is your name? Wendy. Thank you. Wendy, after hearing Queen Paula's account, do you think they have reason to be afraid of me? They did the monstrous deeds, beyond anything both I myself, and the people I came from, ever dreamed of. Yes, I was tempted to lash out, I have to admit it. By the mercy of God and through the good offices of my friends and guardians, I was made to listen to reason instead. You ask me to try to understand? Yes, I was brought to understand. It burned my guts out, as you would say, but I had to accept it. All right, so be it. For centuries, I strove to be a good warrior girl, providing for the weakest and most helpless of your people by doing what I could for those children. I did nothing destructive to your people. I did not threaten them, I asked nothing of them, and I imposed nothing on them, save only to be left in peace and allowed to do the work of mercy He had given into my hand. I even gave myself the trouble of not allowing myself to be seen nude among them, based on what the elves had explained to me. But no—all that was not good enough for them. Dear God, Wendy! Was that asking too much? Do I really have to go on with all the ugly details? I am not speaking against you personally, but you tell me. If you think there is a better answer regarding your people, then you explain to me very carefully what it is."

"You saved some mothers from being made to abandon their children. Those whose plans you frustrated might contest your claim that you were not at all troublesome to my people."

"Yes, I know that. But even that was by way of offering, not demanding or imposing. Surely you understand that." Wendy nodded in assent. "Also, by what the founding of your own land called 'the Laws of Nature and of Nature's God,' their resentment is an accusation against them, not a legitimate challenge against me."

"Yes, of course. I know that."

"Anyway, all that was irrelevant to the assault on me that was tried. The punk who did it knew nothing about any of that."

"All right, fair enough. But given your powers, was it really necessary to kill those men?"

"Wendy, what do you imagine? Do you think I left great mountains of corpses behind me? No, not at all. I killed only during that one active period, and then, in three hundred years I only killed"—here she stopped and thought back—"twelve men. Yes, just twelve. All of them were looking for trouble, and then they pushed it and pushed it and pushed it, until they managed to invoke the protocol for the war your people had provoked against me. Again, I was a warrior protecting the weak against abuse, and those men died as an act of war."

"What about this war? Do you insist on carrying through this war against us? Or would you give it up if you could?"

"Dear God, Wendy, yes! I wished when I awoke that time, and I wish now, that I had heard the voice of God from Heaven, calling it off. I understand that something like that has happened, for the Great Redemption has been accomplished among *your* people. For that very reason, I was *happy* to be held in restraint by Queen Paula's friends, as she calls them. Oh, yes! But then, no—even *that* was not good enough for your people. You have gone from the murder of innocent children to preparing for war with what amounts to blasphemy and sacrilege. By doing so you have ruined these poor girls, and so now they belong to me. But you want me to surrender them to you, after all that has happened! Really, Wendy, where does it end? How long and how far am I supposed to put up with your garbage? Where is the line that is not be crossed, where I have to take the stand for what is right? Not necessary to kill those men, you say? Well, maybe not. Perhaps I acted too harshly, and they were still ugly deeds, in spite of the technical justification. I have wondered about that sometimes and even called on God to forgive me insofar as I was wrong, which I think I may have been in some measure. But then again, really, Wendy, what is necessary with you people? You are the ones who keep looking for trouble."

"Lady Amy, we know our own filthy history well enough, and some of us appreciate all too well how shameful it is. When Queen Paula told us about you, she defended you as a warrior girl as well as she could. May I tell you what she said to us when I challenged her as to whether you were an honest warrior girl?"

"I am sure I know already, but yes—say it."

"Not enough for your life to be spared, but perhaps enough for your soul to be saved."

"Good old Queen Paula! I knew that would be her answer. She is probably right, too."

Now it was Wendy who was greatly surprised. "You admit it that easily?"

"Of course! Now this is important. Did she also say or admit that a warrior has to be ready to pay her price as a warrior by answering with her own life?" Wendy nodded in assent. "Well, there you go! She and the other elves taught me that long ago as part of my basic moral education when I was first growing up, before I was ever started as a warrior girl. Ever since I began thinking for myself, as an adult woman, I have always agreed with that, as well as with almost all of what they taught me. Oh, Wendy, I am not trying to evade anything or to worm out of anything. I have always tried to be honest, about this and everything."

"Then, in view of all this, perhaps I can bring together the question of what I want *from* you with the question of what I want *for* you. Lady Amy, will you submit to be again a devoted handmaid of the Lord God, acting as an honest warrior girl to serve and protect the people?"

"You want me to give your people—another chance."

Weighing her words very delicately and speaking very carefully, Wendy answered, "The short answer is yes, but I think that may be an oversimplification. I think, by the mercy of God, and within the order of Divine Providence, that you and the vampire girls may be the next chance—perhaps the last chance—for each other."

After a very long pause, Lady Amy said, "Yes, you really mean it. You are truly sincere." After a slightly shorter pause, she added, "That is the best I have ever heard, from any of your people, in all the ages of my life." Then, after another moment, she said, "All right, Wendy. What would you have me do for them?"

"I would have you restore them that they may arise as proper women once again, purged of vampiric filth, to resume their lives as free women and fulfill themselves as women through whatever times God may appoint for them."

"Yes, of course—that is the natural and obvious thing to do, at least from your standpoint. But what about the fact that they belong to me now, because of what has been done to them?"

"Well, what about it? Only God enjoys sovereign ownership. No woman of any species may rightly have another person belong to her, save only as a trust from God. But to have someone as a trust from God means in order to bring the one belonging to her to fulfill or accomplish what He has appointed. Lady Amy, you know all this. What, then, are we talking about?"

"You would send them back to your own world of filth, to dwell among the people who caused them to become vampires in the first place. I would spare them that. I would take them away where we can all live together and be happy together."

"Oh, Lady Amy, why do you say such things? Do you really hate my people that much, or do you simply not understand? Yes, I appreciate your concerns. As I said, we know our history well enough and are ashamed of it. And yes, there is an obvious way in which they have suffered too much already for one lifetime. And no, I cannot promise you—or them—that fact will be honored or respected if they go back to my world, as you call it. The problem is, that world is also *their* world. Therefore, what you propose would not be in keeping with either what they need or what they want. To be cut off from those they love would make them miserable, to take only the most obvious thing. Surely you know all this. So, again, what are we talking about?"

"You spoke of what they want. That is not for you, or for Queen Paula, to decide."

"Lady Amy, is that what all this trouble is about? I told you—I would have them be free women. A free woman decides for herself what to do and where to go and which path to follow. I would strive against having anything else happen to them. So no, it will not be about *sending* them anywhere, so far as I can help it. Each will have the widest range of choice I can arrange for her. That is all I can promise, but I do promise that much."

Again, there was a long pause, after which Lady Amy finally said, albeit reluctantly, "Yes—once again, you speak sincerely. All right, then, fair enough. Yes, so be it."

With that, Wendy showed tremendous relief. "Thanks be to God for both of us that we have managed to get all that straightened around and out of the way. Now, as for the rest of it. As I was saying, you must be again a devoted handmaid of the Lord God, acting as an honest warrior girl. With all my heart, I wish and hope to see you restored to that high estate. So, excuse me for speaking bluntly, Lady Amy, but will you submit and allow this to happen the easy way? Please, I beseech you, for all our sakes—especially yours—say yes. Don't make it harder on any of us, especially yourself, than everything already is."

"After all that has happened, *is* there an easy way for me?"

"I believe there is. But perhaps that is the challenge for you. He does not afflict the people any more than He has to. You know that, at least in theory. Perhaps your challenge will be to exercise faith and put that fact to the test."

After a very long pause, Amy said, "Yes, all right—agreed. But please, help me—take me through it that I may get the ordeal over with quickly."

Speaking in a motherly tone to comfort the frightened child that Amy was just now, Wendy said, "Easy, Lady Amy—easy. I am not going to hurt you. You will have to be just a little brave, for just a moment, and then it will get easier as you go along. You know that before the Great Redemption there was a long age of preparation, followed by the age of fulfillment, in which the Redemption finally occurred. All this happened while you slept through the ages."

"Yes, I have been taken through all that history."

"I would apply to you an ancient blessing from the age of Preparation. It was applied to me long ago, and that was the beginning of my own journey home. Will you accept it?"

While she waited, Wendy cried out to God for Amy in her mind. After a long moment, Lady Amy forced out the answer: "Yes." Then, more easily now, "Yes, I shall." Then she knelt, closed her eyes, and waited, with her face contorted as if she were bracing herself to be ready for something dreadful that was about to happen to her.

Wendy smiled sadly, for she knew exactly how Lady Amy felt. It was the same way she had felt upon first eating a banana. Acting quickly, she placed her hands on Amy's head and recited the blessing, which she had long since learned by heart. Then she withdrew her hands.

Lady Amy opened her eyes, relaxed her face, opened her mouth, and then said with astonishment, "Is that it? Is it really just that easy?"

"Yes, at least the first part. I told you I was not going to hurt you."

"Will the next part hurt any more?"

"That depends on you. If you approach Him in docile submission, as I was saying earlier, then no, not at all."

"What comes next?"

And then Wendy knew what she had to say. "As I said, that blessing goes back to the age of preparation. You must go on now to render adoration appropriate for the specific facts of this present age of fulfillment. But how to go about it? The old stories condemn you for having refused to bow before the First Man, at the beginning of our race. Of course, knowing the real history as I do, I know it is all garbage. But even so, it leads into an interesting question."

Before Wendy could say any more, Lady Amy burst out, "No, it is not so simple as that. To tell you the truth, yes—I did refuse to bow before him. But then, you see, I did not meet with him until *after* his defection. Oh, if only it had gone the other way! I expect Queen Paula has told you that part of the story, and so I shall not trouble you with it now." Wendy nodded in assent. "But out of respect for what you have said and done today, I tell you this much—I would have bowed before him very happily, if only—!" Lady Amy was in tears, but by sheer force of will, she kept herself from breaking down and sobbing.

Wendy smiled sadly and nodded again. Then she paused, gathered herself together, prepared, and asked what she knew to be perhaps the great question of her life. "But you see, that was then, and this is now. Yesterday can be left to the mercy of God, if you are willing. For today, the question is what you will say and do about Another far greater, Who has *not* defected. Lady Amy, will you bow before the New Man?—You know Who that is and what He is."

At first she showed astonishment at this proposal. After a shorter moment, Lady Amy said, more easily this time, "Yes. Yes, I shall." Then she broke down and wept.

With great rejoicing in her heart, Wendy comforted her as a mother comforts a wayward child who has finally submitted to be corrected. After that, Queen Paula arrived, smiling beatifically. "Thanks be to God, child, that He has brought you to conversion." Turning to Wendy, she explained, "Alicia told us. All has been made ready." They explained to Amy that Alicia was a prophetess. Then the Queen took them, along with Alicia and Ginger, to meet the officer who had presided over Elizabeth's burial at the house of worship to which the officer was attached.

Beatrice explained what happened next. "They went to the front and faced the altar, on which She deigns to sit in that extraordinary mode, by which the natural world is already turned inside out. Amy first bowed deeply, then stood up, knelt down, bowed her head in docile submission, stretched her arms forward with her palms up to indicate even deeper submission, and began to speak. All the others knelt and followed her as she cried out, in one language after another, 'Glory to Thee, O Lord, glory to Thee!' Again, they call Her 'Lord,' for they speak of Her in the masculine.

"Amy spoke first in the language Wendy had learned from her mother, and then she went through hundreds of different languages, almost all of them from Wendy's people, but also the language of the mermaids, and finally the language of the elves. The others followed along by simply repeating what had been said at first, except when they happened to know the other language Amy was speaking at the moment.

"When finally the recitation was completed, Amy bowed deeply, straightened herself, stood up, and bowed again from a standing position. Then she lowered her arms and went to the officer. Did he understand that she was in fact an alien being, even though she looked like them? Yes, Queen Paula had discussed it with him. Was it true that an alien being would be granted formal initiation into the order of Divine Redemption, but only if she asked? Well, yes, that too.

"Summoning her courage, she said, 'Then, sir, I am asking. I would be formally initiated and brought in, to be kept within the flock of the Divine Shepherd.' Did she know what she was asking for? Amy smiled sadly. 'I have studied history, philosophy, and theology. On that limited basis, yes. I understand well enough. But I have learned enough to know that I shall never truly understand so long as this life continues in this world."

And so it was arranged. Lady Amy was enrolled as one being prepared. That evening they were all back home, where Wendy and Ginger and Alicia were all staying in Queen Paula's realm. Amy asked Wendy, "Is it really all just that easy?"

"As an adult convert myself, I can answer that. Yes. Yes, it is."

"Wendy, this has never been offered to me in this way before. I have never been invited before as you have invited me. But still, I have been living in dread, thinking someday I would be called upon to go through this dreadful torture. I have been a fool!"

"Well, you need not be too unhappy. That is kind of standard. A whole lot of us—very much including me—were fools until He cut through the nonsense for us. If you think you should have known better, so should a whole lot of us, but we were fools anyway. Just relax, and look to Him, and let Him take care of it for you."

⁂

The next day, Queen Paula sat them all down for a special conference. "This is all going very well. It is easier than I had hoped, for Amy has agreed to cooperate with no need for any fighting at all."

"Your Majesty, I thank you for being polite and speaking mildly, but that is not necessary. I have surrendered. It will be best to call things by their right names."

The Queen smiled, bowed her head in acknowledgment, and said, "Very good, Amy.—Now, what about restoring the vampire girls? First of all, as I have said before, they must be set free from the tangle of laws and rules in which they are caught. Only Amy has been authorized to execute the formalities, but those formalities must be prepared. The exact procedure must be laid out and developed, step by step."

"Why, Your Majesty? Why should I not simply go into the hall where they are and declare all that garbage canceled?"

"Well, but what garbage? Will you, as Princess Regent, declare all the laws and rules of your realm abrogated? No, of course not—because if you do, the special provisions allowing vampires to be kept alive under restraint in protective custody will also be wiped out, and they will be pure outlaws. At least in legal theory, we shall then be obligated to kill them all off at once. You see, that is just the problem. No, it has to be done carefully and correctly."

What had to be done was to work through systematically by unraveling the logic of the situation, step by step. The starting point, of course, was the fact that Wendy's people had violated the rules under which they enjoyed autonomy. Apart from this, Amy as Princess Regent would have nothing to say about it. These violations were mapped out in detail, and then they went from there. It took that day, the next, the next, and the next. But finally, all was ready.

The fundamental law among the mermaids made the situation somewhat tricky. There were restrictions and requirements on their queen as a minimal safeguard against tyranny. No one had anticipated the queen would someday have to act totally alone. The last queen had given Amy full power, but she could give only what she had, and Amy had only what the queen had given her. However, by a curious trick of the fundamental law, the queen—and thus the Princess Regent as well—could act totally alone in order to implement policies regarding foreign relations by invoking appropriate protocols. It was Ginger who thought up the way to resolve the situation with the vampire girls on this basis.

The problem was that the evil their government had done had spilled over to reach the elvish queen and her concern for Amy—and thus ultimately the realm of the mermaids and its laws. For this reason, severe criminal penalties had been incurred. But the provisions of law involved had been stated in archaic language. As a result, when applied to those of Wendy's species, what happened ended up being twisted so as to make the penalties far more harsh and cruel than had been originally intended or anticipated. From the standpoint of their law, the sixty-four original vampire girls were considered to have agreed to accept these penalties on behalf of their people. Those girls could never be restored until this situation was resolved, one way or the other, through true death or whatever. This was what was to be resolved by Ginger's gimmick.

The first thing to do was to resolve those provisions of law. This would both remove any danger of having such problems arise again in time to come and also serve as the basis to free the present victims. So, a few days after the planning and preparation had been completed, Lady Amy stood at the lectern at which Wendy had stood not long before. Only Queen Paula and the other elves could of themselves withstand the force fields that made up the matrix. Lady Amy, Wendy, Ginger, and Alicia depended on their elvish escorts. Now Lady Amy spoke, her speech full of standard formulas.

"In the name of God, Amen." Then followed formulas invoking the protocols that allowed her as Princess Regent to act alone, and then followed standard formulas for legislation. Finally, she got to it. "From this moment, all provisions of law authorizing any person to be condemned or subjected to punishment for violating the laws of the realm are restricted in application to mermaids only. This restriction applies to treaties and regulations and to the law of nations as well as to statutory provisions. No person other than a mermaid shall hereafter be condemned or subjected to punishment, in the name or under the authority of the realm, for violating any provision of law whatsoever." Then came further formulas, then the statement of the place, date, and time at which the legislation was given, and finally, "In the name of God, Amen."

Then Lady Amy relaxed and said, "This part of it is done. It was never imagined or intended that anyone should be punished like this by the laws of the realm, and it will never happen to anyone again. Punishment—even severe punishment if need be—yes, but nothing like this. Not at all. Even those on the wrong side of that final war would have been appalled. This is just too harsh and cruel. It reaches the basic question of the difference between punishment and torture. If anyone should ever try such evil again, the heroic girls who submit to answer for their people will simply take sick and die in just a few days, peacefully and without torment, with their minds clear up to the end. For the attacks on those gifted with healing will have to be spent somehow. But there will be no more of this kind of nightmare horror, thanks be to God. But the problem for these girls is that retroactive legislation is clearly forbidden in all cases. These girls are not yet set free. The obvious answer is of course for them to be pardoned. But here too, the legal situation is somewhat tricky."

The queen could pardon, but the pardon would in most cases have to be ratified. This could be done by any one of a number of lesser officials—the queen had her choice. But once again, she could ordinarily not act totally alone. Wendy asked, "Well, but you could act totally alone to legislate away all future danger. Why not this as well?" So they went through the old provisions and checked it out. No, that would not work given the way the protocols were set up, or at least not just based on what was given to the queen in the protocols themselves.

This time, it was not a question of finding some crafty gimmick—it was merely a question of digging up something very old. Consequently, it was Queen Paula who found it.

The fundamental law recognized the need to clean up leftover situations after a change of law as providing a special basis to pardon. Thus, the queen was authorized to pardon just by herself in the wake of a ratified new law, unless the act of ratification specifically forbade it. In the extraordinary of case of an authorized but unratified new law, the pardon would require ratification. However, once again, there was a trick regarding foreign relations. "But the queen may resolve the leftover situations of foreign people after a change of law by pardoning such people with the consent of a foreign ruler, pursuant to valid treaties, lawfully concluded and ratified, that remain in effect, and such consent shall suffice for ratification." Now there were several old treaties between the mermaids and the elves, of which various scraps and fragments stood down to the present day—at least in legal theory—as still valid and binding. Among these surviving provisions was one concerning situations of war or other extraordinary emergency when some military alliance was in effect. In such cases, it might happen that foreign people condemned under the laws of the mermaids would be committed to the custody of the elves. If this should happen, and there should then be a change of law among the mermaids that would make their situation a leftover from the older system, they could be pardoned by the queen of the mermaids with the consent of the local ruler of the elves within the world of the mermaids. In the present context, this local ruler was Queen Paula. Again, when the elves had finally intervened in the final war, they had not just barged in—they had obtained the approval of the queen of the mermaids. In fact, they had gone through the formality of setting up a military alliance for the occasion. The important thing was that this alliance had not been terminated or dissolved—it stood in place down to the present day, at least in legal theory.

"So," Queen Paula concluded, "Lady Amy can pardon them, and I can consent—with the concurrence of the Presiding Governess—and that will be that. Are there any questions?"

Wendy had two questions. "First, I can kind of see why their fundamental law would say that. So far as may be, a fundamental law has to provide for the widest possible range of situations in order that the people may be equal to any contingency. All right, fair enough. But why would there be a provision like that written into a treaty? Second, I am surprised that you need my concurrence, Your Majesty."

"Well, as to the first question, there was an unfortunate incident that arose in the course of their history. It was resolved eventually, but it was real trouble for them. What the situation was, how it was resolved, and what trouble they had—all that is not important right now. The point is, they wanted to make sure it did not happen again.

"As to the second question—you have proximate jurisdiction over them, Wendy, and that is significant under the laws of the realm. Yes, I could do it without you if I had to, but it would take longer and be more difficult."

"Of course you do *not* have to! What are we waiting for?"

"Oh, well, you see, the formal declarations have to be drawn up."

And so it was done, just a few days after the change of law. Lady Amy stood at the lectern and went through the formal phrases to pardon each and all of the vampire girls, Queen Paula stood and went through the formal phrases to consent to the pardon, and Wendy stood and went through the formal phrases to concur with Her Majesty's action. Then it was over. "So, it is accomplished. Today these girls are restored to be free women by right. Tonight, then, Wendy, you and Amy and Ginger and I shall relax and rejoice while my sisters go through some preliminary preparations. Tomorrow we shall begin the more interesting work of making them free in fact. If all goes well—and pray God that it does—they can all go home in a week or two, or whatever they may choose to do."

But it was not be. On this occasion, Wendy had brought Anna along with her at the Queen's invitation. The child was in bed with her as they slept through the night. The morning after the girls were pardoned, Wendy awoke at dawn in a cold sweat. Something was wrong.—What, exactly? The training and discipline from Ginger and then Queen Paula paid off. This time, she did not panic. She searched systematically with the powers given her.—No, not herself.—Not Anna, either.—No, nothing in her bedroom.—Nothing in that building. She was about to start going through the buildings of the compound systematically when Lady Amy rushed in.

"Wendy, you are awake—you feel it. Good. Come with me quickly. Bring Anna if you have to. It is the hall with the girls. I know not why or how, but the matrix is collapsing."

As they walked quickly, with Wendy carrying Anna, they met Ginger, who was also awake and alarmed by now. Wendy said, "Ginger, I love you dearly, but you are not powerful enough to help in this battle. You can help in another way. Hold onto Anna until it is over. Anna, go with Aunt Ginger." She handed the child over, and Amy took Wendy along.

When they arrived, Queen Paula was absent. Her chief deputy, Nona, was running the campaign. It was obvious what was happening. The elves were gradually failing. Almost all of the elves were totally preoccupied with maintaining fine-grained control, without which it would be over in just a few seconds. Nona and one other were projecting energy to reinforce the matrix, but it was not enough. The matrix would finally collapse in less than a minute now, and then all the girls would arise as full vampires at sunset. There was one chance, and it was very clear what it was. Amy and Wendy looked at each other. Wendy nodded, Amy nodded in response, and then both of them began projecting fire bolt energy to reinforce the matrix—not in violent bursts, but as a lower-level, continuous fire. This turned the tide of battle. The progress was gradual at first, but after a few minutes, the matrix was stabilized again. When everything was fully resolved, Wendy said to Nona, "What happened?"

"Her Majesty will discuss it with you later. For now, both of you get checked out."

"But Nona, we are all right."

"No, no 'buts.' Projecting fire bolt energy is dangerous for both of you, and especially for you, Wendy. 'All right,' you say. No. You go and have the physicians tell you that."

While they were with the physicians, Queen Paula came to them. "I was absent at the time of the crisis because I was away in my own homeland on official business. 'What happened,' you asked. What happened is what we were afraid of. The matrix was for girls merely sick with vampiric filth, not for girls who were already full vampires. We adjusted the matrix to accommodate her. But we knew it was and would remain both jury-rigged and fragile. Indeed, we always knew the odds were against us. Even a lightning strike from a thundershower could be critical. Well, the way it happened was not quite that bad, but it was one notch away from that. Sad to say, this has settled it for Lucy. Her fate is sealed. We are watching to see what happens to the other girls. If they are unlucky, this could cost their lives as well. But enough of this." She turned to the chief physician, Norberta. "How are they?"

"Both of them could be in some trouble, especially Wendy. We shall have to watch them and see how they turn out. Right now, the best thing for them is to sleep and sleep and sleep."

Before this could be implemented, Amy said, "Wait a minute! Did you say all the girls might die because of this?"

"Yes. It is not yet clear. We shall know by the time you wake up." Before either of them could say any more, the physicians had very gently taken them down into deep sleep.

They slept until noon the next day. Aunt Ginger had taken very good care of Anna, who had been very happy with her. Wendy was glad of this, and then she received sour news from Queen Paula about the girls.

"Lucy will have to be brought out soon enough—we must wait and see when. As for the others, we shall have to see once Lucy is removed. But it looks bad for them as well."

"Oh, Lord, those poor girls. Especially poor Lucy."

Lady Amy spoke to Wendy. "You forgive her that easily!"

Wendy stopped, reflected, and then said, "Yes, I do. First of all, there is what the Faith teaches, as you know. Instead of thinking how horrible and immoral and full of it she is—instead of hating her for what she has done—I had better remember how horrible and immoral and full of it I am, how I myself have enough to my discredit, and look to God to provide for both of us. Moreover—and here is the kicker—a case like this makes it easy to see how right the Faith is. She killed Elizabeth to be undead. Well, I killed her to be *truly* dead. I did only what I had to do—well, so did she, although in another way. I am deeply sorry—well, so is she. All this makes us more like sisters instead of enemies."

"But what about Elizabeth?"

"Elizabeth did not die with hatred—quite the opposite. So now I would dishonor her if I insisted on living with hatred. But forgive easily? No, not easy—not at all. Every day, more than once in the day, I wish I could have died in her place. It would be very easy to have that explode into pure hatred and then look for someone to lash out at. I have to take care always to look straight ahead, and not turn to the right or to the left, and submit to have God see me through. That is how it is for all of us."

Amy turned to Paula. "Yes, child, that is how it is for Wendy's people. That is kind of how it is for us elves as well, except we see and know far more. This makes it much easier to trust that by the grace and mercy—and justice—of God, none of the filth and horror that has happened has to be important, and everything will finally be right side up at the bottom of the last page. One who trusts that finds it easy to appreciate, revenge here and now is not important."

Amy found all this genuinely surprising. But she came to understand.

From there, everything went forward quickly and easily enough. Amy's conversion proceeded apace. She was formally sworn in and initiated before the year was out. Her comment about this was noteworthy. "It is very much that He illuminates my soul, but it is also something else before that even begins. It is natural for the elves to live on and on, but I am more of a mutant mermaid, and so it was not natural for me. Thus, I lived through age after age, but it was as if my vital functioning were being kept in a special lock down mode, and that was what kept me from dying. As a result, it was almost as if I were not really alive at all. But now, all that is gone. With my liberation from those points of elvish law, I am at long last rightly alive, even with my own natural life, to say nothing of the other. No, please, do not weep for me—rejoice with me. All that horror is over now. Yes, I am dying now, but so what? I am finally alive enough that I *can* die—that is how to think of it. But, O Lord, when I think of how this living deadness was, and when I magnify it to know how it must have been for Elizabeth, it is almost too much to face, let alone for the mind to accept. Wendy, you do not know what misery it must have been, but I know something of it. 'Undead,' they say. That is a very good word for it. You must never be sorry again that you had to kill Elizabeth to be truly dead. You did it that way so she could be a proper woman again in the final seconds. Compared with how she was when she awoke, it was almost like you granted her some last few seconds of pure blessedness, even before she died. Be sorry for her, not for me."

But Amy was not to go home just yet. After the initiation, there was a great religious festival celebrated at the Queen's estate in Wendy's land. The Queen had Wendy there with her family and friends and Amy. Sarah was quickly and easily reconciled with Wendy and Paula, as she had long since been with all the others. Then she met Amy, whom she found to be an extremely nice lady. The celebration went very well, and they all went home without incident, except for Wendy and Anna and Amy, who went home with the Queen to her realm.

After this, it did not take long. Amy died just a few days after the festival, with that same officer to help her through. This was accomplished with no trouble, and an elvish physician was allowed to make sure her death was soft and easy. After that there were the religious activities, and she was buried with Elizabeth as a sister princess.

⁂

"And so," Beatrice summed up, "she too was shortly at peace in Heaven. We can all be very happy for her, as were Wendy and the others. But that left the question of how—or indeed whether—the vampire girls were to be restored. The way that turned out was as remarkable as anything in Wendy's life."

CHAPTER TWENTY-ONE

At this point, Beatrice would simply have gone on with her narrative, but the others prevented her. "Since we are talking about Lady Amy's conversion and death, what about Lady Amy and her people? She followed the tradition of the right Faith and spoke of God in the masculine. Yes, indeed, very good. But that tradition was established only long after the history of her people as a whole, the mermaids as a race, ended. What was there among the mermaids?"

"Of course they knew well enough that God is above the division between male and female. The thinkers and scholars among them understood as well as Wendy did, and as well as we do, the theoretical points at stake in speaking of God either in the masculine or in the feminine. Also, they were not all female, as we are. But all the adults were female. Only children were male. Consequently, they always spoke of God in the feminine.

"However, among the children, there was the division of the sexes. A girl would simply grow up to become an adult woman, just straight out. With a boy, his mother would arrange for him when he was old enough and mature enough. His body would be capable, but his mind would be at the end of the cycle for a prepubescent child. Then he would be given to five or six or seven women, each of whom would take care of him and provide for him by bringing him into personal intimacy with herself. This was at once how they would work him through the process of breeding and also prepare him for the next stage. When this cycle was completed, those women who had received him would combine and take him through the process of metamorphosis, from which he would emerge as an adolescent girl. The child would then grow up into adulthood in the same way and at the same speed as a girl who had reached that stage of adolescence by starting out as a girl. She would then be more or less equal to other women.

"As a result, they had three sets of feminine personal pronouns in their language. There was one set of pronouns to speak of girls and of women who had grown up as girls, another set to speak of women who had grown up from being boys, and a third set to speak of all females generically, leaving aside the question of metamorphosis. Now, when they spoke of God, they would speak of Her with the neutral or generic feminine pronouns when they were speaking loosely, or explaining to a child, or something like that. But when they were being careful, they would speak of God with the pronouns for women who had grown up from being boys, in honor of the fact that God is really above the whole division of male and female.

"We did not know all this until now, for no Traveler from our people or those allied with us arrived on that world until after Lady Amy was just beginning her last period of activity prior to the advent of Wendy's people. I know it because it was given to me. Lady Amy spoke to Wendy about her upbringing and early education at the hands of the elves, and this was part of what they taught her. I witnessed this conversation, and my mind was taken back to observe the living history they had taught her about. Lady Amy knew all this only because the elves had taught it to her, just like any other history she was too young to know about and remember. Wendy, of course, knew about it only because Lady Amy explained it to her.

"But Lady Amy grew up among the elves, and she had no experience of the mermaids' ways. Therefore, even though she is best understood as a mutant mermaid, she followed the tradition of the elves and spoke of God in the masculine. First of all, there were adults of both sexes among the elves.

"But even more important, the elves had revelation given them concerning the Great Redemption that was to come, beyond what was given to the mermaids. This settled a whole lot of questions for them about God and how to speak of God. I was given to observe that living history among the mermaids, behind their way of speaking about God, as part of the larger process whereby I was brought to appreciate the foreshadowing of the Great Redemption."

After Beatrice had explained all this, she reminded the others that the discussion of the mermaids was only a sidelight in the present context. Then she went on with her narrative.

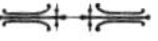

When Lady Amy was buried, the new year had just begun. The next day, the Queen spoke with Wendy. "You were right in saying Lady Amy and the vampires were the second chance for each other. That is very clear now. By projecting fire bolt energy as she did on that day of the crisis with the matrix, knowing the risk to herself, she renewed herself as an honest warrior girl. That did much to promote her moral and spiritual development and speed her journey home." Then her face became much sadder. "It also got her home more quickly in another way. As she knew, she was to die, but she should have lived decades more, until the end of her current cycle. But it turned out she was especially vulnerable on this one point because of—some crazy anomalies inside her. We knew that in theory there would be this danger, but we figured there was no serious danger in concrete reality. This conclusion turned out to be false. We were right relative to what we knew at the time we made the judgment, but we based our thinking on assumptions that we knew to be questionable and that turned out to be wrong. It was what you people call an 'educated guess,' and those can be very untrustworthy. The short explanation is that we did what we had to do at the time, and it turned out badly. Well, Lady Amy knew, and she did what she had to do, and there it is. As it turned out, the tiny tap was enough to send her." Wendy asked about the assumptions and guesswork, and the Queen explained it had to do with some technical points. The problem was, Amy had been unique. There had been no precedent to guide them in working through her development long ago, when she was first growing up.

"Then, Your Majesty, one thing puzzles me. When you first told us about Lady Amy, you said she could have burned down our world in ancient times if your people had not stopped her. Was that statement true, or was it part of your misunderstanding?"

"No, it turns out that part was true, although we did not understand rightly when I said it. The level of energy involved in burning down your world would have been very much less than what was involved in reinforcing the matrix, let alone in projecting even a minimal fire bolt in combat. It would have made her mildly sick for a few days, but it would not have sent her."

The Queen paused, then went on, "The point of all this is that you are not in any immediate danger from the side effects of projecting fire bolt energy, even though you lack the elvish factors that she had. The chief physician tells me that with luck, and if nothing else happens, you could be good for the full normal term at best, and perhaps twenty more years at worst. I know that means your span will be seriously shortened, but if all goes well, you should be able to see Anna through to full adulthood, even if your life is shortened."

"I thank you for trying, but that is not what is foretold for me."

"Yes, I know. We shall discuss that later, when the situation is further clarified."

"Very good, Your Majesty. What then?"

"For the time being, the situation with the vampire girls has been stabilized, with nothing for you to do. So I think it is best you should enjoy this interlude. You and Anna go home to your grandmother's house, relax, and all of you be happy together for a while. If possible, you should discuss all these remarkable experiences with Alicia."

This was exactly what Wendy did. She spoke with Alicia about something that had gradually come together in her mind since Amy had spoken of her liberation from the living deadness of her unnaturally long life. "As you know, Alicia, she was not the first to speak to me of living deadness. What she said reminded of the raving lunacy Pepper spouted when she ravished me, about the basis for everything as nothingness and deadness and all that. Later on, I remembered what I said to you long ago about the ghosts in the parade as living shadows. I am sure it all adds up somehow, but I am still trying to figure how."

"Perhaps you find it hard because it is too simple, too obvious. The connecting thread is the denial or dishonoring of the Lord God. What Pepper said was supposed to be an alternative to having Divine creation with God at the top. The idea of people in the next world as living shadows may be a very good description of what they would be apart from being attached to God so as to rejoice in Him. As for Amy, her whole basis to be what she was—and even to be raised up at all—involved some very serious dishonoring of Divine law. A person is not something to be made up in the laboratory to be used. The fact that she was a hybrid reinforces or underscores the wrongness of what was done. The quality of her life reflected the wrongness of her origin. It was finally resolved only when she was formally brought into the order of Divine Redemption, so as to be remade." Wendy agreed this sounded right, but she wondered how it compared with what happened among her own people. "Well, strictly speaking, something like that applies to us also, as you know. But I think what must have happened is that in Amy's case, the point was much more blatant, because her situation was grotesquely exaggerated." Wendy agreed with this as well. But that led her into the next obvious concern. What about the vampire girls? "I expect she was right in what she said about Elizabeth. As for the others—well, they are relieved of all misery, at least for the moment. Beyond that, we shall just have to see." And so they left it.

Queen Paula was able to stretch out the interlude for a full three weeks. Then she had Wendy come to her estate the next day. "It turns out that the process of stabilizing the matrix went better than we hoped—much better. For that, we can thank Elizabeth. Her presence in the bubble within the matrix turned out to make a whole lot of difference for the others, just as we hoped, as well as a slight difference for herself."

"Enough to be very significant, Your Majesty. In her behalf, it is I who thank you."

The Queen smiled, nodded, and continued. "Lucy has been able to stay at least a dozen weeks more than she could have otherwise, which has allowed her much more healing, which in turn will allow her much more time of being a clear-minded, proper woman again—if only we can figure how to do it. She can stay another week, two at the outside, before being removed. Then we shall just have to see how it goes—'play it by ear,' as you say. As for the other girls, I do not know. They too will have to be played by ear."

A week later, Wendy met with the Queen again, but not to remove Lucy from the matrix. With Alicia, Ginger, and Norberta also present, she spoke of the plan she had developed.

Only Wendy was able to restore the girls. Only Lady Amy could have done it before, but she had known she was dying. So she took counsel from Queen Paula and other elves. Then, before she died, she had raised up Wendy to be able to do it in her place, and so now it was on Wendy.

Lady Amy had explained it to her. "It is not that the elves are not powerful enough—not at all. Quite the opposite is true, as you know. They are plenty powerful enough, and they have the fine-grained control needed. On both of those points, the elves are clearly superior to me and to you. No, but the problem is that they find it hard to understand rightly. This is so even though their minds are clearly superior to both of ours. The thing is that they conceptualize reality very differently from how we do so. Their way is, in fact, better—more adequate or efficient for latching onto what things in fact are as they exist in themselves. However, on this one point I have the advantage, and so do you, as I shall explain. You see, they think of the procedure to restore the girls as a series of crazy tricks and gimmicks strung together in some bizarre way. Strictly speaking, of course, they are right. That is exactly what it is. The reason is that this whole business is so crazy that something crazy is needed in order to resolve it. So yes, their way of viewing it is correct, but it is also kind of useless. Because the elves think of the procedure that way, it would be effectively impossible for them to work it through correctly and to do so in real time. It is in that sense that they find it just too hard to understand rightly.

"On the other side, as a half mermaid, I have this little trick to how my brain is set up. That enables me to see the procedure as the natural and obvious way of doing things. That is why I can do it, but they cannot. Perhaps this is the best analogy. If topsy-turvy world existed with its own coherent structure based on consistent rules, a mathematician could understand that world by working through the rules systematically, and she could understand it much better than people who did not know mathematics. But in spite of her better theoretical understanding, the advantage for practical functioning in that world would belong to the mathematician's kid sister, assuming the sister could adjust her awareness of space at will to be adapted to that world, based on some trick to how her brain was set up. In this context, Queen Paula for example is like the mathematician, and I am like the kid sister."

"Yes, I understand. I think your analogy lays it out very well."

"Right, then. Now, here comes the part that concerns you. In some contexts—of which this is one—it is best to think of me less as a hybrid and more as a mutant mermaid. Well, the people of your species stand with me as a mutant mermaid across various critical dividing lines from the full elves. Along this line, some few of the women of your species can be given to share in our advantages and capabilities. It is really quite rare, but it does exist, and you are one of those few. I can and shall raise you up to act in my place for the vampire girls after I am dead."

And so it had been done. After she was raised up and Lady Amy died, Wendy waited.

Now Wendy was offering her plan. "I know that what I am about to say would not have worked before. The question is how much difference Elizabeth's presence made. There is given into my hands Lady Amy's ability to free the girls from being infested with metastatic charge, as you taught me to call it. As she taught me, what a name for it! But anyhow, what exactly would happen, literally and concretely, if I were to go in on the last day—in the final hours—and disentangle the charge from the structure of exotic energy for Lucy? I am not sure, but I think it might work out, at least partially, given the changes to the matrix."

Queen Paula thought a moment, then said, "Once again, it is just crazy enough that it might work." With that, she summoned telepathically those two elves she had summoned to ask about placing Elizabeth into a bubble. Speaking in the language Wendy had learned from her mother, the Queen explained Wendy's proposal and asked them, "Would that work out?"

"Well, it would be a little tricky, and it would have to be done exactly right, but yes—it would, at least partially. Full disentanglement would not be possible, but Lucy could enjoy some serious measure of benefit, assuming Lady Amy was able to make Wendy powerful enough." The elvish woman asked and received permission to place her hand upon Wendy and scan her. "Wow! That is more powerful than I thought one of your species could be. But yes—quite clearly, you are powerful enough. So yes, it should work if it is done very carefully."

"Is there any question about being able to see it through?"

"Not exactly, but we shall need to have Wendy guide us every step of the way based on what Lady Amy gave her. Other than that, no—it should be easy enough."

Then Wendy asked, "Alicia, so there is no question, what about the end game? Do I kill Lucy when her time runs out? Is it given me to knife her down and send her when she reverts?"

"Yes, you do, and it is. Once again, that is what is given to me."

"Right, then. So be it.—I assume you will want me to stay where the girls are—on the home soil of the realm—until this business is resolved?"

"Yes, of course. That would be best."

"What time, if any, do I have to prepare?"

It was agreed that Wendy would be taken from Queen Paula's estate to the home soil of the realm the next day, at the middle of the afternoon. Anna would go with her.

The day after her arrival, Wendy went through the dormitory with an elvish escort and examined Lucy and the other vampire girls with her extra senses. Afterward, she said to the Queen, "Yes, it will work. I can weaken or diminish the influence of the metastatic charge. Then Lucy can have weeks instead of hours before she has to be knifed down. She can live and be awake, and sleep, and wake again. She can walk about in daylight, rejoice in the beauty of butterflies and flowers and sunshine, and exchange love calmly and soberly with her family and friends—not just farewell kisses through tears. Most of all, she can engage in full Divine worship, not just final hymns and prayers as she is dying. The other girls can have at least the same measure of benefit later on, and perhaps full healing if we are very lucky."

Everything was prepared and arranged based on Wendy's guidance and direction. Three days after Wendy examined the girls, Lucy was removed from the great hall and taken to another room. Her elvish governess took direct personal action to maintain her inert body against deterioration. Then Wendy provided for Lucy as well as she could. And so, by sunset, all had been made ready.

Darkness fell, and Lucy arose as a full vampire but with her mind already cleared. She was greeted nicely by the governess who had tucked her in—what seemed to her just a moment before—who then helped her through as Lucy came to realize she was still afflicted and had arisen only to die. She received from her governess gown and slippers and submitted to be clothed and shod as a formal act of being delivered from vampiric savagery. Then the Queen gave the short explanation of what had happened and comforted her as well as she could. After this, Wendy spoke to her as nicely as she could, led Lucy again through the hymns she had taken the girls through before they had been tucked in, and pronounced that old blessing.

After that, it went for her as Wendy had said. Lucy enjoyed the luxury of going back to her mother's home, albeit escorted by her elvish governess, and living out her final days as if she were once again a proper woman—fully normal, pure, and healthy. She had the pleasure of daylight, the calm and sober exchange of love, and the deep joy of full Divine worship.

There was one complication. The local public officials of Lucy's place had already known about the violence she had done to her father, and they had been informed of how this had caused his death. But they had been given to know the truth, and the question of liability for criminal wrongdoing had been resolved. Now Queen Paula assured them Lucy was presently no danger. Her mind was lucid for the time being, and she would be under guard by the Queen's agents as continuing to be in the Queen's protective custody. Their own central government backed this claim, and so they agreed to what Queen Paula asked, albeit reluctantly. Consequently, Lucy was able to live out those final days without being disturbed.

This concluding interlude lasted six weeks. At the end, there was no trouble, for Lucy knew within herself that her mind was beginning to deteriorate, and so she appreciated what was to happen as what had to be. Instead, she rejoiced with gratitude at being able to conclude her life the right way. But it was also something else. Lucy knew she had blood on her hands: that of her father, which was bad enough—indeed, monstrous—and even more, that of the poor woman she had turned into a vampire. (What was her name? Yes, Elizabeth—thank you.) She understood that she was morally blameless as having been mentally deranged and thus not responsible. But Lucy understood also that this was not the end of the question. If she herself had to die in order to resolve the mess she was part of...well, that would be kind of appropriate. Indeed, it would be the exactly fitting way to keep faith with those she had killed. After discussing all this with her elvish governess, she asked that the one who killed Elizabeth to be truly dead might kill her also. The governess said she promised nothing, but she would see what she could do.

On that last day, as the fateful hour arrived, Lucy turned to her elvish governess at the right moment, declared herself ready, and asked to be taken back to the home soil of the Queen's realm. The governess answered, "Your request has been granted. The person who provided for Elizabeth, a woman of your own species, will provide for you too. You will be taken to the place where it was done, an estate Her Majesty has in your own land far to the west, not the home soil. From that place, you will be dispatched as Elizabeth was." Lucy assented and asked that all be done quickly, before she became too much afraid. The elf assured her what was to happen would be as soft and easy as possible, just as it had been for Elizabeth. Then she took Lucy to the estate.

By the time darkness fell at the estate, Lucy was standing ready. Wendy had explained how it would go in the remaining hours. She spoke of her own experience of being knifed through the heart, just as she had done with Elizabeth. At this, Lucy broke down and wept. "Oh, Wendy—dear, sweet Wendy! From that lullaby speech you gave, and the way you spoke to me when I was tucked in, and the way you spoke to me when I awoke, and the way you spoke to me just now, you love us all so much, I wish it could be you who would send me. But I asked that it be the one who sent Elizabeth."

Wendy smiled and said, "Well, Lucy, you will have both wishes together. Queen Paula gave me the office of Presiding Governess so that I could provide for Elizabeth legally as an official act. A knife that has been specially prepared to kill vampires is waiting down the hall in the room where Elizabeth died. You will go there with me now, and in a little while, you will die on the same table, by the same knife, at the hand of the same woman." At this, Lucy brightened up considerably and was almost happy, at least for the moment.

What happened next was very much like what had happened to Elizabeth. There was the same process of having the vampire speak to get the filth out of her soul. But instead of explaining why she had retreated, Lucy explained why she had spared her mother and sister. "The old stories are right about one thing. I found that classic symbol of the Faith to be unbearable. Tell me, did the same thing happen with Elizabeth?" Yes, indeed it did. "Well, there you go! I was going to start with my little sister, God help me. But then my father intervened. He offered more resistance and held me off longer than I would have thought possible, given that he was only a man and not a vampire. By the time I had drunk his blood, my mother was shielding her. I would have drunk Mama's blood next, but I saw she was wearing one of those symbols. My impression was, to advance upon her would have been to get myself even deeper into the unbearable filth I already was inside. So I ran away."

After this, there was the same process of prayers and hymns, then the same process of bidding goodbye to her mother. Then there was the same urge to strip and the same answer. Lucy complied, paused, composed herself, and said, "I am ready now."

With this, Wendy placed Lucy onto the table and took her through the procedure as she had done with Elizabeth. Then it was finally over for the poor girl.

Lucy concluded her life very well. She died nobly and heroically, exercising devotion and crying out to God in praise and prayer. But alas, she did die that night.

The formalities involved with Lucy's real death were resolved quickly and easily. A few days after that was the day appointed for the chief ritual of Divine worship. The day after that ritual, in turn, Lucy was buried with appropriate religious activities. As a full vampire, Lucy was buried in the Queen's realm. By the Queen's invitation, at her own request and that of her mother, and with the approval of Timothy and Theodora, Lucy was buried beside Princess Elizabeth as her guest.

The day after this burial, Alicia, Ginger, Norberta, Queen Paula, and Wendy met and spoke again. Wendy began, "Lucy arose as a full vampire only because she was already that way. There will be no more full vampires from this group, thanks be to God. In the worst case, all the remaining girls will arise only to die, but they will die from mere sickness, being and having always been proper women and not monsters. But I am afraid that may well be exactly what happens. All too likely, they cannot be restored. I am only a direct recruit and not an elf, but even I can see that much."

Queen Paula answered, "Well, we shall know one way or the other in about three weeks. You may go home and be happy with your daughter, Wendy. I shall send you word."

"Very good, Your Majesty. I thank you."

But something was obviously on her mind, and so the Queen asked, "What is it, Wendy?'

"Your Majesty, I am wondering about that old prophecy you described to Theodora concerning their eternal destiny."

"Will the other girls be covered, given that they do not reach the threshold of vampiric filth? Lord love you for being concerned about this. But yes, Wendy, they will, with no question. With what was given to us, what translates as 'vampires' includes incipient vampires, such as the other girls, as well as full vampires like Lucy and Elizabeth. That is very clear in the original language. So yes—they are covered, and all will be well with them, and there it is."

Alicia spoke up. "It is given to me to know. Yes, it is as Her Majesty just said. Everything will work out all right for them."

Ginger commented, "At least, everything will be all right, given that this whole thing happened in the first place. Given that, then yes, all the rest follows. But –!"

Queen Paula said, "Yes, I know. But what else can I do? What can any of us do? It is what you said to Wendy back on that night when she had to take care of Elizabeth. As you pointed out, Ginger, all we can work with is what is given into our hands. As it turns out, we can be happy it is given into our hands to do even this much."

Three weeks later, Wendy, Ginger, and Alicia heard from the Queen what was given into their hands and what was not. "First of all, there is what you call the bottom line. None of them can be fully restored. All of them will arise afflicted and will die from sickness on that basis. But they will die *from sickness.* As Wendy said, none of them will ever be a full vampire. All will be and remain proper women. Again, all will enjoy the same benefit Lucy had but for a much longer time. All of them will be good for twenty-seven or twenty-eight weeks. Before I explain, are there any questions or concerns so far?" No, there were not.

So the Queen began again. "You people speak of what may happen—win, lose, or draw. Well, we are certainly not going to win this one, for none of the girls will be restored—all will die from vampiric affliction. On the other hand, what can still be achieved is enough of a victory over the evil that we think of it as a draw instead of a mere loss. To begin with, they suffered distinctively vampiric affliction because old points of law from the mermaids were applied to these girls. Among the mermaids, a penitent malefactor who had been pardoned would be released from all restraints and discharged from custody at once, but she would regain her—her full freedom and dignity as a citizen, as you would say, only after a third of a year. Well, the time they will have is more than that. I discussed it with Lady Amy before she died, and we arranged the formalities. There will be a joyous celebration in my realm on the appropriate day.

"Moreover, even among your people, half a year can often be a significant time frame. As regards the present concern, half a year can be long enough to be a serious period of remission from a deadly sickness and not merely a brief interlude. Again, the time they will have is also more than that.

"Lucy was good for six weeks, based on what Wendy was able to do for her. Since the other girls were never full vampires, their structures of exotic energy are much less entangled with metastatic charge, and so Wendy can do much more for them. On that basis, they will be good for eighteen weeks instead of just six. Then, beyond that, we have learned much from Elizabeth and Lucy. Consequently, Norberta will be able to piggyback nine or ten extra weeks onto what Wendy can provide them.

"With Lucy's departure, we have had to reconfigure the matrix. This has been a little tricky, but we have done it. The girls are now organized into a seven-by-nine array, with the organizing theme being the specific concern to counterbalance vampiric filth. A vampire is a monster of night and darkness. So within this master array, there are seven...pavilions, I think would be the best way to say it in your language. Right, then. There are seven pavilions, with nine girls each, representing the seven colors of the rainbow.

"Each girl represents some color and belongs to some pavilion. Within each pavilion, each girl represents some one of nine points of glory for the relevant color. No girl represents more than one color, and no girls represent the same point of glory for the same color. Which pavilion she goes into and which place she has within that pavilion are based on the distinctive facts and features of each girl—facts about her body, to be sure, including her structure of exotic energy, but chiefly about the distinctive character of her personality. Of course, there are many girls in the world who fit each of the sixty-three points, and so there could be terrible confusion, but then this whole affair was never about luck. It is all within the order of Divine Providence."

Wendy asked, "What is to be done when for their restoration?"

"They are to be awakened one week from today. The procedure will be about the same as it was for Lucy except that it will be in the daytime instead of having to wait for nightfall, and it will be done in the great hall instead of in another room. When they are awake, each will receive special therapy from Norberta and her colleagues and then special care from her own governess. Then I shall speak to them, and you will speak to them, and then they will go home, each to her mother's place, after being invited to return for the celebration in a third of a year."

And so, on the appointed day, the work was accomplished, and the girls awoke. Each girl had her governess greet her nicely and then take her through the awareness of her continuing affliction. Each girl submitted to be clothed and shod, as Lucy had been. Then each received from an elvish physician the special therapy that had been prepared. A few minutes later, each girl complained of being very thirsty.

The governesses smiled and explained. The response of one governess was typical: "Good. That shows the therapy has worked. The affliction is largely subsided, although not fully, and so you are enough of a proper woman again that of course you would be thirsty, for that is how it works with your species." Then each governess gave the girl in her charge water she had ready. A few minutes later, each girl received another beverage from her governess and was told to drink—it would improve her electrolyte balance.

Several minutes after all this, when the girls were ready, the Queen explained briefly what had happened and what was to come. Then she had Wendy lead them through the hymns they had sung before going down and pronounce that old blessing on them again. Finally, the Queen sent them home with the invitation to return for the celebration in a third of a year. Since technically they were still in protective custody, their elvish governesses went with them.

Wendy had figured she would be gone just the one day and that she would be busy through the day, so she had left Anna at home with her own mother. But at the end of the day, the Queen prevailed upon her to stay overnight as her guest. The next morning, she awoke feeling idiotically euphoric. Then she saw Samantha, Lucy's old governess, who took her to the Queen. Norberta, Ginger, and her aunt Amanda were also there. Wendy wondered about this for just a moment. Then it hit her. "Three physicians and also a governess—Your Majesty, is something wrong with me? Is that why you brought me here?"

"Very good, Wendy. I am glad to see you are still both so rational and also so docile. Yes, there is, and that is why." Then, with a gesture, she directed Wendy to Norberta.

"Lady Wendy, I am sorry. This is my fault. I should have known better. No woman of your species can do the work you did on the vampire girls all in one day without paying a great price. You see, when you worked on the girls, a little of the metastatic charge from each went into you. There was no way to prevent it that would not also prevent you from accomplishing the work. It could and should have been spread out so that your body could gradually neutralize the effects. For you see, the charge absorbed is cumulative, and so now you have enough metastatic charge inside you to kill five or six ordinary women. No ordinary woman of your species with that much charge inside her has to worry about becoming a vampire—she is past that. As it is, you survived the night only because you are a direct recruit. But all this is why you feel idiotically euphoric. You will not survive this day without therapy."

"What happens now?"

"Happily, the charge has not yet begun to coalesce into a structure, and so it can simply be bled off. This will be done by placing several needles coated with silver into your body at strategic points. But Wendy, any person of your species would find the process extremely painful—indeed, unbearable. It would feel like you were being burned alive with intense cold fire. Also, it is not something where you can be brave for just a minute or two and then it is over. Only by doing it very slowly can you survive. It will take about twelve hours. So you will be anesthetized, but not with drugs. With the capabilities we have, your mind will be blanked out telepathically, and you will experience only an inert dreaminess. Then you will be incapacitated for many weeks. But we must begin at once. Your mother and grandmother have already been informed, along with your aunt Amanda. So if you will come with me now, here we go."

Wendy looked to Amanda, who nodded in assent. She looked to Ginger, who also nodded and promised to look after Anna. Then she went with Norberta.

After the process was completed, Wendy was in and out of delirium for fourteen weeks, and then it was another week before her mind was fully restored. Finally, she proved her rationality by asking the Queen a serious question.

"Your Majesty, when I asked about the wondrous quality of Fairyland, you pointed out to me what the Book said—even the ground was cursed because of the evil of my people."

"Yes, I remember that."

"Well, but when you were explaining about Lilith—I call her that because it was before her conversion—you said such hereditary evil ran through the mermaids as well. I have wondered:

What about you elves? Does hereditary evil run through your people? If so, there would seem to be a conflict here."

"Very good, Wendy. First of all, we are superior beings, and so our natural capabilities enable us to work on a higher level, in spite of whatever evil we may have. It is kind of like how among you, a wicked adult is naturally superior to a wicked child, other things being equal, and so the adult can do more and act at a higher level. Also, life, death, and reproduction work differently among us from what happens among you people, as you know."

Then the Queen paused briefly before explaining. "The short answer to your original question is yes. But that answer is too short. There is no quick version. We have to go back to underlying principles. So be it, then.

"No person can come into existence otherwise than through direct creation by God. With pure spirits, what happens is straightforward enough. With material persons, it can be more complicated, but the basic fact remains. The best traditional thinkers of your species know this. Now the point is that with material persons, there is a range of alternatives for how much is directly given versus how much is provided by means of animal generation and development. We are near the high end of the spectrum for what is directly given. You people are near the low end of that spectrum and near the high end for animal generation. This is why we live and function on different principles from you regarding both body and mind—we are not simply rational animals as you are only more advanced along the same line. Consequently, with us, the question of moral standing is more about personal choice, and less about what is inherited, than it is with you. The short way to say it may be that the old stories are right once again. For they speak of us as midway between you people and the Messengers."

"Yet newly arrived children among you are still formally consecrated."

"Yes, of course. Indeed they are, or at least they were, for the same reasons as with you. First of all, they arrive with some measure of internal degradation, although a much lesser measure. Like you, we must look to God to see us through. Second, as with you, they must be brought into right relation with God, both to honor God and so that they may receive what He would give them."

"You say 'at least they were.' What then? What happens with your children now?"

"I am sorry. I had forgotten that you do not know. Among us, all reproduction, both in this world and in the homeland, was concluded long ago—about fifteen hundred of your years prior to the beginning of the age of Preparation leading up to the Great Redemption."

They discussed all this, and Wendy understood very well. Her recovery was as complete as might be, but there would be residual damage. And so she went home, to be with Anna and the others, and to clean up her affairs, and to prepare what she would say at the celebration.

⁂

Beatrice commented, "In the meantime, the vampire girls were not mere children—they had begun as adult women. Again, the time they had was not a brief interlude so as to be only a long goodbye; it was a serious remission. Consequently, they accepted that they were called upon to engage in some sort of adult activity. It worked out nicely for them, as it had for Wendy years before. All of them acquired mild jobs in local flower shops. This was very good for those girls, as counteracting the vampiric filth that had touched them—even though comparatively slightly—in two ways. The concern with the generation and growth and development of beings genuinely alive stood against the minimal taste they had suffered of living deadness, and the concern with the beauty of color stood against the love of darkness they had just begun to feel. In addition, all of them enrolled for a minimal load of academic study. Of course, they knew they would not go on to further work based on some serious educational background. But they discussed it with their parents and governesses, and then they enrolled to study mystical poetry.

"Most of all, of course, they spent a whole lot of time in extra thanksgiving and prayer and praise as well as the regular rituals and functions of Divine worship, and they strove to learn as much as they could about God and the things of God. Their families found these girls to be especially dear and sweet in those days and to have even greater concern than before about the right things for the right reasons, very much including points of what was right and wrong.

"But time marched on, as it always does, and all too soon that third of a year was used up. Now the day was come for the great celebration. When all were assembled in the great hall, the Queen greeted them and then had Wendy speak." With that, Beatrice resumed her narrative.

Wendy looked upon the vampire girls, smiled, and bowed to them. (*But no, the whole point is that they are not vampire girls any more. Enough of this.*) She began to speak.

"Dear ladies, once again, I salute you as classic heroines. But now I salute you on your success as well. By the grace and mercy of God, it has been accomplished. The evil you ladies submitted to swallow up and keep confined within yourselves has not defiled you—it has been neutralized. The tangle of laws and rules in which you were imprisoned has been resolved. The last vestige of that web is finally dissolved away, gone as though it had never been. Sad to say, this success is not complete. You will still die from this work. It is not given to me or to the Queen to spare you that. But all women die, and your deaths from this affliction will be merely deaths from sickness, which is along the general line. No nightmare filth will be involved. You will die very soon, as you know—but then, any woman may die young, and your deaths will not be especially harsh or cruel. Quite the opposite, in fact. Your departures will be very soft and mild.

"In addition, the success has failed to be complete in another and even more serious way. Women have died as monsters of vampiric filth, who had to be and were simply killed off as classic nightmare horrors. One was your sister Lucy, who was already a full vampire when the Queen's agents found her, as you know. The other was an innocent victim whom Lucy turned into a vampire, a woman named Elizabeth. Not to dwell on horror, both women have died, and both are at peace in Heaven, as was foretold long ago. Everything will finally be right side up for them when they are given to return, in God's own good time. But as always, we must wait upon God's own good time for such victories to be perfected. Until then, there is always what was said in ages past. The Lord gave, and the Lord has taken away. Blessed be the name of the Lord."

At this, Wendy had to pause to control her emotions. Then she resumed. "Yet for today, the thing to note is that there *is* the victory to be perfected. Much remains to be fulfilled, but something great has already been accomplished. This one nightmare has been broken through and burned away. Wherefore, let us lift up our voices in honor of this limited daybreak He has already granted us." With that, Wendy led them in singing another hymn. It was different from the hymns she had led them through before. It compared the freshness of each dawn to the morning when their species was first created and still primally innocent.

When the hymn was concluded, the Queen called forth the next phase of the celebration. "Dear ladies, my friends, an appropriate celebration of solemnities has long since been conducted for Elizabeth. Today we would celebrate the appropriate solemnities for Lucy. Like you, your sister Lucy was a classic heroine. She fulfilled this office by dying well, submitting honorably and very bravely to what must be, and finally exercising devotion as the handmaid of the Lord God when her mind was cleared. As we have been given to know, and as Lady Wendy has told you, she is at peace in Heaven. Ladies, I call upon you to honor your sister Lucy by sharing in the celebration for this fallen heroine. My sister elves will assist you with festal garments and other preparations. I say 'festal' because ultimately it is about rejoicing with thanksgiving for the victory He has granted her."

The girls did not have to be commanded—they were happy to share in the celebration. When they had been made ready, they were brought back, and the celebration began.

The festal garments were worthy of some note. All the girls wore silvery-gray sandals. But each girl's dress was unique. Each girl chose her own dress. Each dress was, in fact, what the elves had prepared to represent some one of the points of chromatic glory. Accordingly, each girl chose the dress that she saw instinctively to be appropriate for herself—which was, in fact, the dress that matched what she herself represented, although the girls were not consciously aware of this until it was explained to them later on. At the time, it was simply that each girl thought her own dress to be at once the most beautiful garment she had ever seen and also the most fitting for herself. Yet all the dresses were, on the whole, fairly modest. It was just that each girl's dress allowed her to perceive and appreciate some aspect of beauty more than ever before and to feel how this awareness was her own special gift.

But the joy each girl felt at her own dress was only the beginning. When they were brought back and saw each other in the hall for the celebration, their joy was heartbreaking. One's own point of glory was wondrous. The full combination of all these points was almost too much to bear. Almost.

⁂

"Indeed," said Beatrice, "to speak of those people as girls is exactly wrong in this context. That experience led to a further coming-of-age for them. At the beginning of the celebration, all of those ladies had been worn down by the burden of their continuing sickness, much more than they themselves knew, and were merely ready to have it finished and go home—again, more than they knew. But this experience of beauty went far beyond being a very great pleasure for them. It involved a serious awakening and deepening for them, with a great renewal of mental energy.

"The celebration ran long, but finally the solemnities were concluded. Then every one of the vampire ladies accepted the Queen's invitation to stay on as her guest and leave the next day. When they awoke the next morning, all found themselves remarkably happy. Along with this, all found themselves to be enthusiastic, and indeed even grateful, for the privilege of staying on for several more weeks to complete their service. They discussed these facts with Alicia, and with the governesses, and with the Queen, and with Wendy. When all this had been talked through, their governesses took them back to their mothers' homes, there to await further developments.

"As the Queen had said, those ladies completed the work of fulfilling their destinies and then went home, quickly and easily enough. The day after the twenty-seven weeks had ended, they began dying. Those ladies died very mildly of sickness over four days, without even any need for anesthesia. Their bodies were adorned in their festal attire and buried by their families in various local cemeteries. I was given to know in my vision that they are all in Heaven now, as was foretold."

CHAPTER TWENTY-TWO

Beatrice continued. "With that, the affair was ended—at least for them. All the original vampire girls accepted the hard task of bearing the nightmare filth within themselves without being defiled by it. None of them failed. All of them were called upon to ride the tiger all the way through the minefield and out the other side, and all of them succeeded in doing so.

"Only with Lucy was there any serious question, but she too succeeded. Her mind and body were ruined, but that had happened against her will and through no fault of her own. Consequently, what happened to her was not the same thing as being defiled with evil. When her capabilities were temporarily restored, first Lucy displayed the right combination of care and concern with docile submissiveness as she was put to bed. Upon awakening, she lived out the interlude virtuously. Finally, she submitted bravely to her fate and died heroically. In this way, like all her sisters in the matrix, Lucy triumphed, in spite of everything."

Beatrice paused for a moment, then began again, her face and voice much sadder now. "So there it was, and that was how it went. I hoped, along with Wendy and the others, that it would work out well for those girls. But I suspected it would not, and my feeling was that I knew too much to take their hopes all that seriously. Afterward, looking back, Alicia, Ginger, Queen Paula, and Wendy agreed. They discussed it and came to understand that they should have known better. What they had tried to achieve was really too much to hope for. It was Ginger who summed it up for them: 'With this business of the vampires, we have been working on a level where the questions of life and death, the concerns over the mysteries, the heights and depths, are especially pointed. In one way, of course, to work and explore on this level is a thing beyond dreams, but the price to be paid is correspondingly great. No woman—or man—can enter into death even as deeply as these girls have and then return, apart from some special Divine gift. Evidently, that gift was not one of the things given to these girls.' The others agreed, and their discussion went on from there." After a moment, she added, "Of course, regarding the most critical question of all, it did work out well for those girls—very well indeed, for they all went home to be at peace in Heaven, rejoicing in God forever. This too was discussed, agreed upon, and appreciated among Wendy and the others."

Beatrice's teacher said, "Queen Paula gave Wendy the office of Presiding Governess. Then, Wendy should have been able to command the elvish governesses attached to Lucy and the other vampire girls. But that seems not to be how it worked out."

"Right. Strictly speaking, yes, Wendy could and did command the other governesses. Very early on, even before Elizabeth was knifed down, the Queen had Wendy issue a series of carefully crafted basic commands. The idea was that the governesses were to take appropriate action based on elvish knowledge and understanding. That allowed them to act without consulting her and even to tell her what was necessary. All this was a technical formality. But in legal theory, Wendy's office gave her dominion over the elvish governesses. Queen Paula took very seriously the sworn duty from her coronation oath to honor all relevant laws and rules. On the other side, there were the obvious pragmatic necessities. So the Queen did what she had to do."

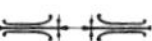

Time marched on. It had been three weeks since the last of those ladies had been buried. The original basis on which Wendy had been pressed into service by her own government was to aid Queen Paula in working through the project with the vampire girls. Now that project was ended, the basis was dissolved, and Wendy had no further obligations or commitments. "But we both know our adventures together are far from over." Yes, indeed. "Then, with your consent, Wendy, you are *not* discharged from your office as Presiding Governess. Instead, you are relieved of active duty and placed on minimal reserve status. That way, the next episode can be taken care of quickly and easily. In the meantime, you are free to pursue your own concerns, with no need to obtain approval." Wendy consented, and they left it there.

Sure enough, Queen Paula called on Wendy one week after this conversation. They met late the next day at the Queen's estate near Wendy's home. But on this occasion, the whole group was there, including Timothy but excluding Sarah. Margaret's sister Florence, whom Elizabeth had visited, was also there. After introductions and greetings, the Queen began.

"Ladies, Timothy, once again, I bid you welcome. Madame Florence, has the background been explained to you?" Yes, indeed it had been. "Very good. I have called in Wendy to speak to her on business, but the first part of the business pertains to all of you. The reason to call you in, Wendy—well, first of all, I am always happy to see you and speak with you. But the concern on this occasion has to do with two things. First of all, I have something for you as the old Presiding Governess over the vampire girls. For the rest of you, there is some background having to do with Lucy. Wendy finished it for her and had her speak of her experience as a full vampire first, just as she did with Elizabeth. The scene was recorded, just as the scene with Elizabeth was. Come, now—let me show all of you the recording."

When Wendy and the others had seen and heard all, they discussed it and agreed that what Lucy had said about her craving and how it dominated her mind, as well as about her abhorrence of that classic symbol of the Faith, was more or less the same as what Elizabeth had said.

Then, after a long pause, Timothy said, "Your Majesty, I am very grateful you have shown us this. It makes it much easier to forgive Lucy for what she did to Elizabeth."

Theodora agreed. "But," she added, "what about Sarah? Dear God, that poor girl. Will she accept it? Will she ever be able to accept it?"

Florence answered, "I believe she will. If she needs to blame someone, she can blame me. I was both the older lady with years of experience and the accomplished mistress teaching the novice about her gift. I should have known and headed off the danger. I did know there was something strange. It was just that I had never sensed anything like that before. By the time I understood enough, it was too late. I found her and took her to the hospital, but all they could do was to buy time and then watch her die—to be undead, as it turned out."

Queen Paula tried to comfort her. "My own direct recruits tried and failed to stop her from hurting anyone else. Once a woman is a full vampire and out free, it is very difficult. My people managed to track her down, finally, but only because of the training—and vastly superior powers—we elves gave them. There was nothing else you could have done."

Florence smiled sadly. “You are very gracious, Your Majesty. I thank you for trying.” Quite clearly, she wanted to say more, but she begged off and said only, “Later.”

And so the Queen said, “There is sour news concerning Lucy—very sour indeed. The failure of the matrix turns out to be even more tragic than we knew. Further investigation shows that it would presumably have worked out for all of them to be fully healed, if only—!”

“What is it, Queen Paula?”

“There is no nice way, so here it is, straight out: very probably it all would have worked out, if only Lucy had not turned another woman into a vampire. Yes, the pardon was carefully written, and it covered the predations she committed as a vampire, but that did not cancel out the natural consequences. If she had merely consumed and killed other people, whether boys, or men, or girls, or even adult women, it would have been all right—not to approve what she did, but you know what I mean. But what she did to Elizabeth distorted her own structure of exotic energy. That being so, there was never any real chance for it to work out.”

After the missing pieces of background for this news had been given to the others, Florence said, “I think I can tell you the rest of it now. Theodora, you told me what Elizabeth said before she left, and we have discussed how it was almost as if she knew. Well, she spoke to me as well. On her last morning, the day she met Lucy, Elizabeth asked me, ‘Aunt Florence, is this the fateful day for me? Will today be when my nightmare comes true?’ I sensed something strange, but I did not know what it was. I told her so and added, ‘So yes, it could well be, but I cannot be sure.’ Then I reminded her that anything could happen to anyone, any day of her life, and the thing to do was look to God, always and in all things. With this, she went and fell to her prayers all the more. Then she returned and said, ‘I must die sometime, of course.

Given what has been promised me, I guess it will not be too horrible. So, if this is what He has appointed for me, then glory to God in the highest.' Then she put her hands together, looked upward, and cried out in prayer, 'But please, God! Let it end with me! If I must be turned into something out of the worst nightmares and be killed as a monster, then I beseech Thee, O Lord, let my death be what turns the tide of battle somehow.' Then she broke down and wept. I comforted her as well as I could.

"Later, when Elizabeth was about to leave on that errand, I was reluctant to have her go. But I had to admit, I did not sense it would be more dangerous for her to leave than to stay. 'Then it might be equally or even more dangerous for me to stay,' she said. She reminded me of that old story about the poor fool who tried to escape his fate by running away from Death—but instead, his flight took him to *meet* Death. What could I say? She went out after having me promise to pray God that she might return safely and that He would see her through whatever might happen. Oh, how well I kept that promise! But He had other plans." Then, barely holding herself together, she concluded, "The Lord gave, and the Lord has taken away. Blessed be the name of the Lord."

Alicia spoke up now. "Madame Florence, you have seen the recording of Elizabeth's death—her *real* death, to be truly dead. You have also been informed about the old prophecies, as well as what has been given to me. So you know He has brought her through. She died as His devoted handmaid. Her death was noble and heroic, even exemplary, and she is at peace in Heaven. But there are other things that have to be shared among us. I am given this, but I do not yet know what they are. Wendy and Queen Paula have one of the missing pieces of the puzzle, and Timothy and Theodora have the other."

Wendy understood and said, "Your Majesty, I am the one who told them about Elizabeth's sickness that would soon have sent her anyway, and so it might be best for me to take this one."

The Queen nodded, and Wendy said, "Aunt Florence, it looks like her prayer was granted. Her death was what turned the tide of battle. To turn any other woman into a vampire would have ruined Lucy's prospects. But with most women, that would have left Lucy very hard to track down. They would have tracked her down her eventually, to be sure, but it would have been a long and very hard job. She could have killed many others, and even turned many other women into vampires, before they caught her. Then there would be the new vampires she made to worry about and those of their victims in turn who became vampires and on and on. Instead of being merely a serious project, the campaign against vampires could have been the most terrible war this world has ever seen, going on for untold years, perhaps even for generations or centuries. But by the mercy of God, and through what happened to Elizabeth, all that was prevented. How to say it...the—signature of her body as regards exotic energy was extraordinary, not least because of that sickness. So, when Lucy did what she did, the specific way her structure of exotic energy was distorted left her plainly marked and easily detectable for the Queen's direct recruits."

Then Alicia turned to Timothy and Theodora.

Timothy objected, "Alicia, I know about Elizabeth, but not about all these other things." Turning to Theodora, he said, "You have your family's gift. Do you know what she means?"

"Yes, I do. Enough has been said about the other things for a while. But Elizabeth must also be considered. It is about her now." She paused, then began again. "Dear, sweet Timmy, if she had not met Lucy, and if she had survived the sickness somehow, what then? Where could she have gone? Which way could she have turned? What path could she have followed? It was kind of like, she was a woman of destiny in some special way, but with no way to fit into the world to accomplish great works. We had wondered about that and discussed it for many years, long before that horrible conference at our house, two years before...what happened to her." Then, turning to the others, she explained, "We loved her dearly, of course, and she was very lovable, but she was almost an impossible challenge—perhaps most of all for herself—and she knew it. It was like, she was to be both a full-blown warrior girl, and also a full-blown mystical contemplative, all rolled into one, impossible as that sounds. We figured that the best she could hope for was probably to act energetically, and speak out boldly, and insist on calling things by their right names, and then be shot through the head for the Faith. But if not that, then it was just totally mysterious what there might be for her. Evidently, it turned out to be totally mysterious. Given that this had to happen to someone, it looks like Elizabeth was raised up for this work."

⁂

Beatrice explained to the others about being shot through the head as one of the easier ways to die. Then she went on with the story.

⁂

Queen Paula spoke up. "Did this have to happen? In the present context, yes, of course, from which follows what Theodora said. Did there have to be this context? Well, we elves live a very long time. We have seen much, and learned much, and watched how things work out, and how old prophecies are fulfilled. So what can I say? History in this world is a tissue of what ended up happening instead of what should have happened 'if only.' Some of you people are truly worthy, and we honor you quite sincerely, and we rejoice in what God has done among you—but we really would like very much to leave your world for the last time and go to what is now our own homeland as alien beings. What I said about your history is a big chunk of the reason why."

It was Ginger who objected. "But Your Majesty, surely among you also there must be the interplay of chance, choice, and destiny or fate, with all the complications that entails."

"Yes, of course, in one way. But it works differently among us.—I spoke too harshly. The way it works among you is what you need; indeed, it is how it *has* to work, given the kind and level of beings you are. The only alternative would be if you people had never adopted evil in the first place. Given the basic choice whereby that failed, all the rest follows. Beyond that—well, it is not your fault there was the old situation that we had to stay in your world and clean up." That was all she would say about it, at least on that occasion.

After this there was an intermission, and they all had dinner together. Then the Queen accepted one question from Timothy.

"Your Majesty, when we were discussing where Elizabeth should be buried, I said she never heard of you or your realm within her lifetime. Now, of course, I know better. That was an oversimplification, if not exactly false. For she had the rare privilege of concluding her life and then dying in Fairyland, with its wondrous quality. Wendy and Ginger and Alicia have explained it to me. But did Elizabeth know what was happening at the time?"

Queen Paula gave this question to Wendy, who had been in much greater telepathic contact with Elizabeth's mind.

"No, Timothy, she did not. She observed the wondrous quality, to be sure. But she mistook that aspect of her experience for a feature of her vampiric functioning."

Then the Queen dismissed the others, explaining she had to discuss some things with Wendy alone. When they were gone, she began their conversation again. "Wendy, I have called you in and told you all this because of your office as Presiding Governess. I have told the others because I figured that after our old conversations and all that has happened, Elizabeth's family—which includes Alfreda in this context—was entitled to know. I have not told the other families, and I do not intend to. As I said long ago, most of Elizabeth's people are kind of like experts in this area. But it is bad enough some select few have to know all this, and it is bad enough the other families have to know as much as they do."

"Yes, Ma'am."

"Well then, enough of this. Oh, Wendy. I am sorry for Elizabeth—very much so. But then there is what we have just discussed about her. I am of course sorry for all the original vampires as well—but after all, they did offer and submit to act as classic heroines. I am also sorry about Lady Amy. She and you helped to stabilize the matrix, and that turned out to be—well, not in vain, exactly, but not many notches above that, either, given that no one was fully healed. That work sent her very quickly, as we have discussed. But then, as we have also discussed, given her personal history, it was kind of necessary for her moral and spiritual development. What I am chiefly sorry about is you, Wendy. Your life span may end up being seriously shortened, again for work that was almost in vain, even though not exactly."

Wendy collected her thoughts and weighed her words before speaking. "Your Majesty, I am sorry for the other people. But as for myself, what else should I have expected? Given my ancestry, I was born into the involvement with wonders and mysteries, heights and depths. A woman descended from soothsayers and all that has to expect certain things. Then I was trained and initiated as a volcanic witch by my governess. After that, by the mercy of the Real God, I left that and was sworn into the order of Divine Redemption, which has wonders and glories, heights and depths, beyond what my governess and her ancestors ever dreamed of. Later, I was ravished by a *real* paranormal mistress and conceived through parthenogenesis. That makes my life and experience exotic right there.

"Finally, I have been intimately involved in this complex of wonders where the mysteries of life and death—and of other things as well—come together. In view of all these facts about me, it might be kind of bizarre if my life span did *not* end up being shortened, one way or the other. And all that is before we consider, given my clinical situation, I spent much of my life, starting before I was born, living on borrowed time, as they say. So, no. I thank you for your concern, but I cannot complain—quite the opposite." She paused, then added, "But perhaps all that is not even the main thing. In the lullaby address, I spoke of the vampire girls as heroines above my own level. Lucy proved how true that was, and that is leaving aside the more serious issues of what the whole thing was about in the first place. Lucy killed two people only because she was demented, and yet she was more than content to answer for it with her own life. I killed two people as a willful and deliberate act each time. Well, hey, what can I say? I reckon what was good enough for Lady Amy and for Lucy can be good enough for me. It has to be good enough for me, or I break faith with Lucy and perhaps Elizabeth as well. No, I am only sorry about the prospect of leaving my daughter motherless." Before the Queen could respond, she concluded, "Also, I may have to face Lucy's kid sister Wilhelmina someday with the truth, just as I had to face Sarah. I cannot face her if I break faith with her sister."

"Well, what you have said is right, of course, and Lord love you for it. But as for Wilhelmina, that will not be a problem. She is already reconciled. Lucy explained it to her in that last interlude and left her a long letter, and her mother explained it to her, and Lucy's elvish governess explained it to her. But the way it worked out would be rather amusing if it were not pathetic.

You see, what finally brought her around was the same thing that brought Sarah around. She saw the dramatization of a fictional story about vampires, and that made her appreciate what the other alternative was.—Hey, at least Wilhelmina did not run away screaming." After they shared nervous laughter, the Queen added, "The full reconciliation came when she was brought to understand how Lucy really died, as opposed to the fantasy of being held down and writhing in agony as a wooden stake was slowly driven through her heart. Again, kind of like Sarah."

"Very good, Your Majesty. But what about Lucy's mother—what was her name?"

"Veronica. The poor woman is carrying on as bravely as she can for the sake of Wilhelmina, and she is reconciled to it as Wilhelmina is. But still, much more time is needed. Someday, when she is ready, what was discussed here today will be revealed to her."

Then she continued. "As for the other, now. Yes, indeed—what about Anna? We must discuss that in detail sometime. For now, I say only this. A mistress is responsible for the harm that befalls her handmaid, including by taking care of the dependents she leaves behind. That point will not be forgotten or dishonored."

"Very good, Your Majesty. I thank you." Then, "But you said there were two points of concern, two reasons to call me in."

"Yes, I did. But now, with the meeting and this conversation, the discussion of the first point has run longer than I anticipated. The hour is late enough, and you have enough to think about, that I believe it is best to conclude for today."

"And so," Beatrice commented, "Wendy's next great adventure was about to begin."